The House of Peril

By Louis Tracy

Originally published in 1922

The House of Peril

Published by Resurrected Press

This classic book was handcrafted by Resurrected Press. Resurrected Press is dedicated to bringing high quality classic books back to the readers who enjoy them. These are not scanned versions of the originals, but, rather, quality checked and edited books meant to be enjoyed!

Please visit ResurrectedPress.com to view our entire catalogue!

ISBN 13: 978-1-937022-08-2

Printed in the United States of America

OTHER RESURRECTED PRESS MYSTERIES

By Louis Tracy
The Strange Case of Mortimer Fenley
The Albert Gate Mystery
The Stowmarket Mystery

By J. S. Fletcher
The Orange-Yellow Diamond
The Middle Temple Murder
Scarhaven Keep
Ravensdene Court

By A. A. Milne
The Red House Mystery

By Agatha Christie
The Mysterious Affair at Styles

By Arthur Griffiths
The Passenger from Calais
The Rome Express

From the Dr. John Thorndyke Series
By R. Austin Freeman
The Red Thumb Mark
The Eye of Osiris
The Mystery of 31 New Inn
John Thorndyke's Cases
A Silent Witness
The Cat's Eye

By Arthur J. Rees
The Hampstead Mystery
The Mystery of the Downs
The Shrieking Pit
The Hand in The Dark
The Moon Rock

Visit ResurrectedPress.com to see our entire catalog.

FOREWORD

It will strike those readers familiar with such works of Louis Tracy as *The Strange Case of Mortimer Fenley* and *The Postmaster's Daughter* odd that detectives Winter and Furneaux have moved to New York and are members of the New York Detective Bureau. To readers new to the pair of sleuths, it should be explained that their usual haunts are London and the environs and that they are normally Superintendent Winter and Detective Inspector Furneaux of Scotland yard, but in *The House of Peril* they have been transformed into Americans.

That mystery, at least is easily solved. Louis Tracy, though British, had for some time before the novel was published been splitting his time between London and New York. A number of his later works first appeared in American editions before being published in Britain, often with minor changes to reflect the different markets. Such is the case with *The House of Peril*.

However, *The House of Peril* does seem to have been an extreme case. Winter, typically described as a large man looking like a country squire, now appears as a big man who might be taken for a stock-broker who breeds pedigree cattle as a hobby, while Furneaux, a native of the Isle of Jersey, is now of French-Canadian descent. In all other respects, they maintain the same personas as their counterparts from Scotland yard. To confuse things further, when the British edition was released a few years after the American, it had been renamed *The Park Lane Murder* and the locale had been moved to London. I have not read this version, but assume that Winter and Furneaux are back in their proper positions at Scotland Yard.

Whatever the location, Winter and Furneaux are in top form, exchanging banter and bickering like an old married couple while they track down the murderer. They, or at least Furneaux, is also not above engaging in a little behind the scenes matchmaking. The various subplots and by play make this one of Tracy's better mysteries.

Resurrected Press is happy to bring its readers this edition of *The House of Peril*, another entertaining mystery by Louis Tracy featuring those two engaging detectives Winter and Furneaux in whatever guise they chose to appear.

About the Author

Louis Tracy (1863-1928) was a British journalist and author. He wrote numerous books both under his own name and using the pseudonyms Gordon Holmes and Robert Fraser. He shared these pseudonyms and collaborated with P.M. Shiel on a number of works. Among his books are The Wings of Morning (1903), The Stowmarket Mystery (1904), and Number Seventeen (1916).

Greg Fowlkes
Editor-In-Chief
Resurrected Press
www.ResurrectedPress.com

TABLE OF CONTENTS

CHAPTER 1: WHAT THE BUTLER FOUND..1

CHAPTER 2: MARY DIXON EMULATES THE SPHINX.................15

CHAPTER 3: MARY DIXON REMAINS INSCRUTABLE.............29

CHAPTER 4: MR. FURNEAUX'S DEDUCTIVE METHOD...........45

CHAPTER 5: HOW FLANAGAN DIED...61

CHAPTER 6: THE RING—IN FACT, THREE RINGS....................75

CHAPTER 7: AN EMISSARY—FROM WHOM?............................89

CHAPTER 8: WHEREIN A PICTURE INTERVENES.................103

CHAPTER 9: MR. WINTER REVIEWS THE SITUATION..........119

CHAPTER 10: A FRIENDLY DINNER.......................................133

CHAPTER 11: AN UNEXPECTED JOURNEY............................147

CHAPTER 12: THE HOUSE WITHOUT A CARE.......................161

CHAPTER 13: FURNEAUX'S THEORY......................................177

CHAPTER 14: THE GAGE OF BATTLE.....................................193

CHAPTER 15: THAT NIGHT..207

CHAPTER 16: THE BOATING PARTY......................................221

CHAPTER 17: A DISQUISITION ON NEUROSIS......................235

CHAPTER 18: A PIECE OF CARDBOARD.................................249

CHAPTER 19: BEFORE THE MOON ROSE...............................263

CHAPTER 20: NEARING THE DAWN......................................277

CHAPTER 1: WHAT THE BUTLER FOUND

MARIE, the parlour maid, tossed her head indignantly. She jerked a thumb toward the stairs and the upper regions of the house generally.

"A nice lot!" she cried. "Not one of 'em gone home. This joint ain't a fit place for a decent girl. I'll beat it at the end of the month."

The butler looked puzzled. He was, as all butters should be, tall, portly, bald headed and English. It is almost impossible to imagine an American butler. He glanced up the stairs, as though expecting the comparative gloom of the hallway landing to yield some sort of confirmation or denial of the girl's statement.

"Sure?" he inquired.

"Of course I'm sure." Indeed, Marie was vehemently so. "Didn't I peek in when I kem down? Dead drunk, all of 'em. And, oh, the smell! Like passin' a corner saloon in Seventh Avenue on a Saturday night before prohibition."

"Well, well," said the butler. "I'll just go an' see what the trouble is."

"Better ring up the Fire Station, an' get 'em to lend you a hose," snorted the parlour maid.

The man turned on the stairs, apparently wishing to say something. But he repressed the words, whatever they might have been. Repression was a habit he had cultivated of late years. He walked on, treading with the remarkable lightness of step often found in big, heavy men.

The house was a Fifth Avenue mansion, but not typically so, since its architecture was simple and pleasing. It stood on the south corner of a crosstown street not far above the main entrance to Central Park, and its rooms were arranged in the shape of an "L," whereof the longer part faced the street and the shorter the avenue. In the inner section were the stair case, elevator, and a series of bathrooms, linen closets, and store cupboards. A gallery gave access to the main rooms on the first floor, and the butler made for the spacious drawing room, which had three windows facing west and two north. All of these opened on to a balcony, protected by a wrought iron railing. The door was situated near the south wall.

The first whiff of air from the interior more than justified the parlour maid's disagreeable recollection of the week end odours of certain parts of Seventh Avenue, although her sarcastic comment had, to a some extent, prepared the butler for the extraordinary scene that met his eyes. The blinds were drawn, and clusters of electric lights shone through a slight haze of tobacco smoke. Mostly lying on the floor—three being sprawled awkwardly across a long dining room table—were thirteen young men, all in evening dress, all apparently sodden with alcohol, and quite insensible.

Neither the parlour maid's glimpse of this disreputable gathering nor her scornful description of it prevented the butler from being surprised and slightly alarmed. Never before had the members of the singularly named Ace Club indulged in such an orgy. He knew at once that something out of the common had happened. Being a butler, his first thought flew to the quality of liquor the revellers had imbibed, but, unless some uncanny chance had intervened, that question could not arise, as every bottle on the table came from one of the best-stocked cellars in New York, and bore a pre war label.

Yet these well dressed youngsters seemed to be helplessly intoxicated. Their stertorous breathing and abandoned attitudes gave first evidence of that apparent fact. Then the butler sniffed, not willingly, it is true, but rather with the air of an expert testing some suspected compound. "That's neither champagne, nor whisky, nor brandy, nor any liqueur that I know of," he muttered. "I wonder what it can be?"

Naturally he sought a more Wholesome atmosphere and a better light, there being few things on earth so thoroughly ghastly as an all night debauch illuminated by electricity struggling against the beams of a summer morning's sun, even if these found but occasional chinks in dark blue blinds.

So he rather hurried across the room to the nearest window overlooking Central Park, trying, as he went, to ascertain with sidelong glance whether or not Anthony van Cortland, his employer, was as utterly hors de combat as the twelve guests. Yes, so far as he could judge, van Cortland's plight was in no wise less discreditable than that of any of his friends. Indeed, the host was stretched on his back on the hearth rug, in front of a fireplace which stood between the two northern windows.

So the butler raised the blind and opened the window both above and below. He had closed the door when he entered the room. Hence, there was not a pronounced draught, but the inrush of air was nevertheless wholesome and effective. He went to the second, or centre, window, but was brought up with a distinct shock.

In a large glass bowl, nearly filled with water, and standing on a high but narrow round table, was a plump gold fish floating on its back—quite dead.

The butler uttered a most un butler like expression. This little creature had been his pet for many months. Mechanically his hand went to a pocket in the loose jacket he wore at that hour of the day.

He brought forth a paper bag of ant eggs with which he was wont to feed his tiny friend, which should now be darting in meteoric flight up and down and around the basin in anticipation of a speedy meal.

But never again would those opal hues flash from the iridescent body. It was lying motionless, up side down on the surface of the water.

"You poor wee thing!" said the man. "You poor, harmless, wee thing!"

Lifting it with a tenderness he knew to be of no avail, he tried to restore vitality by the warmth of his fingers. The least wriggle would have brought hope. But the fish was dead without any manner of doubt, had probably been dead some hours. He put it back in the water. Some drops fell on the paper bag, and a shower of ant eggs streamed on to the carpet. Again the butler muttered an oath.

He glanced angrily at the thirteen prostrate men, and was tempted to arouse them by no gentle means. But his habit of self restraint came to his aid. He placed the package on the table, and raised that blind as well.

He was about to open the window also when, out of the tail of his eye as it were, he noticed a peculiar expression on his employer's face. He described it afterwards as "a waxy look." It was really that tint of camailleu gris which the illustrators of mediaeval Psalters and Horae lent to all saints and early Christian martyrs, whereas, Anthony van Cortland's skin was usually a dusky red, he having been a healthy young man and so physically fit that he could, and did, live a strenuous life.

The butler was thoroughly scared now. He hurried to the upper end of the room, and knelt by his master's side, lifting his head and speaking to him.

"Wake up, Mr. van Cortland!" he said, quite loudly. "Wake up sir! It's nearly half past seven."

The sound of his own voice was almost affrighting. It seemed wholly out of place in that room of awe. Then, as gently as he had handled the goldfish, he lowered van Cortland's head to the rug, for his young employer would not wake up in this world. He, too, was dead. There was no doubting it. Eyes, mouth, lips, were eloquent witnesses of the great silence. Even the fingers of each hand were claw like in their contraction.

After a pause of breathless horror the butler nerved himself to conduct a hurried examination of each of the remaining occupants of the room. He assured himself that they were alive but insensible. They reminded him of men under the influence of an anaesthetic, and the conceit added to his distress. Pulling himself together, in the manner of one accustomed to military drill, he stepped over the body of one of the revellers, and stretched a hand toward a decanter half filled with liqueur brandy.

But he drew back.

"No," he muttered. "That won't do. This is no time for Dutch courage. God only knows what will happen if I make a mistake now. I must keep my head clear until this affair is out of my control for good and all."

Again he glanced around the room. Beyond the raising of the blinds and the quickly abandoned effort to restore van Cortland's consciousness he had literally touched nothing, he assured himself. Nothing, except—

"By jing!" he said. "I am forgetting the goldfish. Poor thing! Why should it have been killed, too?"

At that moment he did not stop to ask himself why he used the word "killed" rather than "dead." He was more than a little dazed and terrified. He really needed a nip of brandy, but resisted another prompting in the direction of the decanter.

"No, no!" he commanded himself again. "Not yet. Not till the police have come."

The definite thought of the police, and of what their visit would mean, steadied him. He literally stole to the door, as if fearful now of awakening any of the sleepers. In turning the knob he touched a key, which he withdrew, and locked the door from the outside, putting the key in the pocket which had held the ant eggs. He did these things stealthily, first looking about the gallery, up and down the stairs, and along a passage running parallel with the northern rooms to make certain he was not observed by any other member of the household. Then he descended the stairs, with the slow step of one who has a crushing weight on his mind.

"Well?" said the pert parlour maid, though modulating her voice somewhat. "An' what about it?"

He halted, giving the girl a lack lustre stare ;which she did not appreciate, in either sense of the word, as she was by way of being pretty, and the butler was a highly presentable man.

"Yes, Mr. Brown, it's really me," she went on.

"So I see, Marie," he replied, uttering each word as though weighing it. "Will you kindly ring up the garage, and ask Morrison to bring the limousine at once?"

"Why, Morrison'll be in bed!" said Marie.

"Yes, he may be, but he's to come here as quickly as possible."

Marie believed her master might appear at any second, so she tripped away to the telephone booth on the ground floor. She did the tripping very neatly, as the butler was watching her, she imagined. He was a steady, good looking fellow, who kept very much to himself. Anyhow, a girl never knew.

Mr. Brown passed a hand over his forehead and eyes.

"That's got rid of her," he mused. "What to do next? Perhaps I'd better find the nearest cop. He can phone the right people."

He crossed the hall quickly, unlatched a heavy door of glass and iron, drew the bolts of an outer door, and seemed to surprise a young man who had a hand out to press an electric bell.

"Good work, Brown!" laughed the newcomer. "Is it thought reading or Christian Science?"

"Oh, Captain Stuart, I am so glad to see you," gasped the butler, closing the glass door behind him.

The slender, well built soldier was probably surprised at the warmth of his welcome, but it conveyed nothing to him otherwise.

"No more than I'm glad to see you," he said. "Mr. van Cortland and I are riding in the Park at 8.15, and I ventured to come here early, hoping to join him in a cup of coffee and an egg. They're a lazy crew in my place. So, please don't look so solemn, and shut me out."

"Oh, sir, I didn't mean to say I was glad," muttered Brown, agitation mastering him now that he had companionship far more than when he was alone. "A terrible thing has happened here. Mr. —Mr. van Cortland is dead!"

"Dead? Are you crazy?"

"No, indeed, sir. I'm telling you the dreadful truth."

"When did he die? And how?"

"Oh, I don't know. I can't even guess, sir. I went to the drawing room five minutes since—I can't be sure to a minute, I am so upset—and there I found him dead, and the rest of 'em lying around him."

"The rest of them? Do you mean that infernal Ace Club?"

"Yes, sir."

"Are they all dead?"

"No, no, sir. The other gentlemen—it seems to me— are drugged, or half poisoned."

"Let me in! Let me see them!"

"Yes, sir. Of course. But—do you think it's wise?"

"Have you sent for a doctor, and the police?"

"Not yet, sir. I was coming out "

"You're damn well coming in. Open that door! I think you're out of your senses."

Now it was the younger man who yielded to excitement, whereas the butler was recovering his shattered nerve. The mere bubbling forth of his frightful news had partially restored his poise.

"Please listen a moment, sir," he said, with something of his natural dignity of voice and manner. "I'm not a murderer flying from justice. I am only trying to repay many a kindness shown me by a good master, an' I don't

want half New York about the house as soon as the story
gets into the early editions of the evening papers. You, an'
me are the only people who know of this thing yet. I want
you to help, sir. A false step taken now cannot be put
right a bit later. I think Providence must have sent you
here this morning. Will you come in, and go upstairs with
me? Don't say anything before the other servants."

Evidently taking for granted the young officer's
acquiescence Brown produced a latch key, and unlocked
the glass door. Stuart followed him into the hall, keeping
a wary eye on the butler's portly form, being altogether
doubtful whether to regard him as a criminal or a
maniac. At that instant the parlour-maid flounced out of
the telephone booth.

"Morrison was at the garage," she cried. "He'll be
round in five minutes. An' let me tell you "

Then she became aware that Brown's companion was
not, as she supposed, a valet or groom from the opposite
set of flats, for Captain Stuart wore a smart riding
costume, and his shining boots were the dernier cri. He
looked what he was, a quite capable cavalry officer.

"Beg pardon, sir," she said, blushing.

Brown explained, in the best butlerian style.

"I have sent for Mr. van Cortland's car, sir. It may
prove useful."

Long afterwards, Stuart realised that he had never
seen a more superb piece of acting. As matters stood, he
only became more suspicious of Brown's sanity. Not for
an instant did he dream that he was thrusting his own
head into a thorny thicket by interfering in a tragedy at
this early stage of its discovery, nor, indeed, to do him
justice, would he have hesitated at all in any dilemma
where the interests of a friend were concerned.

He spoke no word, and, naturally, Marie thought
herself snubbed, since the woman does not breathe who
fails to give the most trivial action a personal
significance.

"Wonder who the swell guy is?" she thought, eyeing the two covertly as they climbed the stairs.

She was actually so flustered at not receiving so much as a glance from the stranger that her sharp ears failed to detect the unlocking of the drawingroom door.

"Anyhow, I should worry. I'm skipping out of this, quick."

Once the two were inside the room Brown seemed to take the lead. While Stuart was looking with amazement at the strange scene before him the butler said impressively:—

"I wish to warn you, sir, not to touch anyone or anything. I have some experience of police methods, an' know that detectives regard their difficulties as increased a hundred times when well meaning folk butt in before them.

"No offence, sir, I hope, but I can't exactly pick an' choose my words this morning. . . . Come this way, sir. Never mind them others. They're alive all right. . . . Here's my poor master. He's been dead hours. This is a bad business. A lot of people will suffer before it's cleared up Did you know he was going to be married?"

Captain Stuart could only nod. He had seen death too often in France not to recognise its dread presentment here in New York. But this pallid husk of life had been his friend, a wild, tempestuous-souled one, it is true, yet a youngster without vice, with a nature oscillating between the fine impulses of a cavalier and the red eyed moods of an unbroken colt.

Still, Stuart was a soldier, and he literally pulled himself together. His first words showed that he had cast aside his momentary doubts.

"Tell me, if you feel up to it, just what has happened, Brown," he said.

The butler, almost calm now, began to tell his story. He was interrupted by a knock on the door, which was partly opened before he could reach it, though he sprang

forward with a catlike agility. It was Roberts, the valet,
whom he was just in time to stop from entering.

"Sorry, Mr. Brown," said the man, "but Mr. van
Cortland told me to call him at seven thirty. He's not in
his room, an' his bed hasn't been slept in, an' Marie sez "

"That's all right, Roberts," said the other. "He was to
go riding with Captain Stuart. Isn't that correct, sir?" and
he turned his head without letting the valet advance an
inch.

"Yes, quite correct," agreed Stuart, marvelling the
while at the butler's presence of mind.

"I'll let you know when you're wanted Roberts," said
Brown, and Roberts went away without the slightest
suspicion that anything was wrong, save that he agreed
with Marie that the party upstairs must have made a
fierce night of it, judging from the whiff of air which he
got in the doorway.

Stuart, who had been examining the faces and
postures of the twelve insensible men, broke in firmly
when Brown would have resumed his narration.

"Look here!" he said, "we really must do something.
There's no use in staring and wondering. A doctor must
be sent for, and he will want assistance. These fellows are
not so much under the influence of alcohol. They've been
doped. I suppose you are right about the police having the
first innings, and I fancy that no one else is going to die.

Luckily I happen to know the chief of the detective
bureau. It's early hours, but he or one of his deputies may
be on hand. Where is the telephone?"

"The private 'phone is in Mr. van Cortland's room, sir.
The first door on the left in the corridor."

Marie was on the stairs as Stuart went out. Realising
her errand, he said:—

"Is the car here?"

"Yes, sir."

"Would you mind asking the chauffeur to wait?"

He forced himself to smile, and Marie smiled back.

"Used his eyes this time, I s'pose," she mused.

When she heard the truth later she deemed herself a quite unfairly treated girl, in whose good sense and strength of character neither Brown nor his gentleman friend had placed the slightest trust. Stuart was beginning already to sympathise with the butler. The whole affair was most awkward and perplexing. The tragedy of van Cortland's death was yielding swiftly to the difficulties imposed on those who had to deal with its terrible legacy. The soldier, like the man servant, was vastly puzzled to decide how to act for the best.

His first notion had been to dash half a glass of water into the face of Harry Holgate, one among the men whom he recognised, and see if this rough treatment would not restore the roysterer's senses, but, somehow or other, Brown had managed to infect him with a suspicion of foul play in regard to van Cortland. The dead goldfish figured nebulously in this theory, as the butler was convinced that his pet not only was in the best of health overnight, but had survived many heavy evenings of smoking and drinking by the members of the Ace Club in that same room.

If van Cortland had actually been murdered, who could have done this thing? No young and healthy man in all the city was less likely to have a secret and deadly enemy. And what would Mary Dixon think when she knew that her promised husband had met his death in such a way? Stuart did not know Miss Dixon—öhad never seen her, he believed, save in certain hardly recognisable pictures in the Sunday newspapers—but she had the repute of being a most charming girl, a leader of the Junior League, New York's galaxy of youthful beauty and social prominence, and in every way fitted to become the mistress of van Cortland's house and fortune. Crime or no crime, the death of her promised husband must be a dangerous ordeal for her. Certainly, the butler was right. They must tread warily that morning, or further mischief would ensue.

He was greeted somewhat curtly by the man on duty in the detective bureau. All matters calling for police enquiry must be reported to the headquarters of the local precinct. If people didn't know this it was time they did.

"Mr. Winter will not be pleased when he hears how a friend's civil request for assistance was received," said Stuart decisively.

"Oh, a friend of Mr. Winter's, are you?" answered the voice. "First you've said about that. What's the trouble?"

Stuart gave a brief and by no means lurid account of the tragedy, or accident.

"Tell you what," said the voice. "Mr. Winter lives in Brooklyn, an' won't be here for another hour. Why not ring up Mr. Furneaux? He has a flat up your way, an' he can get the Chief quicker'n me if he thinks it necessary."

So, after a slight delay, another voice came over the telephone, a queer, high pitched, somewhat illtempered voice, which, however, did not break in on Stuart's explanation of the call.

"All right," it said, after a pause. "Have that butler ready to admit me. I'll be there in five minutes. And, for the love of Mike, keep any doctor out of the room till I've had a look around."

Well within the stipulated five minutes Brown had to tackle another problem. He was chatting to the chauffeur, and trying to show cause why there had been such an urgent demand for the car without any apparent reason, when a diminutive, dapper little man, who might be either a fashionable jockey or a popular comedian of the song and dance type, hurried up to the door, and announced that he was "Mr. Furneaux."

Brown nearly blurted out:—"Of the Detective Bureau?" but sheer incredulity tied his tongue. Something of this must have peeped from his eyes, because the newcomer said acidly:—

"Hurry up, John Bull. I haven't kept Captain Stuart waiting, so you just bring me to him on the run."

Brown simply turned and opened the glass door without another word. He preceded the detective up the stairs, announced him, and waited to see what effect "Mr. Furneaux" produced on the young officer. He was not disappointed, Stuart gazed at the representative of the law with an expression of blank astonishment.

"Now, which of you two knows anything about this business?" said Furneaux crisply.

"Mr. Brown—the butler—can tell you something about it," was Stuart's hesitating reply.

"And you?"

"Nothing."

Furneaux wheeled on Brown with the rapidity of a jack in the box.

"Shoot !" he said.

Stuart had not failed to notice that Furneaux's curiously unprofessional guise did not prevent him from summing up the room and its bizarre contents with an extraordinarily alert glance. While the butler talked the detective listened, without the slightest interruption. At the end he hurried to the fire place, and knelt beside van Cortland's body.

"Why do you think he hasn't died a natural death?" he asked Brown, raising his head in a pert way that reminded Stuart of a sparrow.

"I—I don't like his look, sir," was the answer.

"Have you seen other dead men?"

"Yes, sir. A great many."

"What were you? An undertaker?"

"No, sir. A policeman, and afterwards a soldier."

"A policeman in London?"

"Yes, sir."

Furneaux rose.

"Ring up Dr. George Bright, East 83rd Street. Tell him I want him to hurry. Then get someone to help you to carry Mr. van Cortland to his own room and lay him on the bed. Is there another man servant available?"

"Yes, sir. The valet."

"Good! Make sure he holds his tongue! Stun him with a punch on the solar plexus if you can't be certain of him."

As the butler left the room Furneaux went to examine the goldfish. He smelt the water, and even tasted a few drops of it. Then he fixed his extraordinarily brilliant black eyes on Stuart.

"Your friend has been poisoned," he said. "Of course, I cannot say yet whether he was murdered or committed suicide. But that fellow, Brown, is a gem. What luck to have an ex policeman first on the ground in a case like this! Anybody else would have raised hell half an hour ago, and spoiled every due that may offer itself."

CHAPTER 2: MARY DIXON EMULATES THE SPHINX

THE soldier, far from being favourably impressed by the appearance of Mr. Winter's aide, though subconsciously aware of some dynamic quality in the little man's personality, thought it would do no harm if he took up the detective's concluding words.

"Clues!" he said. "Are there likely to be any?"

"Sure," cried Furneaux, who seemed to cackle rather than speak. "This is either a simple affair or a complex one. There is no middle way. It can either be solved by the first flat footed cop who blows in from the street or it will worry the best brains in the Bureau. Now, let's see. You're in the army?"

"Yes."

"Cavalry?"

"Yes."

"American Expeditionary Force?"

"Yes."

"Know any of these fellows?"

"Mr. van Cortland is my friend. I remember meeting Harry Holgate in Paris, and—yes—this youngster, I think, is called Bolton—Billy Bolton. All three were in the Flying Corps."

"And the others?"

"I am not acquainted with them, but I have heard that they all have experience in flying. Hence the name they went under—the Ace Club."

"But an Ace is a man who has crashed five enemy machines."

"Yes."

"Do you think all these empty headed nuts have done that?"

"Of course, I cannot tell. And van Cortland was certainly not empty headed."

"There must have been a vacant lot in his skull somewhere. Do you believe the butler has told the truth, the whole truth?"

"That is my opinion, up to the present."

"It pays to be cautious. But there are corroborative details of his story."

"Indeed?"

"Yes. He came into the room, and thought these guys were dead drunk, so he raised the first blind and opened the window. Then he saw the fish, and was a bit peeved. Quite mechanically, he produced the packet of ant eggs, burst the'bag with his wet fingers, spilled the eggs on the floor, stuck some to his clothes, left at least one in van Cortland's hair, and smeared two or three on the door key, which he put in the pocket where he kept the eggs. That's a clear trail of his actions if ever there was one. He's either an honest man or a genius, and I'll swear he isn't a genius. By the way, are you a friend of Miss Mary Dixon?"

Stuart, listening with growing respect to Furneaux's analysis of Brown's movements that morning, was slightly nonplussed by this sudden change of topic.

"N no," he said, hesitatingly.

"Aren't you quite certain?"

"Yes, of course I am. But, to be candid, Mr. Furneaux, your line of talk rather takes my breath away."

The detective's face wrinkled in a grin. For a second he had the semblance of one of those grotesque ivory masks which Japanese artists find delight in carving, for his skin was sallow and his features were remarkably expressive, though, again in the manner of Nippon, it was most difficult to tell what mood any definite expression revealed.

"Well," he said, "if you wish to do that charming young lady a good turn, you'll go now and break the news of her fiance's death to her."

"I!"

"Yes, you. Who else? You know enough about it, but not so much that you can't be vague. Poor van Cortland has no relatives in America, and we cannot send one of the precocious asses lying here. We might depute Brown, or get hold of van Cortland's lawyer, but I would vastly prefer entrusting a delicate task to you."

"Really, Mr. Furneaux "

"Don't refuse, there's a good fellow. It's a nasty job, of course, but that is just why I want you to tackle it. And, by the way, take van Cortland's car. It's standing outside. Miss Dixon lives in Park Avenue. Don't let her come here, on your life. Stop alongside the first cop you see, and tell him that Mr. Furneaux needs the help of two 'tecs from this precinct—at once. Make him jump to the 'phone."

So, before he actually realised the nature of the mission thrust upon him, Captain Alec Stuart, of the 5th. U. S. Cavalry, was hurrying his lithe frame down the stairs and explaining to the waiting chauffeur that he would commandeer the car for a brief while. But, like a good soldier, he thought first of his horse, and alighted near the park gate at the rendezvous where many early morning riders mount for a gallop around the reservoir. Sending his own horse back to the livery stable where he kept it, and assuring van Cortland's groom that his master's hack would not be wanted that morning, he took the opportunity to speak to a policeman on point duty near General Sherman's gilded statue.

The man gave him a sharp look when he mentioned Furneaux's name, but did not question the accuracy of the message.

"Right," he said. "I'll fix that right away."

Then, resolutely facing a most ungrateful undertaking, Stuart told Morrison to drive to the big apartment house in Park Avenue where Miss Mary Dixon lived with her father and brother.

The elevator brought him to a solemn little marble lobby on the sixth floor, in which two steel doors, painted to represent walnut, faced each other starkly. Somehow, the gaunt aspect of this enclosure increased his diffidence in an embarrassing mission. He almost stuttered a request to the maid who answered his ring that he might have a word with Miss Dixon.

The girl looked surprised.

"Miss Dixon is not up yet," she said.

"I hardly expected it, but my business is urgent. Will you tell her I come from Mr. van Cortland—from Mr. van Cortland's house?"

The maid was doubtful, and asked his name. He gave it.

"Pardon me," she said, and closed the door.

He waited some minutes, probably not five all told, but it seemed more like half an hour. Indeed, he was on the point of ringing for the elevator again when the maid reappeared and invited him to enter. He was ushered to a library smoking room, and found a slim young woman awaiting him. She was standing with her back to the dim light which came through a large window opening into the well of the building. She wore a blue kimono, and her bare feet were thrust into slippers. It was evident, too, that she was still attired in pyjamas, and her hair had been coiled into a loose wisp on the nape of her neck. It was brown hair, and there was plenty of it, framing a charming oval face. A pair of big blue eyes, which had a violet tint in shadow, peered at the visitor. Her right hand clasped the back of a chair, and the left toyed somewhat nervously with the girdle of the dressing gown. But her voice was quite self possessed.

"Has the maid been mistaken?" she said. "Do you really want to see me, Captain Stuart?"

"Yes, if you are Miss Mary Dixon?" he made no reference to Anthony van Cortland.

"Y yes, in a sense."

Stuart's utterance sounded laboured and out of time in his own ears. Three times in less than twenty minutes he had almost stammered—he, who could make himself heard by a squadron at the gallop. Luckily, however, the girl was so obsessed by her own notion as to the cause of his presence that she did not grasp his obvious unwillingness to admit that he was Anthony van Cortland's actual deputy.

"It there anything the matter with Willie?" she demanded rather breathlessly.

"Willie?"

"Yes. My brother, of course. He has not been home, but we know he was with Anthony last night."

"Oh, I see. Yes. I mean 'No.' Your brother is all right. In fact, I have heard nothing about him."

"Do you mean he was not there?"

"No, no. I'm very sorry to appear so stupid, Miss Dixon, but the fact is I hardly know how to explain my errand."

"But, please, what is it?"

Naturally, in the conditions, and at that hour of the morning, Stuart was not invited to be seated. The door of the room was wide open, and he had an uneasy belief that the housemaid was listening from the passage—probably had been warned by her young mistress to remain there. Nor could he attempt to allay Miss Dixon's disquiet by an amiable grin, though, in his positive distress, he did think of that very thing. Still, he had to say something, and, making a soldierly decision, he broke out, with what seemed to his own censorious judgment to be a horrible brusqueness:—

"I am the bearer of bad news. Will you ask your mother to join you?"

"My mother! My dear mother has been dead eight years."

Stuart's face and neck were promptly bathed in a violent perspiration. But his wretched tidings had to be told somehow.

"Please forgive me," he said. "I am only trying to prepare you for a great shock. Mr. van Cortland, who was

my very good friend—perhaps you have heard him speak
of me?"

Mary Dixon's lips quivered. She merely shook her
head, and he regarded it as a bad sign that she could not
trust her speech.

"Well," he went on, deliberately sinking his eyes,
though forcing himself to keep very much on the alert, if
she gave way completely and fell in a faint, "there has
been a tragedy in his house. Van Cortland must have
been taken gravely ill during the night. This morning he
was—found dead."

"Anthony van Cortland dead!"

"Yes. An idle chance brought me into the sad position
of having to convey to you this awful happening. I cannot
tell you how I regret the cause of my presence here, no
less than the tactless way in which I have carried out a
dreadful mission."

Yet, though he now had command of himself, and was
greatly relieved by Mary Dixon's failure to yield to
hysteria, he was aware also of a profound astonishment
at her attitude. He was heart whole and fancy free,
having devoted eight years of his life to his profession and
to nothing else, but it was not in such wise that he would
have pictured a young and beautiful woman receiving the
news of her lover's death, practically on the eve of
marriage.

"Are you quite sure he is dead?"

Each word came in a slow staccato which gave sudden
warning that the girl's composure was unnatural. He
walked forward and caught her arm.

"Won't you sit down, Miss Dixon?" he said gently.

"I'm not going to scream, or faint, if that is what you
fear," she murmured. But she obeyed him, and sank into
a chair, burying her face in her hands, and leaning
forward until her elbows rested on her knees.

"W was he murdered?" came the most unexpected
question from tremulous lips. It was the last thing in the

world that Stuart expected to hear, and it startled him greatly.

"I do not know how he died," he said. "No doctor had examined him when I left the house. I was sent here by the police."

"By the police!" she repeated, under her breath.

"Yes. In fact, it was I who had to summon them. The circumstances are strange, almost beyond belief. Do you think you can bear to hear what occurred?" —

"Oh, yes. Please tell me. I must know the facts before—please tell me. And—and—-sit over there, will you?"

She was weeping now, but not with the frenzied grief of a distraught creature reft of her promised mate. Rather did she convey to Stuart's fairly keen perception a certain hopelessness, an utter misery, a benumbing of the faculties. Was this how love would act? the man could not avoid asking himself. He would hardly have known that tears were welling from her eyes if he had not seen them dropping between her fingers. Indeed, he realised that the little gesture with which she indicated a chair whence he would view her in profile betrayed a desire that he would not see she had yielded to feminine weakness even thus far.

In slow, cautious words he described the incidents which led up to his presence at that moment. Underlying the recital was a feeling of surprise that he had so much to say. It was hardly credible, he thought, that so many tragic details should have crammed themselves into so short a time, as barely half an hour had elapsed since he hurried up the steps of the van Cortland mansion with no more serious purpose in life than a joyous gallop in Central Park. The girl did not interrupt. She merely listened. When he made an end she brushed her eyes with her hands, and raised her head, but did not look at her visitor.

"You do not know my brother?" she said, and again Stuart was frankly amazed that there should be no reference to Anthony van Cortland.

"No," he replied.

"Yet, he is there. He is one of those foolish boys. Will you do me one more favour?—you have been very kind already in coming here—please see that he gets home safely."

Stuart took this as a dismissal. He rose.

"I'll do my best," he said. "Of course, you realise that the police are in charge of this sad business?"

"Oh, yes, yes. . . . But poor Willie did not kill his friend."

It was on the tip of his tongue to ask why she insisted that van Cortland's death was not due to natural causes—to that mysterious organ the heart, for instance, which is so little understood by laymen that people are supposed to drop dead from its sudden failure without having given the least premonitory sign of disease during life. But he was too glad to escape from an ordeal without prolonging it by questions.

"Won't you let me call your maid before I go?" he said.

"Catherine!" said the girl, raising her voice ever so slightly.

"Yes, miss," came the quick response. Stuart had been right in his assumption as to the domestic plan of attack if he proved a bare faced interloper.

"Please ring for the elevator. . . . Good bye, Captain Stuart. I am more obliged to you than I can tell you now."

As he went out he saw that her head was again bent, but she was no longer crying. Her wan cheeks were puckered by the pressure of her clenched fists. She was thinking deeply. Of what? he wondered.

He believed, though he could give no reason for the belief, that she was far from being crushed by the tragedy which had come into her young life. She suffered, but her distress was for others rather than for her own loss.

He found the chauffeur munching an apple, and the sight brought a sharp reminder that he was hungry. If, as was highly probable, he might have other work to do that morning, he must certainly eat.

"Morrison," he said, "like me, I suppose, you have had no breakfast?"

"That's right, sir," said the man.

"Well, drive to some quiet restaurant, where you can park your car for a few minutes, and we'll attend to the commissariat."

"The nearest hotel, sir?"

"No. There's half a dozen places on Sixth Avenue where we can be served more quickly than in a hotel."

Within very few minutes the two were supplied with coffee and eggs. They faced each other across a small table covered with white Italian cloth. Morrison was busy with a grape fruit for a little while. Then, while stirring his coffee, he looked at Stuart anxiously.

"Is there anything wrong at the house, sir?" he said.

"Why do you ask?" was the non committal answer.

"I dunno, sir. Marie, the parlour maid, said there'd bin some queer doin's upstairs."

"Nothing unusual, is there, in a set of boys indulging in a wild night?"

"No, sir. But they've never bin as bad as this, except one week end in Paris."

"What? Were you there, too?"

"Yes, sir. I drove Mr. van Cortland's car all the time. I piped you once or twice, at Giro's, an' one hot night at the Acacia.

"Did you, by gad? Well, don't tell anybody about the Acacia. I had an awful head next morning, and said, 'Oui, ma cherie,' when my brigadier wanted to know if there was a train for the front at eleven o'clock."

The chauffeur smiled, for he, too, had been one of the American Army of Occupation, as the Parisians described the A. E. F. during a certain phase of the war—in fact, had fought valiantly in the Second Battle of the Cafe de la Paix. But, for all that, he avoided the red herring drawn across the trail of current events.

"It's a pity Miss Dixon didn't marry Mr. Coleman when he kem back," he said. "She's a fine young lady, an' she'd ha' kep' hin straight. But, there! Wimmen are queer. I don't believe she ever really fancied him."

Stuart had made it a practice not to listen to the tittle tattle of subordinates; he shut off the flood of Morrison's gossip peremptorily.

"I am hardly acquainted with any of these people," he said. "Mr. van Cortland—" he had to repeat the name in order to stop himself from using the past tense—"is my friend, and I am concerned in his matrimonial affairs only to the extent of wishing that they might have turned out happily."

Morrison took the hint, and gave his undivided attention to the meal. They were soon at the Fifth Avenue mansion again, where the butler admitted Stuart. The chauffeur was told to wait. Another car was at the door, and Brown whispered:—

"The doctor is here, sir. He says Mr. van Cortland has been dead four or five hours. Mr. Furneaux and a couple of 'tecs are frisking the others."

"Frisking them?"

"Yes, sir. Goin' through their pockets, you know. I think he's finger printing 'em, too."

"You know Mr. Willie Dixon?"

"Yes, sir."

"Well, his sister wishes me to see him home. Do you think Mr. Furneaux will have any objection?"

"You can ask him, sir. My orders are to bring you upstairs as soon as you arrive."

Stuart could hardly avoid speculating as to the detective's motives in thus keeping him in close contact, so to speak, with the tragedy, but he followed Brown without another word.

In the drawing room he found Furneaux and a couple of quite obvious plain clothes policemen in consultation with a stranger, Dr. Bright, to whom he was promptly introduced.

Other windows were open by this time, and the atmosphere of the apartment was decidedly more wholesome. The doctor was stooping over Holgate's body when Stuart entered. He held in his hand a bottle of smelling salts, and was evidently on the point of applying it. One of the detectives was sponging some black marks off the ends of the fingers and thumb of the right hand of a man who lay near the centre of the table. This man, whom Stuart recognised as "Billy" Bolton, showed unmistakable signs of returning consciousness. He was moving slightly, and was almost aware of the sponge rendering his fingers cold.

Dr. Bright eyed Stuart rather attentively. The young officer's clear skin and alert figure certainly offered a curious contrast with the hectic and, indeed, debauched appearance of the men, some of whom, the detective had given the doctor to understand, were his friends.

"Do you know where any of these fellows live?" he enquired.

"One only," was the ready answer. "Oddly enough, I don't know him personally. Miss Dixon told me her brother was here."

"Ah!" Furneaux broke in. "How did she take your news?"

"Remarkably well, considering."

"Considering what?"

"The fact that her affianced husband was dead, of course."

"Did she say that, in so many words?"

"No, not exactly."

"What did she say?"

Now, Stuart had an alert brain, as the occupants of many a German "pillbox" in the Argonne could testify if they were alive, and he was dealing with a man, not a distraught woman. He divined instantly what had been in Furneaux's mind in despatching him on an extraordinary errand. Had a policeman, or any official, gone to break the news to Mary Dixon she would probably have kept a closer guard on her tongue than in the presence of a personal friend of van Cortland's. The soldier respected the law, and knew that he, like all other good citizens, ought to help its representatives, but, to use his own phrase, "he'd be hanged before he gave away a lady."

So he temporised.

"She was certainly very much upset," he said, "but she really seemed most concerned about her brother. Indeed, she asked me to bring him home."

"Took van Cortland's death for granted, in fact?" snapped Furneaux.

"I hope I have not conveyed that absurd impression," countered Stuart, keenly sensitive of the gimlet like action of the detective's beady eyes, which seemed to pierce into his very soul.

"She must have said something bearing on the crime," went on Furneaux. "How long were you with her?"

"Very few minutes. I was kept waiting till she was called from her room. I'm afraid I bungled the affair rather badly—blurted it out, you know. At first she thought I was talking about her brother. We were at cross purposes for quite a time. Then she wept, and—and I came away."

"Hum!" muttered Furneaux, as much as to say he didn't believe a syllable of the story. In very truth he was greatly annoyed that a trustworthy agent should have failed him.

Stuart was in no doubt as to the detective's meaning, and the doctor did not help matters by gazing darkly at him.

"I thought at the time you were making a grave mistake in sending me to interview Miss Dixon," he began stiffly, but Furneaux merely snapped his fingers in an irritated way.

"Don't see why you should kick at being introduced to a charming young lady, especially at eight o'clock in the morning," he cried. "If you are ready to constitute yourself her faithful knight errant at first sight, before she could so much as use a stick of lip salve or a powder puff, what the devil will happen when you meet her in all the glory of the mid day sun or the midnight arc lamp?"

Stuart disturbed already by the detective's eccentricity no less than his uncanny gift of guessing correctly at things he could not possibly know, was convinced now that the man was half crazy.

"We seem to be wandering away from Miss Dixon's request as to her brother," he said.

"Anyhow, you won't wander away with him to Park Avenue," came the sardonic retort. "These boys are going to the police station as quickly as Dr. Bright can bring 'em round, and they can be bundled into a patrol wagon. Please get busy, 'doc.' "

"Do you mean to say you will arrest them?" demanded the astounded Stuart.

"Sure I will—every mother's son of 'em. One, if not more, of these twelve young sinners killed van Cortland. How, I don't know, yet. They'll have to tell me. And it would be better for all concerned if you were a trifle more communicative, captain."

"But don't you realise that I was in this house only a few minutes before you—that you came here literally at my request?"

"Pretty smart, for the army," snapped Furneaux. "I'm not charging you with committing a crime. I want you to give me a full and true account of the words and behaviour of that interesting young lady, Mary Dixon." —

"Who's—talking—about—my sister?" said a muffled voice from the floor. "Who—are—you, anyway? Mind—I don't—flatten your face for you!"

Willie Dixon was awake, and gathering his faculties with much rapidity.

CHAPTER 3: MARY DIXON REMAINS INSCRUTABLE

ONE of the recumbent figures was trying to rise. Furneaux sprang as a weasel might tackle a rabbit, and shook the drowsy boy almost violently.

"Pull yourself together, Dixon," he cried shrilly. "Tell us how it's you are in this state, and why your friend, Anthony van Cortland, should be dead."

"Dead!" repeated the other vacantly. "Tony dead! What bunk! An', who the? "

"I am Inspector Furneaux, of the New York Detective Bureau. Mr. van Cortland was killed during the drunken orgy you have taken part in. Who did it?"

"Look here! Leg go my arm, or I'll punch you between those black eyes of yours, pronto. Why should anyone kill poor old Tony, you—you little cockatoo?"

Willie Dixon, now that returning animation lit up his features, bore a family resemblance to his sister. He rose unsteadily, and Furneaux loosened his grip. Not yet were those addled wits completely restored. He gazed around at his prostrate comrades and, for a second, a sheepish grin indicated a growing conviction that he and his friends had certainly made a night of it. Then he seemed to remember the detective's strange words, and gazed at the place at the head of the table where he evidently remembered last seeing van Cortland. Slowly his thoughts took cohesion, and he turned to look at Furneaux.

"You said you were a detective, and that Tony was dead, didn't you?" he muttered.

"Yes. Was he all right when you gave up the ghost? Was there any quarrel?"

"Of course he was all right. Never better. And what was there to quarrel about? We had the best time ever. But, bar jokes, Mr. Policeman—if you are one—what's this all about?"

"Try and answer my questions. You'll know the whole story soon enough. What was the last thing you had to drink?"

"Punch! A perfectly glorious punch."

"Who mixed it?"

"Tony himself. But I guess we all helped. Dash it all, what time is it?"

Dixon, nearly in his normal senses, was aware of the sunshine flooding the room; the day long roar of traffic in Fifth Avenue came through the open windows.

"Never mind the time," chirped Furneaux. "What was in that punch?"

"Are you serious?" came the somewhat strange question.

"Absolutely. I want you to remember now."

"Well, well. Tony—Mr. van Cortland—Tony is short for Anthony, you know—shoved in two bottles of champagne, and Monty Straus added a bottle of white wine, and I contributed half a decanter of liqueur brandy, and Buddy Owen shot three syphons of soda into the bowl, and Billy Bolton cut the lemons, and Harry Holgate—"

"Hello! Contact!"

A bleared face raised itself slowly from the carpet, and a pair of bloodshot eyes gazed reproachfully at the speaker. Then the eyes rolled about the room, and an indignant voice demanded:—

"What the blazes has been going on here?"

"Ask me another, Billy. But this cop, this gentleman, wants to know what you put in the punch."

"Some Curaçoa, of course. That's what gave it the right tang. Anyhow, Willie, for the love o' Mike, wise me up. What put all our crowd on the blink?"

"Wish I could tell you. Just woke myself to hear someone saying something about my sister. Here, you!" and Dixon's angry eyes found Furneaux. "It was you. What were you saying about my sister?"

"That she had requested Captain Stuart to take you home."

"How could she do that? Does she know him?"

A policeman in uniform, whom Stuart had not seen before, came in and gave the detective a slight nod. Furneaux screwed up his eyes, and examined young Dixon as though he were some museum specimen labelled "the Neanderthal Man."

"I've changed my mind about you," he said. "Captain Stuart, if you wish to oblige this young idiot's family again, take him away. Then return here, if you please, as I want you to meet Mr. Winter."

Dixon was about to make some acrimonious retort when Stuart intervened.

"I believe there is a patrol wagon at the door," he said in a low tone. "If you don't come with me in van Cortland's car you will be taken to a police station."

The sight of a uniform had startled the boy, and he made no further protest. As the two went out Stuart overheard Furneaux telling one of his aides that Bolton was to be sent to his own home in a taxi. This prompt volte face on the detective's part was singularly illuminative. It was clear that he would be swayed a good deal by the disjointed utterances of each member of the party when aroused from a strange stupor as to whether that particular individual should be interned or not. Knowledge of this fact, joined to the finger printing operations and Furneaux's most disturbing guess at certain oddities in Mary Dixon's words and behaviour when told of van Cortland's death, caused the soldier to harbour a new, if temporary, respect for the official.

"There's no reason why you should keep mum, is there?" muttered Dixon while they were crossing the hall.

"What game is everybody playing? Is poor old Tony really dead? Are you a friend of his?"

"Wait till we are in the car," said Stuart.

He looked for the police wagon, and saw that it was drawn up by the curb nearly half a block away. A few idlers, those nondescripts always produced instantly by a great city at any hour of the day or night, were hanging about awaiting developments. Thus far, the police had hoodwinked them effectually.

During the short run to Park Avenue Stuart gave his companion a brief but accurate resume of the morning's remarkable happenings, and Dixon's wits were now sufficiently restored that he should appreciate not only their sinister import but also his own close escape from being held in custody as a material witness.

"Say," he cried, seizing Stuart's hand, "you seem to have done me no end of a good turn. I'm tremendously obliged. You must have some pull with the Police Department."

"Not the least. I am beginning to understand Mr. Furneaux's ways, I think. You persuaded him that you knew nothing of the actual crime. So did Hoigate. That is why he freed the pair of you. Moreover, he can lay hands on you again, if necessary."

Some of Dixon's new born enthusiasm for Stuart evaporated under this cold douche of common sense.

"And you tell me he sent you to break the news to Mary, my sister?" he cried.

"Yes."

"Had you met her before?"

"No."

"Queer little cuss, ain't he? But I recollect now hearing of him in some attack by Chinks on a downtown banker. He's a holy terror, they say, on the war path after a bunch of crooks. But how did Mary take it?"

"I fear I blundered badly in my part of a miserable errand," said Stuart. "Your sister behaved exceedingly well. She was dreadfully upset, of course, but she kept her self control wonderfully, and was more than anxious that I should endeavour to rescue you from an unpleasant predicament."

Dixon winced at this.

"I suppose you look on me as an infernal fool," he said.

"Well, I cannot imagine any young and sane American, with all his life before him, going in for wild orgies like that of last night, even though they took no tragic turn. Please don't misunderstand me. I'm out for an occasional good time as much as any fellow with red blood in his veins. But, as one who served in France, I hate the false pretence which labels a gang of boozers by an honourable name, and, in any case, the present is no time for flouting public opinion in such fashion."

"Every single one of us had flown," protested Dixon hotly.

Stuart did not answer, and the younger man went on, with a shame faced smile:—

"I see you don't know what the Ace Club really stood for. It had nothing to do with downing Fritzies. Alcohol, Chloroform and Ether—A. C. E. D'you get me? Pretty mad, wasn't it? ... However, I'm through with that kind of stuff now, for keeps. Here we are! Come along, and hand me over to Mary."

"Surely that is not necessary," protested Stuart who had the strongest disinclination against thrusting himself a second time into the girl's presence.

"Oh, yes. I'm under your escort, you know. I learnt that much in France, anyhow. As a prisoner I'm not out of your charge till I'm signed for."

Stuart was well aware that this light headed boy counted on escaping the first burst of family displeasure by returning home in the company of a stranger.

"I'll take you as far as the door," he agreed, and would have held strictly to his pact—indeed, he asked the attendant to keep the elevator waiting—had not Mary Dixon herself admitted them. She appeared to have been on the alert for their arrival.

"Please come in, Captain Stuart," she said. "I was
sure you would rescue this bad brother of mine, and I
suppose you have had nothing to eat this morning.
Breakfast is ready, and then Willie must go to bed."

Now, there was nothing new for Stuart in the
discovery that life is made up largely of trivialities. He
remembered that at dawn on a bitterly cold morning in
October of 1918, while repelling a German counter attack
on the trench held by his company,* his chief concern was
lest a kettle should boil over and extinguish a charcoal
fire which had with difficulty been kindled in a dug out
by the efforts of three devoted men and two matches, the
remnants of the last box owned by a whole platoon.

*On the Western Front cavalry acting as infantry took
the infantry formations.*

Similarly, when confronted unexpectedly by the girl
whom he had left in tears, or nearly so, he recalled
Furneaux's impish comments on the varying beauty of
the female sex at different hours of the same day. Mary
Dixon was dressed in black, but not even the pallour of
her face or the wearied expression of her eyes could
conceal the full tide of life that pulsed beneath her skin.

It was pleasant, too, to see the maternal severity of
her scrutiny of brother Willie. That young scapegrace, of
course, scoffed at the notion of retiring to rest.

"I've slept soundly for the past five hours," he said,
ruefully, "but a cup of hot coffee is a bully idea. Tell you
what, Mary, although we're all awfully sorry about poor
old Van, it'll do no good if we talk things over during
breakfast. Let's eat first, and I'll tell you everything I
know afterwards."

Stuart smiled involuntarily, and found the girl's eyes
dwelling on him in a rather searching way. He smiled
again, and she seemed to read his meaning, which was
simple enough for one of her acute mentality, as he only
sought to convey that she was far better posted already in

the details of the tragedy than the boy who had unconsciously taken part in it. So Stuart joined the two at breakfast, there being no sign of the elder Dixon. As a good soldier he had not the slightest difficulty in disposing of an egg and some toast, on the principle of the immortal Captain Dugald Dalgetty, who held that when a cavalier finds an abundance of excellent food at his disposal he does wisely to victual himself for at least three days, since there is no knowing when he may come by another mess.

As might well be expected, Willie Dixon himself was the first to break his own ordinance of silence on the one topic on their minds.

"They talk about somebody having done for Tony," he said, after a refreshing draught of coffee. "Do you believe that Mary? Who could have such a grudge against him as to take his life?"

"Why is it assumed that he did not die from natural causes?" enquired the girl, and Stuart did not fail to note that she neither answered her brother's question nor admitted that her own first thought had been of a crime.

"Well, I can't say exactly. Someone told me—oh, the detective—Furneaux his name is—queer little duck, with eyes like a parrot—said . . . No, he didn't, now I come to think of it. Wasn't it you, Captain Stuart, who suggested that Anthony had been killed?"

"I believe we are all jumping at conclusions," said Stuart. "There is no proof whatsoever as yet that van Cortland was—well, there is only one word for it— murdered. It is the atmosphere of suspicion created by the presence of detectives and police that makes one look for the worst explanation. The butler added fuel to the fire by his annoyance about the dead goldfish."

"The goldfish!" broke in Dixon. "Has that little beggar croaked,too?"

"Yes. He was found dead in the bowl when Brown entered the room this morning."

"Poor little thing! I tried to feed him with some crumbs last night, but Tony stopped me. He said Brown gave him ant eggs. He was lively as a cricket at ten o'clock—skipping around merrily."

"That fact, plus Mr. Furneaux's announcement that he meant taking the twelve of you to the police station, has led us to suppose van Cortland's death was not merely untimely, or accidental. But it is early days to build any sound theory. We must await events. The police will enquire into the affair fully. I, for one, hope the mystery may turn out to be no mystery."

"What do you mean?" said the girl.

"A man can pass away in such an extraordinarily easy manner if the heart or brain is affected. Van Cortland crashed twice in France, to my definite knowledge. How can we tell that he then escaped some vital damage which may only now have revealed its existence?"

There was a slight pause. Then Dixon said, with obvious discomfort:—

"Will the police want to examine me again?"

"That is quite certain. They will delve into every bit of history with regard to the Ace Club, and especially as to last night's gathering. If I may venture to add my advice to your sister's, I would recommend a hot bath and a few hours' proper sleep. You may need your wits later in the day."

"Is the police enquiry likely to go beyond the bounds of the actual crime, if it be shown there was one?" put in Mary.

"You may take that for granted, too, Miss Dixon. Judging from what I have seen of Mr. Furneaux's methods, I am sure he will not hesitate to cable the Pope if he thinks the Holy Father can throw light on any branch of the investigation."

"Will the whole story be published in the newspapers?"

"Not yet, not for some time. Furneaux seems more than anxious that nothing should appear in the press—

prematurely, that is. Of course, the death can be camouflaged for a little while, but full publicity cannot be withheld at the inquest."

The girl nearly, but not quite successfully, repressed a gasp of terror at the sound of an ominous word.

"I had forgotten the inquest," was all she said, yet Stuart was so convinced that she was yielding again to stress of misery, or, though he hated to admit it, of fear, that he excused himself on the ground that he himself was a witness of some importance, and that the Chief of the Detective Bureau wished to see him.

Mary Dixon accompanied him to the door.

"I feel that in you my brother may have a reliable friend," she said. "Will you tell me where we can find you?"

He gave his private address, and that of his club. This time their hands met.

"I am heartily sorry for you, Miss Dixon," he contrived to say rather gruffly, since men of his type find it more than difficult to express sympathy.

"I know it," she murmured, with such a piteous quivering of her lips that he was relieved when the door closed.

He was beginning to hate the van Cortland mansion in Fifth Avenue. Outwardly a thoroughly respectable house, of fine proportions in the best Georgian style, it now revolted his every sense. It had become a morgue rather than a millionaire's residence. He hoped that this time he would get away from it speedily.

A limp youth, whom he failed to recognise, was being assisted into a car when he reached the door. Less robust, probably, than either Dixon or Holgate, this unfortunate felt very ill, and his face had a yellowish green tint which brought jeers from a group of onlookers. The belief was spreading that the police had raided a resort of aristocratic dope-fiends; indeed, this version of the affair was encouraged by those who knew the truth. So strangely constituted is social life in the chief city of

America that not one in a thousand persons passing that morning the succession of minor palaces which constitute upper Fifth Avenue could name accurately the owners of a dozen. Yet, like all democracies, the New York crowd is ever ready to sneer at the idle rich.

"Search me!" guffawed one of the unwashed, noting Stuart's trim appearance. "Here's a guy who missed the party!"

"Shut your mouth!" said another. "If that gentleman doesn't do it for you I will."

Stuart would have left the jibe unheeded, but he could not help glancing at his unexpected champion. He turned, and looked again. A tall, thin, scarecrow of a fellow grinned, squared his shoulders, and saluted.

"Yes, Cap," came the greeting. "It's me, all that is left of me—left of two hundred—pounds."

Luckily, Stuart recalled the man's name, a trooper in his own regiment.

"That you, Benson?" he asked, with a surprise that was not assumed, since he had last seen this old comrade in arms doing certain noteworthy stunts while engaged in the congenial task of mopping up a German trench.

"Yes, sir."

It was greatly to Benson's credit and ultimate gain that he did not embark on any hard luck story. His ragged attire and poor physical condition told a wretched enough tale.

"Why did you leave the service?" said Stuart.

"Disability. Discharged. Then I lost all I had in a Get Rich Quick Scheme."

Stuart had the soldierly faculty of prompt decision. He wrote something on a leaf torn from his note book, and gave it to Benson, with a ten dollar bill.

"There!" he said. "Call on me at three o'clock, and we'll talk things over."

The man's tanned face grew sallow with emotion.

"You've halted me at the gallop, sir," he muttered. "Can I do anything for you now? Shift this bunch, for instance?"

"You can hardly do that single handed."

"If there's another young spark inside who looks as sick as the last one, send him out right away, an' leave the rest to me."

"No rough house stuff, Benson?"

"Not one short arm jab, sir."

Beyond the glass door Stuart met the butler and a detective escorting another much disturbed youth downstairs. Sheer curiosity led him to step into a vestiaire which had a small window commanding the street. The moment the sufferer appeared, and was practically lifted into a waiting car, Benson skipped hurriedly into the middle of the roadway, and after whispering confidentially to some man lounging there, made off at a sharp pace. The others imitated his example. Within five seconds the crowd had vanished utterly.

Stuart was mystified, but had to wait some hours for an explanation. Benson it appeared then, had told the sightseers that several bad cases of smallpox were being taken to the Hospital for Infectious Diseases on Blackwell's Island!

It was disconcerting to learn from Brown that Chief Inspector Winter, head of the Detective Bureau, had not arrived as yet. In the first place, the soldier had no wish to hang about that plague-stricken mansion. Secondly, he did not want to be drawn into any further connection with the enquiry as to the cause of van Cortland's death, and, lastly, he was afraid that at any moment he might be led into open denunciation of police methods. Furneaux, possibly an erratic genius, was not the sort of man he, Stuart, would have entrusted with an affair of this magnitude, and it certainly did seem an amazing thing that the Chief of the Bureau had not been summoned urgently. True, his assistant had announced that he was on his way. But what prior investigation that day could have stronger claims than the apparent murder of a popular young millionaire?

Stuart glanced at his watch. Ten o'clock. Two full hours had elapsed since he telephoned police headquarters.

"Sharp work, Captain," came a high pitched voice from the top of the stairs.

Furneaux's quite uncanny trick of thought reading rendered Stuart chary of open criticism. But he could not help saying:—

"Is that what you call it, Mr. Furneaux?"

"No. No. For me it's merely normal, but you now, a smart soldier, clever young chap, and all the rest of it, what do you really know about this business? You were here first—barring Brown—always barring Brown—a Heaven sent specimen of a baldheaded butler to be in charge of the exhibits in a case like this—yet you passed clue after clue as though you couldn't see or smell or touch. There must be something gravely lacking in the curriculum of the Army School of Scouts, if you even possess such a thing. Come and join me in some breakfast, and I'll discourse."

"I'll join you with pleasure, and perhaps profit, but I'm dashed if I eat a third breakfast," said Stuart, following the detective into a room overlooking the street, which Brown designated as "the morning room."

"Three! Where did you have the first two?"

Stuart told him.

"Good!" cackled Furneaux. "If a man cannot think let him at least eat."

"I have met people who looked as though they did neither."

The detective lifted the cover off a dish of bacon and sausages, which he sniffed with much gusto.

"You're riding for a fall, young man," he announced. "You are now going to see me eat, and, when the gross claims of appetite are satisfied, I'll make your cerebral outfit look like a thin dime."

"Let me pour out the coffee, anyhow," said Stuart good humouredly. There was no sense in quarrelling with this vainglorious little man, who evidently prided himself on showing off the few professional tricks which he could hardly help gleaning from the varied experiences of the Bureau. "How do you like it? Half milk?"

"No, sir. No milk. On the rare occasions when I need a draught of coffee to stimulate the brain, and this is one, I do not dream of spoiling an excellent tonic by clouding and thickening it with milk or cream. Now you, I suppose, smoke?"

"By Jove! I never thought of it. But I'll hold off till you've finished your breakfast."

"Well, that is quite nice of you. I'll take your offer. The fumes of that beastly mixture of chloral hydrate nearly overcame me, and I don't think I could stand the noxious odour of nicotine now on an empty stomach. Winter, when he comes here, will be consuming his second Havana since leaving Brooklyn, where he grows sweet peas in the backyard which he calls a garden. Sweet peas! Ye gods! Was ever delicate flower tended by so bulky a mortal? You, 1 suppose, are a cigarette fiend?"

"No; pipe."

Stuart was girding himself for a battle of wits with this strange little man. Now the two were together again that display of intellectual dominance by Furneaux over others, which the soldier resented, and which really accounted for his slight feeling of petulance, made itself felt once more. He had a queer notion that his thoughts were printed legibly on his shirt front, and that Furneaux could read them at a glance.

"A pipe, eh?" repeated the detective. "Strange thing, but scoundrels hardly ever smoke a pipe. You cannot picture a murderer or a forger enjoying his baccy, can you? Cigarettes, now—they're criminal, if you like. They cover the whole gamut of rascality, from the defaulting bank president to the peccant bellhop. I can almost classify the crook by his brand of cigarette. Cigars are more cosmopolitan. A man may remain a decent citizen and indulge in a good Havana. Of course, I pay no heed to the wretched fellows who poison the air with a home grown tufa—they are beneath contempt, and seldom rise to any height, even in villainy. But beware of the big, blond, bullet headed, round eyed cabaleros who puff giant clouds of smoke out of imported Cubans. They "

"What's the trouble, Frog? Somebody or something worrying you? You always pitch into me when the pieces of the puzzle won't fit."

A tall, strongly built man, whose physical characteristics Furneaux had described aptly, came in, and, smiling cheerfully, held out a hand to Stuart, who was utterly at a loss to know how the diminutive detective was either aware of his chief's presence or could so time his caustic comments that the latter must overhear them.

"Don't let our funny little friend annoy you, Captain Stuart," continued Mr. Winter. "He always gives tongue when on the chase. Stop Furneaux from talking and a wonderful brain would die of sheer atrophy."

"That's the chief's great new word," snapped Furneaux, digging a fork viciously into a second sausage, "He dallied with co ordinate and differentiate, passed through bad attacks of meticulous and connote, and is now "

"Going to ask Captain Stuart to join me in an imported Cuban."

"I knew it," almost shrieked Furneaux. "Here have I been sniffing ammonia during the past hour as an antidote to Chloral flavoured with Glyl Rosae, and now I cannot be allowed even to eat in peace."

"Are you sure of the flavouring?" put in Winter quietly.

"Yes. Dr. Bright recognised it, too."

"That helps some. Van Cortland himself had that prescription made up two days ago at the drugstore on the next block!"

CHAPTER 4: MR. FURNEAUX'S DEDUCTIVE METHOD

FROM that moment Alec Stuart realised he was moving in a new world, a world in which it behooved him to pick his way with exceeding care. He valued a certain reputation for calm and clear judgment earned while on a Divisional Staff, and he certainly did not want to lose it at the hands of a pair of New York detectives. He abandoned at once any thought of criticising their peculiarities, and had not to wait long before thanking his stars for the decision. Of course, he fully expected Furneaux to manifest surprise at the Chief Inspector's statement; not yet did he grasp the complexities of the little man's character. It was almost a point of honour with Furneaux that he should never be surprised at anything.

"Dear me!" was what he said, pouring out another cup of coffee.

"Does that simplify matters?" enquired Winter.

"No. It's the most annoying thing you could have told me."

"Why?"

"Because it introduces the element of suicide, which I have completely discarded."

"Which you had discarded, you mean?"

"Not a bit. I am precise of speech, and use the simple phrases beloved of Lincoln and John Bright."

Winter winked brazenly at Stuart, who, having nothing to say, kept quiet. He himself had thought of suicide as a solution of the tragedy, though it was a theory difficult to reconcile with van Cortland's

approaching marriage to a delightful girl like Mary
Dixon.

"Well, my pocket Vidocq, give us your yarn in words of
one syllable," said the big man.

"You may smoke now," said Furneaux.

"That's a good start, anyhow," and Winter offered
Stuart a well filled cigar case.

"By the way," put in the latter, "do you gentlemen
really wish to discuss this ugly business in my presence? I
am deeply interested, of course, but— "

"We need your help," said Furneaux. "I have employed
you already as a cavalry screen, but you don't seem to
understand your duties. When you get the hang of this
affair you may make up your mind to tell us what you
know."

"What I know?" cried Stuart.

Furneaux waved a hand in air as though impatient of
these childish interruptions, and Winter said earnestly:—

"Captain Stuart, you are spoiling a good cigar by
lighting it on one side."

"I give in," smiled Stuart. "Carry on!"

"I'm about to make a speech," said Furneaux
sententiously, "and I don't want to be interrupted by
either crude humour or military ineptitude."

Winter produced a note book, and wrote the word
"ineptitude" in large script across a blank page,
whereupon Furneaux gazed at the sky through the upper
part of an opposite window.

"Anthony van Cortland may or may not have expected
to die soon," he continued, "but I am sure he did not think
he was destined to pass out last night. His life had been
threatened, however. No later than yesterday, if the date
be correct, he received a type written slip telling him he
would not be allowed to marry Mary Dixon, and that, if
he did not take certain definite steps to break off the
engagement, he would be removed without further notice.
The note alluded to a previous warning, and is couched in

broken English, meant to simulate the effort of an uneducated Italian to express himself."

"Can we see the note now?" enquired Winter meekly.

Furneaux, who certainly was an actor of no mean rank, produced a soiled scrap of paper, apparently the lower half of a folio sheet, which had been torn, not cut, and folded twice. He handed it to the Chief with a fine air.

It bore a date, June i8th., and contained some typed lines, which ran:—

"You kno alredda you have not to marri la Signorina Dixon. I nede not tell you the wy. It is forbid, see. I not tell you again. You stoppa la nozze or you die in twenty four hour, see. You putta littel wite car in windo tomor morning, 8 ora, an I not kill you tomor. Nex day you say in jornal no marri Miss Dixon an Mr. Cortland. Beliva this. It is alright. Maka big blac X on littel wite card."

Winter scanned the message with close attention, and passed it to Stuart, who noticed at once that the letters "r," and "y," and the capital "S" were out of alignment on the typewriter. He passed no comment, however, but placed the paper on the table in front of Furneaux, who still seemed to be seeking inspiration in the blue vault of heaven.

Waiting until each of his hearers had scrutinised the threat, he continued:—

"Three of last night's party of thirteen admit that van Cortland spoke of this warning having reached him in a typed envelope, bearing the Grand Central postmark of midnight the night before. He scoffed at it, attributing it to the craze among low class Italians for sending anonymous letters. Indeed, he went so far as to say that some girl in the opera had probably inspired it. It will be easy to find the girl, and this will be done as a mere matter of form. The note was neither written nor composed by an Italian, but by someone adpting that disguise, someone who knew about the girl, probably a trivial bit of half forgotten folly, and seized on that

pretext to threaten van Cortland with death if he married
Mary Dixon. I spit at the Italian side of this romance. It
centres right here, in fashionable Fifth Avenue. The man
who committed this murder was in that room last night.
It was he who placed a strong dose of chloral hydrate,
disguised by Ghyl Rosae, or glycerine and rose water, in
the punch, well knowing that the mixture of wines and
liqueurs would hide effectually the unpleasant taste of
the chloral, granted even that the tortured palates of a
dozen half drunken fools were capable of detecting it. He
himself of course, took a glass of the brew, but contrived
to spill it unseen into the bowl which held that wretched
goldfish. No respectable chemist, by the way, would
supply one tenth of the quantity needed to dope thirteen
men. Then, when the twelve were down and out, he killed
van Cortland—poisoned him—by some hypodermic
injection. As soon as he could be sure that van Cortland
was dead, or, at any rate, so comatose as to be on the
point of death, he raised the blind of the third, or most
northerly, window overlooking Fifth Avenue, opened the
window, went out on the balcony, and threw the bottle
which had held the narcotic right across the road into the
shrubbery of Central Park. It probably contained, too, the
instrument—I don't think it was a syringe or needle—
with which he had administered the active poison to van
Cortland, but that has not been found. Practically all the
pieces of the broken bottle are accounted for. A man is
now going over the ground with a tooth comb and a
magnifying glass for the other thing—let us call it a
syringe—but I fear it will not turn up. The murderer
closed the window, drew the blind, took a strong dose of
the doctored punch, and awaited developments, trusting
to his own force of will not to betray himself when he
awoke, which, he foresaw, would probably be in the
presence of the police. And, damn him, he didn't!"
    Furneaux's voice broke in a squeak on that last
forcible sentence. It was the protest of a genuine artist
against unkind fate. He had relied for guidance on the

first disordered utterance of the one man among twelve who knew what sort of deadly peril he was facing when his scattered senses returned, and who knew, too, that his period of greatest danger would be the few seconds prior to complete consciousness. But, the test had failed, or Furneaux said it had.

Stuart was certain that the detective was practising no deceit, but the certainty did not preclude possession of other clues which he had not mentioned.

"The window was neat work, Charles, very neat," said Winter composedly. "How did you get it?"

"Each blind is controlled by a spring at the side of the roller. Brown drew all the blinds at eight o'clock last night, and arranged them properly, of course. The murderer—we'll bracket him Mr. X., for short—pulled down that blind too forcibly, and the roller shot over the spring. The accident must have disconcerted him more than enough, or, if premeditated, was the finest thing I have ever heard of in the annals of crime, as it pointed straight to the only direct evidence we have, barring the typed letter. The rest was easy—too easy."

"How—too easy?"

Furneaux turned a basilisk eye on his chief, and was on the point of making some biting answer when he seemed to recollect that Stuart was in the room.

"Oh, yes," he cackled almost apologetically. "You see, Captain Stuart, if a clever criminal, one of the really brainy sort, wants to lead a sleuth gently but firmly up to the arrest of the wrong man—an innocent man, I mean—he blazes the trail with quiet hints, relying on the equally clever and brainy detective finding them. Let me illustrate. Mr. X. had not forgotten finger prints. There are none of his on the glass bowl or the window sash, because he took care to wipe them off with a pocket handkerchief, marked with the initials 'R. K.', and found, of course, in the pocket of young Bob Kerningham. That, by the way, is a secret. Mr. Kerningham himself is not aware that I know it, and I doubt very much that he

knows it himself. In fact, as a clue, it is a trifle too
obvious, but it must be enquired into. Never shall it be
said that the Detective Bureau failed to see the wood for
the trees. Another item—the footprints in the dust on the
balcony were purposely confused by shuffling the feet. In
fact, the man who killed van Cortland forgot very little."

"And now, Captain Stuart, you will tell us your story,"
said Winter.

"I?" cried Stuart.

He looked for no such flank attack by the Chief
Inspector, whose acquaintance he made during some
departmental investigation of a series of pension frauds.
Thinking things over calmly afterwards, he likened the
time spent with these strange detectives to a passage
along an apparently open road on the Western Front
which had been mined. He never knew the second when a
verbal bombshell would burst on him.

"Yes, you. If my quaint little friend will permit, I
should like to interpret him. Apart from all Italian
vendettas or slighted ballerinas, the projected marriage of
Miss Dixon and Mr. van Cortland strikes me as supplying
the key to this mystery. Mr. X., as Furneaux so politely
puts it, killed van Cortland to stop that marriage, and did
so only when the bridegroom scoffed at the notion of
abandoning it. The' e we have a direct and obvious motive
for the crime. Now, it is difficult for us to approach the
lady. The mere mention of a detective's name will either
seal her lips or throw her into a hysteria of denunciation
which will be hopelessly beside the point. But you met
her as a social equal and a friend of van Cortland's. How
did she take the news of his death? Give us your full and
free impressions, no matter how mistaken they may
prove later. That is why Mr. Furneaux chose you as his
messenger, and I am sure you will not, from any absurd
notions of chivalry, refuse us your confidence."

Stuart looked in silence at the men who awaited his
answer. Probably, in no other detective force in the world

were there two members so unlike each other as these two. Winter was a big, round man—round headed, round bodied, round limbed. His prominent blue eyes were rather more kindly than stern, but the width of his head between the ears, no less than the strength of a massive chin, proclaimed the courage and tenacity of a prize fighter, a simile well borne out, too, by his close cropped hair and the size of his fists, of which one rested on the table and the other held the cigar he was smoking. He sat back comfortably in his chair, but was in such fine physical condition that he could have sprung at an adversary in a tiger leap if need be. He was dressed in a loose fitting blue serge suit, and wore a cat's eye tie pin. The third finger of his right hand carried a huge signet ring, which could become a highly effective knuckle duster in an emergency. He looked utterly unlike a policeman. A shrewd observer of men might have classified him as a successful stock broker who bred pedigree cattle as a hobby.

His colleague, Furneaux, was exactly half his weight; Stuart had already taken him for a leading jockey or famous comedian. His hands and feet were tiny, even for one who scaled about a hundred and twenty pounds. It was quite impossible to determine his race from his features. Winter was of pure Anglo Saxon stock, but Furneaux was named Charles Frangois after his French father, and his mother was of mixed New England genealogy. Winter was a fighter, Furneaux an animated thinking machine. The veins of the one held red blood, of the other quick silver. Individually they were a terror to evildoers: when they ran together on a criminal trail, as they almost invariably did, there was no social wolf in the United States but endeavoured to gallop fast and far to cover at the first hint of the chase.

Glancing from Winter's blandly agreeable face to Furneaux's intent one, Stuart could not help smiling.

"Let us in on the joke," said Furneaux tartly.

"It is no joke, gentlemen," said the soldier. "I have read of a bird being fascinated by a snake, and I was just wondering how the wretched fowl would make out if it were stalked by two snakes."

"I've been called all sorts of things in my previous life, but never a snake," said Winter.

"I was thinking mainly of the bird's predicament. . . . Well, I see no way of escape. I must warn you that I am a mighty poor judge of the feminine temperament, but I came to the conclusion this morning that Miss Dixon was less appalled by van Cortland's death than terrified as to its outcome. She dreaded rather what I might say next than what I had said already. I mean that while overwhelmed by my news, as any decent minded woman must be, her thought leaped at once to its possible consequences. She assumed he had been killed, not that he might have been the victim of an accident or unsuspected disease."

Furneaux's face wrinkled in an appreciative grin.

"Hum! Ha! Excellent!" he cried. "I seldom err in choosing my man."

"You would have failed in your choice this time had I guessed what lay behind it," said Stuart quietly.

"Don't you want your friend's slayer to be discovered?"

"Yes. If my personal efforts—"

"Suppose," broke in the other, "Miss Dixon were replaced by some shrew of an Italian ballad squawker, would you feel so aggrieved in the matter?"

Shut up, you imp!" said Winter. "You must make allowances for professional zeal, Captain Stuart. Furneaux would use a pet lamb to stalk a lion if a pet lamb were the best lure. He would even tie a bow of blue silk ribbon round its woolly little neck. But what harm has he done you or Miss Dixon? Please don't be offended if I say that every word spoken here will be, must be, forgotten on both sides. And no one dreams that the lady is a party to her fiance's death. We want to find out the circumstances which led up to it, and what you have just told us may be of exceeding value. Your summary is fine. Won't you go a step farther, and give us the exact words that were used—just what you said and what she said."

Stuart obeyed. Having taken the plunge it was hopeless now to dream of temporizing. He had a retentive memory, and was able to repeat, practically verbatim, the two brief conversations between him and the girl that morning. Having made an end, he rose.

"I have done all that you asked, and a good deal more than I anticipated," he said, with a stiffness of tone not lost on his hearers. "This case does not interest me so particularly that I should wish a closer connection with it."

"You're a bit sore with me?" chirped Furneaux.

"Well, I suppose I am. It is difficult to define—"

"Don't try. I hate to mention eating to a man who has done so nobly twice already to day, but I shall be glad if you will join Mr. Winter and me in a little dinner to night."

"I—er—"

"Please come," urged Winter, winking again.

Stuart had no notion what that portentous wink meant, but he changed an imminent refusal into a hesitating acceptance.

"Good," cried the Chief heartily. "As there is an Italian flavour in this affair, suppose you meet us at the Restorato Milano, in West 46th Street, at 7:30. Don't wait at the door. Walk upstairs, turn the handle of the first room on the left, and, if we are not there, and any son of a gun asks your business, say 'Serpe.' That'll stop his mouth."

"But 'serpe' is the Italian for 'snake.'"

"Exactly."

Stuart could not help laughing, even in that house of gloom.

"I believe you two could persuade me to keep a suspicious eye on my own mother," he said.

When he had gone, Winter rubbed his hands. "A find!" he said cheerfully. "He may kick like a steer, but we can surely get him to pump that girl."

Furneaux shook his head.

"You're wrong, James. We may want to use him in other ways—hence the dinner. But he's on to our game now, and the girl is off the map where his help is concerned. However, he did us a good turn, an' mebbe we've done him one."

Winter's eye brows curved in two perfect arches.

"Match making again, Charles? Such haste is quite indecent," he said. "Poor van Cortland is hardly dead yet."

"She never cared a straw about van Cortland. She almost hated him when it came to marriage."

"How do you know?"

"Because, James, that streak of femininity in me which you think you have discovered assures me, if it exists, that no woman who loved a man would behave as Mary Dixon did two hours ago, and a woman not in love loathes the very thought of matrimony. Next?"

"Have you any sort of plan founded on your analysis up to the moment?"

"No. I must think things out. I need to know a heap more about three men, whose rooms I am now going to search. The three are Robert Kerningham, whose handkerchief wiped the vase, Philip Durrane, and Francis O. Baker."

"Why Durrane and Baker?"

"Because they, like Kerningham, have long thin feet. Mr. X., when on the balcony, forgot to shuffle his feet lengthwise as well as sideways."

"Luckily for us, Charles, they always do forget something. Do you want me?"

"Of course. How am I to force my way into three uptown mansions unless I have your inert and obese mass behind me?"

It was a sore point with Furneaux that the public would never believe he was a detective. Even those policemen to whom he was a stranger suspected him, and his badge had not saved him from being arrested twice, once in Detroit and again in Atlantic City, for asking questions which showed he knew far more about some crime then under investigation than the local authorities themselves.

"Do we go now?"

"I am waiting for the doctor's report. He and an expert in toxicology from the Roosevelt Hospital are making a thorough external examination of the body. It may help some. I suppose the post mortem is the only sure test, but we cannot delay operations for that."

"We must watch our steps. These young asses belong to the best families in New York. They are all in the Social Register."

"One is even an F. F. V., because Durrane hails from Virginia."

"And the girl is in the Junior League. Charles, you must restrain yourself."

"Oh, it is a pretty case, and no mistake. I've known Chief Commissioners lose their scalps for affairs which were not Point One per cent of this in public interest."

"Ah!" sighed Winter.

"Yes, I had to drag you in. I couldn't pull the weight unaided."

"You little devil! Even over the 'phone I felt your fine Italian hand."

"Don't mix your metaphors, Chief. It sounds bad at this hour of the morning. And cut out the Italian stuff. There's nothing in it."

"I don't agree with you. You're sharp, I admit, but your survey is limited to the area of a flashlight."

" 'Sharp?' 'Flash light?' If you said my intellect was 'clear' or 'piercing' I might let the insult pass."

"You'll make a fortune out of boobs by your cheap wit when you take your pension and set up a Private Detective Office."

"I'll find you a strong arm job as bouncer. By the way, the butler here is in your line. Let's put him through it!"

Furneaux leaped to the bell. Anyone hearing these two bandying unpleasant personalities would have believed that the City detective force was about to lose the services of one if not both of its best men, whereas, as the Chief Commissioner well knew, the cleverest crook in New York ought to tremble when the Big 'Un and the Little 'Un of the Bureau were not only yelping at his heels but snapping at each other.

In crossing the room Furneaux happened to glance into the street, so, when Brown came, his first query was:—

"Who cleared the mob away from the door?"

"A rough looking fellow who spoke to Captain Stuart, sir."

"How do you know?"

"The chauffeur told me, sir."

Winter and Furneaux exchanged a look of enquiry. Even their omniscience could not solve that puzzle. Then the Chief took up the examination.

"I hear you were in the London police, Brown," he said.

"Yes, sir."

"Why did you quit?"

The butler's placid face flushed slightly.

"Do you really want to know?" he asked.

"Sure."

"Well, I was getting on all right for five years when a sergeant stuck his knife into me."

"Stabbed you?"

Brown smiled gently.

"No, sir. That's just a manner of speaking. I couldn't do right with that fellow. He made my life a misery, so, when the war broke out, I resigned, and joined the Guards."

"Good egg! That sergeant must have been a mean cuss."

"He was just conceited, sir. But I got square with him."

"Indeed, how?"

"In the interval, when I was out of the force, an' before I passed the doctor, I went to the pub—the saloon, sir— where I knew he might be found occasionally when off duty. I ragged him a bit, an' got him to put his hands up."

"And then?"

"I gave him one or two."

"Soaked him in the jaw!"

"Yes, sir."

"Excellent. And how about the army?"

"I got a machine gun here," and Brown tapped his left shoulder, "three times during the attack on Loos. They invalided me out, and I came to America with one of our Embassy gentlemen. That's how I took to butlering."

"No butler in New York has a better record. By the way, what size was your sergeant?"

"About your size, sir."

"What! Do you think you could soak me in the jaw?"

"I'd try to, sir, if you were to put on me, week in an' week out, for months."

"Ha!" cackled Furneaux. "Perhaps, when this affair has blown over, and before the house is closed, I can persuade Mr. Winter to come here some quiet afternoon, and give you the once over."

The chief endeavoured to look stern, but there could be no doubt that the two big men were estimating each other with a measuring eye.

"My left shoulder still troubles me a lot," said Brown in an explanatory way, and the two detectives smiled.

"Did they blow your hair off in France, too?" enquired Furneaux.

"No, sir. I am proud of my bald head. Hair seldom goes with brains. Look at women!"

Now it was Winter's turn to chortle, for his tiny subordinate owned a shock of black hair.

"Well, let's see how far your brains go," snapped Furneaux, who never expected such a retort from this bland person. "How did Mr. van Cortland meet his death?"

"I think he was stabbed, sir, or maybe that is not the right word. Someone shoved a poisoned needle twice into his neck over the jugular vein."

"Ah, you saw that, did you?"

"I noticed the two little wounds when I lifted his head."

"Just as a mere guess—who did it?"

"Someone who didn't want him to marry Miss Dixon, sir."

"Why do you say that?"

"Miss Dixon and her father came here this day week, and there was a serious talk, in this very room. Mr. van Cortland opened the door for them as they went out, and I couldn't help hearing what he said. It was:—'I'm inclined to laugh at the whole business, Mary. You and I will get married if I have to borrow a suit of armour and clank my way to the church through a hedge of stilettos.' Those were his very words, sir."

"Did you see Miss Dixon just then?"

"Yes, sir."

"How did she look? What effect had Mr. van Cortland's assurance on her?"

"She looked worried, sir."

No one spoke thereafter during some seconds. Footsteps were heard in the corridor without, and Winter nodded to Brown.

"Thanks," he said. "We'll have another chat later. Here come the doctors. Tell them we are in this room."

For a brief while he and Furneaux were alone.

"Ca marche!" murmured the little man.

"It gallops!" replied the big one.

CHAPTER 5: HOW FLANAGAN DIED

DB. BRIGHT and his associate expert from the Roosevelt Hospital pledged themselves definitely to the opinion that van Cortland's death was the outcome of an irritant poison injected into the blood through two small punctures on the left side of the neck. They were quite unable to classify the poison.

"The post mortem may or may not tell us," said, the expert. "Unfortunately we did not examine the subject until some seven or eight hours after death, when rigor mortis had set in, but there are indications that a species of paralysis was induced. Assuming that a state of almost complete coma had been created by a strong dose of choral hydrate before the poison was administered, the latter must have been exceedingly, indeed inconceivably, powerful if it brought about speedy death, as the action of the heart and the arterial circulation would be much retarded by the drug. In some respects both the appearance of the tiny wounds and the subsequent condition of the body reminded me of snakebite."

"I thought of that," said Furneaux, "but dismissed it as too far fetched. The distance between the punctures argued an unusually large head for a poisonous snake, as the poison fangs are set close together, and the unseen conveyance of such a reptile into the room was practically impossible. Of course, these strange things do happen. If a snake did the trick we shall soon have some blood curdling stories from Central Park. I wonder if the creature would find the zoo!"

The Roosevelt Hospital man, who had not met Furneaux before, eyed him curiously.

"Why should you look to Central Park for developments?" he enquired.

"Isn't that the natural place an escaped snake would make for?"

"Well, yes."

Furneaux did not desire that a needlessly wide circle should share his knowledge that the assassin had stood on the balcony overlooking Fifth Avenue about two o'clock that morning. For once, his quick wits had betrayed him into saying something he meant to keep hidden, but Winter never failed him in an emergency.

"When do you gentlemen wish to hold the postmortem?" he enquired.

"This afternoon," said Dr. Bright.

"Very well. I'll see the coroner and make arrangements."

The doctors went out, and the detectives followed, taking the key of the fatal room.

"By the way," said Winter, after giving the butler certain instructions, particularly as to refusing all information to the press, and warning the other servants to keep still tongues, though the presence of a policeman lent some protection from prying visitors, "if that room was used as a dining room why is it known as the drawing room?"

"It is the largest room in the house, sir, so the dining room table was taken there on Club rights."

"How often did the Club meet?"

"Once a month—every fourth Thursday. This was to have been the last meeting."

"Because of the marriage?"

"Yes, sir."

Probably Brown expected a question as to the reason underlying the Club's name, but the police knew the facts already. The Ace Club had attained a certain notoriety. Even the underworld of New York was jealous of a really notable idea!

"Charles, my lad, that doctor man nearly surprised you into an admission by his snake bite suggestion," said Winter when the two reached the street.

"It's these queer coincidences," grumbled the other. "Didn't you give 'serpe' to Stuart as a password to the Milan Restaurant?"

"Oh, blame me, of course, you rat!"

But both men were destined to be startled by a much more remarkable coincidence before the day ended.

"By the way," purred Furneaux, failing to accept the proffered cue, "hadn't we better hammer out a line as to that soldier?"

"Shall we drop him?"

"I dunno. Let's wait till after dinner."

"He may become an active nuisance, and if he won't help with the girl he's no good at all."

"You never can tell. Great events hinge on the most trivial ones. I remember once seeing a brilliant red bird in the tree lined Main Street of a Georgia townlet, and there was a moccasin snake curled up in a near by garden on the bank of the Savannah River. It may be that such sights affect the mentality of the inhabitants. Suppose the dour Scots in a grey Argyleshire village habitually saw orange-coloured parrots on the eaves, and Irish peasants found emerald green vipers in their bogs, wouldn't these things have changed the history of the world?"

Winter took off his straw hat; and fanned himself vigorously.

"Gee!" he said, "those tints are too hot for a day like this."

But a long experience of the workings of Furneaux's mind, with its wild extravagances and fitful gleams of an almost phenomenal intuition, warned him that all this irresponsible chatter about snakes had stirred into activity some germ of seemingly insane thought which would develop into a quite tangible and demonstrable theory. So they walked a whole block in silence. When Furneaux spoke again it was only to say with conviction:—

"Yes. We need the services of the gallant captain. I guess he can stick on a horse. Yes, we'll use him, boot and saddle, whip and spurs."

Stuart, back in his 57th Street flat, was proffered a fourth breakfast, which he declined. The elderly housekeeper, who "did for" a number of tenants, explained that she had given "the man" the suit, shirt, collar, tie and boots, as requested by "the letter."

"That's all right, Mrs. Riordan," he said. "His name is Benson. I am thinking of employing him as a valet—for a time, at any rate."

Mrs. Riordan's face and hands betrayed suspicious incredulity as to Benson's fitness for the post.

"You are taking the book by the cover," laughed Stuart. "He is, or used to be, a good soldier, a cheerful, hard working one as well. Anyhow, we'll try him out. But don't start by condemning him. He has had a bad time. Under a steady course of your cooking he will blossom like the rose."

For which wholly unwarranted tribute to Mrs. Riordan's catering skill, may Heaven forgive him! The other residents in that apartment house never would if they heard it.

After a bath, and a change of clothing, Stuart lit a pipe and sat down to do some hard thinking. As it happened, he was on leave for two months, and only a week of his furlough had expired. With the exception of week ends in Paris during the war, and a month's respite at home in Vermont after the regiment came back, he had not enjoyed an idle hour since 1917. Instead, therefore, of loafing on some sea front, or joining a fishing party in Maine, he had decided on a thorough rest in New York, unless the weather became unendurably hot. He kept fit by a daily ride in the Park, a sharp turn in the courts at the Racket Club, and a swim in the tank afterwards. For the other hours of the day he had books to read, plays to see, and notes to make for an essay on "Cavalry in the

Great War," which he hoped to find sometime in the pages of a service magazine.

Being a regular, he had not obtained the lightning promotion of the special service troops, but had acted as major on the staff, and was expecting a speedy "lift" in his own regiment, which would be at Monterey in California during the fall. In a word, the world was going well with him, and a legacy of three thousand dollars a year from an aunt had made smooth the financial path.

So it was no tangle of personal affairs that occupied his attention. He reviewed each circumstance known to him of the tragedy in which Anthony van Cortland supplied the central figure, and ever the line of reasoning led to a dimly lighted room in a Park Avenue flat where Mary Dixon had received the news of her affianced husband's death with such singular self possession. He knew little of the ways of women, and less of the idiosyncrasies of the modern society girl, but, judged by the only standard he could apply—that of manners and appearance, supplemented by the hidden psychic forces which attract like to like and repel opposites—he appraised Mary Dixon as high-minded, loyal, and honourable.

It is, therefore, a tribute to Stuart's intelligence that he should have decided, without being aware of Brown's statement to the detectives, that the girl had been told of threats against her lover's life. And the mere mental use of the word "lover" brought its corollary—was the love all on one side? Among those twelve left in the room was there one whom she preferred? And did she suspect that man instantly. If so, what a lamentable plight was hers.

"By jing!" he muttered, rising to find a match, for his pipe had gone out, "this is Grand Guignol stuff. What does it matter to me, anyhow?"

Deliberately diverting his thoughts to the Chief of the Bureau and his singular aide, the young soldier realised suddenly that such thrilling mysteries constituted their normal day's work. They would accomplish hardly

anything if they tackled their job with the sombre mien of
mutes at a funeral. Pursuing, and generally capturing,
law breakers was their business. Winter, he had no
doubt, would give a a cigar with a cheery word to a
criminal in the condemned cell, and Furneaux would
certainly have some quip for the official who switched on
the current at the execution. Recollection of the little
detective's ingenuity brought Mary Dixon back into the
picture.

"I suppose he still believes he can use me as a cat's
paw," he mused. "That's why I'm invited to the dinner to
night. I'll see him boiled in oil first! My best plan is to
clear out. . . . But I wonder who the other man can be!"

He had a hand on the telephone directory to find the
number of a friend who would surely know the names of
all the members of the Ace Club, but recalling Winter's
pledge of secrecy, refrained, as the mere enquiry might
start some rill of comment which would soon swell into a
torrent. As to the Ace Club, no one had ever said
anything really scandalous about it. It was just a set of
silly young fools, too well off, sated with pleasure seeking,
devoid of any higher purpose in life than that of killing
time. And Willie Dixon was Mary's brother. Did family
traits come out in women as in men? Then what a hell on
earth it would be for a decent-minded fellow to be tied to
a wife who developed such a mania! The idea was so
utterly unpleasing that he picked up a book written by a
German which gave the Boche's opinion of the American
army. The writer had good ground for posing as a critic,
since he had fought at Belleau Wood, St. Mihiel, and in
the Argonne.

He walked to a near by club for lunch, and actually
heard van Cortland's name mentioned before he had been
in the dining room five minutes. A corporation lawyer
was talking of some rubber combination, and spoke of a
Mr. Dixon.

"Mighty good job that pretty daughter of his drew
Tony van Cortland in the matrimonial lottery," ran the

comment, "or he,'d have been squeezed dry by the Consolidation. As matters stand, Tony's half million cleared off a mortgage debenture which had nearly fallen in, and Dixon is well fixed now for the rest of his life, unless he sells his shares, and dabbles in more high finance."

"But didn't van Cortland hold the mortgage?" enquired someone.

"That's the amusing part of it. The Consolidation had to buy him out, with arrears of interest. But dealing with a prospective son in law was a very different thing from gouging old Dixon through a bank. Tony cleaned up thirty thousand dollars in about three days, and they tell me he weighed in half of the plunder on a pearl necklace for the girl. Another instance of how money makes money."

"And spends it—on a woman," laughed a man.

Stuart noted the speaker, whom he disliked already, though for no reason. Now he loathed him.

The lawyer protested quietly.

"They are to be married early in July," he said.

"Independence Day?" went on the other.

"Well, that's one view of matrimony. Hope you keep to it, Monty."

The retort seemed to score with those who knew both speakers, and "Monty" dropped the subject. Later, Stuart learned from a friend that the would be cynic was Montagu Toyn, an unimportant type of man about town, who was always to be seen at theatrical premieres and the newest dance clubs.

At two o'clock the hall bell rang in his flat, and soon a tall, straight limbed fellow, who wore Stuart's clothes with as much distinction as Stuart himself, appeared at the door, and saluted smartly.

"Glad to see you, Benson," said Stuart. "How much have you spent of the ten dollars I gave you?"

It was an abrupt question, but he had planned things that way, since he was really taking some risk in even

thinking of employing a man of whose character he knew
so little.

"Seven dollars, sir," was the prompt answer.

"Have you, begad? Been going some, eh?"

"One fifty for a hair cut, shave an' bath, fifty cents for
a meal, an' five dollars for a room till this day week.
Couldn't get a decent one for less, sir."

The well to do man invariably sustains a mental
shock when he analyzes the budget of the poor, and
Stuart at once made amends.

"I'm glad I asked you, anyhow, Benson," he said. "You
must have been thoroughly on the rocks."

"I had been on them, an' was slippin' off for the last
time," said Benson simply. "There was no rock for mine to
night."

"What would you have done? Held up some other poor
devil?"

"No, sir. I was goin' for a long swim. I meant to pass
out clean, anyhow."

The conversation was taking an unlooked for turn.
Stuart laughed, almost nervously.

"Well, well," he said. "Let's get away from serious
topics. I've had a surfeit of them to day. I want a valet for
a couple of months, perhaps longer. If you have your
meals here, and I look out some linen for you, can you
make out on twenty five a week?"

Benson did not reply for a moment. He was afraid to
speak. At last he muttered in a staccato voice:—

"Sure I can, sir."

Stuart turned away, fumbled with some papers on the
table, and said in the most matter of fact tone he could
call to his aid:—

"Good! Take up your quarters in the kitchen. You'll
soon find things to do—just like old times in Picardy, you
know. And—don't quarrel with Mrs. Riordan. She's a slut,
and a rotten cook, but she means well."

It was a long afternoon. More than once Stuart found
his thoughts dwelling on Mary Dixon. He experienced an

odd desire to "put himself right with her" in the matter of the police enquiry. Only when he rehearsed what he would say, and pictured her somewhat disdainful surprise that he should have deemed it necessary to warn her of a danger that did not exist, did he abandon the scheme.

At half past seven he approached the door of the Restorato Milano in West 47th Street. Gilt letters and an electric sign announced that the proprietor was V. Pucci. He entered. An ill lighted staircase led straight to the upper stories. Beneath, on the right, lay the public restaurant, which was crowded and noisy.

He was halfway up the stairs when a sharp eyed Italian waiter, all hair, eyes, moustache and white apron, came snapping at his heels.

"Hi! Mistare! Vot you vant?"

"Anti pasto," said Stuart, not disinclined for a few moments' respite from the tragedy which had overshadowed all his waking hours.

"Ebbene! Coom dis vay."

"Tutti frutti!! Corpo di Baccho!"

"Vill you say vot you vant? Si?"

"Buenaserte!"

"Maledetto!" growled the Italian, rushing up a few steps. Then he took Stuart's measure in a quick glance, and rushed down again more hastily.

"Signore! Signore Pucci!" he almost screamed.

A fat, placid man, who resembled a large consignment of lard that had been poured into a dress suit, appeared from the restaurant.

"Now! What is it?" he demanded, after the waiter had explained in torrential Neapolitan that this mad American would only talk nonsense.

"Serpe!" said Stuart meekly.

V. Pucci's eyes nearly bulged clean out of the lard as they withered his satellite. He uttered no word, but the man vanished. "Pardon," he said, bowing to Stuart. "You know the room, yes?"

"First on the left, isn't it?"

"Si signore. It is ready. Your friends haf arrive."

Stuart thanked him, and found Winter and Furneaux seated near an open window in a small apartment with a table laid for three. Furneaux consulted a wrist watch. So did Winter. Not to be outdone, Stuart shot back his left cuff.

"Not late, I hope," he said.

"On the dot," agreed Furneaux. "Kindly push that bell, and we'll start with a grape juice cocktail."

"Please don't order one for me," said Stuart. "I never could tackle grape juice, even before I went to France."

The same waiter answered the bell, and gave Stuart a frightened glance. Furneaux held up three fingers, and he whisked out again.

"You seem to have scared Antonio," he commented.

"I don't think he understands my Italian."

"Do you speak it?"

"I know about six words. I tried four of them, and one in Spanish, so he called for help."

"Oh, you saw old Pucci, then? Some bird, Pucci. There have been three Delmonicos in New York but only one Pucci. But you're good at scaring folk. How did you empty the street this morning?"

Luckily, Stuart had asked Benson the same question, and was able to explain. Winter chuckled.

"I must remember that," he laughed. "Usually I tell the crowd that Furneaux is a violent lunatic; they always believe me."

"Because you look like a warder," said Furneaux.

The waiter brought a tray, and Stuart, who had never seen amber coloured grape juice, tasted the contents of his glass. Then he finished it.

"Converted?" enquired the little man.

"Absolutely."

They began an excellent meal, which was assisted by some admirable Chianti—three star Torino.

"I believe I can guess why V. Pucci nourishes like the green bay tree," said Stuart.

"Then you'll guess wrong," said Winter. "The password is never the same, and is seldom used. Furneaux and I have had a busy day, so we needed a proper dinner. What have you been doing since we parted?"

"I engaged Benson as a valet, and learnt why Miss Dixon may have agreed to marry van Cortland—if any persuasion was necessary."

"Oh, that rubber deal? Yes, that may be it. Certainly the engagement was announced rather hurriedly, since not even rumour bracketed the young lady's name with any other man."

For some occult reason, the statement pleased Stuart. In an unguarded moment he refilled his glass, evidently appreciating the Chianti more than ever.

"Now will you be good?" chirped Furneaux.

"If you want to pry into Miss Dixon's affair—"

"Nothing of the kind. We want you to cultivate her brother. We don't quite know enough about his fellow members of the Ace Club. He may tell you. Then there's Holgate, if you shy at the Dixon family. And we want you to get hold of Mr. Francis O. Baker and Mr. Robert Kerningham."

"I shall be a poor dub as an amateur detective," temporised Stuart.

"Very likely, though it's a sign of grace that you should admit it. But that is not your job. We need intimate details of these young men's lives—what they think, or think they think—how they occupy themselves during the hours when they are not drinking."

Antonio staged a roast capon, surrounded by six plump quails, so Furneaux was silenced for the moment. Winter had removed a leg and a wing with one masterly sweep of the carving knife, when V. Pucci wheezed in.

"Pardon," he said. "Captain Crossley wishes to see Mr. Wintare, yes."

"Is he below?" enquired the Chief, with a surprised air.

"Si, signore."

"Ask him to join us ... Crossley," he told Stuart, "is the police captain for this district."

A solidly built man came in. Evidently he had hurried, and his face was somewhat drawn.

"What's up?" said Winter.

"Bad news, Chief."

"Have you dined? Tell us while you eat."

"I can't eat, but—"

"Yes. Use that large glass. Signor Vittorio—another quart of the same."

The proprietor crooked his finger at his assistant, and the two went off. Crossley fortified himself as recommended, and set down the glass.

"There's hell to pay," he said. "Flanagan is dead!"

"How?"

"I dunno. It beats me." He glanced at Stuart.

"Go ahead. This gentleman is in it up to the neck, if you mean the van Cortland case."

"I suppose I do. I can't tell. Anyhow, here's the story in short. Last night a hobo made up his mind to sleep in Central Park. He crept among the bushes until he reached the boundary wall of Fifth Avenue, as he thought he would not be spotted there, and the rumble of the traffic sort of kep' him company, he said. But he was a long time in getting to sleep, and thought he had made a mistake, as the cars and busses rattled by till after one thirty. Then he dozed, but was awakened by a window being raised rather slowly, as though to avoid disturbing anybody. He got up, and had a look, and saw a tall man in evening dress standing on the first floor balcony of an Avenue house. It was van Cortland's house, I may say."

Antonio, wiping the neck of a flask of Chianti, interrupted the speaker, and, such is the queer reticence of some great events, had no more notion that he was disturbing a most thrilling recital than that he would find a hundred dollar bill on the stairs, which he did not.

"Even though the heavens fall I must eat," said Winter, almost vindictively. "I breakfasted at 8:30, with a cup of coffee in one hand and the telephone in the other."

"Don't make any more noise than you can help," suggested Furneaux.

"Well," went on Crossley, reaching for the wine, "the hobo—says his name is Jackson—was disappointed, as he half expected a burglary. While he was peeping over the wall, the man on the balcony seemed to throw something at him, so he ducked. An empty bottle crashed into the bushes. Then Jackson took a second look. The man flung something again, a small object, which struck a branch of a tree. By this time Jackson was scared, and kept hidden. He heard the window lowered, and knew by the light that the blind had been drawn. Not for some minutes did he realise that the man in the house opposite could not possibly have seen him, and could only be getting rid of something in that way. So, as soon as the light permitted—he. thinks it was about a quarter after four— he made a search, and found a curiously shaped gold ring, while lying about were pieces of the broken bottle, which he smelt, and recognised the scent of some strong dope. About six he got clear of the Park, and begged something to eat from the driver of an all night taxi outside the Great Northern Hotel. He hung about until after ten, when he offered the ring for sale in a Broadway pawnbroker's. The Jew boy assistant thought it was a genuine curio, so he said he personally didn't know its value but would enquire, and suggested that Jackson should return in half an hour. The hobo, of course smoked a trap, but thought he would go through with it, as he had a straight story to tell. At a quarter to eleven Flanagan grabbed him and brought him in. You see, Chief, at that time I knew nothing of the van Cortland affair, but Flanagan did, and kept quiet."

The policeman paused, and his eyes clashed with those of the two detectives. Winter grunted, and Furneaux stuck a fork into a quail. Stuart was aware that some ray of intelligence passed between the three, but could not sense its meaning until he heard later that this particular detective, a fairly able man, was regarded as a bit of a fool by his colleagues because he tried invariably to retain for his own use some scrap of information which ought to have gone into the common stock. Meanwhile, Stuart was much impressed by the fact that neither Winter nor Furneaux, each obviously consumed with impatience, urged Crossley to go on with his narrative though, indeed, the man had wasted no words hitherto.

"Well," he said, with a sigh, "Flanagan entered the charge very briefly, and got Jackson remanded. There was no question of bail, though Jackson, I am told, repeated his story before the magistrate. Flanagan came away with the ring, for enquiry purposes and was fiddling about with it in the charge-room at five o'clock when he contrived to scratch his finger with a hidden claw which darted out when something was released in a seal shaped like a lion's head. He thought nothing of it until he complained of feeling faint or paralyzed. In half an hour he was so ill that we sent for the police surgeon, who dosed him with brandy. But it was no use. Flanagan is dead. He quit about twenty minutes since, and is lying there, all doubled up, and his skin yellow."

"Norn de Dieu! That's our snake!" cried Furneaux, his voice cracking with excitement. "Where's the ring, cap?"

"I've got it here. Catch me leaving the damned thing around for anybody else to monkey with!"

Chapter 6: The Ring—In Fact, Three Rings

CROSSLEY produced a small package from his waistcoat pocket. Unfolding a linen wrapper with great care, he sought the end of a second covering of tissue paper, held it up, and allowed a gold ring to tumble forth on to the table cloth. It was a solid article, and bore an embossed design known in heraldry as a "lion couchant," with the head crouched between the two front, paws. In these the claws were of steel; the eyes were simulated by tiny rubies, which shone viciously in the electric light.

"Don't touch it!" Crossley warned the others in an awed tone. "Those claws work somehow. I don't know the trick. Poor Flanagan discovered it, and it did him in!"

Furneaux and Stuart pulled their chairs closer. Winter rose, and bent over the three heads.

"That isn't a seal," said Furneaux.

"No, I suppose not, but I'm so upset that I just can't think quite right now."

Furneaux picked up the ring, despite Crossley's renewed protest.

"Oh, it's all right," said he. "The most deadly snake is powerless when you grab him by the scruff of the neck."

Holding the ring by its narrow part, he squeezed the lion's mane between the thumb and forefinger of the other hand, and the centre claw on each foot raised itself instantly, remaining upright when the pressure was relaxed. A groove ran down the inner side, and, with the next movement of the detective's hands, some specks of matter, in colour a dull green, dropped to the cloth.

Crossley watched this demonstration with evident fear.

"It's hard to believe that such little things could kill a man, but they outed Flanagan, or I'm a Wop," he muttered.

"You're no Wop, Jim," said Furneaux, "and, unless I'm greatly mistaken, this ring has killed two men within the day. It strikes me as an Italian poison ring, though I have never seen one before. Why not show it to a real Wop? What do you say, Chief?"

"Meaning Pucci?"

"Yes. He's a knowledgeable fellow."

"Sure. I'll send for him."

Antonio was halted on the stairs with a message, and soon the oleaginous Pucci was in the room.

"What's that, professor?" enquired Winter, pointing to the ring, now reposing again on the table cloth.

"No; don't handle it. Look."

Pucci did look, witn eyes pursed up between rolls of fat. Then he grew excited, and murmured something very wicked in Italian.

"It is bad, bad!" he gurgled. "Un' anello di mortal Vot you call a'death'ring. It was made in Venezia, two, three hundred years ago. Von leetle scratch, and, p sst, you die. Madre di Dio! I did not tink dare was anozzare one in all New York!"

"Another ? Where is the first one?"

Winter's question came like a pistol shot, and Pucci straightened himself until his face lay in the shadow cast by a screen above the cluster of electric lights which hung over the centre of the table. With a mighty effort, he recovered himself, but Stuart felt the fat hands clutch the back of his chair with a nervous tension that was eloquent.

"I am wrong. I speak carelessly. I mean there is not one like this in New York."

It was noticeable that his English was nearly perfect now, whereas, in those first few seconds of bewilderment, he spoke like an Italian not well versed in the language.

"Capital, Vittorio! A supreme pose!" said Winter pleasantly. "But it won't work, my friend. This is serious, very serious. You must tell us where and when you saw the other one."

"You ask more than you can imagine," was the reply.

"Can't help that. I give you my word of honor I'll never reveal who told me."

"There is a girl in the chorus at the Metropolitan—Carlotta Grisi—she has one."

"Was she ever friendly with young van Cortland?"

"Si. I have seen them together."

"Is this her ring, do you think, or one like it?"

"No, it is not quite the same. Her ring has a coiled snake, and—and—I believe the poison in it is dead."

"Why do you believe that?"

"Because Carlotta tried it on me four years ago."

Somehow, the statement, though tragic enough, relieved the tension, and three men laughed. Even Crossley, much upset by the untimely death of a friend, could not help smiling.

"Gee! It must be fierce to be an Italian and in love," said Furneaux. "But don't worry about Carlotta, Vittorio. She is not on in this act. Van Cortland was killed early this morning by the ring you see on the table, so when we tackle La Grisi, as we must do, it will be by way of Fifth Avenue, not 47th Street. I tell you this just to make sure you will keep mum, and assist us, perhaps. . . . What sort of poison is this stuff?"

V. Pucci was now mopping his domed forehead with a handkerchief, but he answered at once:—

"I don't know. No one knows. It is one of the lost arts."

"Well, I suppose an admirer of Benvenuto Cellini, like yourself, would describe it that way. How long since you saw Carlotta?"

"Four years."

"What? Do you never go to the Opera?"

"I got married."

Clearly Signor Pucci did not understand why these strange beings should laugh again.

"Say, Vittorio," cried Winter, "if you have a few thimble fulls of that '65 brandy left, they wouldn't do us any harm."

"Cover that ring," said the proprietor, as he touched the bell.

"Do you think Antonio would recognise it?" enquired Winter.

"You never know. These young Wops know a lot of mischievous things. I tell them nothing."

So it was quite a hilarious party to which the unsuspecting waiter purveyed five liqueur glasses. When Pucci had gone, Furneaux turned his attention to the ring once more, much to the distress of Crossley, who literally feared it. The detective found that by pressing the back of the mane, the claws closed. With the tip of the smaller blade of a pen knife he collected the few grains of matter on the table, and placed them in a separate piece of the tissue paper, having first examined the whole of the wrapper to see if any particles had fallen out from the receptacle earlier.

"I wonder how those claws got back into their places when Flanagan opened them," he murmured, as though speaking to himself.

"Flanagan pushed them back. He told me so," said the police captain.

"How long before he felt ill?"

"Not more than fifteen minutes."

"Is it possible," said Stuart, who had kept silent throughout all that tense scene, "that poison hidden in that way would retain its potency after a couple of centuries?"

"Some unhappy guinea pig will answer that question to morrow morning," said Winter. "Mineral poisons last longer than vegetable ones—that is, some of them, as there are virulent minerals which disappear entirely after a few days in the body. This stuff will create a sensation in the Johns Hopkins University, which has the best laboratory in the States. . . . Well, boys, we must go and see poor Flanagan. Are you coming, Captain Stuart? Can you stand it?"

"Are you with us, rather?" put in Furneaux.

"Up to the neck, now," said the soldier. "By the way, it was an odd coincidence not only that you should have called the ring a snake but that Pucci should speak of the Italian girl owning a snake ring."

"Furneaux has been dabbling in coincidences all day," laughed Winter. "I'll tell you later what I mean. We have no more time to spare now. I have to see the Commissioner about this case before I go to bed to night, and I have heaps of notes to make. Talk about an eight hours' day for working men. We seldom average less than sixteen, and often go right round the clock three times. Isn't that so, Frog?"

"The only difference is that I generally go the other way," snapped Furneaux, who disliked being called " Frog" before members of the uniformed force. For the same reason he had to bottle up the more biting retort which otherwise he would assuredly have flung at his Chief.

Passing the newspaper stand at soth Street and Sixth Avenue on their way to Crossley's police station, they all saw a scare head, "Strange death of a New York detective" across the front page of an evening journal.

"Hello! The press have got it," growled Winter.

"That hobo was before the magistrate, and the place where the ring was found was mentioned," said Crossley.

"Not van Cortland's house!"

"No, but the the exact spot in the Park. I suppose, when the Flanagan incident was given out, some sharp reporter connected the two items."

"Which two items?"

"The throwing of the ring from a room in the Van Cortland mansion, and Flanagan's death."

"That's a nuisance," said Winter irritably. "It adds another couple of hours' work to the night—that's all."

Stuart did not understand, but asked no questions.

He could not see what the detectives could do at that late hour, hardly realising yet that they lost not an instant on the trail, and that, if possible, in view of the new evidence, not only Carlotta Grisi but several members of the Ace Club would be crossexamined at length before any of them got to bed.

Flanagan's body showed the same characteristics as van Cortland's, except that the contortion of paralysis was more marked. The skin was quite yellow, which seemed to bear out Furneaux's comment that the poison, whatever it might be, must exercise an extraordinary effect on the blood corpuscles. Singularly enough, the police surgeon's report gave as the apparent cause of death "virulent blood poisoning."

Furneaux accompanied Stuart to his flat—it lay on his path, he explained. The little man seemed to abandon his cryptic style of speech during that short stroll. He sympathised with the soldier on having been literally dragged into an unsavoury case, and promised that, even when publicity became unavoidable, his connection with it would be minimised to the utmost degree.

"In fact," said the detective, "I have a notion that this affair may never cut much ice in the courts. Someone is playing for a high stake, and, when he feels he has lost, he'll save us further trouble by blowing his brains out."

"Do you think there is money at issue?"

"Avarice and sexual passion are the causes of ninety nine in a hundred of planned crimes," said the philosopher, "and avarice comes easily first. Sometimes the two combine; that simplifies matters—for the Bureau, I mean. But, this time, the problem is rather more complex, I imagine. We are up against a thinker, Captain Stuart. Now, I wonder if that hobo, Jackson, could possibly recognise the man in evening dress who threw the bottle and the ring across Fifth Avenue. No, it's too much to expect. We seldom or never get a piece of luck like that . . . well, here we are. Going in? Goodnight. I'll give you a ring here sharp at noon."

Stuart's rooms were on the second floor. He had not rented an expensive place, so there was no elevator, or hall porter, but callers were admitted, after ringing a bell, by a latch controlled by each tenant when at home. He had told Benson not to wait for him that night: hence he was surprised to find the lights on, and Benson himself in the hall.

"There's a gentleman waiting to see you, sir, so I thought I had better stick it," explained the valet.

"Who is it?"

"Mr. Dixon, sir."

"Even my day isn't finished yet," thought Stuart, as he gave Benson his hat and cane. Entering the sitting room, he was met by Willie Dixon, looking a much more spruce young man now than at nine o'clock that morning.

"Hope you don't mind my intrusion," said his visitor, with a forced cheerfulness that revealed shaken nerves. "I'm under orders, and just had to hang on here till you came."

"I am very glad to see you," said Stuart, giving a hospitable eye to a tray with decanter and glasses.

"Why didn't you help yourself to a drink?"

"Not taking any. New leaf, and that sort of thing, you know."

"Not a bad idea. Sit down a minute. I want to send my man home."

"Doesn't he live here?"

"No."

"Keep him a little longer, please. That's part of the scheme."

"What scheme?"

"I'll tell you in a sec'. But you'll make me stutter if you stand there and look at me."

Stuart smiled.

"That would never do," he said. "S'pose I fill my pipe, and listen while you talk. But, bide a wee. I'll tell Benson to hold the fort against all comers."

When he came back he saw that Dixon had lighted a cigarette, but was still in a highly nervous state.

"I'm the last man in the world to persuade a youngster to drink," said Stuart, "yet I do honestly think you need a high ball. Good resolutions are fine, but steady improvement is the thing to aim for rather than a Salvation Army conversion."

"Do you mean that?"

"Sure I do."

"Well, here goes I The first to day—since I woke up, that is."

To put the boy at his ease, and, incidentally, to rid himself of false pretence Stuart explained that he would not join in the festivities because he had been dining with the two detectives engaged in the van Cortland case.

Dixon literally beamed at the news.

"That sister of mine is some girl," he said. "She guessed the Bureau had roped you in, even if you didn't know it yourself."

This certainly was news to Stuart, and it must be confessed he was gratified to hear it, though Mary Dixon's powers of divination were puzzling, to put it mildly.

"I am very pleased to hear that," he said. "Of course, it was an accident that I happened to be on the door step at the very moment the butler was coming out to find a policeman. Furneaux, the little detective, sent me on a sad errand to Miss Dixon, on the ground that van Cortland had no available relatives. Is that correct?"

"Oh, quite. Did he tell you anything about us—about Pop and the rubber deal, I mean?"

"No. But I overheard some men talking at my club. I gathered that van Cortland had helped your father to clear off a troublesome mortgage on your property."

"That all?"

"All I would wish to repeat. But, really, young man, you are catechising me rather than explaining why you are here."

"You're right. I always was a beggar for shoving the cart before the horse, but, as you will soon see, we've cleared the ground pretty well already. Anyhow, here goes! This afternoon Pop came back from 120 Broadway, and I was hauled out of bed to attend a council of war. First thing, Pop, who's under the weather, asked me what I meant to do during the remainder of my days, and I took the wind out of his sails by suggesting that I might fill a stool in his office, starting to morrow. And, by jing, that's fixed. Me for the East side Subway at 8:30 a.m. sharp, to morrow as ever is."

"Splendid! Out of evil has come good, for you, at any rate."

"Yes—that's all right so far. But I'm out on my own. Pop and Mary left for our camp in the Adirondacks about two hours ago. They'll be away all the summer. Mind you, I fell in with the notion. New York is no place for Mary when the fuss about poor old Tony starts."

Stuart managed to conceal his surprise at this wholly unexpected announcement, which, he guessed, would not suit Winter's and Furneaux's plans in the least degree. But the comings and goings of the Dixon family was no business of his, so he only said:—

"Rather a sudden decision, wasn't it?"

"Yes, and no. Van and Mary were going there for their honeymoon, as she likes the place. It's a log hut, near Paul Smith's."

Stuart thought that, in the conditions, no more extraordinary choice of a summer resort could have been made, but again contented himself with a platitude.

"I'm sure your sister will be happier well away from this city just now," he said.

"I wish you wouldn't keep on agreeing with me all along the line," cried Willie petulantly. "Why don't you say, 'Hell, you don't tell me,' or some thing of the sort.

You see, it's this way. Mary has taken quite a shine to you. Says you're a sensible, straight forward sort of cuss, worth a whole truckload of sap headed millionaires and society roustabouts. She got on the 'phone to Polly Langrishe—you know her, eh?"

Stuart nodded. Mrs. Langrishe served on the Red Cross in France, and was attached to his division.

"Well, Polly said you were here on two months' leave, and rather at a loose end, so Mary hopes—hopes most sincerely I was to say—that you will come to our flat as my guest for the balance of your leave. . . . Steady, now, for two ticks! You've got to have it all. She says there will be an awful lot of worry and trouble before Tony's death is cleared up, and I shall be sadly in need of someone to guide my juvenile steps, or words to that effect. If I'm left alone, I'm sure to go wrong, whereas, with your eye on me, I may pull through. This doesn't mean that you are to have me always in a leading rein—not a bit of it. I'll be downtown five days in the week from 8:30 till 5, and you can dine in or out just as you please. The point is that it'll be good for me to feel there's a pal I can rely on, if only to talk things over of an evening, or for a chat by 'phone if there's any mix up during the day. You understand, Mary believes there will be dirty work if it turns out that Van was really murdered. It would never do for me to skip to the Adirondacks, and she doesn't want me to be left alone altogether. You're in this affair already. Will you stay in—for two more months?"

To describe Stuart's mental state during the boy's appeal as one of amazement would be an underestimate. He was literally stupefied. That he, of all men living, should be invited to reside forthwith in the Dixons' flat was the most unlooked for and staggering development that could possibly have come at the close of a day which had long since transcended any twenty four hours within his previous experiences. He seemed to see Furneaux grinning at him over Dixon's shoulder. He could almost hear Winter's big voice guffawing at the plight of a puppet who had vowed not to dance to the Bureau's piping. He was so utterly flabbergasted that Dixon feared he had put the case badly.

"Please, be a sport," he pleaded. "You'll have better meals, anyhow. I knew a fellow who lived here, and old Mother Riordan gave him such a go of indigestion that it took a month's pummelling at Hot Springs to get his tummy right."

"But I have never been quite so surprised by any request in my life—never," gasped Stuart.

"What is there to it?" urged the other. "Just packing a grip, while I 'phone for the car, which, by the way, is at your disposal all day and most nights. Your man can close up here to morrow."

"Do you mean seriously that you want me to go with you now?"

"Sure thing! I can't stick that empty flat by myself to night. I'd—I'd see things. There's a room for your man, and Mary left the house parlour maid, who is a bully good cook for breakfasts. When we dine at home we get our meals from the restaurant downstairs."

"There are twenty good reasons why I cannot act on the jump in that way."

"But Mary's one reason is worth them all, and more. She has a notion that the wrong man will be blamed for doing in poor old Van, and you and I may be able to stop it."

"How?"

"I can't tell you, of course. You see, it's this way— Mary isn't specially struck on anybody. Four or five fellows were after her, as she's an uncommonly nice girl, which you saw for yourself. Frank Baker swore he'd get her—all fair and square, you know—but Pop found himself tied up in a rubber deal, and Tony came to the rescue, so, there you are! Frank Baker said all kinds of nasty things, and wrote 'em, too. You could have knocked me down with a feather when he turned up at the Club last night, though he couldn't very well refuse, that being the lastest last meeting of the boys. Now, Mary and I are sure he didn't kill Van. He isn't that sort of fellow. Plenty of bounce and bluster, but he really wouldn't hurt a fly. Still, it's awkward. There's so much on record, and it's bound to come out. Even at the table yesterday evening he said he'd rather wring Van's neck than drink his health. So, come along, if only to oblige a lady."

And that is how, half an hour later, Captain Alec Stuart found himself installed in the bedroom of Mr. Dixon, senior, while Benson had orders to transfer himself and his master's baggage to the Park Avenue flat next morning.

He and Dixon did not indulge in any more confidences that night. Both were too tired. The boy was physically worn out, and Stuart felt that his brain was crammed to capacity. Next morning they met at breakfast, a meal which fully justified Mary Dixon's faith in Catherine as a cook, and Dixon hurried off to his new occupation. Benson went to attend to the packing in 57th Street, and Catherine asked if Captain Stuart would be at home during the next hour, as she had shopping to do. This arrangement suited him well. He wanted to telephone the Bureau early, since Furneaux would give him a call at noon at the old address, and would be puzzled by his failure to keep the appointment.

He filled his pipe, and glanced through the morning papers, intent on finding how much, if anything, New York knew of the van Cortland tragedy. Almost to his dismay he learned that the City knew a good deal. The police court proceedings against Jackson, followed by Flanagan's mysterious death, had sent reporters hot foot to the van Cortland mansion—at first to enquire into the truth of the hobo's account of his possession of the ring, but ultimately to ferret out the vastly more intriguing story of Anthony van Cortland's death. The history of the Ace Club, of course, was almost common property, and its members were discussed fully and frankly. Happily, the only allusion to Mary Dixon was a sympathetic account of her projected marriage, now so woefully thrown into the limbo of events which might have been.

He was reading certain details about Holgate, Kerningham Baker, Monty Straus, and the rest—Willie Dixon, of course, had a whole paragraph to himself—when the telephone rang in the hall.

He went to answer it, and a man's voice said:—

"Miss Dixon, please."

"Who is speaking?" enquired Stuart.

There was a marked pause. When the voice came again it had acquired a sudden huskiness, plus a quasi foreign accent which had certainly not been there in the opening words.

"Ees dat Plaza, Number ," it enquired.

"Yes."

"Meestare Dixon's apart e ment?"

"Yes."

"Who is speakin', plees?"

"That's what I'm asking you?"

"Bud, I vant Mees Dixon."

"She is not here. She has left New York. I am Captain Stuart, a friend of her brother's."

In that instant Stuart was aware he had erred in saying too much. He could assign no cause for the belief, but felt that it was so.

The voice was taken aback, too.

"You meestake," it said. "Mees Dixon canned 'ave gone away."

"Tell me who you are," said Stuart, "and I may be able to give you further details."

"Bud I musd speak mit her."

Either emotion or anger had thickened the accent more than ever.

"I assure you you cannot—now. She is not at home. Give 'me a message, and I will promise it shall be sent to her."

A broken "Damn!" reached him as the transmitter was hung up.

Somehow, Stuart realised that this call might be of vital importance to the police. He called the Plaza Exchange, and tried to persuade the operator to trace back the call to its originating number. He failed, of course, as that sort of request is made too often for trivial reasons. So he got on to the Bureau, and asked for Mr. Furneaux. Soon a squeaky voice assured him that he, Furneaux, was in the office by a miracle.

"I am in the Dixons' flat," said Stuart. "I'm staying here, in fact, but don't ask me why now. There is something much more urgent. A call came here three minutes ago for Miss Dixon. I answered. It was a man's disguised voice. Will you ask the Plaza Exchange to find out who made it?"

"What's the rush?"

"Because I have a crazy sort of idea that I have just been speaking to the man who killed Anthony van Cortland!"

"Gee!" said Furneaux.

CHAPTER 7: AN EMISSARY—FROM WHOM?

TEN minutes later the telephone rang again.

"Forty second Street call office," announced Furneaux. "Cigar store manager says he keeps no record, as customers pay their own calls by dropping coins in the box. Sorry. Probably, we are missing something good, but, if your mad idea is correct—and mad ideas mostly are in this business—it helps a lot, as I can locate some of the suspects right now, and the circle narrows accordingly. But tell me more about it, avoiding names, if you please."

Stuart realised then that in his eagerness he had mentioned van Cortland in such a sensational way that any telephone operator listening in—as she might well be doing after the scurry by the Bureau to trace a certain number—had obtained what she probably would describe to her associates as "an earful."

So, like every other amateur who is allowed to see how the strings move the marionette show of public life and its greater events, he became ultracautious.

"Won't you be passing this way?" he enquired.

"I have a lot to tell you."

Furneaux took thought. He seemed to be weighing the pros and cons of the situation in a way not customary with him.

"I am due for a rehearsal at the Metropolitan Opera house at 10:30," he said finally. "The duet will last probably half an hour; so, wait in."

Stuart believed the soprano's part in the duo would be taken by Carlotta Grisi, and could not but admire the detective's ready wit. He almost found himself wishing he could have been present at the interview, and looked forward with interest to hearing Furneaux's account of it. The scent of the chase was now strong in his nostrils, and he was eager to keep up with the pack, though well aware that only the quite exceptional circumstances which thus far had attended the enquiry into van Cortland's death permitted the Bureau to take a member of the general public so fully into its councils.

He had hardly returned to his newspapers when Catherine came back, so, when the telephone rang again, he thought it wise to make her the intermediary. It was a long distance call this time, and the maid's eager reply:— "Oh, yes, miss. Captain Stuart arrived last night with Mr. Willie," told him that Mary Dixon, too, had her anxieties. Evidently there was an interchange of small talk about domestic affairs, and certain instructions were given so precisely that Catherine had to repeat them. Stuart paid no heed till he was summoned.

"It is very good of you to help my brother and all of us in this way, Captain Stuart," said a sweet clear voice. "I cannot tell you what a load it has taken off my mind. I hope you don't think it strange of a girl like me assuming responsibility in a serious matter of this sort, but my father has had many business troubles of late, and now must be given a complete rest, mental as well as physical. Willie's reformation is so very new that I simply dare not trust to it."

"Do you speak French?" enquired Stuart.

She assured him, with a Paris accent, that she did, whereupon he explained the necessity there was to prevent any leakage of information already in the hands of the police, and gave her a resume of all that he knew.

He was quickly alive to the fact that the story of the poisoned ring distressed her, and was conscious of a species of satisfaction when she said promptly that Frank Baker had made a collection of Italian antiques while flying in Italy before the United States entered the Great War in 1917.

"I tell you this," she added, "because it is common knowledge among his friends, and I am sure Frank will be the first person to give every sort of assistance to the police."

Stuart was thankful that he had not happened to mention the fact that Kerningham's handkerchief was used to remove finger prints from the glass bowl and window in the van Cortland mansion. He did not wish to distress her needlessly, but took care to say that Furneaux would be with him about noon, and might like to give her a call.

She supplied her telephone number readily. The Dixon house, she said, was about a mile across the lake from the railway station and landing place known collectively as Paul Smith's Camp, and she would be at home all day, having on hand many household matters that demanded attention.

"It is nice that you can talk French so well," she confided, with a little laugh, "though we do sound rather like conspirators, don't you think?"

Altogether, Stuart was satisfied with Mary Dixon's attitude. It was entirely correct, if a trifle callous in view of her affianced husband's fate. Not once had she mentioned Anthony van Cortland's name, though he had perforce introduced it several times. He had yet to learn that the marriage constituted a living nightmare for the girl, and that her mind had not recovered its poise. Indeed, it was just as well that the somewhat impressionable young soldier should be a trifle dismayed by the lady's seeming apathy in this respect. It kept his wits balanced, and he would need all the long headed sagacity he undoubtedly possessed before he might write "Finis" to the van Cortland case.

He retained his real surprise for the last moment. Mary was about to say "Goodbye" when he sought her attention for one more moment.

"If you had not gone North did you expect a 'phone call from anyone in particular this morning?" he enquired.

"No," she said. "A lot of people mostly girls, are always ringing me up, but I cannot imagine any really important message coming through to day."

"A man who used a low, reserved tone, spoke here from a call office in Forty Second Street about half an hour ago. I was alone in the flat, Catherine being gone shopping, and, when I answered, he instantly adopted a disguised accent, half Italian, half German, though I have a faint memory of having heard him speak on some other occasion. He was greatly disappointed when told you were not at home, but refused to give any sort of explanation. He even swore as he hung up."

Mary's stock of exclamations in the French language had been exhausted by Stuart's earlier disclosures.

"Well, of all the extraordinary things!" she cried in English. . . . "Yes father—coming at once, this minute. ... I can only assure you, Captain Stuart, that I have no acquaintance who measures up with that curious standard. . . . I'll think, and let you know later. ... I really must go now. I have been nearly an hour getting this call."

It was an odd circumstance that the husky voiced person, whosoever he might be, had himself contributed, in all probability, to delaying the long-distance connection from up State, since his enquiry had led directly to the flurry raised by the Bureau. Assuredly, thought Stuart, he would have enough to tell Furneaux at twelve o'clock!

But he was by no means ended with the telephone for that morning. Within five minutes the bell clanged again, and Catherine seemed to be too busily occupied to answer.

This time it was Willie Dixon.

"Gee! I'm glad to find you in!" cried that young man breathlessly. "I've just heard that the police are keeping Bob Kerningham, Frank Baker, Phil Durrane and Charlie Spence in jail—holding them as material witnesses, they say. Can't something be done? It's an outrage. None of those birds killed old Tony !"

"Someone killed him, and the detectives are sure it was one of the twelve other men in the room. How can I interfere? And, look here, Willie—you mustn't speak of these things over the 'phone. I've been called pretty sharply already for doing it."

"But I've just met Buddy Owen, and he "

"Is lucky he is not with the others. Now, you really must wait until you come home this evening. Then we can discuss the whole business. Your friends cannot complain if a little harshness is used. To day's enquiries are vital. What time will you be here?"

"Sharp at five thirty. Do you know anything about "

"No questions."

"Oh, they're welcome to listen in on this—foreign exchanges, I was going to say?"

"Not much. Only that when I was in France the dollar was supposed to be worth seventeen francs, and that prices went up as francs went down, so the good old dollar hardly managed to keep at par."

"Well, throw in milreis, kronen, marks and lire, and you'll guess why my head is buzzing. See you on the dot at 5.3.0. Shall we dine at home?"

"Yes."

Taking thought, Stuart went to find the parlour maid, who was banging about industriously in the kitchen.

"Catherine," he said gravely, "you know by this time, I have no doubt, that Mr. van Cortland is dead?"

The girl, not quite realising his drift, said that she couldn't help hearing what he had said the previous morning—in fact, Miss Mary herself had asked her to remain within earshot.

"You understand, then, what a very serious affair it is," he went on. "That is why Miss Dixon and I spoke in French just now. We can't have all the world sharing our knowledge. It will help immensely if you don't discuss our worries with anyone. You are sure to be asked to assist in various ways, and I would like to feel that I can depend on you."

Catherine vowed that she would do anything to oblige the Dixon family and their friends. Nevertheless, Stuart felt that he had removed a slight pique on the girl's part by letting her know that the camouflage adopted by her mistress and himself was not intended for her benefit. Indeed, when the next ring came, Catherine flew to the 'phone.

Mr. Billy Bolton speaking!

There was no stopping him. If Willie or his sister weren't in, who in Hades was? Stuart? Who was Stuart? Oh, he saw, which he did not really do, by any means. What was this about some of the boys being lagged? If the Mayor or District Attorney couldn't do anything, he, deponent, stood well in with the Governor of the State, and was about to wire that potentate at Albany forthwith.

Stuart managed ultimately to pacify him, and came to the conclusion that if the sharp witted young ladies employed by the New York Telephone system were not well posted by this time in a good many phases of the van Cortland mystery it was certainly not the fault of that unfortunate young man's chosen cronies.

After a quiet hour, Furneaux came.

"What a life!" he squeaked, subsiding into a comfortable chair in the library, which room Stuart had adopted as his quarters. "I've just gone through a sort of boiled down version of Cavalleria Rusticana and Pagliacci, with Carlotta Grisi playing each character in turn. However, I got the ring, on loan, and managed to keep Pucci's name out of it. The fat old rascal! I'm anxious to see Mrs. Pucci now, as Carlotta is certainly a good looker.   But, ere nom, there's no wonder these Italians retain their love affairs strictly among their own people. Just peep at this for a token of affection!"

He handed Stuart a heavy gold ring, which carried a snake twisted four times around the section usually filled by a signet or seal. The head, with jaws open, and the tail, were pointed outward.

"Hold the ring between your left finger and thumb, and press the tail firmly backwards with your right forefinger," he said.

Stuart obeyed, and a tiny steel dart shot out between the jaws. It was grooved, like the lion's claws in the "death ring," but no suspicious substance was rendered visible thereby.

"Carlotta tells me a legend that the poison used in that ring was a mixture of arsenic and belladonna," said the detective. "Fortunately for Pucci its virus had gone when she scratched him, as she hinted she had reason to know it was no longer venomous."

"I wouldn't trust the infernal thing," said Stuart, placing it carefully on a table.

"Still, it's useful as a type—all the more so because when Carlotta and some other girls shared in certain festivities arranged by van Cortland, she exhibited this ring, and it was seen, and its properties understood, by van Cortland himself and at least four of his friends."

"Kerningham, Baker, Durrane and Spence," said Stuart, smiling grimly.

"One hundred per cent efficient," cried Furneaux.

"Who posted you so thoroughly?"

"Willie Dixon. He wanted me to get them set at liberty. Another young gentleman, Billy Bolton, spoke of appealing to the District Attorney and the Governor of the State."

"Let him!" snapped Furneaux. "He's too late. This time, thanks to the butler and you, the Bureau has had twenty four hours' start of the Coroner, District Attorney, Mayor, Commissioner, Governor, and all the rest of 'em. You don't appreciate, of course, the obstacles which these well meaning gentlemen will place in our path. Political and social influences are brought to bear on them from every sort of angle, and, be they as impartial as Solomon, they simply cannot avoid becoming serious hindrances to us. You'd hardly guess what Winter is doing this morning—holding off those gentry till ten o'clock! After that they butt in. If we fail to find the actual murderer today, and prove him guilty beyond the possibility of doubt, several estimable officials now drawing salaries as assistants to the Mayor, Commissioner and District Attorney will probably lose their jobs as the outcome of rows between the various interested parties, while the real criminal escapes."

"Meanwhile?"

"Meanwhile we hope to find out, at least, who is guilty. It is up to us subsequently to prove it, if we can."

Stuart's army training had taught him when not to ask questions. He waited a second or two to allow Furneaux to go on talking if he chose. But the little man did not choose.

"Well, he said, after a pause, "I have a small budget for you. It may or may not prove important. That is for you to judge."

Then he explained fully why he was residing in the Dixons' flat, and gave Furneaux a practically verbatim account of the various telephone conversations. He had to confess to a secret feeling of disappointment that his companion should show no sign of excitement at Mary Dixon's revelation anent Baker's collection of Italian antiques. This, plus the mystery man's telephone call, was his prize contribution to that day's potential evidence, but Furneaux remained cold, almost uninterested. His attitude struck Stuart as that of a man waiting in vain for something that did not happen. He was listening, peering, pondering, but he might have been applying those senses to the expected apparition of a ghost rather than weighing the actualities of the hour.

"That all?" he enquired, when Stuart ceased speaking.

"Absolutely all. I was vain enough to think that some of the items would prove valuable."

"You mean Baker's curios, for instance. We examined the lot at eleven o'clock last night. The lion ring was his. It was taken from his collection. I don't believe he either knows it is missing or that it was poisonous. Some fat headed cops would have had him before a magistrate to day on the charge of murder. As a matter of fact he will be liberated before lunch. Winter and I may be mistaken. We often are. But we can get him again if wanted. You've had no visitoi here, I suppose?"

"No."

"Naturally. Otherwise you would have mentioned the fact. Well, I may be wrong again in an assumption, not for the first time, or the twentieth for that matter."

A bell rang, and Furneaux instantly displayed those indications of intense mental excitement which Stuart had seen in him on two occasions only, the first being when he, Stuart, refused to divulge what took place during the early morning meeting with Mary Dixon, and the second when Police captain Crossley told the story of Flanagan's death.

"That the door bell?" hissed the detective.

"Yes. I believe so."

"Stop that girl for a second. If anyone asks for you let him be shown in here. You get under that table in the corner, and I'll pull the cloth down so as to hide you. Cut a slit in it so that you can see. But don't show up, no matter what happens, unless I signal you. Can we depend on the maid?"

"Yes."

"Well, maybe. We've got to take a chance. Grab her, quick, and tell her what to do. I'll tip her the wink when the door is to be opened."

Stuart obeyed orders, and was soon well screened in the darkest part of the room, though in a cramped position, as the table was a small one. Furneaux seated himself with a newspaper, and both men heard someone ask if "Captain Stuart" was at home.

"I believe so, sir," said Catherine. "What name is it?"

"Oh, he doesn't know me," was the offhanded reply.

"I'm sorry, sir, but I can't admit anyone who refuses to give a name."

"All right. Say Mr. Luke Forster wishes to see him."

"Will you please step this way, sir?"

Stuart's heart had not pounded at such a rate since a day in France when a meinenwerfer exploded within six feet of him, but luckily just around the angle of a fire bay. He had recognised the stranger's voice! It was that of the man who swore because he could not get in touch with Mary Dixon that morning!

"S s s t!" he whispered tensely.

"This is the fellow who made that 'phone call!"

"Shut up!" hissed Furneaux. "I knew that two hours ago."

Mr. Luke Forster came in, and was conducted to the library, where he found some person quite hidden behind an open newspaper, and obviously immersed in its columns.

"Ah! Captain Stuart," said the newcomer affably. Furneaux jumped up, with such a jack in the box air that Mr. Forster was almost startled.

"Captain Stuart vanished a few minutes ago," said the detective. "Anything I can do for you?"

"Vanished!" repeated the other.

"That's the word, sir, I assure you. He's a speedy artist. Learnt some funny tricks in France, I expect. I wouldn't be surprised at anything he did, though if he passed you in the elevator he must have excelled himself."

"Well, I haven't the pleasure of Captain Stuart's acquaintance. I called here really on behalf of a friend, who desires news of the Dixon family. May I ask who you are?"

"Sometimes I hardly know myself, for we all live in a strange world since the war, but my friends call me Vidocq, when they're polite. Often I get 'Frog' or 'Funny little codger.' Yesterday morning a young blood likened me to a cocatoo."

Mr. Forster probably thought that if Furneaux's friends called him a maniac they would not be gravely mistaken. But it was evident, too, that he had hailed the presence of this crackpate with relief. He sat down, uninvited. Furneaux sprang on to the edge of the table in the centre of the room, where even he had momentarily forgotten that the snake ring reposed. The library, being in the well of the building, was not brilliantly lighted, and the detective's body cast a shadow over the ring, which was at once covered by his right hand.

"Miss Muriel van Buren asked me to convey a message to Miss Dixon," explained Forster. "I rang up here about ten o'clock, and was told that Miss Dixon was not in New York. My informant said he was a Captain Stuart, whom neither Miss van Buren nor I recognised as a friend of this family, and we are quite intimate with all its members. Captain Stuart's statement so astonished me that I have come in person to find out what has actually happened—I mean with regard to Miss Dixon, who was certainly here yesterday."

"Miss Muriel van Buren, of Vanderbilt Avenue?" queried Furneaux.

"Y—yes." The visitor was rather taken aback by such prompt recognition of the lady.

"Why do you say 'y—yes'? Aren't you sure?"

"Oh, quite sure."

"That's all right, then. I'll 'phone her straight away."

Furneaux leaped off the table, and was nearly in the hall when Mr. Forster recalled him urgently.

"Please don't do that!" he appealed. "Miss van Buren would never forgive me if she thought I had entrusted her private affairs to a stranger."

"But I am only going to tell her what she wants to know."

"Yes, yes, of course. But—don't you see—these young ladies are apt to take offense at nothing. I'd sooner fail altogether than let the information reach her so—so unexpectedly."

Mr. Forster was so perturbed that he rose and followed Furneaux into the hall, but the detective allowed himself to be persuaded unwillingly.

"All right," he said. "Let's discuss," and he backed the visitor into the room, he himself subsiding into the chair which the other had occupied, and thus manoeuvring Forster into one which was farther from the door, and with its back to Stuart's place of concealment.

Beyond doubt the man was bewildered by Furneaux's strange antics and stranger words, but he had come to the conclusion that he had to deal with one who was either eccentric or nearly a lunatic, and the belief simplified matters.

"What is there to discuss?" he said soothingly.

"I only wish to ascertain Miss Dixon's whereabouts, and then Miss van Buren can get in touch with her. Not much in that, eh?"

"Heaps!" snapped the detective. "You're too anxious about it, for one thing, Mr. Forster. For another, I don't suppose you ever exchanged a syllable with Miss Muriel van Buren in your life, unless it was to say, 'Yes, mam,' when she ordered you to bring her an ice or a cup of coffee."

"What do you take me for—a waiter?"

"That's what you look like, and a damned poor one, too!"

"But, my dear sir, I am a friend of all those people."

"Such a close friend that the maid here was acquainted with neither you nor your name."

"Oh, one doesn't need to be on calling terms to know people."

"That's where you're mistaken again. I'm getting to know you quite well."

Mr. Forster's somewhat swarthy face darkened redly, but he kept control of his temper, being clearly resolved to treat a fool according to his folly.

"I assure you I'm not a waiter," he said, trying to smile. "Aren't we making a lot of bother about a very trivial matter?"

"You tell me just why you need Miss Dixon's present address, and I'll supply it."

"But I have told you."

"No. You've merely lied."

Mr. Forster smiled tolerantly.

"Hard words, Mr. Vidocq, hard words!" he said.

"Yet you are right. I did try to succeed by a harmless subterfuge, but you are too sharp for me."

"Far too sharp!" interpolated Furneaux.

"Exactly. Well, since I find you established in this flat I'm sure are aware of Mr. van Cortland's death."

"Now we're coming to the truth."

"Just so. Everyone in New York society had heard of Miss Dixon's engagement with my poor friend."

"Oh, was he also a friend of yours "

"Yes, for many years."

"I'll enquire from his butler," and Furneaux shot out of his chair.

"Confound it!" cried Forster, rising in his turn, and in a rage now, "leave that dashed telephone alone, can't you?"

The detective, gazing steadily at his victim, bent forward and crooked the forefinger of his right hand.

"Come with me, as the spider said when inviting a dirty little fly into his parlour," he cackled.

"Come with me, and you'll hear something, not to your benefit."

Going out on tiptoe, but looking backward and still beckoning, Furneaux seized the one instant when Forster's eyes fell to glance towards the spot whence Stuart was watching this queer bit of tragicomedy. Forster took thought quickly, and arrived at an equally prompt decision. He might be able to bluff a butler.

"Oh, have it your own way," he said, with well affected indifference, and once more strode after the detective.

Stuart hardly needed that look of intelligence, as he had already interpreted the signalling finger correctly. He crept out, and followed the others noiselessly. Thus, when Furneaux reached the telephone with Forster near, Stuart was standing in the hall. At once the detective's mask like face creased in a truly diabolical grin.

"It's as good as a play," he squeaked, in the falsetto he used invariably when at a high pitch of excitement. "Why bother about a mere butler? Here's Captain Stuart now! Why, the man's a perfect wonder. How does he do it?"

Forster had whisked round, almost in fright, but the red hue left his cheeks, which grew sallow. Too late, he realised what a trap he had fallen into.

"It will save trouble," said Stuart quietly, "if Mr. Montagu Toyn tells us what his business here actually is."

Chapter 8: Wherein a Picture Intervenes

"MONTAGU TOYN!" cried Furneaux, with eloquent pantomime of surprise. "But he said his name was Luke Forster!"

"I saw him yesterday in a Club, and was credibly informed his name was Toyn."

"Ah, in a Club! Young men like you, with a fine career before you, shouldn't visit such disreputable places."

Toyn, feeling that Stuart's recognition had in some sense rehabilitated his social rank, if nothing more, began to bluster. He never imagined, by the way, that Stuart had been concealed in the library, but assumed he had appeared from some other room, having entered the flat unheard.

"Yes, that's right," he said. "I remember seeing Captain Stuart, though we were not introduced. However, as this present farce is played out, I'll be off."

"No. You're going into the library again—by force, if necessary—Isn't he, cap'?"

"Yes. If you say so."

Toyn was not a coward, and he had vital reasons for avoiding the inquisition which he felt impending.

"You have no right to detain me," he shouted. "I came here for a legitimate purpose, and it is no concern of anybody's that I did not choose to give my right name. . . . Ah, would you?" and he swung a vicious left arm blow at Furneaux, who had grabbed his right shoulder. Stuart knocked his hand up, and closed with him. Toyn, who had some notion of the principles of jiu jitsu, ducked suddenly, and caught Stuart's left ankle, meaning to throw him heavily. Stuart stiffened his right leg, and lifted the left one so promptly that Toyn lost his balance, whereupon

the detective took a more decisive part in the struggle,
and the three bodies closely locked, swayed to and fro,
with much stamping of feet and heavy breathing. Stuart's
difficulty, of course, was that he could hardly strike his
adversary merely to detain him, but he had one arm in an
iron grip, and Furneaux was quite capable of mastering
the other, so their combined efforts would certainly have
resulted in Toyn being bundled into the library had not
an irresistible force been applied to all three, and, in a
second, they were sprawling over the centre table.

"I took it for granted you gentlemen wanted this other
gentleman to go into this room, so here he is," said a
calm, courteous voice, and Stuart and Furneaux found
themselves staring at the portly figure of the van
Cortland butler. Blocking the doorway, and grinning
broadly, was Benson.

"In fact, here we all are!" said Furneaux. "Who is the
other stalwart ruffian?"

"My valet," explained Stuart. "Would you mind closing
the door, Benson? And pacify that girl," for Catherine was
giving tongue shrilly from the rear of the hall.

"I wished to see you, sir," said Brown, speaking with
the respectful air of a maitre d'hotel announcing that
dinner was served, "and went to your old flat, where I
met Mr. Benson, so I gave him a hand. All your baggage
is in the lobby. Shall we bring it in?"

"Brown, you're a scream!" broke in the detective. "But
let the luggage wait. Have you ever seen this fellow
before?" and he whirled about on Toyn, who was gazing
red eyed at his captors.

"No, sir."

"So he couldn't very well figure as an intimate friend
of Mr. van Cortland?"

"Not an intimate friend, sir. He may have been a
street acquaintance. He knows where the van Cortland
mansion is, because he called there this morning."

"At what time?"

"Half past nine, sir. He enquired rf Mr. Kerningham had left a handkerchief in the drawing room, and I told him there was no handkerchief there."

"Did he, indeed! That is most interesting. . . .Now, Montagu Toyn, at last you are going to tell us the truth, the whole truth, and nothing but the truth, even if we have to persuade you by ungentle means. You agree with me, Captain Stuart?"

For reply, Stuart took from a pocket a small roll of strong twine. He had not lost the habit, acquired in the trenches of Picardy, where bits of string and rope were often worth more than their weight in gold, of twisting up and stowing away in safety all such useful odds and ends.

"Yes," he said slowly. "Sometimes we had to induce Heine to be candid. Didn't we, Brown?"

"Yes, sir. Personally, I preferred the point of the baynit."

"Not round his neck!" protested Furaeaux, gazing at Stuart's preparation in mock horror.

"No. The thumb suffices. Or a big toe."

"Stop this fooling!" bellowed Toyn, feeling his ribs gingerly, since Brown had applied some scientific method of propulsion practised on "drunks and disorderlies" by the London police. "What's it all about? And who are you, anyway?"—this latter question being aimed at the detective.

"Ah! We are about to see light," grinned his chief tormentor. "I am Inspector Furneaux of the New York Detective Bureau, and it now becomes my painful duty to warn you that anything you say will be recorded in writing, and may be used in evidence against you."

"On what charge?"

"Being accessory after the fact to a murder."

"What nonsense! I haven't murdered anyone."

"You are distraught, and quite incoherent. Evidently, you are incapable of understanding plain English. How about a highball?"

"I could do with a drink, certainly."

"Brown, will you officiate? The lady in the kitchen has stopped screaming."

"Yes, sir. And you gentlemen?"

"Captain Stuart will join his club friend. I am debarred officially."

Toyn, who seemed to be badly shaken, collapsed into a chair.

"Quite right," purred Furneaux sympathetically. "We lead sheltered lives these days, so cannot meet the occasional buffets of adverse fortune with the equanimity of our forefathers. I read recently the autobiography of Vittorio Alfieri, an Italian gentleman and dramatist of the eighteenth century, who had an affair with the charming but frail wife of an English guardsman. He was in a box at the opera in London with the Italian ambassador, and was called out by the irate husband, who had spied him there. The two walked from the Haymarket through St. James Park, to a quiet corner of the Green Park facing Piccadilly—the officer actually stopping on the way to buy a sword—and they fought a fierce duel, in which Alfieri was stabbed through the right arm. As his left shoulder was dislocated by a fall from a horse, and that arm in a sling, the Englishman was generous, so merely cursed him and stalked off. Alfieri knotted a handkerchief around the wound with his teeth, and rejoined the Ambassador in the operahouse. The whole incident consumed exactly three quarters of an hour. Now, you, Toyn, could not have done that, if you are so spent by a rough and tumble of a few seconds."

Brown came in with the refreshments, and Toyn gulped down his share at a draught.

"A curious point about the duel," continued Furneaux, "was that the sun was shining the whole time. They used to go to the opera then during the summer, and at six o'clock."

"Oh, tell me what you want, and let me go," growled Toyn, who was beginning to realise that Furneaux had been playing with him ever since he entered the flat.

"One thing at a time should suffice for you," came the quick retort, the detective's manner changing from light banter to a tone of menace. "You know that Anthony van Cortland is dead?"

"Yes."

"And that he was murdered?"

"There's some queer talk flying about."

"Where did you hear this queer talk?"

"I can't remember."

"Let me assist you. You telephoned from a call office in 42nd Street for permission to visit Mr. Bob Kerningham a second time, though you had seen him at eight o'clock this morning. Didn't he tell you that he and some of his friends were held on suspicion of having caused van Cortland's death?"

"I thought he was raving?"

"But you do remember?"

"What if I do?"

"Only that you have proved yourself an incurable liar. I give you one last chance. You either convince me here and now that you are an innocent accomplice of the murderer, or I arrest you right away."

"I swear I know nothing about the murder. I was asked early to day to visit Mr. Kerningham, and learnt, to my astonishment, that he was in prison."

"Who gave you the message?"

"I don't know. I expect Bob slipped a few dollars to some official."

"And then?"

"I 'phoned the police for a permit, which, after some delay, was given. Dammit, what an idiot I've been. It was you. I remember your voice now."

"I'm glad your memory is improving. And what did Mr. Kerningham say?"

"Don't you know?"

"You tell."

"He gave me a yarn about the Ace Club, and a big supper at van Cortland's house, where he and Frank

Baker blurted out some stupid things as to the forthcoming marriage. Then he doesn't know what happened, but he woke up the following morning in the same room to find some queer little jink of a detective—. Well, I sure am "

"Get on with your story."

"This detective, whoever he might be, was screaming at him to tell why he had killed van Cortland. Bob said he hadn't killed anybody, though he certainly had felt like wringing van Cortland's neck for taking his best girl from him. Then he was bundled into an ambulance, and really came to his senses in the police station. It was some hours before he missed his handkerchief."

"Why should he miss it? Everything he needed was brought from his house in a suitcase."

"How the blazes should I know?"

"One more remark like that and you will be marched down Fifth Avenue in handcuffs."

"You daren't do it."

"Brown!" shouted Furneaux, going to the door.

"Yes, sir," and the butler came majestically from the kitchen.

"Run down and find the nearest cop. Tell him I want him, and he'll come on the jump."

"Hold on, there!" cried Toyn, completely cowed at last. "Dash it all, I can't give you information I don't possess."

"Wait a moment, Brown. This baby is becoming more reasonable. Continue, Toyn!"

"At what? Saying 'I don't know,' all the time?"

"No, indeed.' If your wits are clouding again, I'll help. Why did you return to Kerningham?"

"To tell him I couldn't get his handkerchief."

Toyn stopped speaking, yet Furneaux did not utter a word, but merely surveyed him with a smile of sheer sarcasm and contempt.

"Of course," went on the witness sheepishly, abandoning the pretense of not understanding the detective's mocking glance, "he wanted me to give a message to Miss Dixon, and was thoroughly upset when he heard she had gone away."

"What was the message?"

"That he and the other boys were very sorry for the trouble she was undergoing, and would try to make it up to her when the skies were blue once more. Nothing very deadly in that, was there?"

"Yes, excessively so, if sent by the man who killed her affianced husband."

"But how was I to know that?"

"You are guessing pretty hard now, eh? There are others than Bob Kerningham who wish to stand well with the lady in question."

This mere statement seemed to disconcert Toyn more than anything Furneaux had said thus far—more even than the threat of immediate arrest.

"Speak plainly to me and I'll be equally outspoken with you," he muttered, after a marked pause.

"Good. You see now just where you stand," said Furneaux enigmatically. "I'll make you an offer. Promise you'll work faithfully for the police in this matter, and I'll let you go. I'll come to your apartment at five o'clock, and tell you what I want you to do. But make up your mind to run straight, or I'll drag you into notoriety by the scruff of your neck, and you can't afford that."

Greatly to his surprise and relief, Toyn found himself being escorted to the elevator and to freedom. But the seed of fear had been sown in his brain. He was a cowed and beaten man, and he did not endeavour to disguise the fact from his most secret thought.

"I imagined at one time you were going to bounce more out of that chap," commented Stuart, when the two were alone together.

"You are not quite up to some of the Bureau's ways," said the detective, with an air of gravity he seldom displayed. "That guy may or may not become an effective ally, but I've put the terror of the law in him, and that counts for a good deal. You see, I don't know who is guilty of this crime. Nor does he. But he is well posted in the lives of some of van Cortland's associates, and his knowledge may prove more than useful, if I can keep him on the rails, that is."

"Is Kerningham merely an ass?"

"I—think so."

"Well, I'm cured from jumping at conclusions. I was sure I spoke with van Cortland's slayer at ten o'clock."

"Don't lose heart," said Furneaux, with a queer little laugh. "I've barked up the wrong tree many a time. You did us a splendid turn by getting on the 'phone so smartly. Of course, you don't know what happened?"

"I was thinking hard a few minutes ago."

"Probably you were on the right track. I couldn't enlighten you over the 'phone. When you reported the conversation, the supervisor at the exchange told me that the same man had called up Police Headquarters. Then we had him. I deduced that he would call here personally after seeing Kerningham the second time. I didn't err. Toyn has the criminal's mind, though not actually a wrong doer. He fancies himself as a bluffer, too. Both qualities combined to bring him here. That is why I bothered you by seeming to pay scant attention to what you were saying before he arrived. I was waiting, waiting, longing for the ringing of that door bell."

"You're a marvel."

"Not a bit. The average crook is dead easy. He thinks in the same narrow way, whether he's a callous murderer or a mere pickpocket. Thank goodness, that's the only factor in favour of the police."

Stuart was convinced that Furneaux's unwonted humility only concealed some theory he had evolved but was unwilling, as yet, to formulate in words. So he forebore further questioning, though his own ingenuity was working at full pressure.

"Won't you give Miss Dixon a call?" he enquired.

"Why?" Furneaux's expressive eyebrows "registered astonishment," as the movies put it. Stuart laughed.

"Don't ask me for reasons," he said. "I told her you might wish to have a chat with her, and she promised to be in at 12.30."

"Listen to me, cap'," said the detective seriously. "You'll arrange matters with that young lady far more skilfully than I. If I want to get anything out of her I'll send you."

"You certainly will not," cried Stuart emphatically.

"Well, well. You really must read Vittorio Alfieri. If he were alive and here, and I said that to him, he'd jump on a horse and spur the poor beast furiously all the way to Paul Smith's Camp. He galloped once after a bella Inglese from Turin to Vienna, though even he complained of the roads, yet you refuse to take a night's journey in a train to pay homage to a far more delightful American girl."

"You don't really mean that, do you?" said Stuart, perplexedly, whereupon Furneaux cackled shrilly and went off. Finding himself rather red behind the ears, Stuart waited to fill a pipe before summoning Brown to ascertain the exact cause of that worthy's well timed visit.

A carpet ran the whole length of the hall, so his footsteps were inaudible when he went toward the kitchen, though he took no pains to tread noiselessly. It was evident that the butler and the valet were fraternising with the ready camaraderie of men who had faced a common enemy.

"Gee! I kin fix that day well," Benson was saying. "We had just come down to billets after seventeen days in the front line when a regimental parade was ordered for ten sharp next morning. We cussed a bit, naterally, until we heard that General Mangin was goin' to give him the Croix de Guerre, with double palms. Then it was O. K., as the boys all loved him."

Stuart halted. The conversation struck him as having a distinctly personal bearing.

"Well. I must say it's more like him than the average newspaper portrait," said Brown. "An' it's good of Pershing, too. Curious thing Miss Dixon should have cut it out and kep' it."

"She'd be real mad if he got to know she had it," put in Catherine. "My land! You ought to have heard my instructions this morning. I was just going to pop it into an envelope when that row started in the passage, but I was sure you gentlemen would like to see it."

"What's the date?" said Benson. "July 4th, 1918. Yes, that's right. I was gassed a week afterwards."

Creeping back to the library with thievish feet, Stuart sank into a chair. He had, as his humble friends in the kitchen would have expressed it, "gone hot all over." Mary Dixon, a girl of whose mere existence he had then no knowledge whatever, had cut out of a newspaper a photograph of himself, taken on the great day of his life, for no soldier can regard in otherwise the tremendous occasion when he is honoured by a leader of a foreign army in the presence of his own comrades. What midsummer madness was this? That it was not an idle whim of the moment was shown by the fact that she had retained the souvenir, and had been most emphatic in directing that it should be secured from its hiding place and posted to her immediately, since no other construction could be put on the parlourmaid's disclosure.

At first he felt as though he had sustained a rather severe electric shock, but, in a little space, the modest self depreciation inherent in his character suggested an explanation that was reasonable enough. He recalled the picture quite well. In fact, he had planned to obtain a somewhat more finished copy of it from the photographic agency which supplied it to the press. Probably his Red Cross friend had mentioned the ceremony in a letter to Mary, and the girl had retained the newspaper cutting simply because it gave actuality to the written word. At any rate, the incident showed that she might have remembered his name when given to her the previous day, and it might also account for the curious trust she placed in his integrity.

In five minutes Richard was himself again, but this time he rang, and asked Catherine to send in Brown.

"Didn't I gather that you had something to say to me?" he began.

"Yes, sir. It was about Miss Dixon."

Stuart blushed to a peony red, but managed to laugh.

"That young lady keeps herself on the map," he said, grasping at the first lucid thought that presented itself. "I—er—I have heard her name a great many times to day."

"But this is serious, sir," said the butler, little imagining that his subconscious allusion to the talk in the kitchen was keenly appreciated by his vis a vis.

"Well, if that is so, close the door, and take a chair."

"It's this way, sir," went on Brown. "Miss Dixon 'phoned me early to day, and advised me to make a clean breast of things to you."

"Hold on a minute! Are you going to tell me something which the police ought to know?"

"I can't say, sir. It is up to you to decide."

"Dash it all! Why am I made the repository of everybody's secrets? I—I'm rather afraid of occupying a false position."

"Just what I said, sir. But Miss Dixon insisted."

"Blaze away, then."

"She told me she couldn't sleep in the train last night, an' her mind kep' runnin' on my poor master's death. Although there are circumstances which might make a case against Mr. Kerningham, she is sure, without knowin' exactly why, that he had nothing to do with it really."

"But she hadn't heard of the ring then."

"What ring, sir?"

Stuart coloured, with annoyance now.

"I shall never make a detective, Brown," he said. "But you are to be trusted. Mr. van Cortland was killed by an Italian poison ring, which his murderer threw into the Park, and which afterwards brought about the death of a detective."

"God bless my soul!" exclaimed Brown, startled for once out of his habitual calm.

"But Miss Dixon knows that now, as I told her myself two hours ago."

"Did she say she asked me to call?"

"No."

"And did she think it made things look black for Mr. Kerningham?"

"No."

Stuart, having blabbed carelessly in one respect was not minded to err a second time.

"Then, "said the butler judicially, "my orders hold good. And I've often noticed, sir, that in such affairs a woman's intuition may be better than a man's brains, though I do hold we are a long way ahead of 'em when it comes to real, hard thinking."

His hearer did not fail to recollect Furneaux's partial acceptance of Winter's theory that he, the former, had a feminine streak in him. He certainly wondered what was coming next.

"Of course," continued Brown, "there's a heap of difference between guessin' an' knowin'. But that's as may be. Miss Dixon believes that, among all those young gentlemen at the party, there was three only who had sufficient intelligence an' nerve to plan and carry out a deadly crime—those are her very words, sir. One of the three, Mr. van Cortland himself, was the victim. That leaves two—Mr. Francis Baker an' Mr. Philip Durrane."

"Did Miss Dixon state any grounds for her belief?"

"She's only a young girl, sir, an' now I'm comin', in my opinion, to the reason why she sent me to you. She wanted me to chip in, so to speak, with a bit of guesswork founded on fact. Mind you, she didn't say so. This is my own. Those two were crazy about her."

"What, in addition to van Cortland, and Kerningham?"

"Quite correct. But the real trouble was that she didn't care a straw about any of 'em when it came to marriage. She was—rather afraid—of Mr van Cortland."

"I hate doing it, but I suppose I must ask—why did she ultimately accept him?"

"To help her father, and get rid of the others."

"Had they all proposed to her?"

"I'm not sure, but, bless you, sir, a woman always knows."

"Still I see no just cause for suspecting the men you name."

"Neither do I, sir. I'm only tellin' you what Miss Dixon hinted at."

"All this over the 'phone?"

"She spoke in such a way that I alone could understand."

Stuart took thought for a full minute or more, and believed no harm would be done if he probed this matter more deeply.

"You're a sensible sort of chap, Brown," he said at last, "and have had many opportunities for observing these two men in particular. How do you sum them up?"

"Mr. Baker is a very frank, outspoken lad, and Mr. Durrane is reserved, but I've an idea that what one hides by plenty of talk the other hides by being quiet. Each of 'em contrives to get his own way, an' both were furious when my master's engagement was announced. People forget that the butler may be lookin' at 'em when their eyes are elsewhere, an' I shall never forget the way they took his little speech at the Club dinner before this last one. It wasn't a speech either. He just stood up when the first glass of champagne was poured out, an' said: –'Boys, wish me well. To day Mary promised to marry me!' Mr. Baker has blue eyes, and Mr. Durrane black ones, but they both shot fire. Mr. Kerningham shouted:—'Hell she did!' and drank two glasses of wine straight off. The other two never touched theirs. They didn't seem to trouble about each other. They just wanted to kill Mr. van Cortland then and there."

"We must tell the detectives, Brown."

"I agree, sir."

"There may be nothing to it. It's a mere theory, based on little more than the natural jealousy of a set of youngsters enamoured of the same girl."

"That's the cause of a great many crimes, sir. Gold first, and then women."

"You seem to have studied these foibles of human nature."

"When I was in the force, sir, I wanted to get on, so read Lombroso an' other authorities."

"Why in the world did you leave the police for—for domestic service?"

"I was pushed out, sir," said Brown, with a placid smile. "You know what it is in the army. If the colonel happens to say that a private is a mighty smart fellow, every corporal and sergeant in the regiment has a down on the poor devil. That was my case exactly. But I'm better off as I am. I can save money now, and, if an employer isn't a gentleman, I can find scores of other places. And then, the smash up I got in the war unfitted me for hard work. But this affair certainly does remind me of old times, especially when it came to firing that fellow into this room just now."

"I'll tell you what, Brown. You and I must keep in touch. Come and see me any day you like, and I'll give you a ring if I want you."

"Thank you, sir. I would like to hear what those two detectives think of Miss Dixon's ideas. They're a queer pair, but I'd hate to have them on my heels if I had done wrong."

When Brown went home, Stuart grabbed his hat, and hurried down town to a newspaper office. He wanted a print of a certain photograph taken in France in 1918! Meanwhile, oddly enough, he forgot to telephone Mary Dixon, after having practically arranged it with her.

CHAPTER 9: MR. WINTER REVIEWS THE SITUATION

OF course, he did not fail to recollect his promise rather later in the day; but he then yielded to a new timidity, and thought fit to let Willie Dixon deputise for him, when that young man, somewhat weary after his first day of business life, came home at the appointed hour. Mary had not much to say, and she made no request to speak with Stuart.

Dixon, of course, had been a highly interested auditor of the morning's events in the flat, and did not fail to brighten the story for his sister's benefit. She, poor girl, went to bed believing that most of her household treasures had been wrecked during a fearsome struggle.

Although she had seemed to ignore Stuart, the latter's thoughts dwelt on more serious matters. The newspapers were hounding various authorities to the investigation of a crime "which was stirring New York society to its depths." No one seemed to know just what the crime consisted in, but everybody talked for publication. The District Attorney, a Tammany Democrat, saw his opportunity to flutter the Republican dove cot, and seized it joyously.

"The Four Hundred cuts no ice in my office," he proclaimed. "This mystery will be probed if all the forces of social reaction are arrayed against me."

The Coroner was profound but vague.

"The law must reign supreme in this City," he declared. "My enquiry will be thorough and impartial."

The Commissioner availed himself of an excellent opening to denounce those critics who spoke of a crime wave in New York. "Crime is a steadily decreasing factor in the life of Manhattan," he said. "If a crime is committed it is investigated as closely in Fifth Avenue as in Sullivan Street."

Several reporters called at the Dixon flat, but were repulsed by Benson, who used the same formula to all enquiries: "The family left for up State yesterday. No: I don't know where they have gone." Luckily the pressmen had no inkling of Captain Stuart's presence there, so could not ask for him. Even Mr. Winter found difficulty in gaining admission, but ultimately persuaded the Cerberus to let him through those well guarded portals.

Stuart was unfeignedly glad to see him. The Chief's mere aspect radiated confidence and sound sense. Sometimes it was difficult to follow Furneaux's warped wit, but Winter said what he meant others to understand, and said it with authority.

The two younger men were finishing their coffee when the head of the Bureau was announced. Dixon, who had never seen him, was awed at first; but quickly responded to the great detective's geniality and ease of manner.

"Got anybody hidden under the table?" was Winter's first enquiry, when a third coffee cup was bidden, and a fresh Havana lighted.

"Not to our knowledge," laughed Stuart.

"Had a quiet afternoon?"

"Yes. The bell has been kept busy, but you are our first actual visitor."

"I've had a fierce day," sighed the big man.

"May I ask if you have made any progress?"

"Yes—and No. We have lightened the net, which was rather overloaded by our first haul yesterday morning, but there are queer, almost occult, elements in this business which are not solved yet. Furneaux has gone to the movies, and that is an encouraging sign."

"To the movies!" cried both his hearers.

"Yes. Carlotta Grisi is by way of becoming a cinema star, and one of her passionate films is being shown to night."

"Ah!" again in chorus.

"Why do you say 'Ah,' as though my remark had explained everything?"

"Give it up," said Dixon.

"Because, being essentially artificial, she exhibits her true nature far more accurately on the stage than in real life," said Stuart.

"Not a bad answer, yours," and he nodded at the soldier. "But you haven't yet sized up my strange little colleague's whims. He hardly ever tackles any difficult case, such as this undoubtedly is, that he does not fasten on to some mystic and far fetched bond between its main actors and others who are quite outside the scope of what I may define as legitimate enquiry. Carlotta Grisi has really nothing to do with this tragedy. Her ring and the ring which killed van Cortland are merely of the same period and of similar design. She has not even seen van Cortland since before the war, and certainly has given him no trouble. Yet she is one of Furneaux's links. You, Captain Stuart, are the other."

"I!"

Stuart's astonishment was profound. He thought for a moment that the Chief was borrowing some of Furneaux's stage thunder.

"Yes. Do you know anything about static electricity?"

"A little. It is a minor force set up parallel with a major one exerted between two powerful bodies in mutual magnetic attraction."

"A first rate definition. But does anybody know why it exists?"

"I certainly don't."

"Neither does Furneaux, but he reacts to it. He believes that by sticking to you and Carlotta he will ultimately discover the prime cause of the electrical outburst in the van Cortland mansion. That is why he is now having an undisturbed hour with the lady on the screen, and it also explains why he suggested to Miss Dixon that it would be well if you took up your quarters here with her brother."

"Well, I'm dashed!" cried Dixon.

"Neither Miss Dixon nor Furneaux mentioned that to me," said Stuart, to whom, for some reason, the statement was not altogether pleasing.

"I gathered as much, so I am telling you now."

This, for Winter, was a cryptic remark, but Stuart let it pass.

"I really don't see how I can help to solve the van Cortland mystery," was his quiet comment.

"Neither do I. Furneaux's methods and mine are far apart as the poles—Dear me, how I keep dwelling on these magnetic influences! But we generally arrive at the same result, which is bad for the particular malefactor we have in view. Anyhow, that is enough of vague analysis for to night. . . . I hear you, young man, have taken to the rubber business?"

"Well, that's a friendly way of putting it," said Dixon. "I may strike you as being quite sane this evening, I suppose, but I am really asking myself all the time: 'If the pound sterling equals \$4.11-3/4, and one dollar is worth 974 milreis, how many Austrian kronen are there in five hundred Ceylon rupees?'

Can you beat it?"

"I never was really good at figures," said Winter. "What stock deals did your father have with van Cortland, Durrane, Baker, and others some months ago?"

"Can't say I ever rightly understood. Pop got tied up in a knot when the bottom fell out of the rubber market, and tried to hypothecate his shares for a loan. I remember the word, because I looked it up in the dictionary, and wondered why they couldn't use a simpler one. Montagu Toyn, who got twisted up here to day, introduced those lads, and the deal took various turns, as none of the three could be regarded as a fool. It came out that Baker and Durrane were buying blocks of shares, not lending money on 'em, and then poor old Tony fell for Mary, and came to Pop with a proposition that he should just lift a big mortgage off the property, which he did, with the result that Pop cleaned up two millions in preferred stock when the amalgamation took place. He would have made more, if he hadn't sold so many shares to the other two financiers, who got away with the dough, too, of course. But Tony behaved like a white man all through—never even hinted that Mary was part of the bargain—so she could hardly turn him down when he asked her to marry him."

"Ah! That's clear. That's lucid. Now, excuse this question. Was your sister more inclined, let us put it, to marry someone else?"

"Not to my knowing. Sis hated the thought of getting married at all. She likes a good time as well as anyone, but she wanted her freedom, and had some bee in her bonnet about helping along social regeneration, whatever that may mean."

"So she accepted van Cortland out of gratitude for having saved her father's fortune?"

"I suppose so. She didn't discuss that side of it with me. Girls don't, you know."

"She had other suitors."

"Gee! A dozen, I should think. Baker, Kerningham, Buddy Owen, Harry Holgate—even Billy Hoiton, who has been sued at least four times for breach they were all after her."

"Seriously?"

"I dunno. Mary just laughed at 'em."

"These enquiries are really necessary, I take it," frowned Stuart.

"I'm through," and Winter leaned back in his chair.

"But, say, Chief," went on Dixon, aglow with the consciousness that he seemed to have attained a certain importance in the detective's eyes, "won't you tell us about where matters stand? I haven't much of a head piece, but I might help."

Winter, unseen by either of the others, had given Stuart a quick look. He smiled blandly now.

"It does one good to arrange one's thoughts at times," he said, "and there is something in that notion of yours, too. You, Mr. Dixon, are an interested party, as your sister's matrimonial affairs are closely bound up with the crime, and may have to be threshed out in open court."

"Oh, I say!—" began Dixon, but the other stayed the imminent outburst with a massive hand.

"The law is no respecter of persons," he said. "The only chance of Miss Dixon's not being subpoenaed to give evidence is that, by complete knowledge, we may be able to dispense with her testimony."

"But against whom?"

"No one knows yet. I'm going to let both of you see the inside of this matter, in the belief that you will assist, and, if possible, throw light on certain dim issues. Now, we begin by assuming that van Cortland's death was not even thought of by his murderer until the marriage was announced. That is a useful limitation of time. Five weeks ago he himself broke the news to the same circle of friends as that which gathered in his house the night before last. A fortnight later he received a warning that he must not think of marrying Miss Dixon, or he would be killed. He scoffed at the threat, which was repeated the day before yesterday. Fortunately, we have secured the two documents. They vary slightly in text, but are written on similar scraps of paper. The torn half of a folio sheet which was found in van Cortland's pocket corresponds with the half of a typed letter, making a business appointment, discovered in Mr. Francis Baker's suite in his father's house, and, on the back of this second part is the word 'nozze,' in Italian 'marriage,' scrawled in pencil."

Dixon's wide open eyes and Stuart's involuntary movement as he bent forward to catch the detective's every word caused Winter to lift that admonitory hand again.

"No, no, boys," he said, "you are far from hearing all the facts yet. Don't condemn any man because one or two incidents seem to link him up with a crime. Remember there were thirteen in the party, and, if the circumstantial evidence is to be trusted, one of twelve killed the thirteenth. Don't say to yourselves:—'Baker is the scoundrel,' merely because he leaves an incriminating half sheet of note paper in his rooms. To my mind, such inconceivable carelessness is not the action of a man who could plan the daring and cold blooded murder of a friend. It is almost a tribute to his innocence. Now, assuming we have the motive for the murder, as stated in two written warnings, we ask ourselves why a sort of New York Italian lingo was used? Was it not because of van Cortland's half forgotten association with Carlotta Grisi? But how many of his young friends knew of this? Did you, Mr. Dixon?"

"No. Never heard the lady's name till this evening."

"That's a point in your favour. I believe seven out of the twelve can honestly say the same thing. Next, how many among you had seen Baker's collection of Italian curios?"

"All of us. He was rather proud of that show."

"Including the ring?"

"The ring was pointed out as a queer looking article, but, if he knew how the claws worked, he did not tell me."

"Did any of your friends recognise it as a dangerous article?"

"No, and I'm sure it would have been spoken of."

"We are getting on famously, by a process of exhaustion as Furneaux would call it. Finally, before coming to the actual murder, how many among the company were acquainted with van Cortland's habit of taking drugs?"

"Did he?" cried Dixon.

"Well, drugs is a hard term, but he certainly used a very powerful sleeping draught."

"That's beyond me."

"Yet the man who drugged the bowl of punch so potently brought the same mixture to the house that night. He must be a person of peculiar temperament, and gifted with abnormal self confidence. He not only thought out each detail of an atrocious crime, but took the almost phenomenal risk of betraying himself by his first spoken words, after being aroused from a stupor as deep as that induced in any other member of the party. He survived that test, and I do not remember another similar instance of such remarkable will power in all my experience. It is a great pity none among you can recall events just prior to losing consciousness."

"I'm sorry," said Dixon, "but try as I may, my memory is blank. I can see the fellows mixing the punch now, but have no recollection at all of either Durrane or Baker taking any part in it. I only mention those names because you spoke of them, Chief."

"How soon after the mixing did you drop out of the scene?"

"Mighty quick. Buddy Owen and I were arguing about polo—and as neither of us plays we were getting a trifle hot—when the punch was served. Oh, Durrane proposed Tony's health!"

"Did he, indeed?"

"Yes, and we all put the liquor away—no heeltaps. I sat down, and very soon everything on the table became a blur. Then I curled up—dead to the world."

"By the way, since Mr. Durrane called on the company to drink the host's health, and this particular gathering of the Ace Club was intended to mark the end of Mr. van Cortland's bachelor days, I suppose he, Durrane, was not in the running for your sister's hand."

"No. Not a bit of it. He couldn't!"

Dixon spoke excitedly. The question seemed to be a wholly unexpected one.

"But why not?"

"Well—er—dash it all, Mr. Winter!—this opens up something—I really don't know what to say."

"It is a golden rule to tell the facts. If they are in a man's favour they can be forgotten."

"Yes, but "

"I am more than twice your age, Mr. Dixon. Speaking, not as a policeman, but as a man of the world, I may lay down a principle. Any decent-minded fellow will never betray a woman's secret. But when a man is suspected, among eleven others, of being concerned in the murder of his friend, to conceal something which may tend to clear him is but a poor service. Come! Let me make things easy. Was Mr. Durrane married in France?"

Willie Dixon heaved a great sigh of relief.

"That's it!" he cried. "Tony knew, and so did the rest of us. Phil got a heavy crush on a girl in St. Nazaire, where he had a camp job for six months. They were wed right enough, and the girl saw to it that the marriage was registered in the American Consulate. I believe that was the beginning of the row between them, as Phil didn't Me the hole and-corner way it was done."

"So the marriage was not a success?"

"That's what I think. Phil never spoke of it after we came home, and the girl is not in New York, so we drew our own conclusions. Still, he made no mystery of it. We all knew."

"How long have you been home?"

"Two years."

"Did you all return about the same time?"

"All but Baker and Kerningham. They got leave for a trip to Italy."

"Any complications there?"

"Not that we were aware of. We joshed them a bit, but there was nothing to it."

"After reviewing the circumstances which have come to light, can you suggest why any member of the Ace Club should have a serious grievance against van Cortland?"

"Frank Baker was sore with him about Mary—and said so. But Frank would never "

"Of course not. That is our main difficulty. None of you would poison a friend. Yet one of you did."

"I wish you wouldn't put it that way, Mr. Winter."

"You don't like the inclusive pronoun, I'm sure. But, if I begin to exclude individuals, I create inferences, which I want to avoid. However, it may console you when I say that if Mr. Furneaux arrests you on suspicion I'll resign my job. . . . Well, good night! This talk has been useful. Naturally, I expect you gentlemen will not repeat anything that has passed between us. Until I have proof that will withstand the test of the courts I try to keep an unbiased mind. I count on both of you to do the same."

"The Records Branch of the War Department might assist," said Stuart, as the detective rose.

"It has assisted," and Winter smiled cheerfully. The soldier escorted him to the outer door.

"May I put one question?" he said, in a low tone.

"Certainly."

"Did you know already that Durrane was married?"

"No."

The eyes of the two men clashed, and they shook hands in silence. Meanwhile, Willie Dixon, having endured one ordeal, was battling with another.

"Gee!" he muttered, when the library door had closed on the Chief's bulky form, "I didn't figure on being on the witness stand to night. That big stiff put me through it!"

He grabbed a decanter of whisky from the table, and measured out a strong dose. Then, seeming to collect his wits, he poured back the spirit, and drank a glass of soda water.

"Fine!" said Stuart, who came back in time to see what was going on. "Keep that up and you'll soon be able to count up to a million in your own money."

"Bar jokes, do you think I'll make good?" cried the boy eagerly.

"The man who has conquered himself can conquer the world. It's a copybook headline, but none the less true because it happens to be hackneyed."

Now, three days earlier, Stuart would no more have dreamed of uttering such a trite remark than of walking down Fifth Avenue in a straw hat and a military tunic.

But Willie Dixon was Mary Dixon's brother, and it pleased him to find some traits of fortitude and self abrogation injthe family.

The inquest was opened next morning. Stuart and Brown were the only non official witnesses, and the former, at any rate, wondered at the ease with which all sensational details were suppressed. Van Cortland's legal representatives seemed to act in collusion with the authorities in this respect. A verdict was recorded that the deceased died from the effect of an irritant poison, "how or by whom administered being at present unknown," a burial certificate was issued, and the enquiry stood adjourned for a fortnight.

Of course, the newspapers made capital out of the extreme formalities of the proceedings. Stuart found himself prominent as "a credible witness" whose testimony proved conclusively that his friend, van Cortland, had no intent to take his own life. Why were not the "gilded youth of Fifth Avenue, who participated in the now notorious final dinner of the Ace Club," summoned to the enquiry? The heavy artillery of the Republican press was brought to bear on the District Attorney and the Commissioner. The Democratic journals retaliated by promising that the most stately fortresses of the Four Hundred would be shaken to their foundations before those faithful servants of the people concluded their rigid and unsparing quest into this outrageous instance of plutocratic degeneracy. In every instance, the inquest on Flanagan's death, held on the same day, was bracketed with the van Cortland mystery.

In the meantime, Fumeaux had confided to Stuart at the inquest that a telephonic summary of an analysis prepared by the chemists of the Johns Hopkins University showed that the poison crystals "reacted" to both vegetable and mineral tests. Arsenic and belladonna were the prime constituents, but there was one other substance which had defied all reagents thus far. Strangest of the strange, a negro assistant in the laboratory, who had attracted much attention by his singular aptitude for bacteriological research, insisted that the unknown ingredient was desiccated snake poison!

"Queer, isn't it?" whispered the little man, "how this affair always reverts to first principles."

"I don't quite follow," said Stuart.

"A snake first upset the harmony of Paradise, and, if the legend be true that Cain's descendants turned black, here we have a nigger telling our scientists something they don't know. I like his theory. How thrilling that the dry venom of a viper from the Pontine Marshes should strike at a young American life after lying in wait two hundred years!"

"You must have been stirred profoundly by the movies the other night."

"Ah! Winter told you that, did he? The fat lump! Tolstoi was right, after all!"

"What on earth has Tolstoi to do with this case?"

"Young man, you will never rise to eminence in your cut throat profession if you don't read. The great Russian discovered that nicotine destroys the conscience, and the moral sense of that mound of bone and brawn who heads the New York Detective Bureau was long since vitiated by excessive use of tobacco."

Winter noticed his colleague's fiery glance and the tip of a darting tongue. He scribbled a note, and threw it across the table. It ran:—"You look something like a cobra yourself. Pull your hood up!"

"Can you two read each other's thoughts?" enquired Stuart, for it was utterly impossible that Winter should know by ordinary means what their sotto voce conversation was about.

"I meant him to read that one," hissed Furneaux.

Two days passed without incident. Stuart learned casually that every member of the Ace Club had been examined as to his share in the proceedings on the fatal night, but neither of the detectives sought his company, and sheer discipline restrained him from bothering them for news. He attended van Cortland's funeral at Woodlawn Cemetery, and recognised a good many members of the Ace Club. In glancing over the wreaths, he saw one from Mary Dixon, inscribed "with sincere regret and utmost sympathy." She must certainly be either cold-hearted or very self contained, he thought. What precise sentiments from the girl who was about to marry the unfortunate youth who was now being laid to rest for ever in his family vault!

Dixon, who had accompanied him, saw that he was reading the card on Mary's wreath.

"Poor old sis!" he murmured. "She quite broke down when she 'phoned me about those flowers, and left it to me to write something suitable. Is it all right?"

"Admirable!" agreed Stuart, who resolved then and there never again would he form any sort of opinion on any phase of the van Cortland mystery, because he was invariably wrong.

When the two young men reached home a large flat brown paper parcel awaited Stuart. It was the photograph of the decoration ceremony. Evidently Dixon had never seen it before.

"That's a fine thing to have," he cried, genuine in his boyish admiration. "What did you get the Cross for?"

"Pulling a stout Frenchman out of a hole," laughed Stuart.

"Ah, come off! What did the citation say?"

"Just the usual bunk. 'During an enforced retirement,' which means that we were all running like the devil, a rather solid Colonel of Chasseurs got stuck in a muddy shell hole. He was our brigade liaison officer, so I simply couldn't leave him there. I organised half a platoon and held up the Boches till the Colonel was on dry land once more. By sheer good luck the scrap developed into a counter attack, and I got all the credit for it. You know how such things happen."

Catherine came in to enquire about dinner, and caught sight of the picture, whereupon Stuart resolved to startle her.

"I looked quite smart that day, didn't I?" he said, thrusting the photograph before her eyes. She surveyed it critically, with all the requisite enthusiasm.

"How nice!" she said.

"Do you mean me or the photograph?"

"Both, sir. If I was you, I'd have that painted by an artist. Your people would value it always."

Not by a quiver of an eyelid did the maid betray her mistress. When she went out, Stuart smiled rather grimly as he placed the picture on a sideboard. He could not help agreeing with Kipling, that

The Colonel's lady And Judy O'Grady Are sisters under the skin.

Even Benson, next morning, after being warned by Catherine, was stolid as a Sioux brave, though he was generally full of chatter.

CHAPTER 10: A FRIENDLY DINNER

DURING the next few days Stuart met most of the members of the Ace Club. Although that decadent organization was dissolved, its members clung together. It was only to be expected that the shock of van Cortland's death should have a sobering effect on even the wildest of his companions, but the fact that they were socially under a cloud, and almost ostracized by their own circle, brought about frequent meetings, especially for dinner. In effect, they were herded by misfortune.

When Dixon invited six one evening—making two tables at bridge, he explained—Stuart thought it advisable to inform the Bureau. He enquired for Furneaux, whose extravagances amused him, but was put in touch with Winter. Mindful of the ban on the telephone for explicit conversations, he merely said that Willie Dixon was entertaining half a dozen of his old associates, and he wanted to have any necessary instructions.

"I'm glad you told me in good time," said the Chief. "Neither you nor Dixon have been talking, I hope?"

"No. You can rest assured of that."

"Well, with the exception of you two, none of the others is acquainted with our diminutive friend. They were all far too ill on the first and only occasion they met him to carry away any clear recollection of persons or events. Don't mention him at all. In inevitable references to the affair speak only of me. Know nothing. Let the other fellows tell you. D'you get me?"

"Perfectly."

"Then give Master Willie my blessing, and encourage him to similar festivities every night."

"That may be a bit of a trial for me."

"Anyhow, stick it out. I cannot say more than that we depend on you for any real progress."

"Are you serious?"

"Never more so. I'll come and see you soon. Meanwhile you may accomplish more than you can guess now."

It was while the coffee was being served that Stuart had occasion to prick his ears. The guests were Kerningham, Baker, Durrane, Spence, Billy Bolton and Montagu Straus. He found himself seated between Baker and Durrane, a curiously distasteful companionship, as he could not help associating Baker with the means of accomplishing van Cortland's death, if nothing else.

But Baker was quite friendly.

"Didn't I see you at poor old Van's funeral?" he enquired.

"Yes. I was there."

"Know him well?"

"Not intimately. We met in France, and renewed our friendship here. As you are aware, we had arranged to ride in the Park on the very day of his death."

This fact, of course, had appeared in the newspapers, so he was free to make capital out of it if he thought fit.

"We must have looked a strange lot of roosters that morning," went on Baker.

"Well, yes. If you use that simile I may be pardoned for saying that it seemed as though a fox had been in the poultry pen."

"Who was the detective who shouted at us when the Doctor administered ammonia?" put in Durrane.

"I really cannot tell you," said Stuart. "You forget that I am almost a complete stranger in New York, and there were half a dozen policemen and detectives about the place at the time."

"But I understand that you telephoned the Bureau?"

"Simply because I happened to remember the 'phone number, owing to an embezzlement case which occurred at Governor's Island."

"Foiled again!" laughed Durrane. "I have been anxious to meet you, in the belief you might clear up some part of this wretched mystery. It grows foggier every day that passes."

The man had a pleasant, well bred voice, and the explanation robbed his enquiries of the slightest hint of discourtesy. Baker took up the running again.

"I shall be glad when the police take the lid off," he said. "You've heard about that infernal poisonring, of course?"

"Yes. The newspapers took care of that."

"It was mine."

"Yours!"

Stuart hoped his astonishment was well feigned. By this time the others at the table were aware of the interest this conversation had for all, and were listening.

"Sure it was. All the boys here know it, so Where's the good of making a secret of it?"

"Have you told the police?"

"Naturally. Do you think I'd be such a fool as to keep mum about a serious thing of that sort?"

"I suppose mine was a stupid question," said Stuart quietly.

"Oh, it's for me to apologise. I really had no right to say what I did. The words just blurted out. I didn't mean any reflection on you."

"Why did you keep the d d ring, Frank?" broke in Spence, from the other end of the table.

"That's another of the same crazy—oh, confound it, I must try and guard my tongue. But don't you understand, you poor fish, that I hadn't the least notion it was poisoned?"

"Somebody knew," persisted Spence.

"And I ought to have been charged with poor old Van's murder, eh?"

"Look here, boys," interposed Dixon, "that's no way to talk. If Van was killed by that ring, and I suppose he was, one of our crowd must have done it and the guilty man lifted the ring out of Frank's gem cabinet for that very purpose."

"Why is it assumed that one of us is necessarily a murderer?"

Durrane put the question. It seemed to create a new atmosphere of surprise, almost of tension.

"Who else could it be?" demanded Dixon.

"Any one of the millions in New York," came the unexpected answer. "I think the police are foolish in insisting on our collective responsibility. We were all under the influence of a strong narcotic for nearly six hours. How many people could have entered or left the house in that time?"

"But you are forgetting that the star artist, whoever he was, first put the dope in the punch?" said Kerningham.

"Not at all. My memory is better than yours, Bob. It is you who forget. Didn't you attend a certain dinner in a private room at Voisin's, about January, 1919, when dear old Van himself laced four French airmen so thoroughly that the waiters nearly had a fit when they couldn't get rid of them at closing time?"

Several voices cried out in wonderment. Four men present recalled the incident now, but they had never before thought of connecting it with the murder.

"By heck, Van used the very same stuff that night!" vowed Spence.

"What do you make of it, then?" enquired Dixon, staring round eyed at Durrane.

"I? Nothing. I only point out that Tony was fond of a practical joke, and as this day week marked the last meeting of the Ace Club he might quite conceivably have planned to put us all in the down and out class. Now, hold

on a minute," for several men were about to fire
interrogations at the speaker. "I'm not formulating a
theory, but merely stating possibilities. Suppose it was
part of Van's scheme that someone should come in, and—
let us think of something quite foolish—paint our faces
black, or something of that sort. He would have a
confederate, who would be in the know, and would have a
key, if he were not already concealed in the house. What
was there to prevent such a person from seizing the
opportunity to commit a dramatic crime? You ask for a
motive. Van's earlier life in New York may have supplied
it twenty times over. You point to the ring. Has not
Frank's Italian collection been seen by hundreds? And
which among us is an authority on Seventeenth century
poison rings? Far fetched as this analysis of the unknown
may be, it is not one tenth so unreasonable as the police
certainty that one of us is guilty."

There could be no doubting the conviction wrought in
the minds of his young hearers by Durrane's dramatic
statement of his opinions. Willie Dixon, in particular, was
so carried away that he was in the very act of framing a
question when he caught Stuart's warning eye.

"But—" he began, and stopped abruptly.

"But what?" enquired Durrane.

"I—I was going to remind you that the murderer was
in evening dress, and came out on the balcony."

"Why shouldn't he? If he meant to throw suspicion on
one of us isn't that the very thing he would do? If you ask
me, he had no small grudge against Baker, as he took
very little care that the ring should not be found, granted
Tony was really killed by the ring."

"Can there be any doubt of it, after the death of the
detective?" said Stuart.

"No. I admit that. If the evidence were as clear
against the murderer as it is in regard to his weapon I
should be sorry to stand in his shoes."

Stuart was aware of a very slight movement on
Baker's part. It was almost as though he yielded to an

uncontrollable start, such as results from a convulsive action of the heart. Stuart believed, too, that his neighbour either stifled a laugh, or that some emotion caused a gurgling in his throat. He would have given a good deal to have secured Furneaux's presence at that moment. He was sure the detective would have been ready with some quip or verbal thrust which would lend a sinister and revealing turn to the discussion. Indeed, it had lacked little in this respect thus far, but he searched his brains for a lightning inspiration. Whether he was doing rightly or wrongly he could not determine, but he took a chance.

"Your theory, if I may venture to use the word after your disclaimer, Mr. Durrane, is exceedingly interesting and ingenious," he said. "If it is at all well founded, does it leave out of account the motive for the crime assigned by the newspapers?"

"What is that?"

"Well, we are discussing a matter of real public importance, and that must be my excuse for mentioning the fact. Have not several papers taken it for granted that van Cortland was killed by a rival suitor when he announced his forthcoming marriage?"

"Yes. That seems to bring back the guilt to our crowd," agreed Durrane simply.

"Seems? Damn it, it does!" cried Baker, with a ferocity that was singularly out of place, to say the least, seeing that every youngster present, except Stuart, had attended the fatal party. His sudden fury put a damper on the others, and there was silence for a few seconds. As for Stuart, he was sensible of a creeping horror which almost impelled him to rise from the table. Loyalty to his promise to the detectives alone restrained him, but it did go hard against the grain that he should have to sit in apparent good fellowship by the side of the man whom he now believed to be van Cortland's slayer. He was almost convinced that Baker had betrayed himself. Not only had the other refrained altogether from questioning Durrane

during that absorbing dissection of potentialities which
had wholly escaped the notice of the police, but he had
manifested a strange discomposure when the evidence as
to the ring was contrasted with that against its user.

"Like the detectives, we take everything for granted,"
resumed Durrane, speaking in a contemplative way, and
evidently peering into his own quite capable brain. "We
are all New Yorkers, yet we are sufficiently self confident,
not to say conceited, to assume that none besides
ourselves regarded a certain lady as one of the most
charming and lovable girls in the country. Now, you,
Captain Stuart, since you are a friend of the family,
might be inclined to laugh at our consummate cheek?"

Perhaps unconsciously, Durrane was treading on
dangerous ground. Stuart and Dixon had long since
discounted any enquiry on that head, as the soldier's
presence in the flat could not fail to arouse a certain
amount of speculation. Moreover there was no knowing
what Montagu Toyn might have said to his friends,
among whom both Baker and Durrane undoubtedly
figured.

"I might if I knew Willie's sister better," agreed
Stuart, smiling around the table. "Of course, I hardly
dare enter into competition with the talent gathered here,
but, as it happens, I have only met her twice in my life,
and one of those occasions was when I escorted Willie
home."

"How did you pull off that stunt?" pursued Durrane.

"Oh, I claimed him as an old friend, and the police
took my word for it. Some of you young gentlemen were
not so fortunate, I hear."

The sally evoked but a disconcerted grin from those
who had been detained by the authorities, and
Kerningham caused a diversion by exclaiming:—

"Someone grabbed my handkerchief that morning.
Was it you, Captain Stuart?"

"Did you lose your handkerchief," broke in Durrane,
before Stuart could reply.

"Did I not? Don't you—" Kerningham checked the words on his lips. "It's a crazy thing to raise a kick about, anyhow," he went on. "And where's the use? We could chin here all night, and get no forrarder. If there's nothing more to eat, who's for a rubber?"

A protest came from an unexpected quarter. Montagu Straus, who was by way of being an airman poet, having written certain vers libres on flight, said he, for one, did not care to play cards so soon after his friend's death.

"I couldn't bring myself to do it," he said.

"Once, in London, just before the war, my taxi was held up at a crossing, and in front was an empty hearse, returning from a funeral. The white lace curtains were drawn, but inside, and clearly visible from the rear, were four mutes, as I think they are called, wrangling over a game of Nap. I should feel myself on a par with those callous wretches if I took a hand with you fellows tonight."

"Good!" said Baker. "Pass the Scotch, and let's stick to the morbid. Monty Straus prides himself on never having used the word 'empyrean' in his poetry," he confided to Stuart. "Ever read any of his stuff?"

"No."

"I'll egge him on. Monty, give us your latest."   "I cannot even write in my present disconsolate mood," sighed the other. "I tried to jot down something yesterday, but could not go beyond four lines. You fellows will recognize the idea. It runs this way:—

I am the Eagle of the Night: My stable wings are plumed to reach the stars; Beneath a million tiny points of light— The black earth, the shuddering guns, the rocket's flame, the death ringed Camps of Mars.

"It gives a bit of a picture, but I can't keep the rhymes out of it."

"Why should you?"

The poet's dreamy eyes surveyed Baker with the scorn of pity.

"Rhyme is mere jingle," he said. "It passed with Walt Whitman, even though Boston became Irish."

"I like it," announced Baker. "I saw that view one night from the correct angle. I was forced into a compulsory nose dive by a Taube—the beggar had bunged one into my gas tank. I dropped 4,000 feet in something like four seconds, and it was a queer experience to watch the expanding circle of the guns and Verrey lights. When I tried to straighten the machine I couldn't, so, as I must crash in the German lines anyway, I tried to cant the old bus enough to land in their main communication trench— just to do a bit of damage, you know. Well, by some freak of air pressure, that tilt of the planes did the trick, and I flattened out some 20 feet above the heads of a company marching up in relief. If I was scared stiff, so was Fritz, and I actually got off a drum at 'em while scooting along for about 200 yards. Then I raised Cain among our own crowd, and finally brought up with a bang just on top of a colonel's dugout. Some fellows got a cross for less than that, while I came damn near being courtmartialled. That yarn any good for your poem, Monty darling?"

"No. It serves no useful purpose. It did not even break your neck."

The poet was annoyed, since it was quite obvious that he had other verses up his sleeve, and a favourable opportunity for reciting them had been wrenched away ruthlessly by the very man who gave it. But Stuart was greatly perplexed. He believed that Baker had told of something real, a bit of whirlwind experience which every man who fought in France could match in one way or another. Baker had kept his head, and meant to die game. Could a genuine soldier of that type become the cold blooded and calculating murderer of a comrade? Or was it that war, which ennobled some, debased others?

While Baker was talking, Stuart had seized the chance to turn and look at him. He saw a powerfully built man of 25, or thereabouts, who, while far from intellectual, looked honest and dependable, the sort of

person who meant what he said, and whose tenacity of
purpose might be relied on. Yet he could not shake
himself free of the dreadful thought which had obsessed
him during the past half hour, and, despite his every
precaution, some shadow of the conflict in his mind must
have shown itself in his face, because Durrane, proffering
a match, murmured in a tone he alone could hear:—

"You appreciate the difficulty of this extraordinary
affair, Captain Stuart. You can hardly bring yourself to
believe that a bluff, hearty fellow like Frank Baker killed
van Cortland in such a devilish way—now can you?"

"No, indeed."

"And the same may be said of each one of us.
Speaking for myself, I may tell you, if it interests you to
hear it, that despite my most strenuous effort, I became
so deathly nauseated by the sights and sounds of war
that some kind observer higher up—I never knew him,
but he must have been a bit of a psychologist—got me
transferred to the base at St. Nazaire. I was really
valuable there, I think. At the front I was liable at any
time to ruin myself and do harm to others by some frenzy
of disgust, not panic, as I really did not fear for my own
precious skin. It was just an unconquerable distaste for
seeing horrible things, and I felt it quite as keenly in a
hospital as in the front line."

"You must have suffered a good deal mentally," said
Stuart, who thought he found traces of the storm and
stress of life in the care lined features and prematurely
graying black hair of the oval-faced dark skinned man
thus confiding in him.

"Yes. Too much, considering the sheer futility of
employing a man like me in the air service," said
Durrane. "That sort of thing unbalances a fellow, upsets
his spiritual poise. For a long time, even at St. Nazaire, I
did my work mechanically, but had no sense of proportion
in the simplest matters of every day existence. And I paid
'the price, too. But you are not drinking anything?"

"No. I'm cutting out hard liquor."

"So is Willie Dixon, I see."

"That's good for him, too. He is turning over a new leaf, has turned it over in fact. He goes to business every morning at 8:30."

"I am glad to hear that, though I suppose he doesn't intend remaining here all the summer."

"I rather think he has some such notion."

"Ah! Too bad! I was hoping to see a good deal of him in the Adirondacks."

For some reason, though in this company no secret had been made of the whereabouts of Mary Dixon and her father, Stuart felt the tinkle of some little bell of warning in his brain.

"Are you going there?" he enquired, with the requisite note of civil interest.

"As soon as this beastly inquest is over. I have bought a log hut near the Dixons' camp. Do you know the district?"

"I have sailed down Lake Champlain and Lake George once. Although I'm a Vermonter, I seldom or never crossed over into New York State."

"Perhaps you may visit the Adirondacks this year?"

"I haven't the slightest intention of doing so."

"Sorry. I should be glad to see you at my place."

"Thanks, but it's almost impossible. At the end of September I'm off to California. My regiment will be quartered at Monterey then."

"Well, after all, California offers many compensations."

"Will you be alone in your log hut?" enquired Stuart, thinking he had answered enough queries to warrant one on his own account.

"No. Baker is coming and others, as my two spare rooms fall vacant."

A fresh argument had broken out at the other end of the table. It concerned Durrane's suggestion that a stranger might have committed the murder.

"It's hard on us fellows," Spence was saying, "but I can't discover any outsider with a telescope. Tony liked a joke, I agree, but Durrane's idea of blacking faces is a bit too thin for so much planning and preparation. And why should Tony himself drink the beastly stuff?"

"And, then, why chuck away the bottle and Frank's ring?" chimed in Billy Bolton. "They weren't meant to be found. That hobo sleeping in the park was a sheer accident, one of the things that always seem to happen in the best laid schemes."

"It's another instance of 'murder will out,' said Spence.

Durrane caught the drift of the chatter.

"You boys are perfect ghouls," he said smilingly. "Why not leave the whole business to the police? It's up to them to find the criminal and convict him. And, listen to me, all of you. I've been talking here to night among friends. Don't you go and blab to the Bureau that Durrane said this or that. I have no notion to take more than my fair share of the responsibility, and that is exactly one eleventh."

"One twelfth," cried several voices.

"No. I reserve the privilege of telling each one of you privately that I had always exempted you in my own mind."

He laughed, and stood up.

"Smart guy, isn't he?' whispered Baker to Stuart. "Ought to have been a lawyer, I guess."

Again Stuart experienced a feeling of repulsion, for Baker's face was twisted in a wry smile. By nodding, and rising at the same time, he avoided a direct reply. The leave taking was informal. As there was to be no bridge the guests left early, and, as was only natural, Dixon and Stuart reviewed the session.

"We don't make much progress, do we?" said the younger man thoughtfully.

"Perhaps not," said Stuart.

"That notion of Durrane's was just clever bilge. Gee! The further I go in this affair the deeper I sink. And I nearly made a ghastly break one time."

"Were you on the point of mentioning the typed letter?"

"So you caught it, too? I was sure I understood the look you shot at me."

"At any rate, you extricated yourself neatly."

Dixon coloured with pleasure. He was only a boy, and a word of praise meant much to him.

"But we didn't get any really valuable stuff?" he queried.

"I am not so sure. I wish Furneaux could have heard all that passed."

The door opened, and Benson announced:—

"Mr. Furneaux!"

"People generally yelp something about their post mortem condition when I turn up unexpectedly," squeaked the detective. "What's the matter now?"

"We were just talking of you," said Stuart.

"An excellent subject. You'll tell me why in a minute. Will you ring and ask Brown to step in from the kitchen?"

"Brown!"

"Yes. He has been here an hour or more. Got a crush on the parlour maid, I imagine."

Dixon rang, and Brown appeared, stately, self-possessed, and very well dressed.

"Do you prefer Catherine to Marie?" said Furneaux instantly.

"Yes, sir."

"I don't blame you. I should hate to call any girl Maree, just because she doesn't know better. Now, Brown, I want to ask you a question in Captain Stuart's presence. On that morning did you touch, or remove, or in any way change the position of any article on the table?"

"No, sir. My hands never even touched the cloth."

"And you, Captain Stuart?"

"I certainly did not. It was the first thing Brown warned me about."

"Then I ask you both: Why should there be a wet mark on the cloth from the bottom rim of one of the wine glasses which contained the punch? Could it possibly have remained there six hours or more?"

Stuart looked at Brown. This was a problem for butlers, not for cavalry officers.

"No, sir," said Brown.

"Then the answer is?"

"That someone moved a glass, and even drank some of the punch, not long before I entered the room."

"Capital!" chortled the detective. "When the van Cortland mansion is closed or sold, I'll give you a job in the Bureau."

"Sorry, sir, but I've promised Miss Dixon to go to her. I'm to leave for the Adirondacks as soon as I can be spared from the enquiry."

"Then you'll go to morrow night!" cried Furneaux. "You're wanted there, badly wanted. Stand not upon the order of your going, but git. As you're a good fellow, I'll try and send Catherine after you with the least delay possible."

Chapter 11: An Unexpected Journey

THOUGH Willie Dixon was almost incoherent with excitement, he broke into speech the moment Brown had gone.

"I say," he began, "you've hit it! You always do. You're a regular wiz, you are!"

"Why all these second person pronouns?" demanded Furneaux. "And is that a bottle of Scotch I see before me?"

"It sure is. Help yourself."

"Well, and what other magic is there in the air?"

"What you've just said bears out Phil Durrane's notion that some outsider got into the room."

"Meaning, I suppose, the room in which van Cortland lay dead, surrounded by his cohort?"

"Yes. Oh, I'm too full of it all to talk. You tell him, Stuart."

"Most certainly," said Furneaux gravely. "I'll listen with the utmost respect to any theory Mr. Durrane propounds. He is a remarkably intelligent young man. I wanted to have a good look at him and certain others, so have been hanging around Park Avenue an hour or more."

"I think I had better begin at the beginning," said Stuart.

"Fine! I'm a firm believer in first principles."

Stuart, using the excellent memory which he had already displayed on more than one occasion, was able to give the detective a nearly verbatim account of the talk at the dinner table. It was inevitable, of course, that the recital, taken as a whole, should tend to cast suspicion on Baker. He did not scruple to state his views in front of Willie Dixon, as he argued that the better acquainted his young friend became with the actual facts the less likely would he be to make damaging admissions when meeting any fellow members of the Ace Club during business hours down town.

Furneaux paid the closest attention. It was clear that Baker's behaviour interested him deeply. He followed, too, each word of Durrane's reasoning as to the possible presence in the Fifth Avenue mansion of an unknown person, who, with or without the full connivance of the owner, used the gathering for his own deadly purpose.

He made no comment, except to put his hearers right on one important point.

"The wet stain on the tablecloth at 8.15 a. m. hardly corroborates Mr. Durrane's suggestion as to the way in which the crime might have been staged," he said. "Please remember that everyone in the room was supposedly rendered unconscious at or about 2 a. m. One man, at least, was not. One—man—at least. Que diable! Could there have been two? Hardly. That argues an inconceivable compact. Yet who was it that stirred Kerningham to put up such a howl about the loss of his handkerchief?"

Stuart had not omitted Kerningham's reference thereto, nor Durrane's apparent check on his friend's outcry. He did not interfere now, because the detective, sipping a weak decoction of whisky and water, seemed to be thinking aloud.

"Kerningham and Montagu Toyn were the cat's paws," he went on slowly. "Who was the monkey? Toyn vows he doesn't know, and I believe him, because he informed me voluntarily to day that Durrane's agent paid a stiff price to turn some people named Green out of their house at Paul Smith's."

"The Greens!" cried Dixon. "Why, their place adjoins ours!"

"So I imagined," said Furneaux drily. "But let us return to our sheep, which we left grazing on the tablecloth. Durrane's scheme is ingenious, very. It becomes almost plausible in the light of the Paris affair, when van Cortland doped some innocent Frenchmen, if such beings really exist. But, think what it means! Would such a man, unless he were a lunatic, remain fully five hours in the room after van Cortland died? Why should he do that, and run more than the risk, the positive certainty, of being seen by the servants when leaving the house in broad daylight? The time of the murder is fixed positively by the hobo's evidence, which is supported by the doctors, whose researches, by the way, bear out the nigger bacteriologist's notion as to dried snake venom being mixed with arsenic and belladonna. No. I can't agree with you, Mr. Durrane, though you are a thinker, a deep one. That fellow, Straus, has brains. So has Baker. So had van Cortland himself. Gee! This case will turn my hair grey!"

Both elbows were resting on the table, and his clenched hands dug into his almost emaciated cheeks. His high pitched voice ceased, and his eyes stared into vacancy. But those eyes were bright and piercing, and Stuart yielded to the conceit that they had conjured out of the void and were examining intently certain puppets which resembled some of the guests so recently departed.

Neither of the young men broke in on his reverie. They waited his next sentence eagerly, being assured that some profound thought was in process of evolution. Judge of their disappointment, therefore, when Furneaux threw out his arms, yawned, finished the contents of the glass, and said wearily:—

"Cre nom, I am tired! I spent four hours today learning how to drive a motor boat."

"You do say the queerest things," giggled Dixon nervously, for the strain on his nerves had been relaxed in a way he little anticipated.

"You'd be tired and say queer things, too, if you had to set about acquiring a sudden and complete knowledge of a hot and smelly and oily infernal machine. You need four hands and a skin of leather to deal with those gasoline tanks. Once I nearly used my teeth. By the way, young man, are you indispensable to the world's rubber trade?"

"Not yet," and Dixon grinned more naturally.

"So there's no reason why you shouldn't join your father and sister in a short holiday?"

"Oh, yes there is. I've just corralled a desk in the Broadway office of the Consolidated, and they'd think I was a quitter if I tried to cut my job this summer."

"Suppose I fix it for you, will you go?"

"Will a duck swim?"

"And you, Captain Stuart?"

"I?" Stuart drew himself up as though the detective had said something outrageously personal.

"Yes, you my Lord. The Adirondacks at this time of the year are unequalled for scenic beauty and health giving properties. For convincing details see the local guide books."

"It is completely and absolutely out of the question."

Furneaux sighed.

"Of course, I am asking you to undertake a post of great personal danger, and I have no right to do it."

"Danger!"

"Don't repeat the key words of my sentences. It's a most irritating habit. You heard what I said, and I admitted I was making too high a demand."

"I think you know that any physical risk would not keep me away."

"Ah! Then, what is the obstacle?"

Too late, Stuart saw the net, though it had been spread before the very eyes of the bird.

"There are so many obvious reasons that they are hardly worth while discussing," he said loftily.

"But why not?" came the inevitable interruption from Dixon. "Our camp has loads of room, and my people will be delighted to welcome you. That is, of course, if Mr. Furneaux really wants us to go, and squares things for me with the Consolidated."

"I'm sorry, but I cannot entertain the idea," announced Stuart stubbornly.

"No, it isn't really playing ball," said Furneaux. "You've done such a lot for the Bureau as it is. Still, I think you'll be sorry, because the centre of interest in the van Cortland poison mystery is now about to shift from New York to Paul Smith's Camp. Do you know the place? It's quite charming. A deep lake amid tree clad hills. God's own country, which will soon be the abode of a devil. Can you handle an automatic?" and he whirled suddenly on Dixon.

"Sure I can."

"Take a couple with you. And buy one for Brown, as well. You may need all three to protect that pretty sister of yours."

Stuart stood up, and leaned over the table. Furneaux affected alarm, and drew back his chair. The soldier selected a cigar, bit the end off viciously, which was not the connoiseur's way of treating a good Corona, lit it, and glared at the detective.

"Do you know," he said slowly, "that I vowed once, and not so long ago, that I'd see you boiled in oil before I'd help you in some ways?"

"It would be a most unsatisfactory proceeding," chirped Furneaux. "I'm such a shrimp. Now, there's Winter. He'd frizzle and bubble to some tune. He'd jump and crack like a sausage in a frying pan."

"When is this trip to the Adirondacks to be made?"

"To morrow night, if possible."

"I have a man here, Benson, an ex soldier."

"Take him, too. And don't forget Catherine. I promised Brown she'd go."

"Say!" cried Willie Dixon joyously. "Are you really coming, cap'?""

"Mr. Furneaux orders it."

"Great Scott! You two have a line of talk I don't understand. But it's fine. Everything in the garden is lovely. I suppose we're to tell Mary, though."

"So I should imagine," laughed Stuart half heartedly. "If Mr. Furneaux is quite certain of securing your leave-"

"Quite," said Furneaux. "I 'phoned the President of the Consolidated after quitting that beastly launch, and he will tell the department manager in the morning."

"So you had the whole thing cut and dried before you came in?"

"That's Pretty Fanny's way."

"How about Miss Dixon?"

"You must soothe her over the 'phone."

"Well, as the plan is yours, please give us more particulars."

"There ain't any. You two boys must amuse yourselves, but keep all four eyes open. If I knew what the next move in the game would be I'd set up as a clairvoyant. But I want you to keep my name out of any chatter that goes on. Everybody knows Winter. His shoulders are broad enough to carry the full load."

"Yet you spoke of danger?"

"Certainly. You don't expect me to define it, do you?"

"But—danger to Miss Dixon?"

"Oh, very well, my leader of dragoons. If you want your definite instructions you shall have them. I believe the man who killed van Cortland will be in Paul Smith's Camp before we are many days older. I believe he means to marry Miss Mary Dixon by fair means or foul. I believe he will stop at nothing to achieve his end. That is why the young lady needs a body guard of stout hearted warriors who will recognize the enemy when they see him, and go for him, too, vi et armis. Now, will you be good?"

"But this is America, a land of law and order. A man cannot set up as a robber baron of the Middle Ages, even in the wilds of the Adirondacks."

"He can set up as an unscrupulous scoundrel right here in New York. But I told you I was tired. I'm off. Good night!"

And he was gone without another word.

"Is he bughouse?" asked Dixon, distinctly awed by the developments of the past few minutes.

"No. He's just a trifle saner than the ordinary mortal such as you and I," said Stuart. "I know this—he can play on me as though I were a tin whistle."

"But Mary will be tickled to death when she hears you're coming. She thinks the world of you. Polly Langrishe said—"

"Mrs. Langrishe is the most unreliable woman living, because she invariably says nice things about her friends, and they can't all be true. But, if we're actually travelling North to morrow, let's go to bed."

Willie Dixon was removing his collar, and gazing at his own good natured but somewhat puzzled face reflected in the mirror of a dressing table, when a thought struck him.

"Gee!" he chortled delightedly, "but ain't I the prize dub! That's it, of course! The cap's afraid of Mary. Regular woman hater, Polly Langrishe said he was. Guess Polly herself gave him the once over. Well, well. That sister of mine is sure some girl, an' the poor old cap' thinks his number is up. Now, I wonder! What is little Willie to say or do? Why, nuffin. But that funny little mut of a detective knows a bit, don't he? He expects Frank Baker will cut up rough. I never would have thought it of Frank, never. But, there! Some fellows go clean crazy when they're in love. I'll get some in my turn I suppose, but I'm dashed if I ever murder a pal for love of a woman. No, sir! I'll mosey 'round and find another."

Having thus settled to his own satisfaction not only the philosophy of life, but the true inwardness of the van Cortland case, he was soon sound asleep.

As no further guidance came from the Bureau next morning, Stuart took charge of affairs. Mary Dixon seemed to greet her brother's unforeseen tidings with calm acceptance of the unexpected. She asked him to send Captain Stuart to the telephone, and assured the

prospective guest he need feel no hesitation about joining
the Dixon family.

"The only drawback is that life is dreadfully quiet
here," she went on.

Not wishing to frighten Jthe girl with vague threats of
possible evil, he simply said:—

"That will be vastly agreeable after life in New York,
Miss Dixon. Has Willie made it clear that we are bringing
another man with us, in addition to Brown?"

"No, he didn't. But that doesn't matter at all. We
have loads of room. This old house was built when father
used to give big fishing parties."

"All being well, then, look out for us to morrow
morning."

"I'll come for you myself in the launch."

"Isn't that causing you a lot of trouble? We arrive at
an early hour."

"But you won't care to swim a mile and a half. There
is no proper road to our house—only a round about track
through the hills. You are coming to a strange country,
Captain Stuart. Will you please tell Catherine I want
her?"

For some reason, Catherine was detained at the
'phone a long time. Stuart only heard such replies as
"Yes, Miss—I know, Miss; the one with the stone
marten—Oh, that? I never liked you in that!" and other
unintelligible jargon. He did not realize what it all meant
until Catherine demanded two taxis "for the baggage" an
hour before train time.

About noon Stuart received a call on the telephone.
Mr. Philip Durrane would be delighted if he could come to
lunch at the Bankers' Club!

"It is very kind of you," said Stuart, trying to conceal
his surprise at the invitation, "but I cannot get away, as I
am leaving New York to day to visit some friends."

"Ah. Too bad. Will you return before I leave for the
Adirondacks?"

"I cannot say. When do you start?"

"As soon as this unfortunate inquest is over."

"Well, I may have to come back for that, you know. The police seem to look on me as an important witness."

"Then I shall be sure to run into you. Good by. Hope you have a pleasant time. Where are you going?"

But Stuart had expected that final question, and his "Good by" cut into it.

There was no guessing why the man should be so interested in his movements. He had not been particularly attentive to him during the previous evening, yet this pressing desire on Durrane's part to see more of him would be an awkward factor when they met at Paul Smith's Camp. However, in true soldier like spirit, he resolved to jump that fence when he came to it.

Brown awaited the others in the Grand Central station. Stuart, with the democracy of the army, would have had the whole party dine together on the train, but Dixon, wiser than he for once, vetoed the notion.

"They'll be on parade if we're with them," said that sapient youth. "Let 'em keep to themselves. Besides, there's things I want to tell you."

"Has something been going on to day, then?"

"Mary asked me to warn you that Pop must be kept out of our troubles, if we have any, and I've a hunch that we'll tumble into heaps. You see, when I went to buy those automatics, I found a permit was necessary, so I rang up Mr. Winter, and he fixed things for me at the City Hall. I've got licenses for all four of us—you, me, Brown and Benson."

"Did Winter suggest such a large firing party?"

"He did."

"I wonder what the deuce he and Furneaux think may happen!"

"I dunno. But I bought eight guns and five hundred rounds of ammunition. The guy who sold 'em to me will be looking in the papers to morrow for a sensational bank robbery?"

Then Stuart laughed long and loudly. This bloated armament seemed to supply the comic relief with which dramatists lighten the heavy blank verse of tragedy.

Later, when Catherine had retired for the night, Stuart came across the butler and Benson in the smoking room in the Pullman. He wished to know how Brown had contrived to leave the van Cortland service so promptly.

"The executors were glad to be rid of me, sir," was the explanation. "The house is to be closed, till Mrs. Symington, Mr. van Cortland's sister, returns from France with her family. She has two girls and a boy, and they come in for part of the property."

"Only part?"

"Yes, sir. So I'm told."

"Have you heard who gets the remainder?"

"There was rumors downstairs, sir, but I never rightly got the hang of them."

Now, Stuart had put that last question with the idle curiosity of one interested in all that appertained to the affairs of his unfortunate friend. He dismissed the matter from his mind. Long afterwards he had reason to regard Brown as a British Machiavelli, because the butler knew right well whose name it was that figured in van Cortland's will as chief beneficiary in his estate.

The journey passed without incident. At eight o'clock in the morning the train rumbled into the terminus at Paul Smith's Camp, and there stood Mary Dixon, waiting to receive them. The sun was shining gloriously, and the mountain air was intoxicating, and the girl looked very young in a grey sports costume, else Stuart would never have dared to say straight away:—

"You seem so pleased to see us that I'm going to call you Mary. May I?"

Mary's face, flushed with exercise already, took on a deeper tint, but she laughed cheerfully.

"Of course, you may," she said. "And am I to call you Alec?"

"That is certainly in the compact."

"Good!" put in Willie. "Now all that's left is to give the old man 'Pop' for it, and the trick can be turned and quitted."

Mary instantly became very businesslike.

"We can load the baggage on to a barrow," she said. "It's only about two hundred yards to the launch."

Then she attached herself to Catherine while they walked to the landing place on the lake front. Stuart, who all his life long had envied those breezy mannered young men who have the faculty of striking up a close friendship with young women at a moment's notice, was rather tongue tied when the whole party was seated in a roomy motor boat, but the great natural charm of the place absorbed his attention, so he did not notice Mary's furtive glances at him. She chatted with her brother, but her thoughts centred in Stuart. In truth, he had puzzled the girl by his cheery greeting. She had been living in the shadow of an indescribable foreboding for many days, and imagined that he, too, could not have escaped the same sinister influence. When she knew later why he had come to Paul Smith's camp she reproached herself for even a moment's unbelief in her hero.

Meanwhile, each was conscious of a tiny barrier having made its presence felt, and Mary's sense of a hostess' duties led to a gallant attempt to remove it.

"Are you tired after your journey, Alec?" she said at last, hoping that no one would guess the effort the words cost.

"I? Not a bit," replied Stuart. "I had a most restful night."

That did not help a great deal, but the girl persevered.

"We are a long way from New York," she said, "but," with a graceful gesture such as a woodland nymph might use in showing her domain, "this is what we gain by coming so far. Our house is round the next point. It is completely shut in/ We hardly ever see a soul unless someone passes in a boat."

"Have you no neighbours?" he enquired.

"Yes, some people named Green. We know very little of them. I believe they lounge in hammocks all the summer, read novels, and eat candy."

"How idyllic! You will be sorry to lose them."

"No fear of that. We'll find them slung beneath the trees if we come out after breakfast."

"They're goin', all the same," broke in the boat's pilot, a mahogany coloured native whose generic title was "Skip," and was by way of being an old retainer of the family. "They quit by to night's mail."

"Well, wonders will never cease!" cried the girl.

"How did all this happen?"

"Some feller on the Noo Yoik Stock Exchange has bought 'em out, lock, stock an' barrel. I haven't heer'd his name."

"The new owner is Mr. Philip Durrane," put in her brother.

"Oh, Willie, you don't mean it!"

"Yes. It's right enough."

Stuart wondered why the pretty face should so suddenly be clouded.

"Is he coming here soon?" she went on listlessly, though a less acute ear than Stuart's might have caught the tremor in her voice.

"In less than a week, I'm told. Isn't that what he said, cap'?"

"Yes."

"Have you met Mr. Durrane?" asked Mary.

"He and some others dined with Willie and me the night before last."

Stuart's eyes flashed a warning that nothing more should be said at the moment, though the servants were chatting among themselves, being obviously much interested in their new surroundings. The launch passed a long low house, and Dixon laughed when they saw a man taking down a couple of hammocks slung by the side of a small lawn.

"There you are, sis!" he cried. "What more proof do you want? 'Information' is my first name nowadays."

She made no comment. Stuart was certain that the news they brought had disturbed her greatly. The boat slowed up at a rustic landing, which ran out beyond a roomy boathouse. A path of boards and wooden steps wandered up among the trees to an astonishingly large house built of rough stone and unhewn logs. The forest growth had been cleared sufficiently to allow space for a tennis lawn and a garden. Otherwise the ground ran steeply to some outbuildings, and the whole hillside was a mass of well grown timber. The name of the house, "Bellagio," appeared in gold letters on a black board, and Stuart was at once enlightened.

"All the way across the lake I have been wondering what locality this place reminded me of," he said. "I know now. It's a miniature replica of Como."

"Mother had the same fancy," said Mary. "I was a very small girl when we stayed at the Italian Bellagio, and my recollection of Lake Como is that it takes a steamer the whole day to go from one end to the other, whereas we can scoot round our lake in a couple of hours or less."

"Funny how this Dago stuff keeps turning up," mused Willie Dixon aloud, but none paid heed to him, as the "Skip" was making fast.

Mr. Dixon, senior, came to meet them. He had very agreeable manners, and greeted the stranger with old fashioned courtesy. He did not evince the least curiosity as to the reason of his son's presence, and disappeared when they reached the house.

"Breakfast will be served in ten minutes on the verandah," said Mary to Stuart. Then she added hurriedly:—

"Don't expect to see much of father. He is not quite himself these days. Mr. van Cortland's death gave him a great shock, and he imagines that it will affect our fortunes in some injurious way. There is no ground for the belief. The president of the Amalgamated told me himself that everything is quite in order, but father, always the most extravagant and hospitable of men, thinks now we are poor. Promise me you won't let anything he says in that sense distress you at all."

"My dear girl," said Stuart, looking at her so intently that her eyes fell, "my only hope at this moment is that I may be able to lift some of life's troubles off your young shoulders. Please regard me as an elder brother. I am here to justify the relationship."

"I know that," she said, with a fine attempt at cheerfulness. "That is why we are 'Alec' and 'Mary' to each other, isn't it?"

As he went to his room he remembered that for the first time in conversation with him she had mentioned Anthony van Cortland's name, and even then with the formality of one who might, indeed, be saddened by a tragedy, but whose interest in it was of the slightest. Her attitude in regard to her fiance's death was certainly puzzling.

"Human nature may be complex in man," he communed, "but it's a jolly sight more complex in woman. However, here we are, or, at any rate, here I am, and my first concern is to keep myself from being a bigger fool than is absolutely necessary."

He did not try to explain what he meant, even to himself. He felt like a man following hounds over an unknown country, and quickening the hunter's pace to clear a high hedge. What lay on the other side he could not even guess. It might be smooth pasture or broken ground. But he was going over, neck and crop, and be hanged to the result.

CHAPTER 12: THE HOUSE WITHOUT A CARE

THE three young people who so unexpectedly found themselves enjoying a holiday in the summer playground of New York State enjoyed every hour of the following week. Fishing, boating and tennis alternated with long tramps through the lonely hills. They saw lakes and mountain gullies which none but those endowed with youth and energy can ever hope to see. Once, standing on a sugar loaf mountain which cost three hard hours to climb, they snatched a far away glimpse of the mighty St. Lawrence, backed by the blue ranges of Canada.

During these long rambles, and in many a quiet hour by the side of the lake, Stuart found himself almost insensibly gaining Mary Dixon's confidence. Of course, when her brother and he had told her all they had gleaned with reference to the mystery of van Cortland's death, they soon tabooed the subject altogether. But it cropped up in unforeseen ways.

Once, while going ashore—they invariably referred in that fashion to a visit to the little township where hotel, postoffice, railroad station and a few shops and houses clustered together—they met a boatload of hired furniture coming to "Sans Souci," the Greens' house. Preparations were being made for Durrane's reception.

"I don't think I would care to live in a place of that name," commented Stuart. "It seems rather like defying the gods."

"What's wrong with it?" demanded Dixon. "It generally gets San Sowsy here, and leads to ribald remarks, but the Greens drank ginger pop all the time."

"I have a very ignorant brother, Alec," said Mary, smiling.

"Don't you believe it, kid," came the indignant retort. "I know it means 'without care,' all right."

"I had another and more famous 'Sans Souci' in mind," explained Stuart. "In fact, two of them, as there was one in Germany named after its predecessor in France."

"Well, if Baker comes along, this outfit will gain a new glory, because that lad can shift Scotch like a cowboy."

"Surely Mr. Durrane will never invite Frank Baker to join him here?" cried Mary.

"Why not?" said her brother. "They're thick as thieves these days."

The girl simply dropped the subject, but Stuart did not forget. He had an impression that his hostess did not like Durrane, whereas she usually had a kindly word for any of the other young men whose names happened to be mentioned casually. He wondered whether or not the girl might have been attracted by Baker or Kerningham, the two she seemed to know best. It would be a dreadful thing if the former came on the scene now in the guise of a suitor. Yet what could be done? If the police took no action it was certainly quite impossible for an outsider to interfere.

That same day, during the return journey across the lake, they met a smart motor boat coming around the point which hid the two houses, "Bellagio" and "Sans Souci," from general view. It was empty save for the engineer, a small, dark skinned man in the blue overalls of his occupation, who waved a hand in salute as he passed.

"Isn't that the Greens' launch, Skip?" enquired Willie Dixon.

Skip said it was.

"Then where is Evans?"

"Took a holiday. That's his wife's sister's husband, a Frenchy from Montreal, name o' Pierre."

Evans was evidently the regular attendant of the next door launch. On the lake everybody knew everybody else, their business, and their relations to the nth degree.

"That's news," said Dixon. "When did Pierre show up?"

"Yestiddy. Bob an' his wife have gone in a tin Lizzie to Saratoga fur a spell."

On the following morning, the Dixon family, having met in rather prolonged conclave after breakfast, Stuart stuffed a New York paper into a pocket, went to the boathouse, and got out a canoe, in the management of which somewhat cranky craft he was an expert. He paddled past "Sans Souci," and saw out of the corner of his eye that the house was tenanted. Was Durrane in residence already? The launch was tied to a mooring post, so had been in use. Then he recollected that the adjourned inquest had taken place the previous day. He had literally forgotten the date, such was the Nirvana of existence in that lovely solitude of the Adirondacks.

He turned at once and brought the canoe into its accustomed berth, but, wishing to read the paper without being interrupted, sat there, completely screened from observation, except by anyone who chanced to pass in a boat.

He soon found the paragraph he sought, under the caption: "Van Cortland Probe." Then his heart seemed to miss a beat as his fascinated gaze dwelt on the next headline: "Dead man's millions go to promised bride." There was yet another: "Mary Dixon now one of New York's wealthiest debutantes."

Stuart laid down the paper. Like many another man of his race, he had learned in France the trick of finding solace in tobacco during times of grave duress, and now he produced pipe and tobacco pouch without having the remotest notion of what he was actually doing. He filled the pipe carefully, lighted it, and picked up the paper again. Yes, there could be no doubting the truth of the flamboyantly worded article—the girl he had dreamed of making his wife when all the fantasies evoked by van Cortland's death had vanished into the mists of oblivion had been snatched from him by a dead man's hand. For that was the way in which he interpreted the fateful announcement that Mary Dixon was an heiress to the extent of two and a half millions of dollars. Van Cortland's will had been executed three weeks before the day of the murder. In it he stated that he "wished to anticipate a marriage settlement," and had transferred to her name stocks and bonds in gilt edged securities, which transfer would become valid either on the day of his marriage or in the event of his prior demise.

The remainder of the estate, of about the same estimated value, was devised in trust for the benefit of a sister and her children.

The newspaper did not fail to note the uncommon form of the bequest. "It almost argues a premonition of death," commented the writer. "In that respect it may provide a clue for the police, who, thus far, appear to have made no progress whatsoever in clearing up the most tragic occurrence which has shocked New York society in many years. At the adjourned inquest to day no new fact was produced. Chief Inspector Winter, the only witness who testified, was brief to curtness in his statement that the Bureau had nothing to say. In the past the public has had the utmost confidence in this officer and his assistants. It will be a lamentable thing if this confidence is destined to be shattered by complete failure in elucidating the van Cortland mystery."

Stuart read no further. He remained there, not even knowing that he was puffing at his pipe, and his eyes stared into vacancy. The low, wide entrance to the boat house framed as fair a picture as man could desire. The blue waters of the lake danced in the morning sun. From the farther shore rose a magnificent panorama of woodland and mountain. In the middle distance, as though placed there by Turner for artistic effect, two girls, wearing respectively a red and a yellow jersey, were fishing from a boat. But Stuart saw nothing of this. The glowing landscape had lost its beauty and color. He was peering into the vista of his own future life, and found the prospect grey indeed.

For he knew now that that which had been a dream was a reality. He loved Mary Dixon, but the superb generosity of the man who desired her, and whom she had never wished to marry, had raised an imposing barrier which he might never dare to scale. Be it remembered, Alec Stuart was an idealist. On one side of his nature he was a soldier, wedded to his profession, and proud of it; on the other, the less conscious side, of which he became aware only when stirred by some deep emotion, he revealed, in fitful glimpses which alarmed even himself, an intensity of conviction more indicative of a fanatic than of an ordinary man of the world.

He first discovered this unexpected trait of character when on active service. Convinced that he was fighting for the liberty and happiness of mankind, he faced death with an exaltation that quickly communicated itself to the men under his command. He regarded the enemy not so much as an armed foe to be overcome by military prowess and skill but rather as a grossly material obstacle which blocked the path of human progress, and must be removed without counting the cost in life and effort. At such times he radiated an almost supernatural forcefulness. His men recognized the mood. Benson, trying once to describe it to his crony, Brown, expressed it in a curious phrase.

"The cap' seemed to like fightin' for its own sake," he said. "Not that he's a bloodthirsty guy like some I've known, fellows who wanted to chew Germans, an' tried to do it. He kind of reminded me of a Revivalist preacher, who so believed in what he told others that he'd shout 'Halleluya' if tied to the stake with the flames risin' above his head."

And this man, filled with high purpose, devoted to principle, had now to face the utter collapse of his first

great passion. Not only had he never loved any woman
before he met Mary Dixon, he had not so much as given a
serious thought to marriage. He was a soldier, and his
country's fortunes claimed his allegiance to the utter
exclusion of any other mistress. The cynic would hold that
when such a preux chevalier fell victim to a woman's
wiles he would not recover during the rest of his life. And
that was true of Stuart in a way that was almost
lamentable. In Mary Dixon he had found his mate, yet
now he was bereft of her. In his own estimation, and he
admitted no other guide, he would figure as a mere
fortune hunter if he tried to woo and win her. Indeed, his
very position that day in her house was ignoble. On calm
analysis, what did it amount to? He was there as a sort
of ally of the police in the endeavour to track the man
who murdered van Cortland. The criminal, if he were
found, which to day seemed so doubtful, had been
inspired by the self same quest as that which was now
consumed to dust and ashes in his own soul. How could
he continue to fill such an ambiguous role? The thought
was nauseating. He felt that Mary Dixon herself would
recoil in horror from the suggestion that she should wed a
man who regarded her as a reversionary interest after a
malefactor had been secured.

He believed the girl was prepared to like him. She
had certainly given an unstinted friendship, and was
inclined at times to indulge in a hero worship that was
altogether embarrassing. The difference in their social
position, as measured by wealth alone, was already a
grievous hindrance to his suit, since his army pay was
negligible, and his prospects of other income amounted to
about a tenth part of her assured means. And now she
was a great heiress, one marked by nature and
acquisitions to mingle among the great folk of the earth.
Well, just as in a field hospital, when the supply of
anesthetic has given out, the surgeon hands his patient a
bullet to bite on, Stuart now felt the lead between his

teeth, though, in sober reality, he was only trying the toughness of a piece of good vulcanite.

So, with a little laugh that would have caused his mother much suffering if she might have heard it, he got out of the canoe, and walked up to the house, resolving to take train for New York that very day. He meant, if necessary, to be brusque, even with Mary, in stating his resolve. She must not be allowed the least hint of a cause for this sudden departure—of the real cause, that is. He would invent some explanation—what he cared not. Perhaps it would be well to irritate her by a casual statement that he felt he was not making the best use of his furlough, and meant to join the hunting party in Maine, of which, luckily, he had spoken more than once.

He followed the plank path, and noticed that none of the others was visible yet. Then he understood what this gathering meant. The Dixons had only heard of Anthony van Cortland's bequest by that morning's mail. Mary was even at that moment persuading her father, whose health was improving each day, that his fear of poverty would not be realized now. Yes, life could be bitter, though the sun shone and the birds carolled in the trees. He wished he had never met Mary Dixon. Why had fate dealt him this shrewd blow? He reviled fate, silently but in strong language!

So it came to pass, as he approached the house from the lake, he saw Philip Durrane coming through the trees, an unwelcome if hardly unexpected visitor. Evidently, he had crossed the rail fence which divided the two properties.

Stuart loathed the sight of the man just then, and was in no humour to display the tact with which Furneaux had credited him. But unless one or the other turned back they could not possibly avoid meeting, and neither had the least intention of vacating the field. Stuart walked on, covertly watching Durrane, yet resolved not to notice him. But Durrane was not to be ignored. It is true he had stopped for a few seconds, with the aspect of one who did

not credit the evidence of his senses, when first he
became aware of Stuart's identity, but he came forward
now with a cheery "Hello!" though the eyes of the two
clashed with that primitive and challenging glare almost
peculiar to men who have passed the supreme test of war.

"Hello!" replied Stuart, thrusting both hands into his
pockets. He could smell trouble, as the Zulus say, and
was more than ready for it.

"You here?" went on Durrane, with polite surprise.

"Yes. Why not?"

"Only that I had your own word for the assurance that
you were not going to Paul Smith's."

"Nor was I."

"Oh, of course. I understand. You changed your mind.
Been here long?"

"About a week."

"Really. Your plans altered quickly, then?"

"No. I found I had a week at liberty, and this
invitation just filled the gap."

"Ah. Are you leaving again so soon?"

Mr. Durrane's questioning habit was somewhat too
pronounced. Stuart, standing his ground, having decided
not to bring the man inside the house, said carelessly:—

"I've hardly settled on what I shall do next."

Durrane, who certainly was quick of perception,
neither laboured that point further nor offered to shake
hands.

"Mary at home?" he enquired, with a sideways jerk of
his head.

"If you are alluding to Miss Dixon, I believe she is,"
said Stuart.

"Sorry. I spoke as an old friend. And people soon grow
so familiar of speech in these out of the way places. . . .
Ah, there you are, Mary!" as the girl appeared on the
verandah, with her brother a few paces behind. "Captain
Stuart seems as surprised to see me as I am to see him,
yet you knew, I suppose, I was coining here this
morning."

"As a matter of fact, Philip, we had not heard the exact day of your arrival, though we saw preparations being made in your house," said she, smiling a greeting after one swift glance at Stuart.

"How are you? Though I need not ask. You are looking fine."

"That's excitement. It will wear off, and leave me with the sickly pallor of life in New York until the Adirondacks get in their good work. . . . My, Willie, you've been in the sun all right."

"Had a bully time, Phil. How's things?"

"Meaning?"

"Everything. The boys, the girls, the Cascades, Long Beach, and the rest of the caboodle."

"Oh, come now. Don't crow over me because you've got a week's start. I'll soon catch up. I'm a hard worker when I get busy."

"Well, we'll be seeing a lot of you now you're here," said Mary. "I suppose you have heaps to do in your house before you settle in comfortably. . . .Alec, I want a word with you for one minute. Pardon me, Phil, for leaving you the moment you put in an appearance, but what I have to say to Captain Stuart cannot wait, as I have to go ashore."

Three people were momentarily struck dumb by the girl's calm self assurance. Her brother, in his own phrase, would never have believed that this kid sister could hand the frozen mitt to Phil Durrane in that style. Durrane himself was obviously taken aback. As for Stuart, he had an uneasy feeling that his projected stampede to New York was about to be made exceedingly difficult. And, for once, he was not mistaken.

Durrane recovered rapidly.

"All right," he said with a laugh, "if that's how pleased you are to see me I'll pour my woes into Willie's ears."

"I'm sorry," said Mary, "but we shall have lots of opportunities for talk later. I have to send some telegrams, and Captain Stuart is going to help. I always get mixed in trying to be brief."

"That, at least, is a consolation," and Durrane smiled with utmost good humour.

Mary gave him no further heed. She was in such a hurry that she grabbed Stuart's arm and marched him off to the boat house. He thrilled to the touch of her hand, though knowing full well that her action was due to the impulse of the moment. They walked together, keeping step, one of the rare accomplishments in a woman which a man who has been drilled always appreciates.

"Have you seen the newspapers?" was Mary's first question when out of earshot of the others.

"Yes."

"And read all about that horrid money."

"Yes."

At any other time those grim monosyllables would have drawn from her one of those delightfully provocative upward and sidelong glances which Stuart, poor wretch, was beginning to find so alluring that he often tried to invite them. But she was too full of her own bewilderments to notice his curtness.

"Isn't it awful?" she demanded.

"Awful? To be given millions of dollars?"

"Yes. It's blood money!"

"Mary, you should not say that."

"But it is. It's buying me, body and soul."

He had misunderstood her; fortunately she had not read his interpretation of her words. Yet, as she was distraught, and her mind out of tune with realities, he deemed it only straight forward and sensible that he should dissuade her from such foolish imaginings.

"You are excited by your good fortune," he said laboriously, "and probably feeling a trifle overwhelmed by the responsibilities attached to it. You—"

She shook him in quite unsisterly fashion, supposing she had adopted that relationship.

"Alec!" she cried. "Just stop that. I've had half an hour of it from father and Willie. Of course, I won't accept Anthony van Cortland's millions. If I were his wife, which, thank goodness, I shall not be now, though it sounds like being grateful for his death, and I'm sure you don't think I mean that—the case would be different. But do you honestly believe I'm the sort of girl who is likely to go through life labelled 'the van Cortland heiress?' Is that the impression you have formed of me during our week here?"

It was Stuart's first experience of a woman's skill in putting a man on the defensive when she is stating an argument intended to convince him, and probably herself. At any rate, she was victor in a struggle of which she had not the slightest knowledge, and Stuart was completely shut off from announcing his imminent departure.

But he stuck to his guns, though, being a cavalryman, he adopted a flank attack.

"It is not for me to advise you, Mary, in an affair of such great importance," he said. "In any event, it is a grave matter, and not one to be dealt with impetuously."

"You are most disappointing," she complained. "Here have I been carrying on a stand up fight with two perfectly sordid minded relatives, yet I kept saying to myself that I would have a loyal backer in you. And now you tell me I'm to rob a man's lawful heirs merely because he assisted my father in a financial deal, and so set up a claim on my gratitude! I won't do it! Nothing shall persuade me. You're all hateful, and you're the worst of any and I did so count on your help!"

Whereupon Mary dropped his arm, stamped a vehement foot, and burst out crying.

They were on the landing stage by this time, and out of sight from the verandah. Stuart nearly yielded to a frantic longing to take this fair creature in his arms and kiss away her tears. The very sound of her grief maddened him. She was more adorable than ever in her distress. She had, whether unconsciously or not only a woman knows—and even her knowledge is a but fleeting mood—appealed to the protective instinct in the male. But the very modesty of the man, the ingrained habit of years of self-control, perhaps a chilling certainty that it would be unfair and ungenerous to turn a moment of abandonment to his own advantage, restrained him from an action which meant all or nothing. So he crushed his desire with a savage force, little realising that the effort made itself felt physically when his hands grasped her shoulders.

"Please don't do that, Mary," he said, his voice vibrating strangely. "I—I can't stand it. It's not—fair."

"What isn't fair?" she asked, lifting her swimming eyes to his.

"That you—should weep. You are not—meant for tears. And, confound it, what is there to cry about?"

She wriggled free of his clutch, and a wan smile broke through the mist.

"I'm sorry," she faltered. "I just collapsed. But you have horribly strong fingers. There will be ten little black spots on my skin to morrow."

"Scandalous, I call it!" squeaked a voice from the other side of the boat house. "That's not the proper way to treat a lady!"

The two started apart as though subjected to an electric shock. Peering at them around the front of the low building, but ensconced in the trees some yards away, was Pierre, the Montreal brother in law of the "Sans Souci" boatman.

Mary was the first to recognize him, and she flushed with indignation.

"How dare you come spying on this property?" she demanded.

"Don't shout at me, Miss Dixon," came the unabashed reply. "You might be heard at the house, and that wouldn't do, at all, as they say in Cork."

"Great Scott!" exclaimed Stuart, whose ear was more faithful than his eye. "It's Furneaux, the detective!"

"A classical phrase!" chortled the little man, his brown face wrinkling in a very ecstasy of enjoyment. "O, that Winter were here, even in the height of summer! But you, my gallant swashbuckler, what shall I say to you, who so misuse the gifts of the gods that you can only soothe a woman's sorrow by trying to wring her neck?"

Now, Furneaux's name and oddities of speech and manner were already so familiar to Mary by hearsay that she accepted Stuart's astonishing statement without demur. Nevertheless, she was startled, and a trifle confused, it may be.

"Did you come here to speak to Captain Stuart or me?" she asked tremulously.

"Not exactly. I was on the trail of my valued employer, but, seeing you coming this way, I crept down through the trees. You did the rest. A nice pair of conspirators you are, to be sure—bleating out your secrets for all the world to hear!"

"This happens to be an exceptional occasion," said Stuart.

"It sure is," and the sarcasm in Furneaux's tone made the soldier squirm, since one could never tell what this imp of a man would say next. "But the occasion has passed, I fancy. Are you going to the town?"

"Yes," answered Mary promptly. "Captain Stuart is taking me in the canoe, as I want to send some telegrams."

"Take my advice, young lady, and send no telegrams. They are inventions of the devil for the utter beguilement and ultimate undoing of girls of your age. But, off with you! I'll follow in five minutes or less. As I shall pass you on the way don't pay any heed to me. I'll be waiting for you outside the Postoffice. When I walk along the Saranac Road, keep me in sight, and I'll do the rest."

He disappeared, and they caught no sound save the rustling of the branches among the close packed trees.

"What a queer little person he is, but he's a dear, and I'm sure I shall love him," said Mary. "Come on! Let's hurry! He evidently wants to tell us something, and Phil Durrane has quite enough nerve to stroll down here and interrupt us."

But Phil Durrane was then using his nerve to other purpose. He was extracting all possibile information from Willie Dixon. How came it that Captain Stuart was in the Adirondacks? What had the "Bellagio" party been doing with themselves during the past week? What led to the sudden decision to leave New York? How did Mr. Dixon, senior, regard the presence of a stranger? To this, and more, Willie Dixon could reply glibly. Mary thought Pop needed cheering up, and the President of the Amalgamated adopted a sympathetic attitude. And Stuart was one of the best. He'd never see a fellow stranded, and promptly abandoned a hunting trip in Maine to help in the rejuvenation of Pop, who liked Stuart immensely. And it was such a treat for Mary. Brothers didn't cut any ice with sisters, whereas a chap like Stuart had seen so much of the world, and had such a store of yarns about the war—the things that are not written in books, you know—that what between fishing and boating and tennis and walking, and heaps of stuff you'd never heard unless a guy spoke from first hand knowledge—well, the days had simply flown.

Durrane listened, merely putting in a leading question when necessary. He led his companion to the edge of the tennis lawn, which was banked up at one end, and a clearing in the trees gave a bird's-eye view of part of the lake. So, in a few minutes, he saw the canoe and its occupants.

"Mary seemed rather upset this morning," he said casually. "Tell me if I'm butting in on matters that do not concern me—was it about that money?"

"Yes," said Willie, wishing himself well rid of a persistent cross examiner. Then, not without a spice of malice, he added:— "But Stuart is jolly level headed. She says she doesn't want it, won't have it, will chuck it right back at the other heirs, and that sort of tosh. He'll talk her into reason, see if he doesn't."

"I rather agree with Mary."

Dixon was annoyed, and did not care if he showed it.

"Dash it all, the other crowd have plenty. Why shouldn't poor old Tony's wish be gratified?"

"I think I can fathom your sister's mind in that respect. She's a sweet girl, well worthy of all that a man can endow her with, but she would prefer such gifts to come from one whom she loved."

The other was so dumfounded that he said nothing, though he was nearly compelled to bite his tongue to stop an acid comment as to the very different views he had heard his friend express on other occasions.

Relief came from an unforeseen quarter. The chug chug of an engine reached their ears, and soon Durrane's motor boat shot into sight.

"Hello!" he cried. "What's that damn little Frenchman after now?"

"A piece of cheese missing in your place, I guess," said Willie. "Why are you making such a kick about a run ashore? Are you short of gas? or what?"

"No. I want to go to the Postoffice myself. Take me in your launch."

"Sorry, it's out of commission," lied the boy cheerfully. "Something gone wrong with the works. That's why Stuart is paddling for Mary."

Long afterwards, in recounting the incident, Willie Dixon declared that he had displayed an almost human intelligence at a moment's notice. And he had. It was good for the world at large that Durrane should be temporarily marooned that morning at "Sans Souci," the house without a care.

CHAPTER 13: FURNEAUX'S THEORY

THE re appearance of Furneaux rendered the sheer burthen of life somewhat less oppressive for the two young people in the canoe. For one thing, it pointed to the assumption that Durrane's presence in the Adirondacks was connected in some subtle way with the tragedy which was always in their thoughts if seldom on their lips. For another, it kept Stuart's wits in active use while he tried to explain to Mary just what the detective's disjointed utterances really meant.

She did not quote them, as any woman will guess, but she wanted to know what the mysterious fellow was driving at.

"I like his funny cracked voice and the strange way he puts things," she said, meanwhile giving her eyes and nose some furtive dabs with a powder puff and hoping that she did not look a fright after that absurd fit of crying. "But it was difficult to catch his meaning. Of course, he was simply being absurd about telegrams, yet, he seemed to be quite sarcastic with you, Alec."

Stuart, propelling the canoe at a great rate, had good warrant for a red face and was duly thankful.

"It is not so much what he says as what he does not say that is important," was his first weak effort.

"But why did he call you a swashbuckler?"

"That he would describe as a trope. He tries to startle people by the unexpected. I think he regards ordinary mortals as dull folk, who, as Emerson puts it, 'only understand pitchforks and the cry of fire.' "

"Yet he thinks highly of you."

"He did not show any marked appreciation a few minutes ago." The retort was justifiable. Mary had no right to stretch him on the rack in this fashion.

"Oh, I mean when you are not present. He speaks well of you behind your back."

"Indeed?"

Mary waved a greeting to one of the fishing girls in the gorgeous sports coats.

"Yes," she said. "I had a long talk with him before I left New York. Perhaps I should not have told you that, but I do not want to keep any secrets from you to day. I feel lonely and miserable, and I shall weep again at the slightest provocation. But why are you paddling so furiously? We are nearly one third of the way, and the launch has not started yet. Oh, here it comes!"

"Furneaux's mis timed humour reminds me of some lines in an old song," said Stuart bitterly.

" 'Perhaps it was right to dissemble your love, But why did you kick me downstairs?"

I forgot who wrote that, but, the poet, whoever he was, knew what he was talking about."

"Oh, very well! You needn't snap my head off because Mr. Furneaux cracks jokes at your expense."

Stuart's experience of the vagaries of the female of the species was widening daily. Foil a woman in the one direction against which she has pointed her barbed arrows, and she will begin a wholly unwarranted assault from another. He saw that safety lay only with attack, not defence.

"The truth is that Furneaux regards me as a poor spirited fellow," he said seeming to choose each word with care. "Small as he is, I believe he would adopt cave man methods if he were in love."

"Oh!" said Mary.   After that, during a minute or more, there were no sounds but the swish of the paddle and the onward rush of the canoe. For some reason, Mary's gaze was absorbed by the panorama of the lake, while Stuart was sure his skin had turned a sickly yellow. Despite an apparent hesitancy, he had spoken before the precise significance of that concluding sentence dawned on him, and now his brain reeled under the force of it. What in the world was he to say next?"

Mary solved the problem for him.

"I would never have imagined that a launch would travel twice as fast as this canoe at the speed you are driving it," she said at last, "but Mr. Furneaux is overhauling us at that rate, or even more quickly."

"Yet I thought I was getting along famously," he dared to reply.

"You are. But please don't make yourself too hot. The sun is so strong at this time of the year!"

Furneaux passed them at some distance, as a detour was necessary to avoid disturbing the fishers. He landed, and hurried off toward the town. The others followed more sedately. As it happened, this was the first time the two had been out together without Willie Dixon's company, Stuart having never sought the least pretext for being alone with his divinity. They met several friends of Mary's, some of whom he now encountered for the first time, and a most bewildering sense of proprietorship of this charming girl seemed to drop on him from the skies. He would be presented to a clear-eyed, brown skinned young goddess, and she would promptly give him an appraising glance, as much as to say:—

"You're the man I've heard of, are you? Well, Mary Dixon hasn't lost any time, I must admit."

And Mary herself was just as merciless—to the other girl. She used the spoken jargon of conversation, but was actually proclaiming, in a silent language fully comprehended by her hearer:—

"This is he. Yes, the Captain Stuart, who did such wonderful things in France. Isn't he nice, and don't you wish you had my luck!"

When this sort of thing had been repeated three times, and Stuart felt that, come what may, he must adopt one of two alternatives—either go away at once and forever or propose to Mary at the first opportunity—he discovered that, in defiance of all grammarians, feminine ingenuity could always find a third way out of a dilemma.

"Why are you so tongue tied to day, Alec?" Mary asked, during a brief moment when no acquaintance was in sight. "You leave me to do all the talking, and you have no idea what an effort it is, because I really am quite miserable."

"All right," he said, determined to protect himself somehow. "I don't know a soul here, but I'll stop the first decent looking young man we come across, find out his name, and introduce him. Of course, he will thank me on his knees, and you will have a more lively escort."

The girl laughed.

"You say that," she cried, "as though your secret intent is to beat him black and blue. But it's a shame to tease you, and there is Mr. Furneaux, who evidently has seen anybody but us. What are we to do? 'Shadow him' is the right thing, isn't it?"

"Oh, or just saunter along and pretend to quarrel. That will look so natural that no one will take the least notice."

Then Mary frankly stared at him.

"Anybody would think you were angry with me," she said.

"No. I'm angry with myself."

"But why?"

"Just for being a born fool."

"Will you please have pity on an ignorant little girl, and explain that remark?"

"Yes," he said, taking the plunge valiantly. "I know I ought not to be here, yet I cannot tear myself away."

Mary looked at him again. She may have been tempted to urge him to further confidences, but they were in a ridiculously public place, a square of grass lands and roads, with scores of people watching them from the verandahs of a hotel, so she forebore, there being a glint in his eyes and a curiously set purpose in his face which warned her that his next words would leave her in no doubt whatever as to his meaning.

"Perhaps, after we have had a talk with Mr. Furneaux, the outlook may be a little less clouded," she said, edging away to gain a path that cut off a section of the main road.

It was a slight action, but it sufficed. That is to say, it left Stuart in a very frenzy of longing and uncertainty.

"I have been wondering," she went on, with an extraordinary naturalness of tone, "whether I should send that telegram before or after I hear what Mr. Furneaux has to say."

"It all depends on what the telegram is about. But, even if it deals with a personal matter, you had better wait. That was his request, you know, and he always has a convincing reason when he puts forward a demand of that sort."

"That is just why I'm inclined to act first and listen afterwards. I don't want to be convinced. I won't take that money!"

"In that case I cannot presume to advise you. But I'll say this cheerfully. If you persuade the trustees to send you all those dollars in a number of sacks, I'll help you to sink the lot in the middle of the lake."

Mary seemed to be vastly surprised.

"Oh!" she cried. "So you don't really want me to be rich!"

"Why should I? Wealth may spoil you. I should hate to see you clothed in purple and gold."

"I dislike both colors," she declared with emphasis. "Even heliotrope doesn't suit me a bit."

They laughed then with joyous abandon. Evidently she had said something exquisitely humorous. Perhaps they both were glad a crisis had been averted. At any rate, Mary was now well beyond the postoffice, and, indeed, they were deeply interested in Furneaux's movements, because he turned out of the Saranac Road, and soon vanished up a path which led into a wooded gorge. Stuart, gradually recovering his wits, stopped for a moment, ostensibly to light a cigar, but actually to make certain they were not being followed. He did this merely because of a military training which taught that scouts operating in unknown territory must be as alert for an enemy in the rear as for definite dangers in front.

A man was, in fact, strolling their way, a nondescript, heavily built person, who might be an attendant in a garage or one of the lake boatmen.

"Do you know that chap?" he enquired.

"No," said Mary.

"Do you recognise him at all, or is he a complete stranger?"

"I believe he lets boats for hire, and is not above a bit of honest boot legging. I have heard of such a person hereabouts."

"Good! We'll pass that path, and sit on the rock to the right of the road. Then he must either come on or go back. Don't appear to watch him. You and I must be discussing something earnestly, with an occasional laugh thrown in."

"How in the world can we manage that?" giggled Mary. "All the morning you've looked as if you had lost a dollar and found a dime. And you've crushed my best efforts, too."

"I'll tell you some funny stories," said Stuart, with a grim intensity that sent Mary into a peal of merriment. "Did you ever hear this one? When the New York negro regiment went to France they were horribly sea sick during the second half of the voyage. One of two friends recovered slightly the day before the transport reached St. Nazaire, but the other's case was hopeless, and he could only lie on deck and groan. Suddenly the convalescent, who was leaning over the rail, grew excited, and stirred his buddy with his foot. 'Get up, George,' he cried. 'Get up! Dey's a ship close at ban', a real ship.' 'Yo' just lissen ter me, yo black niggah,' said his friend. 'Don't yo' dare distoib me till yo' sees a tree!' Now, shriek, and here's our rock!"

Mary was duly amused, but she contrived to murmur:—

"I was mistaken. I have never seen this man before. And, good gracious, he's taking our path!"

At that, Stuart did not hesitate about turning and watching the intruder, who promptly jerked a thumb in a knowing fashion, and disappeared among the trees. A great light broke on Stuart, and he grinned sheepishly.

"I do believe it's Mr. Winter," he said.

"Oh, let's hurry," cried Mary. "Won't Willie be furious when he hears of our adventures?"

Stuart was not mistaken. A burly ruffian, who revealed the familiar form and features of the Chief of the New York Detective Bureau, awaited them with Furneaux beyond the first curve in the path. Mary was now introduced formally, and Winter was pleased to be complimentary.

"Which of you discovered me?" he enquired.

"Captain Stuart, of course," said Mary.

"Well, it was smart work. I am glad you are taking your holiday so seriously."

"Oh, he is," Mary assured him.

"You think so, too, Miss Dixon?" put in Furneaux.

"No. Not exactly. I only meant that he is very solemn to day."

"Well," bustled the Chief, who sensed electricity in the air, "we can hardly stand here and hold a long session. We are in your hands, young lady, as you are acquainted with the locality. Where shall we go to be free from chance passers by?"

"Let me lead," said the girl. "In five minutes we can be completely hidden."

She left the path after a hundred yards or so, and made her way up hill through the trees. Soon they struck a rocky water course, dry now, but the channel of a raging torrent after heavy rain, judging by the huge rounded boulders they had to climb. They soon found themselves in an open cave hollowed out of an angle of the ravine.

"How will this do?" cried the guide, flushed and almost breathless, for Winter, if no other, had great difficulty in keeping pace with her. He was remarkably active for one of his weight, but was not in training for jumping from rock to rock like a goat.

"Fine!" he gasped. "When I recover my wind may I smoke?"

"Just listen to the man," cried Furneaux. "It is because he smokes he has no wind."

"Do we sit in a circle, cross our fingers, and vow never to reveal what we hear to day?" said Mary, choosing a comfortable rock.

It was evident that Winter did not expect to find Miss Dixon in quite such light hearted mood. He glanced at Furneaux, though his expression remained absolutely blank, but these two could dispense with the spoken word.

"Captain Stuart is responsible," said the latter, and stopped short.

"Responsible for the rules of the meeting, or what?" demanded Mary.

"Very well," said Stuart, arriving at a quick decision to head off Furneaux at all costs. "If I am elected president I call on Mr. Winter for a statement."

"Furneaux is the convenor," explained the Chief modestly.

"We are met for no other purpose than the highly important one of getting to know each other," said the little man, speaking with a gravity that promptly brought Mary to attention. "I look for sensational developments in the van Cortland mystery during the next few days, and it would be foolish for the Chief and me to remain here without the knowledge of our very important aides. Please inform Mr. Dixon, junior, the butler, and that other man, the valet, as to our presence, as we do not wish to be shot if surprised in or around your house at some unearthly hour of the night. It is a nuisance having to take so many people into our confidence, but we cannot help ourselves. I came here some days ago, and the chief of the police at Saranac was able to persuade Evans, the Greens' motor man, to take a holiday. The Chief arrived this morning, via Saranac, thus avoiding any remote chance of being recognised by Durrane on alighting from the train. Mr. Frank Baker reaches Paul Smith's to morrow morning. Then we have all our principals on the stage together. Either Durrane or Baker killed van Cortland, and, if you young folk play the game, it will not be long before we find the guilty man."

Mary gasped with surprise and consternation. She had been in a slightly hysterical mood since a formal communication to hand by the early post from van Cortland's lawyers announced that she was an heiress, and Stuart's fantastic struggles to avoid a declaration of undying love had added to her tremors. Now, here was Furneaux, who figured in her imagination as a person of unbounded humor, a sort of comic detective such as one read of in magazine stories, bringing her back to an earth of tragedy and guile. Somehow the actual death of Anthony van Cortland seemed to be associated with the clatter and restless life of far away New York. She thought she had left that evil thing behind when she fled to the Adirondacks, yet it was stalking her relentlessly in both her lakeside home and the fastnesses of the hills.

"You can't really mean that?" she said, with a fluttered voice that was on the borderland of tears.

"I mean every syllable of it," said Furneaux gravely. "It is sad and unfortunate that we should have to bring you into this miserable business, Miss Dixon, but you must agree there is no other course open. Now, if you want to cry, cry, and get it over."

Stuart shot an angry look at him, but Furneaux dodged it by gazing steadily at the girl, who, on her part, responded exactly according to his calculations.

"I'm not going to hamper you by any absurd weakness," she said at once. "Certainly I did not expect to be drawn further into this affair to day, but you may be sure I will listen carefully to what you have to say, and obey orders, if need be."

Winter nodded his complete approval, and Furneaux, who should certainly have won Stuart's unstinted admiration for his handling of the feminine temperament, took up the parable again.

"It is essential that I should put this matter plainly," he went on. "Though the proposed marriage with Mr. van Cortland was highly distasteful to you personally— Pardon me. Isn't that the right way to express it?" for Mary blushed furiously, and then, with violent reaction, looked rather pale.

"Yes. I think it would have killed me," she murmured.

"Just so. I need not assure you of the Chief's sympathy, and my own. But the fact remains that van Cortland lost his life owing to the insane jealousy of a rival . . . No. Please let me continue in my own way. It was well known in your circle that no definite rival existed. Half a dozen eligible young men would gladly have assumed the role, but you gave none of them the least encouragement. Then a set of curious circumstances developed, and you were forced, so to speak, into a promise of marriage. Soon after this fact became known, Anthony van Cortland's life was threatened. He did not hide the threat; he even told you and your father of it. He scoffed at the notion as absurd, but went so far as to make a will which anticipated the marriage settlement. He was a wild, harum scarum fellow, but he certainly was very fond of you, almost insanely so, if I may use the phrase."

Mary's eyes did then grow suspiciously moist, but she said, quite firmly:

"You are extraordinarily right, Mr. Furneaux. There is no other word for it."

And that, by the way, is the only explanation the girl ever vouchsafed of her apathetic attitude at the news of van Cortland's death. It is more than probable that the headstrong young millionaire frightened her into a state of fear, perhaps of loathing. She was too candid to feel both horrified and relieved. Some natures are like that, just as certain plants will wither and die while others will thrive in the fierce glare of the noonday sun.

"Well, we are getting along famously, and you render a disagreeable task easy," said Furneaux, with a fine display of gratitude which he may unquestionably have felt but which caused Winter to strike a match quickly and apply it to a cigar already well lighted. His colleague seemed to hesitate for a fraction of a second. Then the spasm passed, and he resumed his analysis.

"We come now to a winnowing process among your many admirers. For various reasons, Mr. Winter and I have rejected all but the two men I have named. We do not expect you to help us even by an opinion. We assume that Frank Baker's love making was open enough, but that you were aware of Mr. Durrane's feelings, though they are concealed by a subtlety, an adroit delicacy, much more convincing than the other man's candour. Men have evolved a hundred different ways of letting a woman know they desire her, and she is acquainted with the whole hundred, besides some others in her own equipment. Some men can literally worship a woman yet go out of their way, with a clumsy obtuseness, to conceal their passion. Of course, that does not deceive the lady—I am not sure she is not rather flattered by such humility— but I see that Captain Stuart is growing restive, so—"

Here the incorrigible little cynic paused with dramatic hesitation. Stuart was convinced that the blaze of colour which reddened his face was equally vehement on his scalp, while Mary was so embarrassed that she tittered quite audibly, not from amusement but from sheer nervousness. Furneaux paid no heed to these signs of distress.

"Perhaps I put that awkwardly," he said. "What I mean is that Captain Stuart, who is aware of a barrier probably unknown to you, Miss Dixon, is eager to point out that Durrane cannot possibly be regarded as a candidate for your hand, since he is already a married man. That disability no longer exists. He was married in France about two and a half years ago, but he obtained a divorce in April of the present year, so he cannot now be denied an equality of eligibleness with Mr. Frank Baker. It is the fixed belief of my respected Chief and myself that between them, in a way not perceptible at this moment, lies the guilt of Anthony van Cortland's murder. We are convinced, too, that something, some false step taken in fancied security, some revelation of shrewd and far reaching intent, will offer a solution of the mystery at no very distant date. We look for light to the Adirondacks rather than to New York. That is why we are here. That is why you, Miss Dixon, must not dream of renouncing your heritage. Van Cortland, elated by his good fortune, did not trouble to hide his intentions. Both Baker and Durrane knew he meant to endow you with no niggardly hand. Kerningham knew it. So did a man named Montagu Toyn, who acted as Durrane's intermediary in the divorce proceedings, and had been primed to spread the truth about his friend's freedom when needed. Now, part of my statement is theory, not fact—provable fact, that is. The police often have suppositions of whose truth they are convinced, but which must be absolutely useless in the law courts. Indeed, the mere hinting at any such belief on their part gives clever counsel a means of demolishing the solid foundations of real evidence. It is, therefore, with Mr. Winter's approval that I am showing you our secret thought in this matter. We put ourselves completely in your power. If you throw us down by refusing your full co operation, in every sense of the word, it is more than probable that the van Cortland mystery will never be solved, unless, indeed, it is supplanted by another."

Seldom had Furneaux been vouchsafed by fate such an opportunity to display his peculiar genius, and never, in Winter's opinion, had he used it to greater advantage. With the skill of a dramatist and the finesse of a capable actor he had first disturbed the mental poise of the two young people he wished to win over to his views, and then cast on them the shadow of a deadly intent that stopped at nothing to achieve its purpose. Stuart, of course, was electrified by the news of the divorce, while Mary shuddered at the abyss which yawned under her feet. Furneaux meant to frighten her, and had succeeded.

It was a subdued and distraught girl who said brokenly:—

"But, please, Mr. Furneaux, what can I do?"

"Just be your charming self. Announce that you mean to enjoy life to the limit— Now, please, let me finish— Wild schemes of buying a big estate, owning a yacht, and the like, need not be blared forth by trumpets. I am speaking only of the small circle in which we four are so vitally interested. Then, you must maintain your friendship with Durrane and Baker on its former footing, but take care never to be cut off from your brother or Captain Stuart while in their company."

"Surely you don't think either of them would do me any harm?"

"There is no knowing what a homicidal maniac . will do to attain his ends. Not so many days ago you would have protested with genuine indignation that none of van Cortland's friends was likely to murder him in cold blood."

Winter extended a calming hand.

"Mr. Furneaux, being a small man, adopts a sledge hammer effect in speech, Miss Dixon," he began.

"So my respected Chief will now give a verbal display of thrusts and parries with the rapier," broke in Furneaux.

"Am I alone in danger, or are my troubles shared by my brother—and Captain Stuart?" asked Mary unexpectedly.

Winter was not quite ready with a reply. He halted perceptibly before saying judicially:—

"It is hard to define either the nature or extent of the danger to be feared."

"A perfect example of the carte en tierce," explained Furneaux with utmost suavity.

"You are strange men," said Mary, looking with wide open eyes from one to the other, "but I have real faith in you, and will do what you advise. It is all very dreadful. I seem to be the centre of a tornado, which moves as I move. I suppose it is a stupid question, but I would like to have your opinion as to how long this terrible situation may last."

"When does your leave expire, Captain Stuart?" demanded Furneaux briskly.

"At the end of August."

"Oh, we ought to know who killed Anthony van Cortland long before then."

"And now," said Winter, rising from the ledge of rock on which he had been glad to subside, "the conference adjourns. You young people will make the best of your way back to the Saranac road after climbing this ridge. I return by the footpath, while you, Furneaux, I believe, head for the gasoline depot."

"May I ask you something, Mr. Furneaux?" said Mary.

"Certainly. I'll answer, even though either of these sons of Anak chokes me instantly thereafter."

"I only wish to know how you browned your face and hands."

"With walnut juice. After the first thorough staining a slight application each morning preserves the right tint. Now what do you want to know about Mr. Winter or Captain Stuart?"

"I daren't tell you," said Mary. "You might speak the truth. . . . Come along, Alec. We have a long way to go.

Good bye, you two. I don't believe you are half such ogres as you pretend to be."

The detectives waited until Mary and her escort were out of sight up the gully. Then Winter said:—

"Anything doing?"

"No. There may be developments to morrow, but I don't look for ructions until that fool of a soldier grabs the girl in his arms and she assures him with a shuddering sigh that she is his for ever."

"Well, you certainly brought him up to his fences more than once to day."

Furneaux snapped his fingers in disdain of all shy gallants.

"The fellow is bewitched," he squeaked. "Name of a good little grey man ! This morning she was weeping about her money, and lifted her face to his, and all the poor fish could do was to bleat 'Confound it'! and ask what there was to cry about. I've never met such an ass in all my born days."

"He's coming along nicely," said the big philosopher. "You've seen too much of him. Now, I recognise marked progress."

"Well, perhaps I'm impatient. Anyhow, the pot won't boil over till Baker is here, and both he and Durrane realise that Stuart gets the girl. But, I'm anxious, James, and that's a fact. Mille diables! I don't want either of these young people to lose life or limb."

"If there is the slightest chance of that we must act."

"It would be folly, and do no good, before we have a real case. Anything fresh in New York?"

"Y yes. Something about a dog, which was found dead two days before van Cortland got his. Luckily, the street cleaner who came across the body was a bit of a dog fancier, and the symptoms puzzled him. I'm having the story cleared up."

"D'ye know, I like the sound of that yarn."

"So did I. It may give us a useful pointer, though the dog was a fox terrier."

For once, Furneaux was silenced, though he shared Dr. Johnson's contempt for the man who penetrates a pun.

CHAPTER 14: THE GAGE OF BATTLE

FURNEAUX meant well, but his blood curdling suspicions as to the present and prospective tenants of "Sans Souci" ended any tentative love making between Mary Dixon and Alec Stuart. They said little during an irksome and almost dangerous bit of mountaineering. While walking back to the lake they drifted back to the friendly intimacy of the past few days.

"I see now what you meant when you said that those detectives could wheedle you into doing almost anything they desired," said the girl thoughtfully. "And the big one is just as masterful as the little one. I almost found myself believing that Mr. Furneaux was using arguments invented by Mr. Winter. Yet that cannot possibly be correct, because we know for certain they did not meet here until we joined them, and Mr. Winter only left New York last night."

"In half an hour you have hit upon a curious fact which I did not discover for some days," said Stuart. "They don't need speech. They think alike, though Furneaux would fly into a rage if I said that to him. I have no doubt they quarrelled furiously before they parted."

"Quarrelled!"

"Yes. That is a trick of theirs when the chase is warm. They are an extraordinary pair."

"How far are we to go with Willie and Brown, and Benson in telling what happened this morning?"

"I think we ought to confine ourselves to the limitations obviously imposed by Furneaux—merely saying that Winter and he are here, and how they can be recognised. Willie is a quite candid person. I fear if he knew that the Bureau was convinced of the guilt of either Durrane or Baker, he might be so horrified that his manner, if nothing else, would convey a hint, a warning."

Stuart realised that his words might invite comparisons, but Mary was in serious mood.

"You are right," she agreed. "I took that view myself, but I wanted to have you confirm it. You and I, Alec, have an awfully difficult task ahead of us."

"It is due to Anthony's memory that we should persevere."

Again the girl did not swerve.

"Yes," she said simply. "Poor fellow! He has been brought nearer by death than he ever was in life. But I am really perplexed about that money. If I take no action now I suppose it will become mine after some legal formalities are complied with."

"If I were you," said Stuart, "I would let events take their course. You are not robbing the widow and the orphan. It is said that Mrs. Symington is well provided for already, while she and her children are your co heirs. If you choose, you can regard yourself as van Cortland's trustee, and devote the whole or the greater part of your legacy to deserving objects. There are Rockefeller and Carnegie Foundations. Why not a Mary Dixon Benevolent Trust? The mere annual income will be a large sum. In any event, why not decide how to act for the best after you retuÂ»n to New York, where you can consult wiser heads than mine?"

At that, Mary did lift her eyes enquiringly, but, when she saw Stuart's troubled face, with its look of honest endeavour to solve a knotty problem, she only smiled and said:—

"When we reach the camp you must help me write a letter to the lawyers."

Neither Furneaux nor his launch was visible at the landing place, but they expected this, as their hill climbing had occupied a full hour.

"By the way," exclaimed Stuart vexedly, while the canoe was speeding homeward, "we forgot one very important thing. We don't know Winter's name or address."

"We were not intended to know, or he would have told us."

Then he laughed.

"The Bureau has one thorough going believer here, if no more," he vowed.

In the meantime a somewhat significant episode was in progress at "Sans Souci." When Furneaux arrived at the boat house with a cargo of gasoline, his new employer awaited him.

Durrane was not a man who spoke hastily. Never did his tongue betray his brain. He eyed the pile of cans, and did not speak till Furneaux leaped ashore with the mooring rope.

"Were we short of gas?" he enquired.

"Oui, m'sieur!" said Furneaux.

"Why didn't you get a supply yesterday? You knew I was coming."

"I tell dat to dose canaille in ze store, but day say 'Show me,' and I—I haf not ze dollaire."

"Have you ze dollaire now?"

"Cre mon! No. But day keep open eye, and see you come. By gar, day send beel queek, too. Le void!"

Furneaux thrust an account into Durrane's hand, and forthwith busied himself with the launch, evidently regarding the conversation as closed. The other man smiled; he had more to say.

"What's your full name?" he enquired.

"Pierre Loti!"

Dangerous, but Furneaux loved risks! Durrane could have been no great reader of romance, since he swallowed this amazing information without comment.

"From Montreal?"

"Lachine. Same ting, yess."

"And you are Evans's brother in law?"

Furneaux humped his shoulders expressively.

"I marry his wife's sistaire once," he growled. Even one who knew him well would hardly have recognised his voice. He was a French Canadian voyageur in accent and appearance, with just the requisite colour brand of a half bred parent.

"You could hardly marry her twice, unless under very exceptional circumstances," said Durrane amusedly.

The detective did not reply. He wanted to get on with his work. This was, perhaps, the most finished piece of acting he had indulged in thus far. And with what uncanny divination had he taken the measure of his man, because Durrane only laughed again.

"I think I understand," continued the calm, unemotional voice. "But leave those cans for a while. You and I must get to know each other. I shall depend a lot on you, and you will find me a generous paymaster if you serve me well. Are you acquainted with the people at 'Bellagio,' the next house?"

"I say 'how do,' yess, but I am strangaire here."

"The young lady is Miss Mary Dixon, and "

"Mais oui, m'sieur. Day tell me dans la ville dat she was goin' marry some man in New York, but some ozzaire fellow keel him."

"Yes, yes. That's a newspaper story. Miss Dixon would never have married Mr. van Cortland."

"By gar! Den w'y did he leef her two million dollaire?"

"So you read the papers?"

"I? Nevaire. I haf no time. De store keepaire, he talk, and mak ze big eye. Two million dollaire!" and Furneaux's own eyebrows nearly reached his black hair.

"That's all right. Those matters will arrange themselves soon. Now, I'll let you into a secret. I mean to marry Miss Dixon."

"Grand Dieu!" cried Furneaux.

"Why are you so surprised?"

"It ees, vat you call, queek work."

"Not at all. You don't follow my meaning. I'll tell you again. That young lady could not have married van Cortland. She—hated him, and she certainly doesn't hate me. But you can guess now why I want to find out what has been going on during the past week. How long have you been here?"

"Quatr' jours. Four day."

"And what have you seen?"

"Dere ees a brothaire, yess?"

"And another man—Captain Stuart, an army officer."

"Day go out togezzaire."

"Captain Stuart and the lady alone?"

"Dis mornin', yess."

"But earlier?"

"I not see dem. Dey go feesh, and sweem, and dim' ze 'eel. And dey laugh—ver' jolly, all ze time."

"What other men are in the house?"

"A valet, and a butlaire. Dey say in ze store he ees Mistaire van Cortland's butlaire."

"The devil! Brown?"

"I haf not hear hees name."

"Are you sure?"

"Cre nom! I not know dem. But I see two men, serviteurs, domestiques."

Obviously, Mr. Philip Durrane was not pleased to learn of Brown's presence. It is possible he could not have given a definite reason even to himself for the sense of unease that possessed him, but his dark eyes were brooding and troubled, and he remained silent for such a time that Pierre resumed work. This display of energy seemed to irritate the other man.

"Damn it," he said, "listen to me. You can stow that stuff away later. Is the launch in good order?"

"Oh, yess. For two day—I comment dit on?—I clean ze machine "

"You overhauled the engine," prompted Durrane.

"Peut etre, m'sieur. Je n'ai pas le mot juste."

This queer little man, though willing to mislead his victim completely, would not tell a direct lie. To pose as a famous French writer he regarded as a bit of outrageous humour.

"Very well. Now pay heed to my instructions. I want the launch to be ready at any hour of the day or night I may need it. Don't be surprised if I call on you at unusual times, and shut your eyes and ears to everything except what I order. If you have to go ashore of a morning to bring stores or that sort of thing, always let me know before you start, and return as quickly as possible. In a word, I wish the launch to be at my disposal absolutely. Do you understand?"

"Parfaitement, m'sieur."

"What wages are you getting?"

"Forty dollaire a veek."

"I'll give you seventy five, and a first class pour-boire when I go away, which should be within a fortnight."

"Then m'sieur does not rest all ze summaire?"

"I hope not," and Durrane laughed quietly. "I get busy quick when I start anything. You watch me, Pierre, and you'll see the sparks fly."

The canoe shot past. Stuart was paddling hard, and Mary was so interested in something she was saying that her glance did not wander in the direction of "Sans Souci," though the landing stage with its two occupants was not more than twenty yards distant.

Durrane did not speak again until the ripples caused by the swift passage of the canoe were lapping the wooden piles of the boat house.

"Do you meet any of the servants there?" he enquired then, jerking his head toward the neighbouring house.

"No, m'sieur."

"Try and get to know them. You may pick up something useful."

Furneaux looked dubious.

"Dey only talk fool tings," he said. "Jazz, and liqueur, and ze choke."

"Choke?" enquired Durrane.

"Oui, oui!" Fumisterie."

"Oh, joke! But they may say lots I want to know, such as plans for the evening or the next day, or people who come and go. For instance, I am particularly anxious to find out how long Captain Stuart intends remaining here."

"Two mont'," said Furneaux promptly.

"The devil you say! You seem to be well posted in infernally disagreeable facts. How did you find that out?"

"Le valet, he tell ze cook monsieur le capitaine have two month en vacances. Eef he good soljaire he not leave ze pretty girl all dat time."

"Oh, I see. You're just guessing. Well, he may change his mind. Now, don't forget what I have said."

"Will m'sieur want ze launch again to day?"

"How do I know. You must be ready all the time."

Furneaux shrugged his shoulders.

"Eet ees tres difficile, m'sieur," he said. "Von mineet you say, 'Pierre, you vait ordaire.' Den you say, 'Pierre, you mek luff to ze maid in ze next house, and hear her talk.' Que diable! C'est impossible!"

"You don't look like a fool, Pierre, so why talk like one. Of course, I can always get you from the Dixons' place. That is only a matter of sending one of the servants after you."

"Ah! Ca y est! Je vous comprends, m'sieur."

"Sure you do. You and I should hit it off famously. . . . Well, come to me whenever you have anything to report," and Philip Durrane strolled up the wooded slope to the house.

"So you're the prospective candidate," mused Furneaux, as he bent over the cargo of gasoline. "If that is so, it was you who killed Anthony van Cortland! Why, then, is Master Frank Baker coming here to morrow? Perhaps he'll tell me. If he's half as confiding as you, foxey, I may see light soon, and can look forward to scuttling this filthy launch. I shall never be really happy again till I see Winter driving a ten ton steam lorry on a scorching hot day, and picking cinders out of his hair."

Mary wrote her letter, which stated briefly that she had been greatly surprised by the lawyers' announcement of Mr. Anthony von Cortland's bequest, and that she was ready to sign such documents as were necessary in order to assume the inheritance. She showed the draft to her father and brother. Of course, they gave it their approval at once.

Unfortunately, as it happened, Willie Dixon asked her why she had changed her mind so thoroughly, and she replied, without thinking, that Captain Stuart had persuaded her to take the money. At that, Mr. Dixon, senior, showed an annoyance not wholly unreasonable in the circumstances.

"I am glad Captain Stuart was so sensible," he said, "but it is somewhat strange, is it not, that you should listen to a comparative stranger rather than your own people?"

Mary flushed. Too late, she recognised her mistake.

"I have explained myself badly," she said. "Captain Stuart only urged me to obey you. He personally was afraid of my possessing so much money."

"Ah!" That has a different sound, certainly," agreed her father. But he did not forget the incident, which was destined to cause further trouble much sooner than anyone could possibly guess at that moment.

After lunch, the three young people went off in the launch, which the Skip, duly advised, tested for a few minutes as though he had replaced a faulty valve. They were so anxious to avoid Durrane that they made a trip to an unfrequented part of the lake merely to avoid passing his house, which, as it chanced, was playing into his hands. He saw them go, and waited until the throbbing of the engine had died away in the distance. Then he strolled across to " Bellagio," and found the elder Dixon reading a book in his own particular den.

"Hello!" cried the visitor cheerfully. "Here is the old warrior at rest, far from the battle field of Wall Street. I suppose you don't care a cent now whether the market is rising or falling?"

This was a clever appeal to the one great passion of the old man's life. Only the urgent and solemn representations of his doctor had sent him away from the Stock Exchange, and his children, of course, avoided the subject altogether, while Stuart was not even acquainted with the jargon of finance.

"Come in, Philip," said Dixon. "I heard you were here. Why are you not with the youngsters?"

"I've been pretty busy digging in, as I only arrived this morning. Let me congratulate you on the success of the amalgamation. I held some ordinary shares, you will remember, so I know just how well everything turned out. Then there is Mary's thumping legacy from poor old Van. What a time you will have supervising the investments!"

"No," was the disconsolate answer. "I am forbidden that sort of thing. The doctors tell me I am a back number."

"Doctors talk a lot of humbug occasionally," said Durrane, glancing around to assure himself that none of the servants was in any of the neighbouring rooms. "Off hand I couldn't name one man in New York whose opinion I would value more than yours on any financial question."

Though pleased by this tribute, Dixon still protested feebly that he was permanently out of harness. Durrane dropped the subject. He spoke glibly of conditions in Wall Street, gave his interested hearer some inside information as to a forthcoming Mexican loan, and waited a full quarter of an hour before re introducing the one topic he wished to discuss.

"Of course, Mary's millions will be given her in gilt edged securities," he said at last. "But even that kind of investment needs watching. I suppose you have told her she must abandon her notion of refusing the bequest?"

"Where did you hear that?" came the surprised demand.

"Willie mentioned it this morning. Perhaps I shouldn't have said as much. Please don't let the kid know I spoke of it. And, at any rate, he was confiding in an old friend of the family."

"Well, Mary had some such foolish idea in her mind. But that's all right now. Captain" Stuart is a level headed fellow, and he helped a good deal, it seems."

"Ah!"

Durrane flicked the ash off a cigar, and gazed dreamily at the lake through the open doorway. He said no more, until Dixon shut his book with an irritated movement of his hands.

"It's odd," said the elder man, as though speaking to himself, "but the young people of to day seem to think their elders lacking in intelligence. I nearly lost my temper with Mary this morning when she vowed that nothing would induce her to take van Cortland's money, yet she switches on to the directly opposite track after a trip in a canoe with a soldier who doesn't know what an option is. Still, he did advise her correctly. I must admit that."

"Oh, he would."

"What do you mean?"

Durrane stirred uneasily. He was searching for the right word, it appeared.

"I did not intend discussing this matter when I came to pay a sociable call," he said. "But, now you force an explanation, I may say frankly that friends of yours in New York not only think Willie should have stuck to his guns in the office a little longer but regard the gallant captain as nothing more or less than a fortune hunter."

"Dash it all, man, none of us knew about the will before this morning!"

"Isn't she your daughter, Mr. Dixon? She was a wealthy girl already."

"But—Captain Stuart is a very nice young fellow, and a most reliable acquaintance for Willie."

"He met Willie for the first time on the day of Tony's death. Now, please understand that this sort of thing is highly distasteful to me personally. I wouldn't have uttered a syllable of this gossip were it not for the sake of old associations, and I do think you ought to know the views expressed by some of the men who count in the financial world. There has been quite a lot of talk, I assure you. But please forget every word I have said. Mary and Willie would never forgive me if they heard I had been interfering in your family affairs."

"Who passed that remark about Stuart?" enquired Mr. Dixon testily.

"There was some chatter in the Bankers' Club, yesterday at lunch. But, look here!" and Durrane rose with an air of vexation. "I haven't come here to make mischief. Confound it! It's always the case, if one tries to drop a timely and useful hint, the parties interested combine right away against the poor devil who thought he was doing them a good turn. However, I'll stand by what I've said. There's no reason why Willie shouldn't enjoy life while he's young, but I would hate to see Mary snapped up by the first penniless adventurer who happened along."

"There is no fear whatever of that," said Mr. Dixon.

"I'm very glad to hear it. Now, cannot this confidential talk of ours be regarded as though it had never taken place? Why, if Mary knew I had discussed her in this way she would never speak to me again, and that would be hard measures for one who is her devoted admirer."

"All right! All right! Sit down, man, and don't get hot about trifles. I'm not going to call you as a witness against my son and daughter and their friend. Indeed, I am greatly obliged to you. I suppose I had some sort of collapse in New York, and took things easily up here. But I'm quite recovered now. There can be no doubt about it! Willie should not have left the office so soon. He ought to return. He has a good excuse for a few days' absence in his sister's unforeseen legacy. If he goes back now the Amalgamated people will not give another thought to his lapse. And, of course, with him goes Captain Stuart. That will silence the critics. . . . Have a high ball."

"No, thanks," laughed Durrane. "I've stayed far too long as it is. I can't guess what you would wheedle out of me if I took a drink. But, if you wish to pull me out of a hole, get Mary to ask me to dinner. I am alone to night, and I hate that. Frank Baker comes in the morning."

"Ah! There were queer statements in the newspapers about that young man. My head was so bad I gave little heed to them at the time. What was the story?"

"No, you don't, sir," protested Durrane gaily.

"Enough for the day is the gossip thereof. I'll be seeing you later in the week, when the house is quiet, and then I can tell you the whole yarn. But there is nothing in it. Frank is white, through and through."

He made off, well satisfied with the outcome of his visit. Yet he had not crossed the lawn before the butler was at the window of the attic room above Mr. Dixon's sanctum, where his portly form had been reclining on the floor until he felt quite stiff, while one ear was sore from being glued to a crack between the pine planks.

"So that's your little game, is it, Mr. Philip Durrane?" muttered Brown, with the nearest approach to a scowl his placid features were capable of. "Well, well. What a good job we have your number!"

He hurried to the kitchen, arranged that Catherine should take Mr. Dixon his cup of tea, and then sought Benson.

"Can you manage a canoe?" he enquired, when the ex cavalry trooper was discovered in an outhouse where he drilled a regiment of shoes.

"Ask me something harder than that?" grinned the other.

"I want you to take me to our young people, quick."

"Where are they?"

"We must find out. And I don't want that joker next door to see us, neither."

They consulted hastily as to ways and means. Within five minutes they were in the boat house, and Brown's bulk was being adjusted scientifically in a craft which he regarded with unfounded dread, when a brown face peered at them from among the branches of trees and shrubs that lined the water's edge.

"Hi!" hissed a voice. "Where are you two big stiffs heading for?"

"Mr. Philip Durrane came in just now an' poured poison into Mr. Dixon's ear," began Brown, drawing on some half forgotten memories of "Hamlet."

"Good Lord! Not really?" whispered Furneaux, horror stricken.

The ex policeman laughed quietly.

"Sorry, Mr. Furneaux," he said. "I don't often make a break of that sort. But he is a nasty piece of work is Mr. Durrane. He has got the old gentleman in a rare fret because Mr. Willie is not at work and Miss Mary is being chased by a fortune hunter, Captain Stuart. I could hardly help admiring the way he did it. Must have studied Iago, I imagine."

"Tell me just what he said."

Brown gave an astonishingly accurate resume of the conversation between the two men, and Furneaux uttered never a word till the butler announced that he was now going to warn Miss Mary, at any rate, as to probable developments when she returned home.

"No," said the detective decisively. "Let things hum. If the fat is in the fire, so much the better."

"But she may quarrel with her father."

"And why not?"

"I think she might act differently if prepared."

"Tell her afterwards. She can always make it up with the old man. Don't you see, Brown, we are undone if Durrane has the faintest notion that someone is queering him?"

"Unless I am greatly mistaken, sir, Captain Stuart will pack up and be off at even a hint of old Mr. Dixon's opinions, or the opinions Mr. Durrane has supplied."

"Let him! He had the girl in his arms this morning, and just shook her till her teeth rattled. I have no use for him. He's the biggest ass that ever wore shoe leather."

"See here, mister—" began Benson angrily.

"Oh, shut up. Between you all I'm nearly crazy. Back you go, both of you. Tell Miss Dixon and Captain Stuart after the family squabble, not before. And beg the lady to invite Durrane to dinner. She won't like it, but she'll do it at my request. Now, do as I bid you, or I swear by the sun, moon and stars I will keep the pair of you out of the trouble that must start here within the next forty eight hours, and you'll miss the time of your lives!"

CHAPTER 15: THAT NIGHT

NOT even the incomparable Furneaux could make every puppet dance to his piping. Mr. Dixon, senior, defeated the night attack by not saying a word to his offspring as to the domestic scruples that were troubling him. Brown obeyed orders strictly, and merely informed his mistress that her father might ask her to invite Mr. Durrane to dinner, and that Mr. Furneaux wished her to agree without demur.

Mary, being a woman, did things in her own way. She sent Durrane a brief note, and, when the time came, pleaded a headache and dined in her room.

The party of four was curiously balanced. Mr. Dixon, eager to show an unimpaired mentality, was full of stories of old New York and the days when Jay Gould dominated the Stock Exchange. Durrane, of course, could follow the intricacies of high finance better than Stuart or Willie Dixon, and would have kept the talk on that level all the evening had not the older man. suddenly recollected that the "shop" of the money market was probably unknown and might be quite distasteful to a soldier.

So, by a tactful question, he led Stuart to explain some disputed point in the later stages of the Great War. Here Durrane was equally at home. He spoke with such modesty and real knowledge that Stuart found himself regretting that the man was undoubtedly a rascal and possibly a dangerous criminal.

At any rate, the dinner passed off quite pleasantly. Strange to say, the prevalent harmony was disturbed only by the urbane butler.

Coffee was served and cigars lighted when Durrane said to Brown:—

"I hope Miss Mary's indisposition is nothing serious?"

"No, sir," came the bland assurance. "Catherine has just taken Miss Dixon a second helping of strawberry shortcake!"

Durrane, who had his own reasons for addressing the question to the butler, gave him a weighing look, as much as to say:—

"What, then? Are you, too, an enemy?"

But Willie Dixon sprang to the rescue.

"I'm the doctor!" he chortled. "Mary was off her feed at lunch, and the reflection of the sun on the lake gave her a headache, so I recommended a full dinner, from hors d'oeuvres to demi tasse. She'll be all right in the morning."

"I hope so," said Durrane. "Frank Baker will be here by the mail. We might join forces for a picnic."

Then the elder Dixon joined in. Here was a golden opportunity.

"Do that, by all means," he said. "Willie cannot remain at the Camp much longer, or his absence will have a bad effect in the office."

His son was surprised, and said so.

"Well, there's gratitude for you!" he cried. "I tore myself away from Broadway in July, when the air of New York is notoriously salubrious, just to cheer you up and keep you company, and now you tell me to quit. It was an order from the president, too."

"I am perfectly well, thank you," said his father.

"You had a far sounder reason for coming North in Mary's succession to one half of a large estate. As that matter is happily settled, you ought to return. I assure you your office chiefs will appreciate it."

"Too bad," put in Durrane. "Just as Frank and I get here!"

He had better have said nothing, for Willie Dixon's father was a man of singularly upright character—too much so, indeed, to protect himself from the sharks which beset Stock Exchanges in all lands.

"I rather expected you to agree with me, Phil," he said, "just as you upheld my views about the propriety of Mary's accepting her inheritance."

"Phi ew!" whistled Willie. "You're a quick change artist, Phil. You said exactly the opposite to me this morning."

"There are always two points of view," was the suave reply, though Durrane was cursing the luck which gave this unforeseen twist to the conversation. "One is that of the man of the world. The other expresses a natural phase of human nature. Mary is now my very valued friend. I don't want to see her transformed into a sort of princess. What do you say, Captain Stuart?"

"I think Miss Dixon will be well advised if she falls in with her father's wishes; in fact, I have told her so already," was Stuart's contribution.

Mr. Dixon glanced perplexedly from one to the other. He was an old man, and, despite his recent collapse, had all an old man's experience of his fellows, and some instinct warned him that Stuart's blunt statement rang true, while Durrane was obviously trimming his sails to meet each favouring breeze.

"Well, that matter is settled," he said with an air of finality, as though dismissing a disagreeable subject. "If the president of the Amalgamated sent you here himself, Willie, you may remain until the end of the month, at least, so everybody should be satisfied."

"A first rate way out of the difficulty, if any difficulty exists," agreed Durrane. "It's a fine night What do you say to a spin on the lake in my launch?"

"You boys go," said Mr. Dixon. "I have a book to finish, and our talk this afternoon, Phil, put me fifty pages in arrear."

Durrane certainly wondered what unlucky star had risen over his astrological horizon in that hour. But he made the best of things.

"Perhaps Mary will come, too," he suggested.

"I'll go and see," said her brother. He went upstairs, and found his sister in a very bad temper, since the butler had just told her what had happened during her absence before dinner. Brown felt he was justified in this. He caught snatches of the talk in the dining room, and believed that events were turning out pretty well as Durrane had calculated them. Of course, he was mistaken, but it had been impossible to listen to all that was said.

"Go on the lake with that man!" cried the girl. "I think I'd rather die first!"

"What's the particular trouble now?" enquired Willie, who knew nothing of Brown's revelations. She told him, looking so vexed and speaking with such vehemence that he took thought before replying, which was a rare thing for him.

"Anyhow, Durrane's little plan for getting rid of Alec and me has come unstuck," he said. "Pop has given me until the end of the month, and that means all of another fortnight."

"Wild horses will not drag me out to night," vowed Mary, not to be headed away from her real grievance.

"But, look here, sis," urged her brother. "If a row springs up now Alec will go. He cannot do anything else."

"Very well. What do I care?"

"It will make trouble for Winter and Furneaux, too. They seem to count on our holding the fort."

"They expect too much. Am I to smile and be agreeable to the man who may have killed Tony?"

"If it comes to that, old girl, it is harder on Alec than on any of us."

"What do you mean?"

"He is here simply to oblige us. If ever a fellow got roped into a mess which didn't concern him at all, he is it."

Then Mary's sparkling eyes softened. She was better informed than her brother as to the cause of Captain Stuart's perturbations of spirit.

"Willie, dear," she said, "I just can't come out now. I—I might say something that would be dangerous. Make my excuses, there's a good boy."

In the upshot, the boating trip was abandoned, Durrane suggesting at once that three hulking men had no desire to go and gaze at the moon. A little later he bade them "Goodnight," after stipulating that they should make up no party for the morrow without sending for Baker and himself.

The one person whose views on a rapidly changing situation had not been ascertained was the man whose presence in the camp had brought about nine-tenths of the commotion. Stuart, neither blind nor deaf where men were concerned, had read into the elder Dixon's words their true significance. He was on the point of telling Willie Dixon that circumstances might compel him to leave the Adirondacks at an early date—next day, in fact—when Mary appeared. She had changed a white dress for a dark coloured one, and had thrown a grey shawl over her shoulders.

"If we can get out of our own house without being watched by our neighbours," she said somewhat bitterly, "I would like to go out. There's a concert in the hotel. Why shouldn't we have an hour there?"

"Good!" agreed Stuart instantly. "Let's take the canoe. The launch is about as discreet as a machine gun."

They walked, or rather, crept to the boat house, for the night was extraordinarily still, and the sounds of their footsteps on the boarded path might have been audible beyond the hundred and fifty yards which separated them from Durrane's house. For the same reason Stuart did not avail himself of the oil lamp which hung at the end of the little pier, but, at last, in sheer bewilderment, was compelled to strike a match inside the shed.

"The canoe is not here!" he announced.

"No; it has been gone these ten minutes and more," said a voice from the darkness, and Mary just managed to repress a squeak of sheer nervousness.

'That you, Mr. Furneaux?" demanded Stuart.

"It is. And whither bound the noble three, may I ask?"

Stuart told him, winding up with the natural question as to whether the detective himself had been using the canoe.

"No," came the snapping answer. "I have enough to do with one invention of the devil without bothering my head about another. Mr. Durrane has borrowed your canoe. You surely wouldn't deny a friend a little privilege like that, would you? Send a note to his house, and invite him to accompany you. He can't, because he made straight for the town. Then take your launch, and, if on the way across you meet him and drown him by accident, you will rid the world of a knave and stop a horrible lot of the publicity which awaits you before the moon wanes."

"I suppose you have no idea what Durrane is after?" enquired Stuart.

"No. I am quite human in some respects. But get a move on. The concert waits."

Willie Dixon saw to the writing and despatch of the note, while Stuart went to summon the Skip. This left Mary alone with the detective, whom she could not see. Furneaux was a mere phonograph in the impenetrable blackness of the trees.

"Feeling a bit skeered, Miss Dixon?" he began.

"I'm not frightened, but you certainly startled me, and you cannot imagine how curiously everything has changed during the past two hours."

"Changed?"

"Yes, we were so happy till Mr. Durrane came."

"And now you are miserable?"

"Not quite that, but he has contrived to put us all at cross purposes. The wretch came in and worried my poor father while we were away to day."

"It's all to the good, Miss Dixon. The gods first make mad those whom they wish to destroy. That is not, as many people imagine, an old Latin tag. It is quite modern, and profoundly accurate."

"But there is method in Mr. Durrane's madness."

"Oh, he's shrewd. Nevertheless, his hour has struck."

"Is something really going to happen?"

"Yes. Anyhow, you have no reason to be afraid. You are being well looked after. Here comes your escort. Unless my respected Chief wishes to have a word with you, cut him dead if you meet him."

In the presence of the boatman no reference could be made to Furneaux, but Willie Dixon felt at liberty to draw attention to the singular way in which events had become twisted that evening.

"I blamed you for the latest development, Mary," he said. "I told Phil in my note that you had changed you mind, which any lady is at liberty to do. Won't he be the surprised lad if he sees us ashore?"

"I don't believe he will be at the concert," said Stuart.

"Oh, he's very musical."

"That's just why he won't be there."

Mary refused even to smile. She was distrait. If she had Scottish blood in her veins, which was highly probable, since her mother was a Macdonald, though of an old New England family, she might have been deemed fey.

"I don't think I really want to hear any songs tonight," she said. "Suppose we take a little walk, and return home."

"Now, listen to me, kid," growled her brother. "These constant variations give me a buzzing in the head. You've got to go to that concert, even though you curl up and howl with anguish when a fat man sings the 'Toreador.' And he will, too. I saw the programme in the local paper. Besides, we've given our written word for it."

So, to the concert they went, having found their canoe tied at the landing stage. To lend further pretence to a spurious invitation, Willie Dixon enquired from some hangers on at the lakeside if they had seen Mr. Durrane.

"He landed here a bit since," said one man, "an' hurried to the depot, or in that direction, anyway."

"Is there a train to New York to night?" enquired Stuart, and he was told that the night mail would leave in about an hour. It was improbable that Durrane would travel in a dinner jacket, and without any baggage, but further investigation was not to be thought of, so they strolled to the hotel, after Dixon had warned the boatman, if Mr. Durrane put in an appearance before they did, and asked for an explanation of the "Bellagio" launch being there, he was to let him know about the note awaiting him at the house.

"I never guessed I had so much guile in my makeup," he confided to his sister. "Ain't I the wily boy? Now, you'd not have thought of that bit of artistic trickery in half a year."

"I'm afraid the army taught you a lot of things you didn't know before, Willie," said she.

"What has the poor old army done now?" cried Stuart, who had not overheard Dixon's boast.

"Made my brother artful."

"Is that so?" he said thoughtfully. "I must ask him where he took his course. There may come times when the training will be useful."

"I don't know what has come over you two since you went gadding off in the canoe this morning," grumbled Willie. "You've been sparring all day. There's no sense to it. We three are partners, and should stick together."

This magnanimous declaration was received by the others in dead silence, for the girl's heart was full of she knew not what dire forebodings, while Stuart was now quite determined to defy fate by going away at the first opportunity. If, in other days, he were destined to meet Mary Dixon again, and she had not forgotten him, he would put his fortunes to the test and declare his love. He certainly could not dream of doing so now, when her father had hinted that he was not a welcome guest, and at a moment when the girl herself had become an heiress.

Willie Dixon did not help matters by laughing loudly.

"Gee!" he cried. "We are a merry party!"

He spoke rather loudly, and that very fact drew Mr. Winter's attention, as the Chief was just passing in front of them, and would not have noticed one small group among several gathering for the concert. Although the moon was now shining gloriously, the mass of the hotel threw a deep shadow on the road, and the detective had no difficulty in avoiding them as they made for the concert hall. He kept watch, however, noted where they sat, paid for a ticket, and took up a position at the back of the room. He listened patiently to a pianoforte duet by two schoolgirls, but went out when a young gentleman announced a series of imitations of well known vaudeville singers. Then he hurried to the landing stage. The canoe was gone. By chance he met the men charged with the message to Durrane, and ascertained that the latter had received it, but had said he was tired and would go home.

Straightway he returned to the hall, and sent Stuart a note which brought the three out quickly. As soon as he was sure they had discovered him he walked half way across the green and waited.

"I didn't want anyone to know you had such a disreputable acquaintance as me," he said when they came up. "Would you mind taking a stroll along the Saranac Road? At this time of night it is usually deserted. Meanwhile, I'll disguise myself."

A panama replaced the cloth cap he was wearing. Next his mechanic's overall was discarded, and, in little more than a second, he looked a quite respectable citizen.

"No," he said, "none of your friends will be shocked if they meet us. I am very glad of the chance of a talk to night. I may not be able to see you to morrow or the day after. I hear you are aware that Mr. Durrane came ashore an hour ago?"

"Yes, in our canoe?" said Mary and Willie together.

"Ah. Then he borrowed it?"

This time neither answered, as each waited for the other to speak, so Stuart explained briefly what had happened.

"Just so. Furneaux signalled me to keep a lookout at the landing stage. Mr. Durrane arrived, and went to the railroad station, where he entrusted a letter and a couple of dollars to the conductor of the night mail. The letter was addressed to Mr. Montagu Toyn, so we may hear to morrow what it was about, as that gentleman seems definitely to have thrown his lot in with the police in this affair. The tip, of course, was to secure delivery in New York by a messenger boy early to morrow morning. . . . All right, Miss Dixon, I'll be good, and explain things. Furneaux can get me at eight, nine, ten and eleven o'clock any evening by showing two vertical white lights for a few seconds at the extreme angle of the 'Sans Souci' lot, which is just visible from the farthest end of the landing stage. I don't go to him. He will either come himself, or send interesting company. Naturally, no signal is made except in a case of urgent necessity. The rest was easy, as of course, the train conductor is friendly with the local deputy marshal. So now you know two closely guarded secrets of the Bureau. Then accident helped, as I met you en route to the concert, and even ascertained that Mr. Durrane had decided not to join you."

"Good work!" cried Willie Dixon enthusiastically.

"Thanks! Even a Tammany cop likes to be commended occasionally. But I have serious news of that dog."

"What dog?" enquired all three.

Winter took the cue instantly. Furneaux had said nothing about his disclosure that day.

"How stupid of me!" he exclaimed. "I was sure I had mentioned the dog. At any rate, three days before Mr. van Cortland was killed Mr. Philip Durrane purchased a fox terrier, which he brought to his apartment. The animal, a well bred one, was seen by his man servant and two maids, who promptly made a pet of it, but, it disappeared that night, and Mr. Durrane explained that when he took it out for a stroll late in the evening, it made off and he could not find it again. Probably, he suggested, it had been stolen, and knew its way home again; therefore, he did not wish anything more to be said about it. But the dog was found dead in the gutter eight blocks away next morning, and would have been thrown into a dust cart without further ceremony if a White Wing had not been a dog fancier. He saw it was a valuable animal, and in perfect condition, and wondered what had caused its death, as it had not been run over. He examined it carefully, and came to the conclusion that it had been poisoned by a hypodermic injection, the marks of which he found on its neck. The incident, though trivial, was a curious one to him, and he mentioned it to a policeman, who, in turn, remembered it after the adjourned inquest. He, of course, did not connect the dog's death with the two murders, but spoke of the affair to one of our men. The street cleaner has been questioned by the Roosevelt Hospital expert in toxicology, and the post morten symptoms were exactly the same as in the human cases. There was no difficulty in getting Mr. Durrane's servants to tell what they knew, as the enquiries there concerned a stolen dog, and they described the animal exactly. It is a pity the poor brute's body could not be secured, but it went into the incinerator. Anyhow, that is our first bit of direct evidence again any definite person in the van Cortland case. It is only one link in the chain, but a fairly strong one. We have given up hope of finding out how or where the chloral was purchased. No drug store would sell it in such a quantity. It must have been obtained through the sources of supply so common in the underworld of New York. . . . Why, what is the matter, Miss Dixon?"

Mary, who had contrived to smother her feelings up to this point, now began to sob.

"I cuc cuc can't help it!" she wailed. "Surely that poor little dog might have been spared!"

"I'm sorry if my story has upset you," said the detective, "but I felt you ought to know it, if only to prove the cold and calculating nature of the man whom we have to entrap somehow or other. That is why Mr. Furneaux and I have resolved to tell you everything we know. You will be on your guard. You will hear all and say nothing. You can follow the least innuendo which may creep out inadvertently in conversation."

"But just think of it," blazed forth Willie Dixon.

"That—that— Gosh, I wish you were about ten yards away, sis!—that hell hound was dining in our house to night."

"Yes, and there must not be the slightest perceptible change in your attitude towards him," said Winter firmly. "The Bureau is showing its entire confidence in you young people, and I am sure it is not misplaced. Please remember that Durrane is not yet proved guilty. The balance of such evidence as we possess still inclines strongly against Frank Baker, who is now on his way here. Why is he coming? That is a puzzle, which I look to you to solve. ... So you see, Miss Dixon, I have no option but to ask your continuance of a most unpleasant task. It will not be for long. The man, whoever it was, who killed Anthony van Cortland had a strong, an overwhelming motive for the crime. It must reveal itself soon."

"I'll do my best, Mr. Winter," said Mary, lifting her tear stained face and gazing at him with strangely pathetic eyes. "I suppose all the world, all my world at any rate, thinks to day that I am the luckiest girl alive, whereas I am really one of the most miserable."

"Oh, this shadow will soon pass," was the cheery answer. "Bless your heart, child, before you are twelve months older you will have forgotten all this wretched business. At best, it will only figure in your mind as a half remembered nightmare. Off you go to your launch now. I leave you here. And don't forget you are well guarded. Isn't that so, Captain Stuart?"

"I don't think that any evil can reach her while she has so many defenders," said Stuart slowly.

The detective went off into the night, and Willie Dixon remarked sotto voce to the moon that if events moved at this rate during the next day or two he'd write a dime novel, bless him if he didn't!

As for Stuart, he got Mary to talk quietly and sensibly of the queer incidents related by Winter, but not a word said he of a hurried exit from the Adirondacks. Plainly, such a retreat was now utterly impossible. And, as though to harden his heart against the promptings of pride, he had caught a glimpse of Mary's woe begone features when she made that valiant promise to the Chief of the Bureau. Her beauty then was of the stars rather than the earth. She was not Mary Dixon but the eternal feminine, and the man was beginning to know that the greater part of love is not passion but self sacrifice.

So, come what may, Stuart was determined now to remain by her side until the formless peril which the two experienced police officials seemed to fear had passed out of her life forever.

CHAPTER 16: THE BOATING PARTY

NEVER in his professional career had Furneaux blundered into Carlyle's assumption that mankind is made up mostly of fools. He knew that if there be an element of truth in the cantankerous Scot's dictum it applies only to the ease with which a majority of the people can be beguiled into momentary folly. Any detective who acted as though the servants at "Sans Souci" possessed neither eyes nor ears, was simply courting disaster.

It was necessary, therefore, to provide a plausible excuse for his frequent disappearances and inexplicable Sittings to and from among the trees and shrubs around the house at hours when tendance on the launch would be ridiculous.

So he sought the butler at "Bellagio," and forthwith propounded a problem which has vexed humanity ever since a certain apple was halved and eaten in the Garden of Eden.

"Brown," he said, when the two were alone in the servants' region, "do you trust Catherine?"

The butler, suave but cautious, was not to be rushed into giving an opinion on any such knotty point.

"That depends, sir," he replied.

"Do you mean it depends on Catherine as Catherine, or as a woman?"

"Catherine is a very nice girl, an' she an' me seem to get on wonderfully well, considerin' she's a New Yorker an' me a Londoner. But all women have their limits, Mr. Furneaux."

"Have you ever read any of the maxims of La Rochefoucauld ?"

"I've never even heard the gentleman's name, sir."

"I see. Some men are born philosophers; others can only use borrowed brains all their lives. Well, I must state a case. Would you care to trust Catherine with me alone among the trees, at a spot where it is so dark that you cannot see your hand, and where the quivering leaves of a summer's night whisper of love and romance?"

"Being a fair minded man, sir, I think Catherine herself would be the best judge of a proposition like that."

"You won't feel rattled?"

"Not if you say it is in behalf of the law. Besides, Catherine an' me are not yet strictly engaged, so to speak, an' if she is minded to change, now's her time."

"Brown, you're a scream! But I ought to explain that Catherine's manifest charms have nothing to do with this matter. I ought to have said:—How far do you trust her discretion ? Will she keep tightlipped if we wise her up about this enquiry?"

The butler smiled amiably.

"That's all right, Mr. Furneaux," he said. "Of course, you will have your little joke. That's what I like about you. You're dry, very dry. Now, as to Catherine. She knows a lot already—a good deal more than I've ever told her. Women are certainly cute in some things."

"Very well. Bring her here, and I'll talk to both of you."

Catherine was produced. She looked singularly pretty in the black and white of a parlour maid's regulation dress, which, by some freak of feminine caprice, is one of the most attractive costumes the sex ever devised.

Furneaux avoided the least semblance of humour now. He spoke quite seriously, and made it clear why he wished to be "surprised" that evening in the shrubbery when his employer came back. Catherine was a bit timid at first. In any case, while Brown was present, she had to appear timid. But she allowed herself to be persuaded. The pair took care they were seen by at least two members of the "Sans Souci" staff; then they strolled down to the water's edge, and it was a quite realistic giggle that reached Durrane's ears when he housed the Dixons' canoe, and made a path for himself through the undergrowth.

Now, he had felt exceeding wrath on receiving the message at the landing stage. In two minds whether or not to join the party at the concert, he decided that it would be altogether gauche to thrust himself on them again that night. But he was in a black rage, for his schemes had gone wrong all day, so he knew not what to think when he heard a woman's laughing coo in the unmistakable accents of one engaged in a lively flirtation. It is true that Catherine was only obeying orders, but Furneaux thought fit to startle her into the correct note by clutching her tightly round the waist.

Durrane took thought for a second, to make sure he was on his own land. Then he demanded sharply:—

"Who is there?"

"C'est moi, Pierre, m'sieur," answered Furneaux, with a silent cough.

"Oh! But who is with you?"

"Une jeune fille, m'sieur."

"I didn't imagine it was an old one. I'm going to have a look, anyhow."

He crashed forward, struck a match, and found the two—Catherine, by this time, being quite realistically embarrassed.

"Sorry," he said gruffly. "I didn't really mean to disturb you, but I hardly expected to find anyone here."

"Vare goot, sare," said Furneaux. "I see you in ze 'ouse, toute suite."

Durrane began a further apology, but Furneaux cut him short.

"I tek you 'ome, yess, ma belle," said the detective, grabbing the girl's arm, and hurrying her off. "You did that splendidly," he whispered in her ear. "Now I've got that gentleman just where I want him. Come to morrow night if I send for you."

"Yes, but "

"There are no buts. I had to make you give tongue at the right moment."

"You seem to have had considerable practise," was Catherine's parting shot as she fled.

Durrane was reading Willie Dixon's note, and having the conviction forced on him that, after all, Mary had not excluded him deliberately from the night's outing, when Furneaux entered.

"I tink I queet to mor'," he said, and his black eyes twinkled vindictively.

"Why? Just because I caught you with a girl?" cried Durrane in genuine astonishment.

"Et pourquoi non? You giff ze ordaire, an' me, I obey. Den you mek one dam beeg fool of me. By gar, I go!"

"But didn't I tell you I was taken by surprise. Who would have thought of meeting anyone among the trees at this time of night? Look here, Pierre, don't be an idiot. Here's a ten spot. Make my apologies to the lady, and buy her a present, un p'tit cadeau, eh?"

"No, sare. I not tek ze monnaie. P'raps, eef you say you hav' ze regret, I stop till Mistaire Evans come beck. Den, eef you steel pleased, you giff me tip."

"All right. There's nothing to be so touchy about, anyway. May I ask who the lady was?"

"Ze mait, Mees Dixon, mait."

Durrane swore. He knew now what the man meant by saying he was only obeying orders.

"I certainly was an ass, Pierre," he admitted, trying to smile, "but I have been horribly upset to day. Any news?"

"Cathareen, she say nothing. But I hav' not ze chance. You frighten her."

"Never mind. I shall know better next time. Have a nip of whisky."

"Non, merci, m'sieur. I am vat you call teetotallaire."

It was one of Furneaux's peculiarities that he would never accept any of the ordinary civilities of life from a man whom he believed a malefactor, and who might in consequence come into the clutches of the law. Indeed, at that very moment several eminent financiers in and around Wall Street would have been gravely perturbed if they knew of this trait in the detective's character. Meanwhile, he had quite neatly provided against possible enquiries into his nocturnal prowling around the grounds of "Sans Souci."

Durrane sat in his room until he caught the purr of the Dixons' launch. He lighted a cigarette, went out on to the verandah, and listened. When the party had landed he heard Stuart say distinctly:—

"I suppose Mr. Durrane got your note, Willie? I rather imagined he would join us."

"Perhaps he was tired," said Mary. "It is a long pull to cross the lake twice."

"But he has a launch," put in Willie Dixon.

"Well, I'm really off to bed this time," announced the girl. "We shall hear in the morning what happened."

All of which, of course, was intended for the listener, since the glowing end of the cigarette was quite visible long before the motor boat reached its berth. Durrane was pleased. So was Furneaux, watching him intently from the blackness of a clump of firs.

Durrane stepped out into the moonlight, and strolled to a point on the lawn whence he could see the Dixons' house. In a few minutes a light appeared in Mary's bedroom, the position of which he had ascertained when her brother went there after dinner. Then a queer and remarkable change came over his regular and usually unruffled features. They took on an expression of demoniac intensity. His eyes glistened like those of a wild animal. He seemed to be exercising an extraordinary degree of will power, as though he were some mesmerist, half quack, half cataleptic, seeking to subdue an unwilling or unresponsive subject.

All this was intensely interesting to Furneaux, whose professional zest was only modified by a longing to take part in the seance, and scare this madman out of his remaining senses. At last, after a tension that lasted some minutes, Durrane wilted perceptibly, and nearly fell. Recovering himself, he passed a hand over his eyes, and went into the house.

Furneaux waited until a French window was closed and bolted. Then he, too, crept to his quarters.

"Cre nom!" he muttered, while examining his brown skin in a hand mirror after a vigorous wash, "I wish the Chief could have seen that exhibition. There must have been something in the theory of the ancients that a man might be possessed of a devil. This rascal needs watching every minute of the day and half the night!"

Stuart and young Dixon were smoking on the lawn after breakfast when Durrane and Frank Baker came to them. The latter had evidently been primed as to what to say. He tackled Stuart at once.

"Quite a surprise to find you here," he cried. "I don't know why, but I had a sort of notion you were off to Maine at the first opportunity."

"In a sense, the Adirondacks are on my way," said Stuart civilly.

"Well, yes. It's a case of killing two birds with one stone."

"He hasn't killed either of you birds yet," put in Willie Dixon, with a loud laugh that betokened the belief he had said something humorous.

Baker, whose strong point was certainly not repartee, looked puzzled for a moment.

"Where's Mary?" he enquired.

"Here," said the girl herself. "You're looking very well, Frank. Did you sleep in the train?"

"Nine hours, by the clock. What's the frolic today?"

"Suppose we go to the head of the lake, and tow the canoe, in case anybody wants to fish or swim."

"By the way, I hope you didn't mind my borrowing your canoe last night?" said Durrane.

"Not a bit. Only Alec was sure the boathouse had been burgled when he couldn't find it."

"What happened?" enquired Baker interestedly. He was startled at finding Stuart on such familiar terms with the Dixon family, but had wit enough to realise that he must discover just how the land lay before plunging into the combat.

Willie Dixon explained, and mimicked successfully some of the amateur artistes at the concert. This diversion put the party on a cheerful footing. Brown came with them to set forth a luncheon in a favourite nook, and everything went well until Baker introduced a topic which, though harmless in itself, led to what journalism calls "a breeze" when speakers differ at a public gathering.

He mentioned that some girl known to the Dixons was engaged to an officer on the staff at Governor's Island.

"Oh, I've known him for years," said Stuart. "I hadn't the least suspicion he was a marrying man."

"Are you a good judge?" enquired Baker.

"No. I can hardly claim much experience. In any event, I was only using an everyday phrase."

"D'ye mean to tell me you went to France without having a girl's picture tucked away inside your tunic?"

"It sounds outrageous, but it is quite true. I owned no photograph—of a young lady. I had one of my mother, but I lost it."

"How?" broke in Mary.

"Most disagreeably. The left side of my tunic was ripped off during a scrap, and that is the last I saw of it and some perfectly good dollar bills."

"Was that when you got the Croix de Guerre?" demanded Willie Dixon.

"Well, as it happens, it was."

For no assignable reason, or to be correct, for no reason that could be assigned, Stuart reddened and Mary blushed furiously.

Dixon, who confessed afterwards that he was "out for blood" that morning, grinned hugely.

"What's up?" he cried. "Why are you two getting hot under the collar?"

Stuart, compelled to extricate himself and the girl from an awkward predicament, contrived to laugh quite naturally.

"I'm afraid I am not at all a modern young man," he said. "A fellow should not be ashamed to confess that he had no sweetheart but his mother, yet the statement sounds almost ridiculous in these days."

"It is, let us say, somewhat unusual," said Durrane, whose eyes, after a penetrating glance at Mary, took on an introspective look. "Pity you did not meet Frank on the other side, Captain Stuart. He could surely have spared you one photograph out of a round dozen."

"The blessed girls sent 'em by post," protested Baker rather heatedly. "I differed from you, Phil, I didn't take 'em seriously."

"If you are alluding to my unfortunate marriage I want to make the fact known that it was dissolved early this year. I did not understand what the affection of a husband for a wife really meant when I met Mademoiselle Georgette. Like every other young American in France, I had a dream girl in my heart if not in my brain. So I idealised the first young woman who came along, and paid a stiff price for my calf love, too."

This verbal bombshell silenced all tongues until Willie Dixon came to the rescue.

"I never quite understood why you broke with Georgette," he said. "She was a jolly kid, in her way."

"Did you know I was divorced?" and Durrane turned on him with a suddenness that might have disconcerted any other person.

"No, but I'm a good guesser. She did not show up in New York, and you never even mentioned her.   "Suppose we talk of something else," said Mary hurriedly.

"Please do not think my feelings are harried," said Durrane, with what seemed to be a smile of utter detachment. "Quite apart from any personal bearing, there are few things better worth analysis than the emotional wave created by the war. It led to strange attachments. It plumbed the depths of human folly, and soared above the clouds. I hope some cynical Frenchman observed its vagaries; he ought to give us a strangely illuminating study in psychology."

"Write the book yourself, old top," said Frank Baker rather coarsely, yet with a curious emphasis which the commonplace remark hardly warranted.

"I may, some day," murmured Durrane, with the air of one communing aloud. "Hitherto my researches have been grossly material, but I see a glimmer of light on the horizon. Perhaps the dawn is at hand."

Baker, for no perceptible cause, was inclined to lose his temper, and glared at his friend with an almost bovine fury of expression, but Mary Dixon now spoke peremptorily.

"If we five cannot find something else to discuss than a mythical Frenchman's, or even Mr. Durrane's, researches into the ethics of war marriages I shall ask the Skip to make a bee line for home," she announced.

"Let's all sing!" suggested her brother.

Stuart broke the spell by asking the Skipper what kind of fly would be most effective on the water that morning. Thenceforth the atmosphere cleared. Both Durrane and Baker made amends by indulging in harmless nonsense. They even left Stuart to look after Mary while they adjourned with Willie Dixon to a swimming cove, and went in for hundred yard sprints.

The others were watching the three heads bobbing around the canoe, which Mary insisted should be taken out by the boatman, when the girl said in an awed way:—

"Alec, do you really believe Phil Durrane killed Anthony?"

"I answer that question by asking one," was the grave reply. "Doesn't it seem to you that he is mad?"

"I could have shrieked in hysteria, whatever that may be, when he spoke of his marriage. Did you——had you any—Oh, I hardly know how to put it. But it seemed to me—there was some strange meaning lurking behind his words."

Mary was seated on a tree which had fallen close to the lake. It was anchored securely by its roots, the upper part of the trunk being wedged between two rocks. Stuart, smoking a favourite pipe, squatted cross legged on a patch of grass fully six feet away. He had learnt that tailor like attitude in the trenches, and could sit comfortably thus for an hour or longer. There was nothing in their attitude to betoken love making, yet Stuart thrilled at her broken statement, since he had not the least doubt as to what was in her mind.

"I don't think you will ever be hysterical, Mary," he said. "You have borne and are still bearing a great strain. The existing tension cannot last much longer. Something must crack."

"I, for one, shall not care how soon that happens," she murmured, with a touch of defiance in her voice. "I suppose a man like you hardly understands the subtle ways in which a person of the neurotic temperament can convey things to a woman."

Stuart produced a nail, and loosened the tobacco in the bowl of his pipe. This gave him an excuse for keeping his eyes off the girl's face as he said with calm deliberateness:—

"I should be dull, indeed, if I did not realise that Durrane's rhapsodies on the emotions aroused by the war were figurative, with this poor Georgette, whoever she may be, at the foot and you at the head of the scale."

"Then I was right," she said, in a frightened way. "And—I hardly like to tell you, but I must confide in someone—he pursues me when he is absent."

"Please explain that."

"I am conscious that some force of his mind is centred on me. Last night, for instance, when I went to my room, I found myself compelled to think of him. I had to fight against it. When I said my prayers the feeling, the danger I want to call it, went away."

"Do you know," said Stuart reflectively, apparently stating a fact rather than seeking an answer, "the time is approaching rapidly when, with all due respect to Messrs. Winter and Furneaux, and with utter disregard for the conventions, I shall give Mr. Philip Durrane the hiding of his life. Your brother is hardly equal to the undertaking. I am."

Mary had nothing to say to that. She did not even protest against such a lawless declaration. Indeed, she looked a trifle nervous, nor were Durrane's furtive methods of love making the disturbing factor now. And she was right. Stuart was actually debating with himself whether or not he should tell her straight out that he loved her, that she was the only woman in the world for him—a time honoured yet ever new formula—and that he wished the said world to grasp the essential fact that he was her avowed champion against all and sundry persecutors. Yet the irritating fellow forbore. The rampart of two and a half millions of dollars still blocked the path, and, in his heart of heart (as Shakespeare really puts it) he was aware that the New York Detective Bureau had thrown him into Mary Dixon's society merely as a decoy for a wild beast which had thus far successfully eluded the nets of the law. Moreover, he had actually known her during little more than a week. A day would have sufficed, he thought. But how about her and her people?

And so passed a golden opportunity. While this eminently well matched young couple were avoiding each other's eyes, and quite candidly reading each other's souls, a shout from the Skipper attracted their attention. The man began paddling with furious haste, but a tiny headland soon shut him from sight, and the watchers sprang to their feet.

"Oh," wailed Mary in quick distress. "Something dreadful has happened!"

Stuart, no matter how backward he might be as a lover, was never found lacking in a man's decisiveness in action.

"Brown," he shouted to the butler, "remain here with Miss Mary till I come back Don't leave her for an instant!"

He set off at top speed by the path the swimmers had taken. In three minutes, or less, he was at the strip of beach where they had undressed. He found Baker lying there on his face, and Durrane applying scientific treatment for the half drowned. Even before he could ask Willie Dixon for an explanation, Baker hiccoughed and demanded to be let alone, on the ground that he was "all right."

Durrane continued to work at him, however, and it was soon evident that the sufferer was not yet out of danger.

Meanwhile, Willie Dixon was excitedly voluble.

"It was only a fool stunt," he cried. "We were all equally responsible. We had a couple of races to the canoe and back. Frank won one, and Durrane the other. Then I stood down, as I was tired; and Phil challenged Frank to a decider. Frank looked rather done, but agreed, as Phil seemed nearly all in, too. Then "

Durrane glanced up, though without ceasing to compress and expand Baker's lungs by moving his arms.

"As Stuart is here your sister must know that things have gone wrong," he said with laboured breath. "Run and tell her there is nothing to worry about. And—there is no need—to distress her too much."

Willie obeyed. Stuart saw that the boatman's clothes were soaked.

"You had to jump in?" he said.

"Yes, sir, an' mighty quick at that. This guy was goin' down, an' there's none of yer three rise propositions about this yer lake. If he got tangled up among the ten foot weeds on the bottom—well, good night!"

"Geel" spluttered Baker, when allowed at last to struggle to his knees. "I never swallowed so much water before in my life. An' they call this a dry country!"

In a few minutes, though white and shaken, he was able to dress. Willie Dixon came back with some whisky, but Baker refused it.

"Couldn't touch a drop now," he said. "Gimme a cigarette, an' try me with the Scotch in about half an hour. Guess I'll sit in the sun, an' ruminate on a misspent career. They say death by drowning is pleasant. Well, by gosh, I couldn't have been anywhere near dead, because that was the most infernally disagreeable experience I've ever had. . . . And, say, hand that corpse reviver to the Skip. I'll attend to him later."

"I wonder which was the bigger idiot, Frank, you or I?" smiled Durrane, who also showed the effect of his exertions.

"There's no argument about that," said Baker, with a feeble grin. "Great Scott! I'd never have guessed you were such a good swimmer, Phil. You left me like a streak of lightning in that last lap."

"I simply hate to lose in anything," said Durrane. "The wonder is that I didn't crack up first."

"Well, I saw no signs of it when you went away. However, I've been getting a few surprises lately, and one more jolt won't hurt any. Let's move. I don't like the look of that particular strip of water."

Stuart went to assist the boatman to launch the canoe, which was beached, but Durrane helped as well, and took the opportunity to tell the man that he personally would give him a hundred dollars for his prompt daring; evidently he had been compelled to jump in after Baker.

Despite the latter's protest, Mary insisted that they should return at once, and have luncheon at home, where Baker should rest during the afternoon. It was a quiet party that sped along the lake.

Even the Skipper, a by no means taciturn person when he felt free to join in a conversation, looked thoughtful. Perhaps, in his case, it was the prospect of a thumping reward that tied his tongue.

But what could account for the cloud which so suddenly descended on Willie Dixon? When spoken to by his sister he replied in monosyllables, if possible. But he accounted for this phenomenal behaviour when the launch reached "Bellagio," after landing Durrane and Baker at the adjoining house.

"Tell you what," he muttered in a scared voice, as Mary and Stuart went with him up the footpath. "Durrane tried to drown Baker. I saw it in a flash when Frank said that about Phil drawing away on the return trip! Something ought to be done. What sort of frantic jazz are we up against, anyhow?"

CHAPTER 17: A DISQUISITION ON NEUROSIS

IT transpired, as the newspaper reporter puts it, that there were others who shared Willie Dixon's opinions. Stuart had not reached the house before he was overtaken by the boatman, who caught his eye and held up a crooked finger.

"Jest a minnit, 'cap'," said the man, in a low tone. "I'd like ter hev a word with yer."

"Certainly," said Stuart, "but won't you change your clothes first?"

"I had a notion ez how, p'haps, you wouldn't mind comin' to my shanty. We kin talk kind o' private thar."

Stuart told the others he would joint them shortly, and accompanied the Skipper to the servants' quarters. There he was surprised to see Winter peeping at him through the window of the butler's room, while Furneaux was scurrying back to "Sans Souci."

"Wilson," he said, Jake Wilson being the Skipper's name, "are you going to tell me something about the accident to Mr. Baker."

"Yes, sir. T'wan't no accident. An' I ain't satisfied ter keep things to myself. But what's the use o' speakin' ter old man Dixon, an' Mr. Willie is only a kid."

"A friend of mine has just turned up, and I have the greatest faith in his judgment. Would you like me to ask him to hear what you have to say?"

The mountain and lake folk of Northern New York State seldom care to express themselves openly before total strangers, and the Skip's dubious head shake emphasised the fact.

"I wouldn't make the suggestion if this matter were not serious," said Stuart, looking the other square in the face. "You probably know as well as I, Wilson, that things are far from being right here. Now I can assure you that you will not regret calling into our councils the man who is now in Mr. Brown's room."

"Wall, cap', if yer sez it, it goes."

So Stuart beckoned to Winter, who followed them to the boatman's habitat, which consisted of four rooms built on to the service wing; Wilson lived there all the year round, acting as caretaker during the winter.

His wife happened to be out, since she, like the rest of the staff, thought the boating party would be absent all day. There was no false modesty about the Skip. He procured a dry suit, linen and shoes, stripped with remarkable celerity, and towelled his body vigorously while he talked.

"What's yer name, mister?" he enquired, eyeing Winter curiously. The detective was now clothed in his ordinary attire, a fact in itself of much significance to Stuart.

"Winter," said the Chief. "James Leander Winter, Chief of the New York Detective Bureau."

"Snakes alive!" cried the astonished boatman.

"And likewise 'By heck!' What the trouble?"

"Let me begin, Skip," put in Stuart, and he supplied a brief resume of the morning's outing, stopping short at the bathing incident.

"Wall, gents, it wuz this yer way," went on the boatman. "It seemed ter me, when Mr. Baker an' Mr. Durrane touched the canoe in the fust lap o' the third race, they wuz both pretty well all in, or looked it, so I kep' an eye on 'em, an' even moved the canoe in a bit. Good job I did, or I might never ha' ketched Mr. Baker's hair as he wuz goin' down. But I'm derned if Mr. Durrane didn't draw away like an otter on the return trip. Mr. Baker yelled suthin', but Mr. Durrane on'y went the faster, though he must ha' heered. Then Mr. Baker cried 'I'm done!' an', like every other blamed fool in trouble in deep water, threw up his hands. By that time Mr. Durrane was ten yards ahead, but he never turned. So I chipped in. Two strokes o' the paddle brought me over Mr. Baker. I could see his white body sinkin' slowly, an' the air bubbles tole the rest o' the tale. Over I went, grabbed him, and clung on ter the canoe when he fought a bit. Then Mr. Durrane kern back. 'Good God!' sez he, 'what's gone wrong?' 'Never you mind,' sez I. 'Jest give a hand, an' get this guy ashore.' I'm bound to admit ez how Mr. Durrane did the right thing straight away then, ez you saw fer yerself, Cap', but I hev a sort o' sneakin' idee that the affair didn't turn out 'xactly ez Mr. Durrane calc'lated it."

"You mean that he thought his friend might sink and be caught in the weeds!" said Stuart.

"It sure is a hard thing ter say, Cap', but it looked derned like it. An' didn't he ez good ez tell me ter keep me mouth shut when he offered to gimme a hundred dollars?"

All three men caught the footsteps of someone walking quickly across the paved yard without. Winter, with amazing swiftness, vanished into an inner room, and Stuart had barely time to fling the boatman a warning glance when Durrane entered.

"Ah, here you are!" he cried, as though fully expecting to find Stuart there.

"Yes," said the soldier, smiling. "I thought it my duty to see that the Skip changed his clothes at once. He's a careless sort of cuss in such matters."

"Quite right. I'm glad you did it. I had the same suspicion. And here's your century, Skip."

The boatman was in no hurry to take the proffered note.

"I don't see ez how I earned anything from you, Mr. Durrane," he said stubbornly.

"Oh, you certainly must let Mr. Durrane give you a present for saving his friend's life," broke in Stuart, fearful lest Durrane should have a glimmer of doubt as to the true cause of his presence there.

"Wall," said Wilson, spitting on his palm, "if you two gents agree on this affair I hev no more ter say." "Quite right," laughed Stuart. "And now we'll leave you. ... Is Baker going to bed?" he asked Durrane as they went out together.

"He didn't want to, but I persuaded him. Is Mary very much upset?"

"Oh, no, I believe not."

"Do you think she would see me?"

"Well, I really don't know. Why not send the butler with a message?"

Stuart was swallowing a bitter pill, but he could not help himself. He was bound to act as though life were moving again on its normal plane, and it was wholly essential that Durrane should be inveighled out of Wilson's cottage.

Brown took Mr. Durrane's compliments to Miss Mary, with the request that she would come to the verandah for a moment. Very reluctantly, she did so. Stuart made for the lounge, which opened on to the verandah by two French windows. He sank into a chair whence he could see Mary leaning over the rail, and Durrane standing on the lawn.

"I am here to apologise for this morning's mishap," began Durrane. "I wouldn't have had it occur on any consideration, though it was an accident, pure and simple."

"Why, of course, Phil," said the girl. "You surely don't need to tell me that?"

"No, but you are troubled and distrait, I know, because we are in sympathy, and anything that disturbs you causes me a real agony of spirit."

She laughed nervously.

"Why so serious?" she cried. "I'm sure Frank will be all right to morrow. He isn't the sort of man who would suffer from shock."

"At the present moment he is in a very bad temper, as I insisted that he should undress, and rest properly for an hour. This afternoon he will be playing tennis. It is you I am concerned about."

"But why? I never felt better in my life."

"Ah, don't tell me that. I know. I know!"

"I wish you wouldn't talk so absurdly. I cannot even guess what you are driving at."

"That is my misfortune. I so seldom get a chance of a quiet talk with you, yet you are the only being on earth whom I wish to propitiate."

"Goodness me! I shall be here all the summer. Now, please, run away. I have to see about luncheon. . . . No—I shan't stop another second. I think we are all somewhat nervy over Frank's narrow escape, and you more than anybody."

Whereupon Mary flounced off, crossing the inner room without even a glance at Stuart. Durrane walked slowly to his own house, with bent head and eyes that gave no heed to his surroundings.

At luncheon the young people spoke freely of Baker's escape, though they dropped no hint to Mr. Dixon, senior, as to any malicious intent on Durrane's part. But he was manifestly ill at ease.

"I shall be glad when this atmosphere of tragedy is dispelled, once and for all," he said irritably. "Is nothing being done to discover the cause of Tony van Cortland's death? I have often heard of the gross incompetence of our detective system, and surely this is a genuine instance of it!"

Willie Dixon, as usual, rose to the occasion.

"The hands of the police are tied in that affair, pop," he said. "I don't mean there is any graft, or that sort of thing, but they have to watch their step. You see, the theory is that Tony was killed by one of his twelve friends, and the said twelve are sons of New York's chief citizens. I'm one."

"Why has Frank Baker come to Paul Smith's? His name figured prominently in the enquiry."

"It's my opinion, Pop, that the less we know about the affair the happier we'll be."

"Well, if he really wants to drown himself I hope he will choose some other locality. I've been thinking things over, Willie. You must stay here as long as Durrane and this other man are near. You, too, Captain Stuart, if it is convenient. I don't want my little girl to be mixed up in any more of these wretched accidents, or whatever else they may be."

He certainly did not expect that his daughter would spring up and throw her arms around him, with a hearty kiss, and a whispered:—"You're a dear, good, thoughtful Pop, that's what you are. So, there!"

"Well, well," he blustered. "Why all this fuss? What do you say, Stuart?"

"I shall be delighted to prolong a wonderful holiday," said Stuart, wondering what had occurred to cause such a change of mind in his host. He did not know till much later that Mr. Dixon and Brown had indulged in a long and confidential chat that morning; the butler had experienced little difficulty in making the old gentleman believe that Miss Dixon should not be deprived of the company of her brother and her soldier friend at quite so early a date as he had contemplated.

Reading and sleeping occupied the larger part of the afternoon for the invalid. It has been noted already that once in his sanctum he did not like to be disturbed. So the three were about to take the launch to go ashore, where they could discuss freely the one topic of vital interest for the hour, when Brown came and intimated that Mr. Winter would be pleased to see them "upstairs."

"Mr. Winter?" echoed Mary.

"Yes, he is here," explained Stuart. "I would have told you in another second, but, in any case, it was for him to seek us if he thought fit."

"Where have you put him, Brown?" enquired the girl.

"In No. 3,. the blue room, miss."

They asked no more questions, but stole upstairs on tiptoe, why so furtively it is hard to say, though ninety nine people out of a hundred would behave in the same way in similar conditions. The scent of a first rate Havana reached them on the landing, and the Chief would have thrown away his cigar had not Mary stopped him. Furneaux was there, too. Natty as ever, even in his engineer's overalls, he smiled a greeting to Mary, having evidently adopted that young lady as a friend and protegee.

"We must hold a sort of conference," said Winter. "Brown, I'll tell you our secrets afterwards. Just now I want you to mount guard. If anyone comes from the next house give us timely warning so that Mr. Furneaux may slip down to the kitchen, where, I am given to understand, he is courting Catherine."

When the door was closed behind the butler, the Chief spoke. His aspect was grave, and, it may be, a trifle disconcerted.

"I have various items of news," he began. "In the first place, Toyn rang up one of my men as soon as Durrane's letter reached him this morning. It contained some peculiar instructions. Do any of you recall the strange history of Marie Bashkirtseff?"

Willie Dixon promptly vouchsafed the information that the lady was a prominent member of a Russian ballet which had been staged in a New York theatre during the previous winter. Mary had never heard of her. Stuart had a vague recollection of some famous or scandalous memoirs—he knew not which.

Winter pointed the stub of his cigar at Furneaux. "You tell 'em," he said. "This psychology stuff is in your line."

Furneaux bowed with much grace.

"The chairman's speech is a model of what such prefatory remarks should be," he said. "Marie Bashkirtseff was a young Russian lady who died in Paris nearly thirty years ago. She was aged only twenty four.

At thirteen she had a violent love affair—with a French
Duke—in imagination, since the man had never spoken
to her. At fourteen she tried to become a prima donna. At
fifteen she was a painter. About twice every year she fell
in love, and fell out again. Fortunately, she never
married.   Two years before her death she did really
devote herself to art and studied under Julian. Since she
could write before she was weaned she kept a diary, in
which she recorded her most intimate thoughts, and to
that diary published after her death she owes all her
fame. It supplies a strange and searching analysis of the
feminine and artistic temperaments. My personal belief is
that she touched up the earlier years while writing of the
later ones. Whistler described her as a 'journalistic, born
genius,' and he was no mean judge."

"A pocket marvel, ain't he?" said Winter, surveying
his aide with proud eyes. "When he talks like that he
always reminds me of the yokels listening to the village
schoolmaster in Goldsmith's

And still they gazed, and still the wonder grew That
one small head could carry all he knew."

Mary tittered. It was nearly her first experience of the
manner in which this queer pair of detectives carried on a
discussion of even the most serious topic.

"Having now supplied certain obvious lacunae in my
respected Chief's literary knowledge, and enabled him to
bring off one of his stock quotations, I yield the floor,"
said Furneaux.

"Well, we had to understand the facts about poor
Marie," went on Winter. "Durrane picked up a picture of
hers—a studio portrait—in Paris. I don't know whether
it's a fake or not, but he has it, and his letter to Toyn
requested its dispatch to Paul Smith's. It's on the way
now, by express . . . Oh, I know you're puzzled. So am I.
So is our pocket psychologist, though he hates to say so."

"Let us, then, pursue another line of enquiry," chirped
Furneaux, whose very tone caused the Chief to glare at
him suspiciously. "Mankind, of the lymphatic and

neurotic, a compound which supposed to belong, is made up to three well defined physical and temperamental types—the scrofuletic, the lymphatic, and the neurotic. Marie Bashkirtseff and I are perfect examples of the last named, which is largely responsible for insanity and genius. Mr. Winter is a vivid specimen of the scrofuletic, which is not prone to insanity, but goes in for pugilism and wife beating, and has never been known to produce a genius. Philip Durrane is a blend of the lymphatic and neurotic, a compound which sup plies nearly all our most noted criminals, with a fair sprinkling of lunatics. He is a keen student of a certain class of erotic literature. Marie Bashkirtseff's 'Journal,' the letters of 'Abelard,' the 'Confessions' of Jean Jacques Rousseau, the 'Autobiography of Benvenuto Cellina' and other similar books are at his bedside."

He paused. There was a slow, dignified step in the corridor. The butler knocked, but opened the door, at once.

"I think you're wanted, Mr. Furneaux," he said.

"A hem!" cried the detective. "Never mind!" he went on, with an airy hand wave. "Mr. Winter can now get in some good work annotating my remarks."

They waited to see if he returned, but it was evident that the "Sans Souci" launch was required. So the Chief took up the parable.

"All this is not so confusing as it seems," he told his highly attentive audience. "Furneaux's interpretations of the criminal neurotic mind are almost invariably correct. Durrane probably sent for the picture because he believes that it will place him en rapport with its creator's soul. There may be something in the notion. If you show me a pocketbook, and ask me to smell it, and then find the unknown owner some miles away, I cannot do it without utilizing the newspaper, the printed handbill, or making other enquiries. But a blood hound will pick up the scent, and hit an almost unerring trail if it is a recent one. If an animal can do that, why should not some human beings have means of communication altogether unknown to others?"

"Oh, they do! They do!" exclaimed Mary excitedly.

"For instance, did this man Durrane succeed in bringing himself clearly to your mental vision last night at eleven o'clock?"

The girl's eyes opened wide.

"How can you possibly know that?" she cried. "Alec, did you tell him?"

The soldier shook his head.

"Don't be alarmed, Miss Dixon," and Winter smiled cheerfully. "There is nothing psychic about that statement. Mr. Furneaux, who is wearing himself to a shadow over this case, watches Durrane all the time. He saw him trying to exercise a mesmeric influence on you, and knew exactly when he failed, or when the magnetic current was broken, which would be about four or five minutes after it had been established."

"Never, never, shall I miss saying my prayers before going to bed!" vowed Mary, and her earnestness eased the tension by causing a laugh.

"Well, now, where do we stand?" continued the Chief. "The picture, whatsoever the merit Durrane attaches to it, cannot be here before the morning. My own far fetched theory is that it will be given to you. . . . Yes, I mean that—" for the girl was naturally still more surprised. "People who believe in those media endeavor to use them. Please forgive me, but I must say it. Durrane is crazy to marry you."

She took this quite calmly.

"I have known that a long time," she said, "and I would not be his wife if he were the only man left in the whole world."

"Luckily for you and the man you will wed, he is not. But complications have arisen. This attempt to drown Frank Baker, or more correctly, to get Frank Baker to drown himself—what does that imply? Surely something deeper than merely ridding himself of a rival suitor for your hand? And the scheme can hardly have been planned beforehand. I cannot bring myself to think he invited Baker here to kill him. This morning's attack was a masterly seizing of an unforeseen opportunity. Has, then, something occurred, since Baker's arrival, and after the sending of the message for the picture, to precipitate matters? It would appear so. At any rate, the time for pretence has passed now. You young gentlemen must not let Miss Dixon out of your sight unless you are sure she is in the house. You, Miss Dixon, must not dream of going out alone. And—this is my really startling fact—unless something dramatic happens before to morrow morning, I shall make it my business to interview Mr. Dixon, and tell him that the whole household should leave for New York by the night mail. Certain legal business in connection with Mr. van Cortland's legacy will detain you there a day or two—that is your excuse for an immediate departure. Then the Dixon family should just vanish off the map—go to Europe, for choice."

"Why are we being chased out of the country?" demanded Willie Dixon fiercely.

"To protect your sister," said the Chief of the Bureau, obviously speaking in all seriousness. "We can arrest Durrane, of course, but I must tell you candidly that we have not enough evidence against him yet to secure a conviction. We shall get it. I feel that in my bones. But we must wait. Meanwhile, waiting here is made impracticable. This morning the Commissioner told me over the 'phone that he cannot possibly spare Furneaux and me any longer. We must leave, with you, by to morrow evening's train. Of course, other men will be detailed for observation, and I think Brown should stop here. None of my assistants could be half so valuable."

The positive dismay on the three faces moved him to add:—

"Don't imagine we are abandoning the chase. It will occupy our thoughts day and night until we have laid our man by the heels. But Furneaux and I are the principals of a great department, and we simply cannot devote the whole of our time to a waiting job on the shores of this lake."

"But, Mr. Winter," ventured Mary, "what if my father prove obstinate? He is not—quite himself. He may refuse to go."

"Then we must devise other and dependable means for your protection. But I shall urge him strongly. With you away, Durrane's hand may be forced. You may be sure he will not remain long at Paul Smith's then."

"Please carry your theories or surmises a step farther," said Stuart firmly. "What is the particular form of danger you fear for Miss Dixon?"

"I—really—don't know. Furneaux would give you a dozen ingenious hints. I am not built that way. I cannot project myself into the brain pan of a neurasthenic. I suppose a straightforward bit of madness would be to carry Miss Dixon off and marry her at the point of a pistol, so to speak. That very thing has been done over and over again in many countries, but by the big, blond scrofuletic men, not by neurotics. Then there is—but you've started me talking nonsense. Get hold of Furneaux. He'll reel off sensational film by the thousand feet. . . . Hello, what's that?"

"The 'Sans Souci' launch," said Willie Dixon. "I'll go and see who's in it."

He had only to cross the corridor, and look out through a window commanding the lake.

"Durrane alone," he announced, "with Mr. Furneaux driving, of course."

"Well, this trip may bring another ray of light," sighed Winter, who was honestly perturbed by the unexpected summons to New York. "Meanwhile, Miss Dixon, can I occupy this room to night?"

"Certainly. Let me get you a better one."

"No—I prefer this. It commands the yard, and Furneaux can reach me easily if he wants me. Shall I tell you how?"

"Please do?"

"When I retire, which will be at a late hour, I assure you, I'll tie a piece of string to my left wrist, as I lie on my right side. It will hang through the open window to within four feet of the ground. One or two jerks will wake me. That's a quite effective alarm clock which few people have ever thought of. Now, I want you to show me where each person in the house sleeps."

Mary took him on a tour of inspection.

"What the deuce is he driving at?" muttered Willie Dixon, when he and Stuart were alone. "Why did he shy away from your question as to the danger that threatens Mary?"

"He would not tell us in her presence," growled Stuart, and his voice had a rasp in it that the younger man had never heard there before. "Search your memory of crimes reported in the newspapers, Willie. In the great majority of cases, don't these frantic idiots who confound passion with love try to murder the object of their frenzy if balked of possession? Durrane is a homicidal maniac, and my fear is that Furneaux may contrive to goad him into action. Winter believes it, too. I shall tackle him on the point. Do you remember what he said about Furneaux being ready to sacrifice a pet lamb as a decoy for a tiger? But why should Mary's life be risked in this way?"

"Good Lord! You don't mean it!"

"I do. And this damnable business must end."

Mr. Winter returned without Mary, who was giving Catherine some housewifely instructions. Stuart closed the door, which had been left open. He eyed the Chief for a second or two in silence, being a man whose habit it was to think before he spoke. But the detective merely smiled, and bit the end off a fresh Havana.

"You needn't fly into a rage with me, Captain Stuart," he said pleasantly. "Miss Dixon's life is quite safe while Furneaux and I are here. We guarantee it. But we cannot be sure of her well-being after we leave for New York, and that is why, if the boiler doesn't burst within the next twenty four hours, she, at least, must come with us to morrow evening."

CHAPTER 18: A PIECE OF CARDBOARD

FRANK BAKER, though young in years and physically strong as an ox, had led too dissipated a life since returning from France that he could come near being drowned and not feel any ill effects from the experiment. When, therefore, he went to bed under protest, and yielded to persuasion that he should endeavour to sleep, he soon sank into the Nirvana of sheer exhaustion. He sturdily declined, however, what Durrane described as a "sedative."

"I have no use for drugs in any shape," he said. "Give me a stiff dose of whiskey, and I'll be able to eat nails when I wake up."

He was mistaken. After some hours of unconsciousness he opened his eyes and looked at his watch. To his surprise the time was nearly four o'clock. He bounced up with his customary energy, but found that he was far from well. Then, as he told the story afterwards, he lay down again, and took stock of his present position quite seriously. Among other things, he resolved to eschew spirits, or intoxicants in any form, for the remainder of the day. He decided, too, quite wisely, that the less he ate the speedier would be his recovery. Finally, he made up his mind to have what he called a "heart to heart" talk with Mary Dixon, and subsequently return to New York. He may or may not have formed other good resolutions during this chastened mood. He vowed that he did, but his actual intentions matter not, since circumstances wholly beyond his control swept him and all the other people dwelling on that little wooded spur of lakeland into a whirlpool of tragedy and death which threatened at one time to engulf many lives.

He rose at last, dressed slowly, and went to the living room, where he found Durrane ensconced in an arm chair, and reading. He did not know, of course, that his host had paid a flying visit to the town. The latter might have been merely awaiting his reappearance.

"Feeling better?" came the friendly greeting.

"Nothing to boast of. May I have a cup of tea and some dry toast?"

Durrane rose and touched a bell.

"How have the mighty fallen!" he said, with a smile.

"Well, I dunno," said Baker testily. "I fell pretty badly for that little stunt of yours this morning, but I couldn't bring myself to believe that you had gotten such a crazy idea into your cranium that you could bury every fellow who stood between you and Mary Dixon."

A servant entered and Durrane gave directions about the invalid's fare. When the girl had left the room he turned and looked fixedly at Baker, not at all in a threatening way, but rather with the tolerance of one who believes he has just heard an utterly foolish remark.

"Do you know what you have just said?" he enquired.

"Sure I know. The point is do you realise what I meant by it?"

"Are you light headed?"

"Not a bit. Light stomached, perhaps, but my head's all right."

"Then, although I hate doing it, I must ask you to explain yourself."

Baker's blue eyes met Durrane's brown ones steadily.

"I'll supply all necessary explanations at the right time, if ever it comes. I'm beginning to think it came and passed on the day of Tony's death. But I'm not quite such a fool as I look, or may have acted. It was a damned good job for you, Phil Durrane, that I was hauled out of the lake this morning, because, the moment my death was reported in New York, you would have been arrested. I'm talking by the book, believe me."

"This is most interesting, not to say arresting," said Durrane, speaking with calm unconcern.

"Y—yes. I guess you find it so. But, 'nuff said. You leave Mary Dixon alone. She'll never marry you, anyway. One can see with half an eye that the gallant cavalryman has cut us all out. You dished my chance, and your own, if you ever had one, when you advised me not to lend the old man the money to clear off that mortgage, but to buy his shares instead. That let Tony in on the ground floor. And now, something else has happened—what it is I don't quite understand yet—which has put us again in the also ran class. This morning's little game clapped the lid on tight. Hang it all, you didn't bring me here to kill me, did you? I'm sure now you're bughouse, but even a loony should know enough to save his own skin. So, hands off me, unless you really want to go to the chair." The maid came in with the tea. She arranged a small table, spread a doth on it, set out the china and cutlery, and addressed her employer.

"I brought two cups, Mr. Durrane," she said, "in case you would like your tea now."

"Thanks. Talking is dry work. I think I will take some."

The girl had no more notion that she was interrupting a most remarkable conversation than the Italian waiter in Pucci's restaurant had of the nature of the seance going on in the private dining room when Police captain Crossley produced the poison ring.

She poured out the tea, asked questions about the sugar and milk, arranged the toast, butter, and some pastry, and finally took herself off.

Durrane sipped his tea so nonchalantly that Baker was constrained to say:—

"By jing, Phil, you sure have got the devil's own nerve!"

"I pride myself on that attribute. But you were threatening me, I believe. Pray continue."

Baker suddenly aware that he was ravenously hungry, buttered a square of toast, and bit off half of it.

"Try that bluff—on someone—who hasn't—the whip hand—over you, my lad. You heard—what I said—all right. I meant it—every word."

He was snarling and chewing at the same time. Durrane laughed.

"You're like a dog with a bone," he said.

Baker did not reply. He cleared the plate of toast, and started on the cakes. So, one, at least of those good resolutions had gone by the board already. Durrane finished his tea, and seemed to be deep in thought. Twice he glanced at his companion, but met only an angry glare which did not encourage airy persiflage.

At last, however, after a silence of many minutes, he spoke.

"I want to assure you," he said slowly, "that I did not, to use your own phrase, invite you here in order to kill you. But let that pass. You are perfectly safe in my house. You can go or stay as you choose. But, suppose you are wrong as to Mary Dixon? Suppose I marry her, after all? What then?"

The food, in all likelihood, had brought back Baker's senses to their normal level, which was not a high one by any accepted intellectual standard. He had not actually intended to be so outspoken, but the sight of this man, so smug and self centred, had roused him to boiling point when he came downstairs. He was no coward, yet he loved life, and the bare elements of common sense warned him that he was taking a desperate chance in driving such a cold blooded antagonist to extremities.

"If you marry Mary Dixon," he said, "you win, and I'm through. I don't see what else I can do. What would be the use, anyhow?"

This cryptic remark seemed to satisfy Durrane, but Baker had not done with him yet.

"Look here!" he cried, thumping the table and making the crockery rattle. "There's a lot of talk about what you may or may not do. What about me? If you have one chance I certainly have fifty. Why should I give in?"

"Has anyone asked you to give in?"

"No, but "

"My dear Frank, don't be hysterical. Calm yourself. If Mary prefers you, you will have my blessing and best wishes. And please rid yourself of that stupid notion that I am plotting against your life. I'm not. One should never blunder twice in the same way."

With that, Durrane lighted a cigarette and strolled into the garden. Baker scowled at the retreating figure.

"No, damn you!" he muttered. "Probably I'm safe now. You could hardly stage a second attempted murder and hope to escape. I've acted like a born idiot during the past three weeks, and shall probably keep on doing it all my life, but I think I'm safe from your clutches for the rest of my days. At any rate, I've given you something to bite on, and I hope it'll choke you!"

Then he, too, went out. Durrane was standing at the water's edge, watching Furneaux, industrious with a handful of oily waste and an almost equally oily cloth. The detective took care to be at work at such hours. Owing to the conformation of the house it was absolutely impossible to achieve any successful eavesdropping during daylight, so the next best thing was to remain in evidence on the launch.

Baker gave a glance in the direction of "Bellagio," but none of its residents was visible. He joined Durrane.

"Where's the other crowd?" he enquired.

"I don't know. I have not seen them since we came back from our swim. Have you heard what they are doing Pierre?"

"Non, m'sieur. I hev not spik wit Cathareen to day."

"Well, leave that spotless engine, and tackle her now. You may hear something."

Pierre obeyed unwillingly. It was a pity that his masterpieces of acting, and they were many in those days, had no larger audience than the one man necessarily blind to their excellence. Suddenly his face brightened.

"By gar!" he squeaked. "Eef I go now mebbe she giff me tea." And away he sped, not by the shore, but by the footpath and fence.

"Where did you find the Frenchie?" asked Baker.

"He was found for me. He is the brother in law of the regular boatman here."

"Looks a smart little chap. I must have met him somewhere. I seem to remember his voice."

"He comes from Montreal."

"Oh, that's it. I go up there occasionally in winter for the sports. Wonderful mechanics, the French."

"I don't think much of Pierre in that respect; he's useful in others."

Furneaux would have given a good deal to have heard those few simple sentences. He could have built on that slight foundation a structure that must have amazed even the imperturbable Durrane. But that was not to be. He was many yards distant when Baker put the first question.

By mutual consent, as it were, the two men avoided the topics which usurped their thoughts to the exclusion of all else. They talked of fishing, and Durrane explained the methods most in vogue on the lake.

Furneaux returned sooner than his master expected. The little man looked sulky.

"Cathareen she no mek ze tea," he said. "She ees too dam beezy. Dey giff le grand diner to night to veesitaire from New York."

"Hello!"said Baker.

"Who can that be?" mused Durrane aloud.

"Eet ees a man 'oo haz to do wit' ze law."

"Oh, one of Tony's lawyers," commented Baker.

"And where is Miss Dixon?" Has she taken the lawyer ashore?" enquired Durrane.

"Mais, non, m'sieur. Day all go to ze 'eels."

"That's near where I went a few hours ago," guffawed Baker. His friend shuddered at such coarseness.

"Pierre means the hills. They're off for a walk, eh?"

"Oui, m'sieur."

"Let's go and chin with old Dixon," suggested Baker.

"Cathareen say 'e go, too," put in Furneaux quickly.

That may or may not have been strictly true, but the statement sufficed to stop the projected visit. The detective meant to place every obstacle in the way of further meetings between the elder Dixon and Durrane. The old gentleman's vacillating opinions were a real drawback to the Bureau's plans, and provided the weakest link in an already far too slender chain, since, up to the moment, Winter's contention that a court of law would look askance at any evidence he could offer against either Durrane or Baker was fully justified by the literal facts.

In the conditions, the curiously assorted pair at "Sans Souci" could hardly intrude on their neighbours later, and, as the day wore, it became evident that they were not to be included in the dinner party. They smoked and read until it was time to dress, when Durrane asked to be excused from wearing a dinner jacket that night.

"I'm going ashore about nine o'clock," he said. "I hope you don't mind being left alone. I have an appointment that must be kept."

"Oh, I'll be all right," agreed Baker. "In that case I won't change either, and perhaps I'd better go to bed early. Then, in the morning, I'll be right as rain."

"The best thing you can do. I may be detained longer than I anticipate."

"Something unexpected sprung up?"

"Yes, in a sense."

Baker knew of old that Philip Durrane could be as "tight as a clam" when he chose. Whatever his business ashore might be, he meant keeping it to himself. After a cocktail, which Durrane pressed his companion to make two, not without setting an example, they went to their rooms.

Living as bachelors are supposed by their female' relatives to live, though the critics would be astonished by the Lucullian habits of some New York misogynists, their meal began with soup. A butler, whom Durrane had picked up in the town, removed the plates after the first course, and was vastly surprised at finding under his master's soup plate a white card, about four inches square, bearing a black cross. Baker saw it, too, and stared quite naturally at an object which could only be regarded as an extraordinary one, even though it need have no really sinister purport.

The butler muttered something under his breath, but Baker swore loudly.

As for Durrane, both men were aware that his sallow face had grown livid, though so great was his power of self control—a strangely incongruous attribute of the neurotic brain—that he said not a word during some seconds. When he spoke it was to ask the simplest question.

"Who laid the table?"

"Helen," gasped the butler.

The maid came in at the moment, carrying a dish of cutlets.

"Helen," said Durrane, "did you place this card here?"

The girl gazed at the curious token with evident bewilderment.

"No, sir," she said. "I never did."

"Has any other person been in this room?"

"Not that I know of, sir."

Durrane then looked at Baker, and the latter was conscious of a lambent gleam in the brown eyes which he had never before seen there.

"Is this a joke on your part, Frank?" he said, and his tongue moistened his lips the while as though they were dry.

"Joke!" repeated Baker. "What sort of joke is that? It strikes me as the high sign."

"Won't you answer my question?"

"If you want me to say that I know nothing whatever about that bit of cardboard, I say it at once. Pull yourself together, Phil! If you know what it means you must be equally well aware that I don't."

The reasoning was shrewd, more so than Baker himself guessed, because he went on to spoil the effect of a deadly thrust.

"Just recall the facts," he protested, being somewhat annoyed that he should be placed on his defence before the servants. "I went upstairs before you and came down after you. We weren't gone five minutes, and Helen fixed up the table during our absence. How in hades could I slip the damned thing under your plate? And, if it was put there by a stranger, it might as well be meant for me."

"True," said Durrane. "Perfectly true. I did not think of that. I should not be surprised to hear that it was some boyish trick planned by Willie Dixon."

"I don't quite get the hang of it. Let's have a look."

Baker did not realise then, though he remembered the incident afterwards, that Durrane hesitated a fraction of a second before touching the card with his fingers. Nevertheless, after turning it over, and finding that the back was blank, he gave it to the other. The black cross had been inked in quite recently. The ink still had a bluish tinge.

"There's nothing particularly funny about this design," commented Baker. "It looks to me like a sort of warning."

"Meanwhile our cutlets are growing cold," said Durrane.

"Well, you're taking it calmly, at any rate," and the speaker contrived to laugh. "As for me, I'm not worrying. I think I've had already all that's coming to me to day."

It was not a tactful remark, but it served. The butler and maid were far more distressed than the two diners during the rest of the meal, as Durrane had propped the card against a sugar basin on the table in such wise that the servants saw it constantly. Also, it could be seen by any eyes that peered in from the garden through a pair of open double doors.

The dinner, though simple, was well cooked and served in an appetising way, did not seem to appeal to either of the young men. Baker soon found that he was still on the sick list, and Durrane ate as though unwillingly. There was wine on the table, but he took none of it/ He impressed Baker as being engaged in an absorbing reverie. He was not literally impolite to his guest. His manner implied that Baker no longer existed. During a long half hour the latter felt certain that Durrane did not know he was in the room.

With the arrival of coffee and the proffer of cigars and cigarettes the spell seemed to be broken. Durrane even apologised.

"I have been abominably neglectful, Frank," he said, obviously waiting until the butler had gone out. "But, you, better than any other person living, can understand that I have cause for some degree of mental disturbance. It will pass. Tout passe, tout casse, tout lasse. Are you Frenchman enough to understand that bit of philosophy? 'Everything passes, everything perishes, everything palls?' I wonder if it is all true?"

"I dunno," came the blunt answer, "but if I was you I'd get out of this—make a bee line for South America, or Japan, or, better still, Central Africa. Just persuade yourself, Phil, that you've been more than a little mad, and try to rub a wet sponge over the slate. I'm willing to help—damme if I ain't." He bent forward and whispered:—

"I'll take a chance. Those fool cops have nothing on me."

Durrane favoured him with a curiously contemplative stare.

"I never imagined you were so melodramatic," he purred, with all his wonted cynicism. "But I am sure you mean well. Please remember I said that, will you? Things may happen which will tend to shake your faith—as for instance, that stupid folly of this morning; yet, with time, you may come to see that I am telling you the truth now."

"Oh, forget it!" cried Baker. "You're not the first man who has lost his wits about a girl, and you won't be the last. Confound you, if I didn't know how you felt, d'you think I'd have kept my mouth shut so long, and at no small risk to myself?"

"Yes, it is time you were in bed," said Durrane. "Your mind is beginning to wander again. Please take my advice and retire early."

With that, he lighted a second cigarette, picked up the marked card, put it in a side pocket, and went out.

For some reason, which his rather sluggish brain did not trouble to analyse, Baker felt uneasy. He did not even begin to understand Durrane's pose. The man who had unquestionably tried to take his life a few hours earlier seemed to regret the attempt now. He had gone so far, indeed, as to hint that it was foolish rather than criminal! Again, he (Baker) had as good as told Durrane he regarded him as the murderer of Anthony van Cortland, yet the extraordinary fellow had begun by accepting the charge without contradiction and ended by chaffing him for having made it.

He did not arrange these thoughts clearly in his mind. They consisted of a series of confused images, but one fact stood out clearly: Durrane meant leaving him alone in future. Ah, but would that change of heart endure? If a man had the temperament which permitted him to drown a friend just because the hazard of a moment brought an opportunity which could not be regarded as other than a sheer accident, might not that same temperament seek safety by the death of one who shared a shameful and deadly secret?

Sound sleep was about the last thing Baker courted at that moment. Had it been possible he would have caught the night mail to New York, and he resolved firmly to clear out next day. He actually found himself trying to recall whether or not there was a lock on his bedroom door. Grinning nervously, he took a glass of liqueur brandy, and resolved to smoke a cigar before going upstairs. Where was Durrane going at that late hour, he wondered? Surely he could not be attracted by some momentary dissipation at the hotel, while, as for the scattered dwellings on the side of the lake, their inhabitants probably went to rest at an earlier hour than any other fashionable gathering in the world, unless it were one similarly situated.

While these conflicting and troublesome notions were jostling in his brain he heard Durrane come round the end of the house and walk down the plank path to the landing place. Behind him followed the little engineer, Pierre. Again some vague recollection of the Frenchman's voice, even of his eyes and general appearance, flitted into hazy memory, but the impressions were indefinite, and soon lapsed.

Then he caught the snorting of the engine, and the launch emerged from the boathouse. He was tempted strongly at that moment to stroll across to the Dixons' place. He was alone, and an invalid of sorts. He stood well with Mary and Willie Dixon, even with that interloper, Stuart, and it was hardly likely any business would be discussed with the New York lawyer after dinner, since they had taken him out for a long country walk during the afternoon. He had to summon all his resolution to resist that impulse. Convention has its own fetters of steel, and Baker knew quite well that neither he nor Durrane were wanted by their neighbours that night, or they would certainly have been invited to dine. Baker smiled sourly. He was not accustomed to being "left out" on such occasions.

"What beats me," he said to himself as he rose and went out to smoke in the fresh air, "is why I am here at all. Why on earth did Phil rush me up from New York, making it such a point that I should come at once? What game had he in mind? What game is he playing now? I give it up. Wish I was out of it."

The moon had not yet risen, though a silvery blue sheen was expanding over the eastern hills. The surface of the lake was invisible, a pall of utter blackness, save for the few shimmering streaks which reflected distant lights. But the stillness of the night, and the eerie beauty of a scene suggested to the spiritual senses rather than visible to the eyes, made no appeal to Backer, whose curiosity was greatly stirred by discovering that the motorboat was merely forging along by spasmodic jerks in the direction of the Dixons' landing. He heard it stop there, and straightway jumped to the conclusion that Durrane had simply humbugged him, and was himself making a belated call, probably with the hope of securing a tete a tete conversation with Mary Dixon.

Baker described this proceeding with the richness of diction such double dealing seemed to demand. He waited to make sure he was not mistaken, and soon detected Durrane's tread on the plank path, with its occasional boarded steps,' leading to the Dixons' house. Then he hurried along the track, hardly a path, which gave direct communication between both residences. If he stepped out he would arrive simultaneously with the man who had hoodwinked him so egregiously.

However, before crossing the dividing fence, halted and took thought. If Durrane had pretended he was going to town, he, Baker, had equally pretended he was going to bed, and neither had the slightest right to carry their squabbles into the quiet household next door. Evidently, then, this headstrong young millionaire was still affected by the morning's adventure. Ordinarily bullheaded and pugnacious, that night he somewhat resembled a nervous colt, and was equally ready to shy at shadows and magnify trifles into alarming monsters.

Be the explanation what it might, Frank Baker certainly hesitated and stood still. And that absurdly small cause promptly led to a tragic sequel. Had he gone on, and joined Durrane on the verandah at "Bellagio," it is possible that events might have shaped themselves very differently that evening, even though a volcano of passion blended with insanity was ready to pour out its scorching lava at r.ny moment. But convention controls neurotic lunatics nearly as forcefully as it holds within bounds the sluggish people. Baker and Durrane arriving together must have exercised a wholly opposite effect from Durrane arriving alone. Yet that latter thing is what happened. Bidding Furneaux await his return, which would not be delayed many minutes, Durrane walked up to the house.

CHAPTER 19: BEFORE THE MOON ROSE

MARY decided there was no need for the chief of the New York Detective Bureau to live in hiding in her father's house. As he was fully determined to leave for headquarters by the night mail next day it was quite a natural thing that Willie Dixon should invite him to dine and sleep at "Bellagio" prior to his departure. Mr. Dixon, senior, to whom he was introduced vaguely as "from the Police Commissioner's Office, greeted him cordially, and Winter himself soon made the best of impressions on the old gentleman.

It was actually on Furneaux's suggestion that his colleague consented to appear thus openly. They gained nothing, he argued, by further concealment where Winter was concerned; if, on the contrary, the sense of unease already lurking in Durrane's mind were accentuated by a (seemingly) accidental discovery of the detective's presence, then, even at the eleventh hour, there might be some definite result. Furneaux confided to no one his intention to startle Durrane by hiding under the plate on the dinner table a card bearing the sign asked for by van Cortland's murderer. For one thing, he was afraid that Winter would not sanction the ruse; for another, he had knowledge which his Chief did not possess until he returned from the afternoon's long ramble in the hills, as he knew that Durrane had gone ashore to arrange for a high power car to await him at the landing stage at 9:15 p. m. In that car would repose two well filled suitcases, which certainly suggested a night journey by their owner.

So Furneaux spent a busy and anxious afternoon and evening. Not only had he to secure the presence of the town marshal and a couple of stalwart aides near the car at the right moment, who would lend assistance if called on, but he wished to feel sure that Mary Dixon would not, on any account, trust herself alone in Durrane's company. She had been warned already in this regard, but the little detective made every allowance for the vagaries of the feminine temperament.

"She might easily take it into her pretty head to give that fool of a soldier man a heavy jolt by pretending that we are all treating Durrane and Baker unfairly on the slenderest of suspicions," he argued. "I don't think she would bring herself to flirt with either of them, because she is nearly as convinced as I am that not only is Durrane a murderer, but that, in some way, Frank Baker is his accomplice. But a woman does not stop at trifles when she wants to tease a backward lover. Cre nom, I've done my best to flog into action the dragoon's galled jade, yet I can't get a move out of him. Even now, when all our trouble seems likely to count for little, if only Durrane saw Mary in Alec's shy but longing arms, I think he would give himself away."

Not until the late afternoon did Furneaux hear the true story of the morning's escapade, and then it merely added another complexity to a riddle already baffling enough. However, he warned Brown and Benson to be constantly on guard during and after dinner. Catherine, too, had to be available instantly, since he foresaw Durrane's furious searching for some clue which would account for the appearance of that terrifying bit of cardboard, and if he, Furneaux, were surprised again in the girl's company, the incident might divert those searching brown eyes from himself and his not quite plausible presence in the camp as the permanent boatman's deputy. He had not missed Baker's scrutinising glances. He knew, but had never told anyone except Winter, that Baker was the one man, beyond Willie Dixon, who might reasonably be expected to recall the identity of the detective who questioned him on that fatal morning in the Fifth avenue mansion. Baker was a blustering idiot, in Furneaux's estimation. Yet, just for that reason, he was likely to blurt out the fact that "Pierre" bore, at least, a remarkable resemblance to "the little cop who held us all up in Tony's ouse." In a word, Furneaux was having a heartbreaking time. He had to consider the possible actions of a homicidal maniac from every point of view, and contrive that, no matter what risk he ran personally, no other person's life should be jeopardised. He did certainly secure that end, yet not even he, with his almost phenomenal insight into the workings of the criminal and neurotic mind, was prepared for what actually happened.

The dinner party at "Bellagio" was quite lively. Winter drew on his intimate knowledge of New York life to keep the table within the bounds of general topics, and the elder Dixon was delighted with him. Instead of retiring after the meal, as was his nearly invariable custom, the senior member of the family came out on the verandah for coffee.

When an opportunity offered, he drew his son aside.

"Willie," he said, "I had no idea you were forming such excellent acquaintances as this Mr. Winter. Who is he?"

"Well, pop," said the boy, unwilling to mislead his father, yet not daring to disclose the literal facts, since the older man might incautiously say something next day in the presence of their dangerous neighbours, "all I can tell you just now is that he is the big noise in the police department. But he doesn't wish it known here. Don't press him for details. I've a kind of notion we may hear the whole story in a few days."

Clearly Master Willie was not lacking in tact. He contrived to hide essentials from his parent, yet flattered him by letting him believe he shared an official secret.

"All right," said the old gentleman. "You can trust my discretion. What I really wanted to say is this:—He is the sort of friend I approve of for you. Cultivate such men. One is worth a vanload of fools like the members of the Ace Club."

This was dangerous ground, and Willie promptly got off it.

"It's a pity we can't persuade him to stay a while," he said.

His father took his cue, and gave Winter a cordial invitation to prolong his visit.

"I'm sorry," said the detective, "but Commissioners expect their orders to be obeyed."

"Perhaps we may see you here again before the end of the season?"

"Yes. That is quite probable, indeed."

"Well, then, come straight to us. We have plenty of room. In my young days I have put up a dozen men in this house. And the fishing is first rate in September. Have you used a rod during your present visit?"

Willie took care to join in the chat. He believed that all difficulties had been smoothed away for the night, at any rate.

Mary and Stuart were leaning over the rail a few feet away. Unless they sank their voices they could not, in that place of peaceful stillness, discuss any phase of the mystery not intended to reach other ears, though two young people in love need no training in the art of seeming to talk about nothing in particular yet read occult meanings into quite ordinary words. The girl happened to notice the butler and Benson standing in the shade at opposite ends of the house. She laughed contentedly.

"Are we being guarded?" she asked.

Stuart knew through Brown, who had told both Winter and him, that Durrane was going ashore at nine o'clock.

"Not exactly guarded," he said, "but waiting watchfully. Durrane has ordered the launch to be in readiness at this hour."

"Oh," said the girl. She hesitated a moment. Then she murmured:—

"I suppose I ought to say I am nervous. But I'm not. I really don't think the boldest desperado could carry me off at this moment."

"He would certainly have to be a greater warrior than either of the two next door," agreed Stuart.

"Do you know," she went on, "I seem to be living in a strangely realistic dream. Life goes on in its ordered way, yet it holds events that are fantastic, unreal, altogether mad at times."

"If I had my way I'd whisk you away from it all," said Stuart simply. "Have you ever heard of the magic carpet of Tangu, on which you have but to seat yourself and wish to be in Bagdad, or Pekin, or any other outlandish place, and, hey presto, there you are!"

"But how many people will the carpet hold?"

"I don't know. Two, certainly."

"Are we to desert Father and Willie?"

"They are safe. You are not."

How much further this interesting conversation might have gone will never be ascertained. They both caught the staccato barking of an engine. Durrane had left "Sans Souci." In a few seconds they discovered its course, and, despite her valiancy, Mary moved a trifle closer to Stuart. Their elbows touched.

"He's coming here!" she whispered.

"I half expected he would," said Stuart.

"But why?"

"He and Baker may feel lonely. He may want us to go ashore. There is a cinema show in the hotel to night. One might give a dozen convincing reasons, yet fail to hit on the right one."

Never was truer word spoken, but, like most portents of threatened evils, it passed unheeded by those mainly concerned. Other ears were on the alert. Winter and Willie Dixon suddenly stopped talking. Even Dixon pere realised that something unusual, yet anticipated, was taking place.

"Is that Durrane's launch?" he enquired.

"I think so," said his son, "but, if we are to have
visitors, we'll soon know."

"I'm going in," announced the old man at once.   "I
don't want to meet Durrane or that oaf, Baker, to night. I
am not particularly fond of either of them."

He bade the others "Good Night," and went to his den.
His guardian angel—if that kindly sprite has not
altogether deserted heedless mortals—must have led him
away, because he might have sustained a serious,
perhaps fatal, shock had he remained on the verandah.
He had hardly disappeared when the launch reached the
landing stage, and Durrane leaped ashore, bidding
"Pierre" keep the engine running, and be ready to put off
again without delay.

The night was still pitch dark, but a blaze of light
came through the open windows of the dining room, so
the four figures on the verandah were plainly visible to
anyone approaching from the lake.   Equally visible was
Durrane, when he came into the lighted area.

The footpath curved slightly to avoid the tennis court,
which fronted only half of the house, the remainder of the
open space being filled with flowers and a rock garden.
Thus, he had to come nearer to Mary and Stuart than to
the others, who stood on the opposite side of the four
broad steps leading down to the lawn.

He raised his hat, and spoke without any perceptible
effort.

"I ventured to come and ask a favour, Mary," he said.

"Yes?" she enquired, with the least little tremor in her
voice, since she felt excited, though without any definite
reason.

"It's a beautiful night, and the moon will rise in a few
minutes. Come out on the lake with me."

"No, thanks. Won't you come in?"

"So you will not even grant me one small request?"

"Sis is tired," volunteered the ever ready Willie. "We
went for a long hike to day, and I'm sure she doesn't want
any more aquatic adventures to night."

Durrane ignored this interruption.

"But it will not weary you, Mary, to sit in the launch for half an hour. I really want to have a talk with you about various matters, and opportunities may be few and far between."

"I fear I am to blame, Mr. Durrane," broke in Winter, advancing a pace or two until he stood on the topmost step. "Miss Dixon does not care to desert her guest, I imagine."

Durrane gave heed to this new speaker. He looked at Winter steadily.

"Aren't you the Chief of the New York Detective Bureau?" he said, and his hearers only noticed a slow distinctness in his tone that seemed to imply intense mental concentration.

"Yes."

"Here on business?"

"Unfortunately I can seldom shake off business, even on a holiday."

At that instant, from among the trees on the left, came a crash of brushwood and the sounds of men engaged in a heavy struggle. They all heard Frank Baker's voice shouting:

"Let go, you fool! Let go, damn you!"

The butler, stationed at the other side of the building, ran forward. It may be that in some infinitesimal fraction of a second the controlling nerve centres of Durrane's overwrought brain finally snapped. Possibly he thought that the end had really come, and that he had blundered blindly into a trap. Winter's unexpected presence must have shaken him, and the attack on Baker by an unseen assailant, together with the sudden rush by Brown, may have led him to believe that he himself would be seized forthwith. But these things are merely speculative. What frenzied notions coursed through that warped and tortured consciousness will never be known, but his deadly intent became all too clear.

"Very well, Mary," he cried in high, reedy tones. "I tried, but have failed. Perhaps you and I may meet in another place!"

He whipped an automatic pistol from a pocket and fired pointblank at the girl, who was so close that he could not have missed. But if he was quick, Stuart was quicker. Thrusting Mary aside, he flung himself in front of her, offering his own body as a target.

The pistol snapped, and there came the harmless explosion of the fulminate of mercury in the cap of a useless cartridge. Then Brown fired, for he was still too distant to close with the would be assassin, and Winter sprang down the steps with the tiger leap by which, big man though he was, he had won a respectful dread from the underworld of New York.

The butler's bullet grazed Durrane's ribs, but did not injure him, as Brown had tripped slightly over a peg which kept in position one of the nets surrounding the tennis court. Durrane turned and ran, just avoiding Winter's clutch, and the detective's voice rang out like a trumpet.

"Don't shoot again, Brown! You may hit Fur neaux, and this scoundrel cannot escape now!"

The murderer may have heard, too, and his sensitive if disordered intellect may have pierced Furneaux's disguise in a lightning flash of intuition. Still he raced on, to be met most pluckily by a man half his size, who, at the quite unexpected flash and roar of the butler's pistol, had shoved the launch forward among the bushes and away from the landing, and now awaited the fugitive at the foot of the path.

Durrane almost halted when he came face to face with the detective, although his three pursuers—for Stuart at last had Mary Dixon in his arms, and Willie Dixon was hampered by the bulk of the two men in front of him— were close on his heels. Even during his breakneck flight this neurotic, this man who had confessed to squeamishness even in the comparative safety of a military hospital in France, contrived to eject the faulty cartridge and restore his pistol to a serviceable condition. He fired point-blank at Fumeaux, yet again did that remarkable thing happen, of a detonator exploding with no other result. With a lurid curse at this repeated mishap, he flung the weapon at the detective. It struck the little man fairly on the chest, and nearly knocked him down. But he did contrive to keep his feet, and grabbed the other with a shrill yelp: "The game is up, Durrane! You're arrested for—"

His cry was stopped by a second blow, which shook him, for it caught his forehead. Another found his chin, and still he held on grimly. Then in being borne backward, his heel caught a loose plank, and Durrane wrenched his lithe body free, flinging himself headlong into the lake while Winter's powerful hands were yet within a few inches of his neck. He may have expected to find the launch there, but it was gone, and he could not know that it lay alongside the bank, barely a length away.

Winter pressed the switch of an electric torch; its concentrated beams revealed the black head of the swimmer. He produced a pistol, and shouted:—

"Come back, Durrane, or I shoot to kill!"

But Durrane would not yield. He swung into a side stroke, and the light gleamed intermittently on his white face and the swirling waters. Winter himself never knew whether or not he would have fired—because it is the business of the police to capture, not to execute, criminals—but the ticklish problem was solved for him in an unlooked for way. Brown tore off coat and waistcoat, and sprang into the lake.

"Stop that, you idiot!" bellowed Winter. "He'll drown you as well as himself!"

The butler heard, and waved a hand. He drew away at a surprising speed, and it became evident in a few seconds that, good swimmer though Durrane was, he had met his master.

"Charles, are you hurt?" cried the chief, turning to Furneaux.

"I'm not any better, if that's what you mean!" came the answer.

"Can you possibly start that launch?"

But the launch itself backed up to the landing place. Willie Dixon had leaped after it in obedience to a sign from Furneaux, who was distinctly shaken by the blows he had received, while blood was streaming from a cut on his forehead.

The motorboat had to move in a half circle to get its head lakeward, and Winter's lamp was not strong enough to cover a wide area, so the Chief shouted again:—

"Give us a hail, Brown!"

"Boat a hoy!"

The butler's cry enabled the watchers to find him.

"Take the boathook and plant yourself firmly in the bow," said Winter to Willie Dixon. "Tell Furneaux when to slow up, as if we hit either of those men he will sink. Never mind Brown. He can swim like a fish. Try and hook Durrane's clothes. I'll tackle him when you drag him alongside."

"Swim like a fish!" repeated Furneaux, as though talking to himself. "Like a goldfish, you should have said!"

Winter knew then that his colleague's thoughts had swung back through the whole cycle of strange events which had absorbed their lives to the exclusion of all else since the moment when the butler discovered his tiny pet in the glass bowl floating on its back, dead.

"The end is not yet," he muttered, answering the other's unspoken comment. "Keep a sharp lookout there, Dixon!"

Brown's voice reached them.

"Easy!" he said. Stop her now! I'll be with you straight away."

They saw him, treading water, and then paddling towards them dog fashioned.

"He's gone!" he announced calmly.

"How—gone?" demanded Winter, who had not been so wrought up by any chase during many a year.

"He knew I had his measure, sir, so he up with his hands and sank like a stone."

"How far can a man swim under water?"

"Fifty yards is first rate goin', but Mr. Durrane meant sinkin', not swimmin'. He went down feet foremost into the weeds."

"Hadn't we better circle round a few times to make sure?"

"If you like, sir, just for your own satisfaction."

"How about you?"

"I'll act as a mark. Go round me, and keep lookin' outwards. But, bless your heart, sir, it's all over with him. He meant it this time, all right."

The butler's confidence in his own judgment was justified. He explained afterwards that when a policeman he had practiced swimming with his clothes on, and rescuing drowning people. That is why he had no fear of jumping in after Durrane, whom he would have stunned with a blow before closing with him. Moreover, anyone about to swim under water does not sink in the technical sense of the word, but takes a rolling dive like a porpoise.

At last, Winter was convinced that it was a waste of time to remain on the lake any longer. In all human probability Durrane was down. Brown was hauled aboard, and they returned to the shore. Meanwhile Furneaux had managed to staunch the flow of blood from his slight wound, but he looked rather ghastly under the light of the lamp at the boat house.

"Do you think you will be all right, or shall I send for a doctor?" enquired the Chief sympathetically. He hated to see the little man injured in any way. It was a standing cause of quarrel between them that whenever any physical risk was incurred in tracking a criminal Winter always took it.

"I want a drink, not a doctor," squeaked Furneaux.

"Well, that's the easiest thing to fix in this neck of the woods," said Willie Dixon. "If I dared fall off the wagon with Stuart's eye on me I'd take one myself."

"By the way," said Furneaux, "what has become of the gallant captain? I rather expected to see him in the forefront of the battle."

"He did his share all right," said Winter. "When Durrane fired at Miss Dixon, Stuart threw himself before her, and would have got the bullet if the pistol hadn't missed fire."

"It was bound to get him—pluckiest thing I ever saw," put in brother Willie.

"First I've heard of that," said Furneaux.

"Where did that pistol fall?" enquired the chief. "I saw it strike you, but didn't notice where it dropped."

"It is quite possible we kicked it into the lake while Durrane was punching me. Anyhow, I'll have a look later."

As the four men walked to the house he found an opportunity to murmur in the Chief's ear:—

"I know where that automatic is. Don't let anyone examine it. I substituted dummy cartridges for every live one in Durrane's possession. They've worried me for two weary days, because he always carried a gun, and I was scared stiff that he might do some target practice at any time. I got the pistol while he was having a bath yesterday morning, and the rest was easy. But we must let Mary be saved in the proper spectacular way."

"You're a regular marriage broker, Charles," said Winter, and his hand fell affectionately on his friend's shoulder, for he valued this crabbed little man more than any other person in the wide world.

"Slush!" cried Furneaux. "Before we face the lights and the music, tell me what the rush was in the garden before the shot was fired. And who did fire?"

"Me, sir," said Brown.

"I'm glad you didn't hit him. It's better as it is. But what caused the first scurry?"

"Mr. Frank Baker, for some reason, yet unknown, was making for the house by the short cut from 'Sans Souci,' and Benson collared him in the dark," said Winter. "He seemed rather peeved about it, but Benson held on, and probably brought him along. Yes, there he is, in the dining room. And, what a crowd! Our first job is to get rid of the cooks and housemaids. You go in front, Charles. One peep at you, and they'll all run like rabbits!"

Furneaux allowed the jibe to pass. What he wanted more than aught else just now was a discussion with Frank Baker, "with the gloves off."

CHAPTER 20: NEARING THE DAWN

WILLIE DIXON, however, took on himself the task of clearing the dining room and verandah of "Bellagio" of the flock of servants who had gathered from both houses at the ominous sound of a fire arm. They all seemed to imagine that this was the shot aimed at "Miss Mary." They knew well who was supposed to have fired it; their execrations against the would be murderer were loud as their search for marks of the bullet somewhere on the front of the building was zealous.

Mary, during some few minutes, was too terrified to say anything coherent. Stuart, who had grasped the essential facts, did not enlighten anyone, not even Mr. Dixon, who was brought from his own apartment by the loud snarl of the butler's pistol. He judged it wise to await the detectives' return, while Frank Baker's presence, when that protesting young man was led in forcibly by Benson, offered another reason why little should be said at the moment.

One thing he did do—he requested the Skipper to see that no person should be allowed to approach the landing place.

"None of us can say for certain exactly what is happening," he announced firmly. "Two representatives of the New York Detective Bureau have the affair completely in hand. They will be here soon. Until they arrive we can do nothing. There is no reason for panic. There will be no more shooting, either by accident or otherwise."

But Mr. Dixon had seen his daughter sobbing in his guest's arms, and was also convinced that his eyes were not deceptive when they told him that the said guest was reassuring her in divers lover-like ways, whether by kissing her forehead and lips, or assuring her in the most endearing terms that she was quite safe now and would be for ever and ever if he had any control over her life and fortune. Moreover, the old gentleman was not only a loving father but an easily irritable one.

"That is all very well, Captain Stuart," he said, trembling with fear and excitement, "but some person seems to have made an outrageous attack on Mary. Who was it? What was his motive? And—and—what is this man doing here?"

In search of a fitting object for his wrath, he wheeled suddenly on Frank Baker, who had been forced into a chair by Benson, and was now held captive by the scruff of his neck.

"That is just what I want to know," roared the enraged Baker. "I was simply hurrying along to prevent mischief when I was rough housed by this big stiff, and treated like a drunken tough, for no reason on God's green earth!"

"You take my tip, and shut up, mister," Benson admonished him, not without an ominous tightening of clutch. "The other guy tried to do harm enough, an' it mayn't ha' bin your fault if you didn't help any."

"Confound you, don't I tell you—" began Baker, but Stuart, who had led Mary to her father, stayed him with a quietly authoritative air.

"Benson only acted for the common good, Mr. Baker," he said. "You are not hurt, I believe. Surely you can restrain your anger until you learn what has really occurred. Give me your word of honour that you will remain here until Mr. Winter—whom you know quite well—says you may go and you will be set at liberty instantly."

"Sure, I will, or I won't whichever meets the case," cried Baker. "What I mean is that I won't quit. Why should I? I've not tried to kill anybody."

A nod from Stuart sufficed, but Benson, taking no chances, first "felt" Baker for a gun, and then mounted guard between the two windows. The prisoner on parole began to test his arms and ribs gingerly. In all probability what actually annoyed him most was the knowledge that he had been thoroughly bested in a physical contest with a man whom he would have tackled cheerfully when in good condition and if he had not been taken by surprise.

Stuart persuaded Mr. Dixon to retire with his daughter into his room, and get her to sit down. She would soon recover, he was assured, and would then be able to give him as convincing a story as anyone. So the ground was fairly well prepared for Willie Dixon. He had only to tell the servants to go to their own quarters, and the stage was left empty save for the main actors. He said no word of Durrane's drowning. Probably they all believed the would be assassin had escaped. Even Catherine did not notice that the butler was soaked to the skin, since his coat and waistcoat were dry.

Winter hinted that he ought to change his clothes at once, and Benson was sent off with him. Furneaux waited outside until the domestics had vanished. He did not wish to create a sensation by his appearance, which was ghastly in the extreme. His first act was to help himself to a small glass of liqueur brandy. While sipping it slowly he eyed Baker in such a peculiar way that the latter resented it.

"What the devil," he cried, "are you a detective?"

Furneax did not reply. He merely continued to look at the other with those piercing black eyes of his, which had always suggested to Stuart the strange notion that he could read the soul of any man who wished to conceal a sinister and self committing secret.

"Why, of course," went on Baker, grinning as though he had made a pleasing discovery. "You're the queer little guy who tried to bounce each one of us as we woke up in Tony's house. I —er—"

He faltered. A most disconcerting smile, of what may be termed the Japanese variety, wherein the extreme of merriment is apt to blend into a truly diabolical scowl, crinkled Furneaux's face, which, between walnut juice, blood stains, broken skin, and rapidly swelling lumps, was certainly not prepossessing just then.

"But why hesitate? Pray, go on!" said the detective, to whom even those few words of Baker's were extraordinarily illuminating.

"Oh, I've got no more to say," growled Baker. "What's become of Phil Durrane? And did he really shoot at Mary Dixon?"

"At present, young man, it is your business to answer questions, not to put them. Are you going to tell us now the full story of the murder of Anthony van Cortland?"

"I? What in Hades do I know about it, any more than Willie there, or the rest of the fellows?"

"You know so much about it that you are now under arrest for being an accessory after the fact."

"Me! Arrested! You can't prove a thing against me!"

"We shall make a surprisingly realistic effort. The only slender chance you have of escaping punishment is to tell the truth, the whole truth, and nothing but the truth—now."

"I know nothing and can say nothing," said Baker doggedly. But his assurance was the outcome of a gnawing fear, not of conscious innocence. He glowered at Furneaux as a bull in a Spanish arena meets with eyes of dull rage the steady glance of the matador who is about to pierce him with a sword.

"That simplifies matters for all parties," put in Winter. "If you showed a genuine desire to help, we might be puzzled to know what to do with you. As it is, the constable is now about to land, and he will take you to the jail at Saranac to night. His car is waiting at the landing stage."

Sure enough, the near approach of a rather noisy launch could be heard distinctly. Baker gazed from the one man to the other with a terrified perplexity that was almost comical. Indeed, Stuart had to preserve a severely court martial aspect to stop a smile, because he knew, or thought he knew, suffident of the detectives' methods to feel certain that the last thing they desired was Baker's arrest.

"You can't mean that you're going to rush me to Saranac to night!" bleated Baker, who, by this time, was wilting visibly.

"There cannot be the least doubt about it," said Winter.

"But on what charges?"

"Mr. Furneaux has told you—that of being accessory to the murder of Mr. Anthony van Cortland. I now put to you officially, and warn you that anything you may say will be taken down in writing, and "

"Here! Stop, for the love of Mike! Give me a chance."

"You've had a hundred chances, yet you keep silent."

"Still, you said a good deal a while ago," broke in Furneaux, with an icy contempt in his voice that literally frightened the last show of resistance out of his victim. "It was you who drank some of the doped punch when the butler left the room after discovering that his master was dead!"

"I never told you that!" Baker almost howled.

"Oh, yes you did. You even took care to leave a record of the dose by marking the wet rim of the wine glass on the table cloth. You will sure have a hell of a time persuading a judge and jury that you're an innocent man, Baker !"

The on coming launch was slackening speed. In another minute the vessel would be tied to the little pier at the foot of the garden. Winter nodded to Furneaux, disregarding Baker altogether.

"I'll go and meet the constable," he said. "Then he and I will accompany the prisoner while he packs a grip. I'm sure Captain Stuart and Mr. Dixon will assist you if Baker is fool enough to try and escape."

These cold blooded preparations were too much for Baker's nerves.

"Send that damned constable away," he said sullenly. "I'll tell you the whole yarn."

"Keeping back nothing?" demanded the Chief with a metallic snap in his voice that was unpleasantly reminiscent of clanking fetters.

"Where's the use? Once I start I've got to finish."

"Very well. I'll go and fix things temporarily," and the big man strode off. He was not humbugging Baker in any sense when he spoke of the constable's arrival. That quite capable official, hearing the distant gunshot, and seeing not only the Chief's lamp but the erratic movement of the motor boat's lights on the lake, decided to investigate matters in person. Winter now explained briefly what had happened, and arranged for a party with grapnels to be at work early next morning. Despite the flood of moonlight now available, men who knew the lake all their lives deemed any effort to recover the body that night useless. When he returned to the house he found Baker fortifying himself with a high ball.

"Now," he said, sinking into a chair and addressing the other with some degree of affability, "I suppose you have not begun your story during my absence?"

"No. I only asked Willie for a drink."

"All right. Shoot!"

Baker, it has been seen, was not a physical coward, but his moral force was not of a high order, and the threat of arrest alarmed him. Nevertheless, facing four pairs of accusing eyes, he pulled himself together in a remarkable way. In the first place, he used what lawyers term a preamble.

"You fellows have got to rid yourselves of the notion that I'm an accessory, or whatever you call it, to Anthony van Cortland's death," he said. "I'm not. I never have been. To this minute, beyond what I've read in the newspapers, I don't really know what killed him, or exactly how he was killed. Of course, I'm sure Phil

Durrane was the murderer, but I didn't actually realise it for a long time. I want you to regard that statement as true, and I'll now tell you why."

He emptied his glass, lighted a cigarette, and continued:—

"I needn't say a word about what took place at the dinner. I was sore as a boil with Tony for cutting in ahead of me with Mary Dixon—just as I am now with you, Captain Stuart, but I ain't going to poison or shoot you because you've beaten me again. I hadn't the ghost of an idea that Durrane was in the running. We all thought he was still married—didn't we, Willie?"

Willie Dixon, as was only to be expected, suffered little embarrassment from the fact that his quondam friend and crony was virtually a prisoner on a serious charge.

"Quite correct, Frank," he said. "Both the Chief and Mr. Furneaux know that, and I've always stuck out that you had nothing to do with poor old Tony's knock out."

Baker tried to find in the detectives' faces some appreciation of this tribute. But Winter sat with the impassivity of an image of Buddha, and Furneaux, what between contusions and discolouration, looked positively inhuman. The narrator decided to carry on, and trust to luck for his defence.

"We moved about the room a bit when coffee was served," he said. "Tony was chairman, as you might put it, and I was at the other end of the table, facing the Avenue, and nearest the door. Phil Durrane, at the middle on the same side, said he wanted some ice in his coffee, and stood up to get a chunk from an ice pail on the sideboard, which ran along behind our backs. By mere chance I saw, out of the corner of my eye, that he took something from the left breast pocket of his dinner-jacket, and put it in the empty punch bowl before touching the ice pail. Then he dropped a piece of ice into the pail, and pretended to take it out again. But he really took out with it a small flat bottle, like an eight ounce medicine

bottle, and slipped it back into his pocket. . . . Now, have
you heard how Tony himself put some French aviateurs
on the blink one night in Paris?"

"Yes," said Winter.

"So you'll agree with me, I fancy, that I was justified
in thinking Durrane meant to work the same joke on
Tony. I want you to believe me that I was quite sure of it
then. I kept mum, of course. For one thing, I didn't very
much care what he was doing. For another, I was that
tearing mad about the marriage as to be afraid of being
dragged into an argument with anybody. But I watched
Phil, all the same. I saw that he was drinking very little.
When the punch was made he took care to be first at the
punch bowl with several chunks of ice. Then he moved
right away, to the other side of the room, in fact. I believe
I was the only one who saw him use the ice. Did you,
Willie?"

"No. I remembered most of the fellows who poured in
wine and the rest, but not the ice."

"Well, the punch was brewed just before two o'clock.
We were to finish it, and go home. I managed to spill my
first glass on the carpet. The second one I poured into a
flower vase. Durrane himself was so busy concealing his
own share of the dope that he never noticed me. But I
needn't have taken so much pains, even about the first
dose. One by one the boys began to flop. I was about the
fourth or fifth to collapse, and slid from the table to the
floor. You ask why I did this? Simple enough. I wanted to
find out what Phil's particular stunt was going to be. I
had mine all ready. When he was through, I meant to
burn a cork and black all their faces."

"Why, that's—" Willie Dixon began excitedly.

"Yes, the very thing Phil Durrane said at your dinner
party. It made me jump, I can tell you. Struck me as a bit
of thought reading—the real article. I am convinced now
he had that scheme up his sleeve if anything gave him
away over the mixture in the punch. Well, I was on the
floor, wasn't I? I went there because it was out of the

light, and I could see better. There was no cause for
alarm, of course. I was tickled to death by the notion that
I had fooled Phil completely. He, by the way, simply sat
down, and bent over the table for a minute or two. Then
he straightened up, lit a cigar, and smoked quite a while.
I wondered what the devil the game was, but kept still.
At last, he rose, and examined all of us carefully. That
was the hardest part for me, because he made sure we
were dead off, and I had to sham as well as I knew how.
After a time he seemed satisfied, and went to where Tony
was lying on the hearth rug, all of a heap. I watched
closely, but nothing very serious happened. He turned
Tony over onto his back, seemed to touch his neck, and
that was all. He stood up, leaned over the table, took one
of the wine glasses which still had a few teaspoonfuls of
the punch in it, and poured the lot into the glass bowl
where the goldfish was swimming about."

Here Furneaux rapped his forehead with his
knuckles, forgetting the broken skin where Durrane had
hit him. He swore under his breath.

"Sorry I interrupted you," he squeaked. "Go ahead!"

"In a very few seconds he took out the goldfish and
looked at it. Then he put it back again. Walking to the far
window, he raised the blind, opened the window, and
went out. He was not long out of sight. Not until I read
that hobo's yarn given to the police magistrate was I
aware that he had thrown the bottle and my ring—which
he must have stolen, and which I never knew was
poisoned—into the Park. When he came in again, he
walked straight to Kerningham, got his pocket
handkerchief, and wiped every place his fingers had
touched, including the glass bowl. He put the
handkerchief back into Kerningham's pocket, and had the
nerve afterwards to prompt Kerry to ask Toyn to enquire
about it. It was I who sent the message to Mary. I'll
explain that later. I just want to say right here that if
Kerry looked at all likely to be in trouble I would have
owned up at once. Durrane's next action was to pull down

the blind. He jerked too hard, and the roller at the top ran beyond its spring. He stood on a chair and tried to fix it but failed. Phil never was anything of a mechanic. That's one reason why he was a dud at flying. Anyhow, I heard him say:—'That's a nuisance. Yet is it? I wonder!' Afterwards, he took a long look at Tony, sat down for a few minutes, and, to my very great surprise, drank nearly two wine glasses of the punch. At least, I assumed he did. I couldn't be quite certain from where I lay. Soon he, too, was on the floor, and he fell so naturally that I felt sure about the punch. I waited a bit before scrambling to my feet. Like Phil, I had a good look at all the other fellows, including Tony and him, and came to the conclusion that they were all dead to the world. I was puzzled, I admit, and more than a bit addleheaded, because lying on the carpet had made me feel drowsy. I forgot all about my burnt cork notion, curled up in the arm chair in the far corner of the room, and went to sleep!"

He appeared to expect this statement to be challenged, but no one spoke.

"I suppose I slept nearly three hours," he went on. "It was broad daylight when I awoke. The boys were just as I had left them, except that one or two had straightened out a bit. But I didn't like Tony's appearance. I'm no doctor, but one saw plenty of dead men in France, and I was convinced almost at the first glance, that Tony was napoo. Believe me, I was badly shaken. My first idea was to give the alarm, and I wish to goodness now I had done it. But I took a bracer from a decanter of liqueur brandy on the table and sat down to think. It was a bit of a tangle. Tony was dead—probably killed by Durrane, but, mind you, I didn't know how. It might have been natural causes. I couldn't tell. The great fact was that the way had been cleared for me to marry Mary Dixon. There you have it. I make no secret of my motive. If the whole bunch of you could be cremated by lightning where you sit, and I could creep away and not be mixed up in any tangle of police enquiry afterwards, I'd act in the same way again—always provided I had a chance of making Mary my wife. I thought hard, let me assure you. I saw that if Phil had murdered Tony, not only was I a queer sort of witness, but I felt certain Mary would never look at me as a possible husband if I talked. Remember, I'm not telling you what I think now, but what I thought then. I couldn't size up the whole ugly business for three or four days, and then it was a trifle late to come along with the rather tall yarn I've given you to night. Moreover, I regarded Phil as a madman, and Mary did seem to be brought a little nearer by Tony's death. In a crazy sort of way, Phil had done me a good turn. If I could have saved Tony's life I wouldn't have hesitated a second. But he was dead and being buried before I understood what had actually happened. When Phil invited me here—by the way, do you—have you heard—"

Baker's confused sense of loyalty to a one time friend caused his tongue to trip. Winter had pity on him.

"If you are alluding to his attempt to drown you this morning—yes," he said.

"And where is the poor devil now? Under lock and key?"

"He is out of harm's way. But, finish your story."

"I was going to say that when he asked me to come here I was tickled to death at first. Then I reviewed the situation, and decided to write down everything I have told you. It's in my bank, marked, 'Not to be opened until my death.' I thought it wise to take that precaution."

"It was exceedingly wise. What bank is that statement in?"

Baker gave him the address.

"That is a material point in your favour," said the Chief. "Will you authorise your banker, who knows your voice, I suppose—by 'phone to morrow to hand the envelope to one of my assistants?"

"Sure I will."

"It will help you greatly. Just why did you write it?"

"I couldn't understand Durrane's hurry to buy this property at double its value. It occurred to me that he, too, wanted to be near Mary, and straight away a score of little hints as to his possible objective came into my mind. I saw, then, of course, the reason why he killed Tony. I took a bit of a chance in coming here at all, so, after that fake swimming match I as good as told him this afternoon that I knew where he stood, and had taken care, if he tried any tricks on me, he'd pay the full price."

"And that is why you were glaring at each other over the tea table," said Furneaux. "You were a long way off, but I read your expressions correctly."

He did not add that he was using a pair of high power binoculars at the time. Baker stared, but he had more to say.

"We had another dust up at dinner—" he began, whereupon Furneaux, who wanted no stress laid on the piece of cardboard episode, headed him off adroitly.

"Keep to the incidents in the van Cortland mansion," he said. "You have not finished yet."

"There's nothing more to tell. I wasn't at all worried when you woke me up."

"No. I saw that," said the detective drily. "You didn't deceive me for an instant. But haven't you forgotten certain details? When you heard the servants stirring you lay down on the carpet again. After the butler had gone out to summon assistance, and the door was locked, you remembered, almost in a panic, that you had taken none of the drug, and its absence might be noted. So you rose quickly, poured a quantity into a wine glass, and sipped a little. You were compelled to hurry, because the butler returned with Captain Stuart almost immediately. However, you left a perfect set of finger prints on the glass, to say nothing of the stuff poured into the vase and spilt on the carpet!"

This time Baker stared even more blankly at the little man.

"Gee!" he groaned. "A fat chance I had of pulling any wool over your eyes!"

Winter understood that his colleague did not wish the enquiry carried farther that night. At times the two might bicker to their hearts' content, but in the presence of an important witness each respected the other's hidden intent, even though its exact motive might not be perceptible at the moment.

"Now, Mr. Baker," he said, "you are badly shaken, and ought to be in bed. Will you promise me to speak to no one, go straight to your room, and rest till breakfast time? Of course, I take it you mean to be sensible, and not try any foolish scheme of dodging consequences such as crossing the border into Canada, or that sort of ostrich policy. If you work in with the Bureau now, we, on our part, may do our utmost to minimise the consequences of the somewhat peculiar part you played in this affair."

Baker's face brightened visibly.

"Sure I'll do all that, and more, if you want it," he said. "But, about Phil—"

"I said 'bed' and 'no more talk,' " smiled Winter, rising, so the hint was taken, and Baker went. Willie Dixon accompanied him, lest Benson might still be lying in wait, but that astute young man winked at the Chief as much as to say that Baker would worm nothing out of him. The three men remaining in the room sat in silence for a minute, because they heard Mary Dixon bidding her father good night and going upstairs.

"And now," said Furneaux calmly, "after I've had a wash and changed my clothes, perhaps I may be allowed to eat something. That brute broke up nearly all my face except my teeth, and, while you people were gorging in shameless ease, I was keeping a sharp eye on Mr. Philip Durrane."

Stuart rang, and when the butler came, he said:—

"Brown, a banquet for Mr. Furneaux, please."

"Yes, sir. . . . What wine will you take, sir?"

"A small bottle—I need it," said Furneaux, and he added, when the portly form had vanished:—

"Some lad, Brown, ain't he? Always says the right thing, and does it, too, even in missing Durrane!"

Chapter XXI: A Real Summer

"On, my, but it's good to see the sun shining again!"

That was Mary Dixon's greeting to her lover when they met next morning. The girl's words were symbolical. The sun had shone every day for weeks past, but he knew she was hailing the disapearance of the cloud which had darkened her life and the lives of those she held dear ever since Anthony van Cortland's death was announced to her by the strangest of all messengers—a man whom she had never before seen yet who was her destined husband.

Beyond that kindling of the eyes which betoken a quickening of the spirit there was no hint of last night's dramatic disclosure. Nor was any word of love or longing spoken voluntarily by these two that day, nor for many days thereafter. The shadow of death, though passing, was far too close. Mary's quick intelligence had supplied the true explanation of the long conference in the dining room. She was sure that Durrane was dead. What she did not know, and what Stuart did not tell her until later, was that the suicide's body had been recovered from the lake long before she rose, and was now resting in an undertaker's mortuary until an inquest could be held.

Winter had gone ashore at an early hour to arrange official formalities and inform the Police Commissioner in New York of the strange developments in the "Fifth Avenue Mystery" which would detain him and Furneaux in the Adirondacks yet awhile.

As for the little man, he slept late in the room found for him at "Bellagio." Between mental excitation and physical pain, he did not close his eyes before the dawn. But a hot bath, and a supply of his own natty clothes brought by Brown, worked wonders. Beyond a degree of brownness induced by the dye, a couple of lumps on his face, and some plaster on his forehead, he bore no serious signs of the previous day's ordeal. His worst contusion had been caused by the automatic pistol, but, fortunately, it had struck high up on the right shoulder, and had done no real damage.

He was surprised, perhaps, at finding Willie Dixon and Frank Baker chatting on the verandah. The latter, who had heard of Durrane's death, felt like a lost dog, and came across to seek company at the earliest possible moment. But he did not thrust himself on Mary and Stuart. Evidently, he regarded one page of his life's record as filled.

Furneaux greeted him cordially.

"Hello!" he said. "Been for a swim this morning?"

"No yet," grinned Baker. "I'm in hot water already, and am rather expecting you to give me a cold douche."

"Well, here it is! You may find the effects beneficial. Don't discuss the van Cortland case with anybody. Don't wire for a smart lawyer to represent you at the coroner's enquiry. Don't add a syllable to the statement you made last night, plus the signed story you deposited in the bank. Leave the chief to pull you through. He may do it. He's the only one who can."

That bit of succinct advice explains why no public reference was ever made to the square of cardboard Durrane found beneath his plate. The servants at "Sans Souci" knew of it, of course, but the incident was swamped in their minds by the torrent of subsequent events. Winter was puzzled, for perhaps a full minute, by the soddened mass of brown and white paper pulp, bearing a queer cross shaped device in almost obliterated ink, which was taken from the dead man's coat pocket. He said nothing about it—in fact, wanted to know nothing about it. While pursuing a criminal the police were strictly forbidden to do certain things, and those were the very things which Furneaux almost invariably did.

The detective passed on. Mary and Alec were looking lakewards from beyond the lawn. By accident, probably, he walked noiselessly on the grass, so he happened to hear Mary say "Yes, dear!" in response to some remark by the soldier.

"At last!" cried Furneaux, with a cheerful chuckle.

Mary turned, and blushed furiously, but Stuart only smiled, and said:—

"You made me do it!"

"And a fine old job I had," was the prompt retort.

"Miss Dixon, I have only one good thing to say for him—I'll swear he has never kissed any other girl!"

She laughed, though not so confusedly as might be imagined.

"I haven't much experience," she said, "but he seemed to know a good deal about it last night."

Furneaux did not grasp the true significance of this statement until he heard the Skipper's version of Stuart's behaviour on the verandah after the shot was fired.

"Gee!" exclaimed that veteran enthusiastically. "He handled that gal to rights. Never saw anything better done. He batted like Ty Cobb in the deciding inning."

The detective was not out to embarrass these young people, however.

"I'm joining the Chief in a few minutes," he said, "and may not see either of you for some time. Will you tell me now, Miss Mary, why you had a premonition, or whatever it was, of van Cortland's death?"

The laughter fled from her face, but she answered readily enough.

"Yes. It is all very vague in my mind. Even during the past few hours the outlines of that dreadful time have become more blurred and indistinct. But—Philip Durrane is dead, isn't he?"

"Yes."

"I knew it, though I have asked no one, have I, Alec? It is a strange thing to say, Mr. Furneaux, but I believe that unfortunate man could make me know things. I don't understand. Is it possible to hypnotise people at a distance?"

"I suppose so. Not by hypnosis, strictly denned, perhaps, but some species of telepathic influence can undoubtedly be established."

"Well, that must be the explanation. I seemed to be sure I would never marry Anthony—that some evil agency—I always knew it would be evil—would destroy him. And then, when Alec, when Captain Stuart, came that morning, I was afraid of the consequences, because my brother was at the party, and I dreaded lest he had been mixed up in some terrible quarrel."

"Ah, that's what I wanted to hear," said Furneaux. "It has been an extraordinary case, all through, and your share in it is not the least interesting and unusual."

"Before you go," put in Stuart, "I have something to ask. What about those cartridges?"

"What cartridges?"

Furneaux's eye brows began to arch, but stopped suddenly, because the broken skin on his forehead crinkled.

"You know perfectly well. The cartridges in Durrane's automatic."

"My dear man, I'm a Jack of all trades and master of many, but I cannot teach a soldier anything about fire arms."

He made off: He even took the trouble of searching for and finding the shell extracted by Durrane during that frantic race down the path, because a percussion cap had also detonated when the flying murderer tried to shoot him. If this wizened little man with a golden heart could possibly prevent that one small fact from leaking out, Mary Dixon should never know it.

"What's puzzling you now, Alec?" enquired Mary.

"When that scoundrel fired at you last night the cap detonated in the cartridge, so it was not a dud. It is an almost impossible thing for the charge not to explode."

"You did not think of that, dear, when you thrust me behind you," and the light in the girl's eye was sufficient warrant that her faith in him would never diminish.

The "Fifth Avenue Mystery" flared into prominence again in the newspapers when the up State inquest was reported. The Republican press was much incensed by the failure of the police and District Attorney to probe the affair more speedily, while the Commissioner issued a statement bidding all evil doers, "no matter how highly placed or how assured their social position," beware of the evenhanded justice dealt out by his department. Mr. Dixon, senior, refused point blank to leave his lake side residence. His resolution helped on rather than retarded the date of Mary's marriage, which took place very quietly in the Church at Saranac.

Brown married Catherine, and undertook to bring his employer safely to New York for the winter, while "someone higher up" discovered that a leading Embassy abroad needed a Military Attache who could afford the expense of the post, so Stuart's leave was extended until he and his bride sailed for Europe.

Willie Dixon met a nice girl at his sister's wedding, and is thinking of settling down. Benson is Captain Stuart's "man," and a very efficient one. Even the miserable hobo, who played no small part in the drama, was found (quite naturally) to have some knowledge of poultry, and was given a job on the Vermont estate where Stuart's mother lived. Frank Baker took the first opportunity to join a shooting party in East Africa. The two detectives held firmly to the theory that Durrane had brought him to the house on the lake in the belief that he might interpose between Mary and Stuart. He had no sooner arrived than it was evident he would fail disastrously. His attitude, too, evoked distrust on Durrane's part, hence the effort to remove him out of the way forever when the chance of a moment gave some promise of success, with little or no suspicion attached to the man who had contrived his death.

The last echo of the tragedy came through a letter to Stuart from Furneaux. It read:—

"I forgot to tell you I collared that picture by Marie Bashkirtseff. It is what artists call 'a free drawing in oils' of the lady herself. She has tousled hair and fascinating eyes, of the type which the French call soucieux. I can hardly imagine what Durrane meant doing with it. But, qui diable, how can one read the mind of a man like that? He was a synthetic compound of sixteenth century Italian craft and modern degeneracy. You will follow this quite excellent analysis when you hear that his heirs have turned up in some distant Milanese cousins named Durano, who live on a small estate once owned by Lucrezia Borgia!

"So, as the girls in the down town lunch clubs say:— 'Well, what d'ye know about that?' The classic reply of an Englishman to the question is:—

'Very little!' I agree with John Bull.

"The Chief is flourishing; he still smokes that cargo of vile but expensive cigars you sent him. He is incorrigible. I treasure my new and superb wristwatch. Winter says I gesticulate mainly with my left hand nowadays."

THE END

Resurrected Press Mysteries From Louis Tracy

The Albert Gate Mystery
Four men murdered and a fortune in diamonds belonging to the Turkish Sultan stolen, while the Foreign Office official in charge has gone missing. Was it a common jewelry theft or was it a case of international intrigue? This is the question that barrister detective Reginald Brett must solve.

The Bartlett Mystery
When Ronald Tower is murdered on his way to a bridge game on the yacht Sans Souci it at first appears a common crime. But as Rex Carshaw finds, a tragic case of mistaken identity leads to political scandal among the rich and powerful of New York.

The Strange Case of Mortimer Fenley
When the wealthy Mortimer Fenley is struck down by a shot from an express rifle on the steps of his mansion, detectives Winter and Furneaux of Scotland Yard must find the culprit. Was it the artist who claimed he was painting a picture at the time of the shot? The disaffected younger son? Or is there another suspect?

The Stowmarket Mystery
For five generations the Fergus-Hume family has been cursed. Each of the baronets has met a violent end. When the fifth baronet is found slain by a ceremonial Japanese dagger, suspicion falls on his cousin David. It falls to barrister detective Reginald Brett to prove his innocence and find the real murder in a case that spans two continents and as many centuries.

Resurrected Press Mysteries by J. S. Fletcher

The Orange-Yellow Diamond
When an elderly pawnbroker is murdered in the London parish of Paddington, a young, down on his luck writer is accused of the crime. But then it's found the pawnbroker had had in his possession an extraordinary South African diamond worth over eighty-thousand pounds — a diamond that's now missing. It falls to Melky Rubenstein to unravel the mystery and prove the young man's innocence.

The Middle Temple Murder
When an elderly man's body is found on the steps of chambers in the Midde Temple, one of the Inns of Court, it falls to newspaperman Frank Spargo and Detective-Sergeant Rathbury to solve the crime. The murdered man, for indeed it was murder, was found with no money or identification on his person except for a piece of paper with the name and address of a young barrister. Who is the victim? Why was he killed? Who is the murderer?

Scarhaven Keep
Bassett Oliver, the famed actor, has gone missing. When Oliver fails to show for a rehearsal, aspiring playwright Richard Copplestone finds himself sent to the small village of Scarhaven on the northern coast of England to track down the actors movements. What he finds is mystery. Find the answers as Copplestone unravels the mystery of Scarhaven Keep.

Visit www.resurrectedpress.com

Resurrected Press Mysteries by Fergus Hume

The Green Mummy

Professor Braddock hoped to compare the burial practices of the Egyptians with those of the ancient Peruvians with his latest acquisition, the mummy of the last Inca, Caxas. But on arrival, the packing case proved to hold not the mummy, but the body of his assistant Sidney Bolton. It falls to Archie Hope to discover the murderer if he is to marry the professors step-daughter, Lucy Kendal. Who killed Bolton and where is the mummy? Was it the sea captain Hervey? The mysterious Don Pedro? Cockatoo the Polynesian servant? The professor, himself? And what has become of the emeralds? These are the questions that Hope must answer amongst the secrets of the past in The Green Mummy.

The Mystery of a Hansom Cab

"Truth is said to be stranger than fiction, and certainly the extraordinary murder which took place in Melbourne Friday morning goes a long way towards verifying that saying." Thus opens The Mystery of a Hansom Cab, the best selling mystery of the nineteenth century. When a man is found dead in a hansom cab one of Melbourne's leading citizens is accused of the murder. He pleads his innocence, yet refuses to give an alibi. It falls to a determined lawyer and an intrepid detective to find the truth, revealing long kept secrets along the way. Fergus Hume's first and perhaps most famous mystery... The Mystery Of A Hansom Cab.

Visit www.resurrectedpress.com

Resurrected Press Mysteries from the Dr. John Thorndyke Series

Dr. John Thorndyke - Lecturer on Medical Jurisprudence and Forensic Medicine. Before Bones, before CSI, before Quincy, M.E– there was Dr. John Thorndyke solving the most baffling cases of Edwardian London using the latest tools of medical science. Read about his cases in:

The Eye of Osiris
John Bellingham, noted Egyptologist has vanished not once but twice in the same day. Now Dr, Thorndyke must unravel the tangled claims on his estate, solve the riddle of the missing man and find the "Eye of Osiris".

The Mystery of 31 New Inn
When Dr. Jervis is whisked away in a coach with no windows to an unknown location to treat a man in a coma from undivulged causes it is Dr. Thorndyke who must come up with the solution.

The Red Thumb Mark
The first of Dr. Thorndyke's cases finds him trying to prove the innocence of a young man accused of being a diamond thief despite the fact that his finger print was found at the scene of the crime.

John Thorndyke's Cases
More cases of medical mysteries as told by his trusted assistant Jervis, M.D. Eight stories of crime and deduction in Edwardian London.

Visit www.resurrectedpress.com

Resurrected Press Mysteries by John R. Watson & Arthur J. Rees

The Hampstead Mystery

High Court Justice Sir Horace Fewbanks found shot dead in his Hampstead home, a butler with a criminal past, a scorned lover and a hint of scandal. These are the elements of the Hampstead Mystery that Detective Inspector Chippenfield of Scotland Yard must unravel with the assistance of the ambitious Detective Rolfe. But will he be able to sort out the tangled threads of this case and arrest the culprit before he is upstaged by the celebrated gentleman detective Crewe. Follow the details of this amazing case at it plays out across Hampstead, London and Scotland until it reaches a stunning conclusion in the courts of the Old Bailey.

The Mystery of the Downs

When Harry Marsland was caught in a sudden down pour he sought shelter at Cliff Farm. Met at the door by a young woman clearly expecting someone else he is only too glad to get inside to wait out the storm. When they hear a noise upstairs in the deserted house they investigate only to discover the body of the farm's owner, Frank Lumsden, dead of a gunshot wound. Who then, killed Lumsden, and why? Who was the woman expecting and did she have any roll in the murder? These are the questions that private detective Crewe must answer in The Mystery of the Downs.

Visit www.resurrectedpress.com

Other Resurrected Press Mysteries

Mysteries on a Train

Before the Orient Express there was:

The Rome Express by Arthur Griffiths
A man is found dead in his first class sleeping compartment on the express from Rome to Paris. Who was his murderer? The Countess? The English General? His brother the clergy man? The maid who has disappeared? Is the French justice system up to solving the crime? Read about it in The Rome Express.

The Passenger from Calais by Arthur Griffiths
Colonel Basil Annesley finds he is the only passenger on the train from Calais to Lucerne. That is until a mysterious woman shows up at the last minute to book a compartment. Who is after her? What is her secret? Is she a criminal or a victim? Read about it in The Passenger from Calais

Visit us at www.resurrectedpress.com

About Resurrected Press

A division of Intrepid Ink, LLC, Resurrected Press is dedicated to bringing high quality, vintage books back into publication. See our entire catalogue and find out more at www.ResurrectedPress.com.

About Intrepid Ink, LLC

Intrepid Ink, LLC provides full publishing services to authors of fiction and non-fiction books, eBooks and websites. From editing to formatting, from publishing to marketing, Intrepid Ink gets your creative works into the hands of the people who want to read them. Find out more at www.IntrepidInk.com.

CPSIA information can be obtained at www.ICGtesting.com
Printed in the USA
LVOW120109260612

287655LV00006B/27/P